The
Feet of a
Snake

The Feet of a Snake

by BARRY CHUBIN

ARBOR HOUSE   New York

Library of Congress Catalogue Card Number: 84-070317

ISBN: 0-87795-571-9

Manufactured in the United States of America
10 9 8 7 6 5 4 3 2 1

This book is printed on acid-free paper. The paper in this book meets the guidelines for permanence and durability of the Committee on Production Guidelines for Book Longevity of the Council on Library Resources.

This book is dedicated to all those who lost a piece of themselves in the name of a violent God: the Iranians who lost their country, their loved ones and their self-respect; the American hostages and their families who were brutally and shamelessly used; the media people who once again allowed their Nielsen ratings to cloud their better judgment.

We shall always discover reasons, which we shall proclaim inevitable and divinely ordained, for hating one another.

Paul Eldridge

I have never seen the eye of a needle, the feet of a snake, or the charity of a mullah.

Islamic proverb

CHAPTER 1

It was the dull look on the dead girl's face that had really shaken the old man. Those fixed, dilated eyes, locked onto the ceiling.

The old man stretched and turned on his back in the crisp linen sheets of the king-sized bed. He lay still for a moment, his eyes closed. Gradually he raised his right arm and caressed his mop of white hair, then the fleshy wrinkles around his eyes. He massaged harder, digging into the crevices as though a burning pain lay buried deep in the tunnels of his mind.

Only then did he open his eyes to face a new day. He looked up at the large square ceiling of his bedroom. The agreeably beautiful colors and textures that he had seen last night had vanished. His stomach burned and growled as reality replaced the salacious dreams of his opium sleep. Slowly his young daughter's face faded in, superimposed as a hideous fresco on the ceiling.

It's only the opium, Ali Mahmoudi consoled himself, remembering the depression that sometimes follows the drug's euphoria. But it was of little comfort; there was nothing to look forward to and so much to regret.

"*Heyvanha*, animals," he cursed out loud.

He could not recall how he had returned to his Watergate apartment last night. Nor could he remember the drugstore from which he had so desperately called Gina in Aspen. He remembered only the sorrow, the guilt, the craving for escape; and the urgency with which he had removed the opium cake from the heated laundry cupboard and unwrapped the aluminum foil. He remembered, too, how unsteadily he had carried the apparatus—the brass tongs, the elongated pin, the *vafoor* pipe, the small coal briquets, the opium cake—on a silver tray to the library.

11

Sprawled among deep Persian cushions in front of the blazing fireplace, he had trembled impatiently, waiting for the coal to glow. At last he had lifted the embossed tongs and picked up a small, glowing briquet. Clutching the tongs, he brought the coal to the pipe bowl and then sat back, awaiting the bittersweet aroma of fantasy as the coal began to caress the opium.

And Gina? he thought, massaging his tense scalp again, his first daughter. Had she moved quickly? Had she taken the precautions he had taught her?

He hoped so. Dear God, he hoped so. There was nothing else....

The chirp of the trimline telephone jerked Ali Mahmoudi out of his misery. He turned toward the bedside table and feebly stretched out a hand.

"Yes?" He croaked, his throat dry and lifeless from the opium. The elixir that had drowned out an entire revolution. And now his daughter's death too.

The familiar voice of the operator answered.

"Morning, sir. It's ten o'clock. Your breakfast is on its way."

Mahmoudi murmured his thanks and replaced the receiver, turning again on to his back. Instantly the pain returned. Why had they killed her? An innocent child who knew little and cared less. What possible good could come of it?

The chime of the doorbell sounded and the old man dragged his arthritic body from the bed.

"One moment, Guttierez," he called as he made his way toward the heavy security door, struggling into a bathrobe. He fumbled with the locks and chains and turned the knob.

The door came into him fast. It knocked him sprawling against a chest of drawers in the hallway, sending a priceless antique Ju vase crashing to the floor. Two men in white stepped in swiftly and Mahmoudi knew instantly his time had come.

One of the men raised a pistol and a hiss of air ended in a sharp jab that stabbed his right thigh. He grabbed at the limb and looked down. A small dart had furrowed through the dark blue bathrobe into his flesh, and he fell over and collapsed.

The two men worked with mechanical proficiency.

"Get the cart," said the heavily built one as he knelt beside Mahmoudi's crumpled form. He lifted an eyelid. Satisfied with the fully dilated pupil, he withdrew the dart from Mahmoudi's leg and waited for his companion to reenter the apartment.

12

"Go," signaled the stretcher-bearer as he walked back in.

The two men lifted the body onto the collapsible stretcher cart. The heavy man peeled off Mahmoudi's soiled pajamas—a natural reaction to the anaesthetic—and half-heartedly dried Mahmoudi's groin and thighs before disappearing into the bathroom. He tossed the soiled ball of cloth in the direction of the tub, then washed the paper-thin surgical gloves covering his hands. By the time he returned to the living room, Mahmoudi's corpulent body had been wrapped professionally in a gray wool blanket. The men then strapped down the softly moaning body.

The smaller man unfolded a lightweight cotton pillowcase and wrapped it around Mahmoudi's face, leaving enough space for him to breathe but not be identified. Then he collected a fresh set of clothes from the bedroom and stuffed them into a large paper bag that was folded onto the end of the cart. Together they wheeled the stretcher into the hall.

Seven minutes after the two men had knocked on Mahmoudi's door an unmarked ambulance left the loading dock of the Watergate complex. Twenty minutes later it entered a basement garage across the Arlington Bridge in Crystal City, less than a mile from the Pentagon.

"You awake?" The heavier man tapped Mahmoudi's cheek and lifted an eyelid.

"What is going on?" the drugged man slurred. He was dazed, disoriented.

"You're okay. Just lie still." The accent was heavy Brooklyn.

Mahmoudi squeezed his eyes to improve the focus. He felt a parched, burning sensation in his throat. The feeling contrasted sharply with the sensation of ice running through his limbs. He heard the heavy man say:

"I'm gonna tell you exactly what's happening so you're not surprised by anything. That way you'll have no reason to act irrationally and if you do, you'll have only yourself to blame. We're both gonna pitch in and help. I'm gonna undo the straps and you're gonna get dressed. If there's any resistance we'll put you back to sleep. Only this time it'll be something far blunter than a needle." He released the arm straps and the second man offered Mahmoudi a glass of water.

Mahmoudi took it gratefully and moistened his mouth; the burning in his throat receded and his mind stirred. Perhaps he could

13

negotiate with them, make them an offer. Anything. Any amount. He tried to shake the remaining cobwebs by squeezing his eyelids again and shaking his head.

Gina! A shudder ran through his body. Had she listened? Was she safe in London? He took another sip of water and then a deep breath.

"I will stay here quietly and I will not misbehave or give you any trouble," he whispered. "I will also pay you whatever you wish—say, fifty thousand dollars each—delivered right here within the hour, if you release me."

It was a pathetic attempt and he knew it. Not even the words came out right. But he had to try; the alternatives were worse. Somehow he had to break free to make that call to Gina.

"This ain't Iran. Your rials are no good here," said the heavy man. He emptied the paper bag into a pile at the end of the stretcher.

"Untie me," Mahmoudi said in a cracked voice. His feet flailed at the cuffs still tied to his ankles as he struggled to sit up. The pile of clothes fell to the floor. "You animals you...."

The man stepped forward and placed a massive paw on Mahmoudi's chest. He applied pressure until Mahmoudi's body lay prostrate again.

"Don't get excited, your excellency," he smiled. "The colonel wants to see you."

CHAPTER 2

WASHINGTON: FRIDAY, OCTOBER 19, 1979: NOON

Troubleshooter, thought Mahmoudi disgustedly, as the two men sandwiched him through the doors of the elevator and across a green-gray marble lobby that rose almost three floors in height.

An unrelenting sweep of the eyes posted at various vantage points followed their echoing footsteps. Not for one moment did the armed guards on the catwalk or in the lobby disengage their silent vigil. They followed the three men through the visual identification procedures at the control desk, supervised by a scrawny, owlish-looking man, and into the elevator.

That was the official term—troubleshooter—thought Mahmoudi sardonically. Troubleshooter, consultant, advisor and a host of other names—they had them all. First, second and third secretaries, political officers, consuls, petroleum attachés, private businessmen and even, occasionally, ambassadors were espionage operatives. But of course that was in their "official days." When they reached retirement age or a scandal bared their hidden identities, they became troubleshooters, consultants, advisors.

The high-speed security elevator came to a stop on the twenty-sixth floor but the doors did not open. The smaller of the two men pressed a series of numbers, which changed daily, on the elevator wall panel before the doors separated to reveal a large fluorescent-lit reception area, silent and antiseptically cold. Four uniformed security guards, in various corners of the room, stood at the ready, as the doors slid open.

"All of this for a troubleshooter?" murmured Mahmoudi, glancing distastefully at the two men.

With only the faintest of nods around the room they guided him past a row of plastic shrubbery to a desk that sat before a large double door. An elegantly dressed, middle-aged secretary glanced up momentarily from the screen of her word processor, and with a nod of her half-moon spectacles permitted them to enter.

The two men left Mahmoudi and the door shut behind him with a snap that sounded like an electronic lock. Mahmoudi knew he had been expected. But now, inside Colonel Grover Cleveland Bell's office, he was not so sure. The hunched figure at the polished desk seemed preoccupied with the mound of papers before him.

As Mahmoudi stood waiting, uncertainty and fear gripped his stomach. He knew from experience that it was part of Bell's strategy to unnerve, but the knowledge was of little comfort.

The figure behind the desk glared at the papers on his desk, oblivious to his presence. But that, Mahmoudi knew, was part of the man's psychological arsenal which he tactically deployed to dominate and control. He watched and waited, observing how the colonel wore his leer like a trophy, not as a handicap. It was, Bell had once pompously told Mahmoudi, "a testament to my will, a badge of dedication to my country."

Nevertheless, the muscles and nerves that had been torn to shreds by North Korean shrapnel had been rebuilt with exquisite delicacy by America's finest surgeons. But even they were unable to reconstruct the most sensitive of organs. The otherwise distinguished features were locked into a slight contortion, a stiffness, resulting from nonexistent nerves and paralyzed muscles that froze the flesh from the right lip up to the cheekbone and earlobe. There remained, too, a razor-thin scar that no amount of surgical wizardry had been able to erase.

Trophy or not, thought Mahmoudi, looking away with distaste, it was a sinister image. But one which its owner used effectively— often, and to maximum advantage.

To calm himself, Mahmoudi turned to survey his surroundings.

"Ali!" smirked Colonel Grover Cleveland Bell at that moment. His eyes registered Mahmoudi's head snapping towards him. "It's so good to see you again."

He put down his pen and deliberately removed his glasses before walking across the room to where Mahmoudi stood. He almost had to bend to take the right hand of the plump former cabinet minister to the Shah.

"You haven't been here before, have you?" he asked, attempting to smile effusively and noting Mahmoudi's haggard condition. It belied the fact that only a year ago this was one of the most powerful men in Iran; the man to see if you wanted to peddle anything— armaments, computers, construction projects, refinery equipment, trucks, toys, tankers. With a small commission to this Jack-of-all-trades—*bedeh bestoon*, as it was called—you could sell anything, and at any price you chose if the fee was right.

"How do you like my paintings?" Bell asked, pointing to a wall.

Behind the couch at one end of the vast room hung a small grouping of Leonardo da Vinci cartoons, including the original hang glider and the bicycle that predated its "invention" by four hundred years. Beside these classics were more modern designs—two LeRoy Neiman paintings of the younger Muhammad Ali in full swing and a clashing multi-colored design by Nicola Simbari depicting two beautiful nude showgirls in a torrid embrace. They added both color and contrast to the collage.

16

Mahmoudi looked away.

"I am sure you did not physically drag me here to talk about your office or to show me your paintings," he said, trying to sound haughty.

Bell placed a patronizing arm around Mahmoudi's slumped shoulders and steered him toward his desk. As he did so he noticed how much Mahmoudi had aged. His wiry hair was completely white and brushed straight back, leaving a widow's peak extending into the deep, wrinkled forehead.

"I enjoy paintings myself," he said, sitting down in the ladder-backed chair that matched his oak desk. "Leonardo got to the truth through his passion for detail. Which is why I admire him. It's a philosophy I have lived by, and recommend highly."

Bell's face became a trifle softer as deep lines etched his wide, thin-lipped mouth. But his cold, light blue eyes remained emotionless and his face appeared slightly flat on one side.

"But I bore you, and we have things to discuss."

He picked up a pair of tortoiseshell glasses and placed them on the tip of his aquiline nose. A neat stack of computer printouts rose beneath his folded arms.

Mahmoudi knew the pleasantries were over. He shifted uncomfortably in his seat. Fear, opium withdrawals and the death of his daughter had shattered his world. By comparison the continuing revolution in Iran was a minor aggravation. Nervously, he tugged at his collar, smoothed his hair.

"I'm sorry about the death of your daughter," said Bell in a tone that reflected little sympathy. "But the fault lies squarely on your own shoulders. I guess it's convenient, even natural, to lay the blame on others, but for the record we had nothing to do with it, despite what you may think. She was running with a sick, decadent crowd. Dope addicts, mass sex, that sort of thing, and someone killed her."

"Then how did you find out about the existence of the tapes?"

"Pardon the cliché, but we have ways. And they're a little more sophisticated than killing teenage junkies."

The bastard knows he doesn't even have to lie convincingly, thought Mahmoudi. But he stayed silent; antagonism was counterproductive at this point and his priority now was to keep Gina alive. On the phone last night she had listened to him for once in her life. Not because of her sister's death—for Gina the shock was a surface reaction that would soon pass—but because she had sensed the danger. Usually she never took anything seriously, except her jewels, her clothes, her playthings. But the question was, had the mood lasted? Had she moved quickly? Would she be at the call box at the appointed time? Don't be conspicuous, my darling, he had warned her. Use another name. Call yourself Maria Montez—the actress on whom he had doted in his youth. It was the only name he could think of.

Bell removed the half-moon glasses from his nose and pointed them at Mahmoudi.

"There seems to be an epidemic of irrationality running wild among you Iranians. The Shah's acting like a spoiled brat. Why the hell doesn't he just listen to Washington and abdicate? And you, Ali, why do you refuse to answer my calls? Why can't we meet like civilized human beings instead of your being dragged in here like a common criminal? You'll have to stay with us now until this absurd business is cleared up once and for all." He sounded like a schoolmaster feigning disappointment at a wayward charge. "I can't imagine what prompted you to make those tapes in the first place. You knew how sensitive that information was."

Mahmoudi felt his heart skip, his stomach turn. As he looked away from Bell's menacing glare he prayed that Gina had listened and moved quickly.

He shook his head from side to side and loosened his tight collar.

"You ask yourself why I have to make tapes like those after twenty-five years of friendship with your country," Mahmoudi said in a croak. "They were protection. After so many years, I know all too well what you people are capable of doing in the name of democracy and freedom. No one is ever safe with you. When their usefulness runs out, they are expendable. And there are no exceptions for friendship, are there? Not even His Majesty was immune."

Mahmoudi sighed wearily and looked at the looming figure.

"I am tired, colonel. Sick to death. One of my daughters is dead. I am marked for death, and we both know it. Do what you will."

Bell stood and looked down at Mahmoudi. What he saw, more than what he heard, told him that the man was broken. He was a pathetic shell of his former self and had no cards left to play. Bell banked the observation and correlated it to the computer summary of Mahmoudi's personality on his desk. He didn't need the machine's information and he didn't need to revert to the inquisitor's role: to go for the balls. No need to break down the man's cunning by intimidating him. The computer profile identifying Mahmoudi's likely collapse point in the face of any physical violence was now obsolete. In fact, if he had known the extent of the man's disintegration, he wouldn't have employed such dramatics to drag him in. He would have used more conventional means.

No, he thought again. There was still information to extract from Mahmoudi, but now he had to be careful not to drive the Iranian to despair. He had to offer him solace and hope.

"Nobody," he said with practiced sincerity, "is going to kill anyone, Ali. You're tired and the pressure is getting to you. Leila's death was a hell of an unfortunate incident and you have my deepest sympathy. Besides, I think we can solve this thing without too much of a mess. We've formulated procedures to recover the tapes from your house, presuming, of course, they're still there."

Yes, thought Bell as he paced a few steps. He'd share some information with Mahmoudi and boost his confidence. There was nothing to lose and everything to gain. After all, he would be no threat; he would be in custody for the rest of his limited life.

Bell turned and paced back. Bait him with a little information.

"We've even selected an individual for the job. For various reasons we had to rule out sending in our own people. Under the circumstances, it was considered unwise to involve this country directly. For certain other reasons the president has ruled out the Israelis, and our other allies are willing to help, but only in a superficial way. None of them is prepared to undertake the actual mission, which is typical of the bastards. Always sitting on the fence."

Bell lit a thin Davidoff cigar. Mahmoudi's eyes had ceased darting. The old schemer was nibbling.

"We need a complete plan of your house in Teheran and the combination of your floor safe. Do you have them?"

Mahmoudi stared at Bell as he strained to rally forces that had once functioned instinctively. He tried to weigh the options, assess his interests. But his mental wheels were rusty. There was no solution, only a chance. The information Bell wanted was not crucial; he knew too much already. He knew where the tapes were; all he wanted was the safe number. If Mahmoudi did not comply willingly, Bell could easily circumvent him. He could blow the safe open if he had to. On the other hand, if Mahmoudi cooperated, perhaps it would buy him time. Perhaps he could break free long enough to contact Gina. And there was still the other matter. Yes, maybe there was a chance.

"I will help you," he said finally as he fumbled in his coat pocket. Then he remembered the coat had been taken from the closet by his kidnappers.

"May I please have something to write with?" he said. "Your animals forgot to pack my pen."

Bell slid a pen and a pad of paper across the desk.

"That is the combination number of the safe," Mahmoudi said, handing the pad back. "If I am not mistaken I have a plan of the house at my apartment in Cannes."

"My pen, please," said Bell.

Mahmoudi pushed it across the table as Bell stubbed out his cigar. The ashtray, Mahmoudi noticed, was made from a 75mm brass shell casing, another of Bell's peccadillos.

"How will you do it?" asked Mahmoudi, not the least interested in the answer. What he needed was more time. More time to think. More time to plan. But the answer was more than he had bargained for.

"Michael Adel," replied Bell casually, pleased but not surprised by the shock on the old man's face. "He'll get them out for us."

There was a momentary hesitation as Bell contemplated the skyline through the massive windows again. Just enough time to separate the two subjects and let both effects take hold.

"Gina and he were lovers, weren't they?" he asked slyly.

Mahmoudi looked sharply at Bell.

"He is the father of my granddaughter, Natalie," he answered softly, embarrassed to have his daughter's long affair with Adel dragged into this setting. "But of course, you would know that sort of thing. That is your forte, is it not?"

"Of course," answered Bell. "I know Adel quite well myself. We met when he was at the National Iranian Oil Company and saw a lot of each other while I was on assignment in Iran. There are several reasons why we chose him, but we needn't go into that. Let's just say that a combination of the ancient *qanat* irrigation system of your country and the fact that his father's house is only one away from yours was the clincher."

Mahmoudi shook his head in disbelief.

He had always liked Michael Adel. In fact, he would have liked him as a son-in-law—he had been the only solid, stable influence in Gina's turbulent life. He had to admit, though, in this moment of doubt or that it had never been clear whether this bright young whiz kid was more American than Iranian or vice, versa. He had known Adel's father since boyhood, when they had attended Alborz College in Teheran. After a long stint in the United States Adel had returned to Iran with an American wife and two American sons. Michael, the elder, had grown into a bright, clever and dynamic petroleum engineer. He was wholesome and refreshingly American, yet fully at home in the intricacies of Iranian society. After a few years with the national oil company, he had set himself up in the oil services industry, and hard work, charm and good business sense had been parlayed into great wealth.

The fixer in Mahmoudi, the operator whose survival and success had always depended on up-to-date information, was curious. Had Bell somehow coerced Adel into a role in this venture? Or had he misread Michael Adel? Had he been one of Bell's pigeons all along?

"I find it difficult to believe that a man like Adel would willingly lend himself to this sort of thing. That is very surprising to me. He is a very decent man."

"You surprise me, Ali," said Bell, glancing at the computer printouts on the table. "Nice he may be, but beneath that Lothario exterior lies a ruthless character. Ask your daughter."

This time Mahmoudi did not rise to the bait. "Even if you are right, he had every opportunity to enrich himself at the oil company and he always refused to participate in the simple route to wealth. May I ask under what pretense he would subject himself to danger and help you steal now?"

"No," Bell said, staring at him icily, "you can't."

His hand dropped beneath the table and pushed a button. "There are, Ali, several sides to Michael Adel. And most of them you know nothing about. But don't worry about it. He'll help."

The door of the office opened and the two kidnappers entered.

"You haven't been formally introduced, have you? His Excellency Ali Mahmoudi. Jim Gleeson," Bell said, pointing to the smaller of the two men. "And Bill Davis."

Ali Mahmoudi flashed a contemptuous look at the two men.

"These gentlemen will accompany you for the next few days," said Bell, looking at his watch. "We'll meet in Cannes, in three days. In addition to your house plans, we have other business there." Bell stood and approached Mahmoudi with the same twisted grin. "But before you go, your excellency, tell me just how you obtained those tapes. You've piqued my professional curiosity."

Mahmoudi stared at him. For a brief moment he felt a craving to defy Bell. But he controlled the urge; it would only be a short-term satisfaction. Play along, he thought. Loosen the reins by appearing helpful. It's the only hope.

"It's so simple, you probably wouldn't believe me."

"The best plans always are, Ali," Bell said encouragingly.

"Christmas, 1974, I gave Jacey one of those Eraser-Mate pens. Very good for doodling, scribbling and so forth. I had it encased in gold at Cartier's in Paris. Luckily he liked it and always carried it with him.

"I had something else done to it too," said Mahmoudi. "The pen has a very large eraser on the top and there is—how do you say it—a microphone that works off any noise. . . ."

"A S.A.M.," interrupted Bell, glancing at the two men behind Mahmoudi.

"A what?"

"Sound-activated microphone."

"Ah, colonel, what a professional you are. That is what the man called it too."

Mahmoudi's teasing irritated Bell. "And how did you record?" he snapped.

"Ah, that was more or less luck. I was kept on standby, as you say—waiting outside the meetings in case I was needed. I was in the room next door when Jacey was giving his presentation, a few feet away with only a wall separating us. The microphone taped straight on to an IBM tape recorder in my pocket. I had to change the miniature tapes often through the long meetings, but I was alone in the room and it was not a problem. Later I transferred all the material on the small tapes to regular cassettes and destroyed the miniature ones. I was so happy I obtained them and so lucky that the meetings were so. . . so. . . crucial. I thought afterwards that they would provide me with protection if ever I needed it."

The old man lowered his head and gave a hollow laugh. "Protection," he repeated bitterly.

Bell nodded at the two men, who moved toward Mahmoudi.

"Help Mister Mahmoudi back to his apartment and see that he has everything he needs."

The old man showed no resistance. "Be careful, colonel. There are exceptions to every rule," he said as he turned toward the door. "And Michael Adel may prove to be your exception."

He walked a few feet, then stopped abruptly and looked back.

"Oh, colonel. There is something else you might like to consider. It does compare well with the tapes you seek."

Bell stood up and hooked his granny glasses to the end of his nose. Slowly he walked toward Mahmoudi.

"In many ways the papers are remarkably similar in value to the tapes, colonel. They are my recollections; diaries of various activities in Iran."

Bell's instincts sensed danger.

"Various activities?"

"The stealing."

"What stealing, Ali?"

It was Mahmoudi's turn to smile.

"Oil stealing, colonel."

CHAPTER 3

CANNES: FRIDAY, OCTOBER 19, 1979: 5:30 P.M.

At precisely that moment—six time zones away—the Côte d'Azur was hardly the glamorous place the French tourist industry so proudly advertises. The *mistral* had burst out of Africa like a freight train. It boomed and tumbled through the stormy darkness, building great roller-coaster waves that crashed on the beaches and hurled their fury against the flotilla of deserted private yachts moored in their coves.

In Cannes rain lashed the sparkling promenades and the palm trees bent sadly under the impact. The town's main boulevard, La Croisette, which in the summer months played host to the glamorous jet set, was barely inhabited. The few people who had braved the afternoon's ominous clouds cursed themselves and sought refuge from the steady downpour. With the exception of one man, no one was visible on the more exposed southern flank of the Mediterranean boulevard.

The lonely figure, running at a medium pace, exhaled every fourth step and the spent air vaporized upon contact with the brisk autumn chill. He ran past the Majestic Hotel, past the expensive boutiques—Hermes, Gucci, Lanvin—past the Blue Bar and the Palais des Festivals, where the antics of the Cannes Film Festival signal the start of *la saison.*

This gets harder every day, the athletic figure thought as he broke his run in front of the mecca of the town—the elegant Carlton Hotel. He walked slowly across the deserted street and the pink, paved parking lot that sets the hotel back from the boulevard, and skipped up six steps to the dry sanctuary of the hotel awning. There he bent forward to catch his breath.

"*Vous êtes fou,* Monsieur Adel. Running in this weather," huffed the doorman. He offered him a towel.

"Pull in the stomach, Jean. You're beginning to look like an egg," panted Michael Adel.

The doorman straightened his moustache and then cradled his stomach.

"*Ça c'est présence.*"

"It's fat, Jean," quipped Adel. It was part of their daily banter. "That's what it is."

"No, Mister Adel. We French are not mad like you Americans. Whenever we feel the urge to exercise, we merely lie down until it passes."

Adel smiled, conceding the game.

"Did madame and young Natalie return with you?" inquired the doorman.

"No. They should be here by the weekend." Adel towelled his mop of curly black hair and wiped his blue plastic jacket and running shoes. "You'll probably see them before I do. Natalie is sure to want a club sandwich on the way home." He exchanged the towel for his car keys and the newspaper which the doorman picked up for him every day, saving him the trouble of entering the lobby.

"Stay here, Jean. No use both of us catching pneumonia," he said as he moved away.

"Oh, Monsieur Adel," the doorman called after him. "Did you see your friends?"

A look of surprise crossed the athlete's rugged, handsome face as he turned back. "What friends, Jean?"

"A couple of American gentlemen." The portly doorman shrugged. "They said they'd drive along the Croisette to find you running."

"Didn't see a soul. Did they leave their names?"

"No, sir."

"Well, they shouldn't have any problem finding me. My telephone is listed." He winked at the doorman before turning into the pouring rain. A few steps down the narrow hotel driveway he slid into the front seat of a sleek white Aston-Martin Lagonda and waited for the new V8 engine to warm. Two Americans? he thought. He wasn't expecting anyone. Dismissing the question, he slipped the car into gear.

The doorman smiled and shook his head in admiration as his eyes followed the luxurious car. There goes a fine gentleman, he thought, wondering if Monsieur Adel had looked after himself during the revolution in Iran; whether he had money in America or Switzerland or somewhere. Monsieur Adel had been working in Iran, he remembered hearing; he had a lot of investments there. It would be a shame not to see him again. Like so many others who had dropped out of sight over the years after some distant political convulsion. How many of the wealthy crowd from the Middle East, Africa and South America had suddenly failed to appear at the "usual" time of year. He watched as the car turned right on the Croisette and disappeared. It would be a shame if that happened to Monsieur....

Abruptly his thoughts were jarred by the sound of a motor kicking to life to his left, in the small parking lot fronting the hotel. A dark blue Peugeot 504 pulled into the traffic behind the Lagonda. Inside were the same two Americans who had asked after Michael Adel.

CHAPTER
4

Colonel Grover Cleveland Bell watched the short, disheveled-looking man turn and amble toward the huge photochromic windows. "What oil stealing, Ali?"

"Of course, my papers are not documented with signatures or contracts. Such things never are," said Ali Mahmoudi with stiff precision, "but they are the recollections of an old man who seeks to spend the rest of his short life in peace and quiet."

Brusquely, Bell waved dismissal to his two subordinates as Mahmoudi continued to speak softly into the window, his breath clinging to the cold glass.

"I have written it all down in great detail, colonel. Before the revolution. In the form of diaries, recollections, aide-mémoires. It is all parked in a safe deposit box somewhere in Europe. It was prudent of me, no?"

"I'm not sure I follow you, Ali."

"It is not difficult, colonel. I have made detailed notes of the entire framework by which the Western oil companies used us and how their senior executives enriched themselves. Oh yes, and in the process made some of us very rich, too. But that is all in the past now."

He paused and turned to smile at Bell's puzzled expression. "My notes detail exactly which officers in the old Anglo-Iranian Oil Company pushed their pet Iranian executives after the 1953 nationalization to the pinnacles of power in the National Iranian Oil Company and the Iranian government. After all, we—and I was one of them—were all part of the early cadre trained by the British...."

"What has all this got to do with us, Ali?"

"It is quite simple. Through these corrupt friends, or *doostan*

26

as we were called, your oil companies and their executives enriched themselves outrageously. Oh, what a lovely story it would make one day. Watergate would pale in comparison. Not very good for political stability in the West, would you say, colonel?"

"And how was this stealing purportedly conducted?" Bell pressed.

"Many ways. Having established their network of *doostan,* the foreign oil companies would use us as they wished. For example, after we nationalized the oil industry, the companies came to us to negotiate discounts on future oil sales ostensibly to amortize the investments they had made over the years to develop the oil facilities in Iran. We would engage in tough negotiations and finally concede, say, twenty cents a barrel to the offshore trading company that represented all the oil companies. Of course, that was perhaps eight cents too much and by prior agreement—reached in secret sessions in Geneva—we all shared that eight cents through a complex web of offshore bearer share concerns. By we, colonel, I naturally mean certain individuals in your oil companies as well as a few of us Iranians. And eight cents a barrel for, say, three or four million barrels per day is not an inconsequential amount is it? Especially over a period of some years.

"Don't look so bored, colonel," said Mahmoudi as he turned back. "It's all documented. Names, dates, amounts, bank accounts. Above all, names. And it goes back a long time. Not just the more recent boom."

He stuck his hands in his pockets and took a few steps, then stopped again.

"And once OPEC was established we all, the Western oil company executives and the *doostan,* had such a profitable time bypassing the OPEC equal mix provisions between light and heavy crude. The oil companies would pay us huge bribes—millions per year—to give them a favorable mix of light oil over heavy. We Iranians would supply the light, breaking OPEC rules. We'd bank the bribes in Switzerland. Clean. End of story, colonel?

"But no-ooh. Oooh-noo. Because who would come pecking at those accounts in the middle of the night? People like..."

The significance of the half-dozen names spilling through Mahmoudi's grinning lips was not lost on Bell. He was naming the chairmen and presidents of Europe and America's largest oil companies as well as senior banking and government officials on both sides of the Atlantic.

"That's right. These gentlemen and a handful of us Iranians were partners in perhaps the biggest swindle in history."

Mahmoudi paced toward a leather armchair.

"Oh, I nearly forgot the S.C.T.'s," he said as he slumped on the chair.

"The what?"

"Shuffling Credit Terms," smiled Mahmoudi. "You see, I was a professional too." He burst out laughing at his own joke.

"What were shuffling credit terms?" asked an irritated Bell.

"OPEC regulations allowed its members to offer a maximum of sixty-days'-credit terms and that's what all the contracts between Iran and the oil companies stipulated on paper. But who drew up and policed these contracts on the Iranian side? We did. And do you know what else we—the *doostan*—insisted upon? That the money be paid to Iranian government deposit accounts in Switzerland. The oil companies always paid promptly within sixty days into these accounts. The only wrinkle was that they were not Iranian government accounts. The real government accounts, maintained in Chase Manhattan branches in New York and London, were actually only credited after one hundred twenty days. So sixty days' interest on oil shipments was always unaccounted for. Calculate what that was, colonel, when oil prices had climbed to ten, twelve dollars a barrel. About one, sometimes one and a half, million barrels a day were being treated in this way. That's ten to fifteen million per day earning two months' interest. What's that add up to, colonel? What is that per day? And what happened to it? Why don't you ask..." and out poured the names again "... for the exact figures and where some of that money went. Ah, it was all so cosy, our little partnership."

Mahmoudi suddenly became reflective. "I wonder if they're still doing it with the other oil countries? Is it happening also in Saudi Arabia, Nigeria, Venezuela?" His pensive frown cracked into a broad grin, then a mocking cackle.

Bell stared at him and waited for the laughter to subside. It was unlikely, he thought, that Mahmoudi had made more than one copy of the documents. But unlikely was not good enough. He had to get a precise handle on them. He had to be certain.

"You've recorded all of this?" he prompted after Mahmoudi had got hold of himself.

"And more, Grover—may I call you that?—I have outlined the activities of the myopic meters. Have you heard of them?"

Bell moved his head from side to side.

"That was perhaps the jewel. It was so brazen. You see, we in Iran were equipped to export eight and a half million barrels of oil per day, but even at the highest point only six million barrels were ever officially transferred to tankers. That left two and a half million barrels a day of extra capacity that we never used—not officially. It was for *emergency purposes*—only the 'emergency' was unofficially always there. All we did was bypass the meters with auxiliary pipelines that had no meters, and *voilà!* the oil was never registered."

"Pipelines and pumping stations with no meters, Ali? How's that possible?"

"I said auxiliary pipelines. Lines designed for use in temporary emergencies when tracking output was not important. When the main pipes were inoperative after an earthquake, or during a fire, and so on."

"How much flowed this way?"

Mahmoudi was pleased with the interest he had aroused in Bell.

"It is difficult to put a figure on it. Sometimes it was more, sometimes it was less. But it was always there. Somewhere between five hundred thousand and one million barrels a day. Even at the twelve-dollar-a-barrel price that existed just before the revolution, that is somewhere between six and twelve million dollars a day that was being siphoned off. Twelve million a day, colonel! Think of it!"

"Where did all this money go?"

"I have written down only what I know. Some of it came back to us *doostan*. Much of it went to our friends in America and Europe who were doing the buying on behalf of their companies. Where the rest went I don't know. Your imagination is as good as mine. But what I know is written in detail. Names, Grover. Names, names."

Bell frowned. "And you're saying no one ever questioned the oil company figures?"

"Of course not!" snapped Mahmoudi. "SAVAK—the secret police—were always there, lurking in the background. His Majesty had created a *bête noir* which provided us with wonderfully effective cover. No one dared question what went on because the enormity of these myopic meters meant it had to have been... approved."

Mahmoudi shook his head and chuckled. "The funny thing, colonel, was that it was so impressively efficient. We did not need more than two people at most. Two people in just the right positions in the oil company. And toward the end, colonel, in the last few years before the revolution, it was inefficient to have to go through two men, so both positions were filled by one man, making the operation even more streamlined. Is that not impressive, I ask you?" There was another round of belly laughter.

Bell's eyes squinted and his fingers drummed his bottom lip as he let the silence hang. Then he pushed himself out of his armchair and walked to his desk. "That's a hell of a tale you have there, Ali. Could do quite a lot of shaking up in the world. And that is the last thing we need."

"It is bigger even than Watergate, is it not, colonel? It is the biggest swindle in history. And what poetic irony that its stars are the most upstanding and upright pillars of the American and European business establishment. Up to now it was always us dirty little Arabs that were the thieves. It would be fascinating to see what the American public would say if they learned that what we stole was a pittance compared with the pillars of your society, would it not?"

"You don't want to leave documents like that lying around. Could be counterproductive."

"Rest assured, dear Grover. If I have no worries, you have no worries. For my own protection I have made only one set, which the depository has been instructed to release only on my death. And then only if it is... how do you put it? unnatural."

Bell sifted through a pile of papers on his desk, selected one and studied it for a moment before placing it back in its slot.

"You seem to forget, Ali, that we are on the same side. We have no quarrel with you. There's no animosity between us." He rose and put a hand on Mahmoudi's shoulder and smiled. "Look, Ali, you've been under unbelievable pressure lately. It's all gone wrong for you and it's a shame. But don't let it get to you; don't take it out on your friends. I assure you, you will never need that file— not against us. We are colleagues. We'll always look after you. Even if it means we have to put up with these occasional tantrums of yours," he laughed, his face again showing kindness and sympathy.

Mahmoudi returned the smile. "Perhaps you are right, colonel."

"You need a holiday, Ali. A long vacation away from telephones, newspapers and television. Maybe after Cannes you should just

30

take off—'destination unknown' sort of thing," said Bell. He moved back to the desk and pressed the button again.

"I'm running a little late, Ali. I do hope we can meet again before Cannes. Perhaps you can come over for dinner."

The two men entered the room and Mahmoudi turned toward them. His stomach fluttered as he looked back at Bell. He had to call Gina in London. He had to instruct her what to do.

"I won't need these...these two..."

"Just for protection, Ali," said Bell as he guided Mahmoudi toward the door. "They won't get in your way. We have information that suggests the Khomeini people have hit squads heading this way. I'd feel more at ease if you had someone looking after you."

He turned to the two men. "I don't want you getting in his excellency's way. Stay in the background."

"Well, Ali. We'll be in touch," he said, shaking hands with the old man.

Mahmoudi smiled contentedly. He had the leeway to distance himself from these two ghouls long enough to call Gina from an untapped telephone booth.

"Good-bye, colonel," he said as he turned to leave, "and thank you."

Bell held the door open until the three men had walked through the reception area. Then he walked swiftly to his desk and picked up the telephone. He pressed a button and waited.

"Miss Pringle," he said when a voice answered. "Mahmoudi's file. The papers from his safe deposit box at the bank in Geneva. Have them brought up. I want to see those diaries of his again."

CHAPTER 5

CANNES: FRIDAY, OCTOBER 19, 1979: EVENING

Michael Adel drove carefully through the light evening traffic, heading the powerful car northward, up the narrow winding lanes to the hills of Super Cannes behind and overlooking the city. He did not look forward to the empty house; without Sam and Natalie it was too big, too quiet, too cold. He did not enjoy it without them.

He thought of his daughter. Natalie was still a serious child, observing everything, taking it all in. But she was happier now, the memories of her mother's home were fading, and she was gradually warming to the love and security Samira had so carefully and generously provided.

It was amazing, he thought, from that chance meeting with Samira had begun a love affair that was to affect not only his life but to radically change Natalie's.

It had been—what?—almost three years ago. He was sitting over croissants and coffee at an outdoor table of the Café Flore, the famed Left Bank bistro on Boulevard Saint Germain, after a late night and little sleep. He had glanced at the headlines of *Le Monde* but nothing gripped his attention and the paper remained half-folded beside his plate. The strong, bitter coffee warmed his stomach and activated his sluggish brain. He looked up to see a girl seated two tables away dropping her eyes as they met his. It was commonplace to find women sitting alone in Parisian bistros, but this one seemed so vulnerable sitting alone. She was a small, slender girl, almost delicate. *Recherché*, the French called it, with fine small bones, not unlike thousands of French women with their indefinable air of delicacy and chic. Yet it was her eyes that were startling. They were large and brown and limpid—so openly, nakedly trusting that one's immediate impulse was to warn her against strange men, like himself. He looked at her unobserved and with growing interest. Her long jet black hair was tied loosely by a ribbon at the nape of her neck. Her face was dark and striking, with enviably high cheekbones that gave her wholesome features a starkly sensuous caste. She wore skin-tight Levis over long slender legs which she had tucked into knee-length burgundy boots. A puffy silk chemise matched her footwear and fluttered against her taut nipples with the morning breeze.

Yes, she was different from Parisian girls, not because she lacked their intuitive style—she had that in abundance—but because she lacked their awareness, that self-consciousness of their own sexuality and how to use it. Yes, she was vulnerable; she lacked the protective carapace that helped survival in a harsh world.

32

"*Vous êtes américaine?*"

She looked at Adel with a hint of a smile and nodded. "Yes. How did you know?" Her voice was youthful but husky. Her French held not a trace of an accent but it was guarded.

"It's been years since I saw a lavaliere," he said.

She touched the necklace with its Greek symbols.

"The man must be very dear to you."

"He is." She brought the necklace to her lips and left it there. "But how do you know about lavalieres?"

He switched to English. "I'm American, too."

She smiled and her face was warm and sensuous and disarming. "Well, maybe we should start at the beginning," he said. "What's your name?"

"Samira," she replied. Her large brown eyes looked openly into his, the whites clear, healthy.

"Samira what?"

"Ferragamo. My father was Italian, my mother French. They both emigrated to the States. What's yours?"

"Adel. Michael Adel. And that's half American, half Iranian."

Her eyes held a trace of surprise as she looked at him, her chin resting in the palm of her hand, her elbow leaning on the table. "You look far more American than Iranian."

He smiled. "In the present circumstances, that's a compliment, I suppose."

"You'll laugh, but in Paris I've come to love what everybody mocks Americans for—their simpleness and childlike honesty. There's no guile in America."

They ordered more coffee and talked for a long while. Then they strolled along Boulevard Saint Germain to St. Clotilde, the ancient church sleeping among the trees. Then northward again along the Esplanade des Invalides, onto the sculptured bridge, Pont Alexandre III.

Along the way she spoke of her frustration as a student at the Sorbonne and how she loathed the Frenchmen she knew, both students and teachers, who "treated all females as playthings." She found France, her mother's country, disappointing and pretentious, even though she blended in so well. And she missed her undergraduate years at Brown University, the direct honesty, the purity of the American style.

Adel leaned on the bridge rail beside her, captivated by her open innocence, her candor, and they watched the river. A *bateau mouche* excursion boat moved into view and she waved and smiled at the crowded deck; some of the passengers waved back.

"So what are you going to do with yourself?" he asked.

"I don't know," she said, her eyes on the river. "I've got to come up with something that stimulates me."

He pointed at her necklace. "What does the man in your life say?"

"Nothing. It belonged to my father. And he's dead."

He was amazed that she could provoke such interest in him. She was enthralled by things he had not observed—at least not for a long time. Her concerns seemed so trivial, so innocent, so young. But it was the enthusiasm, the zest, she exuded for them that was catching. Under normal circumstances, boredom should by now have set in and the search for excuses started. But he was captivated by her spirit and charm. It was like a journey back through time, a junket back to the carefree days of a college campus.

Besides, he thought, they had been together for several hours now and she hadn't once mentioned Louis Féraud or Givenchy or Dior—a blessing. She hadn't even brought up Regine's.

Suddenly she smiled mischievously. "Come on, I'd like a crêpe," she said as she took his arm.

"Let's make that a full lunch," he suggested.

For a second her eyes revealed hesitation. Just as suddenly, the doubt vanished. "Okay."

After that they had met every day and Paris took on a new meaning. She managed to organize and program their days according to her own tastes, ignoring his suggestions of more luxurious and glamorous things to do.

"Yech," she would say after every name he mentioned.

And, strangely, he did not object, he found it attractive. Not for her the expensive overrated restaurants, discotheques and night clubs—Lasserre, Maxim's, Regine's, Ruby's, Club d'Artois. Gone, too, was his habitual menu of lissome high-priced call girls that only Paris provides with such facility, taste and class. Instead, he saw the city by day and with Samira it took on a new light. They did the traditional tourist things and he loved it. They walked along the Seine, the Tuileries, the Louvre and watched and made bets on the men playing *boule* in the Luxembourg Gardens.

They visisted the ancient Hostellerie du Bas-Breau in the village

34

of Barbizon and walked its cobblestoned streets to the former houses of Millet and Rousseau. They rented horses and rode the scenic paths around Fontainebleau forest, then returned to Paris to play the slot machines in Passage Point Show till dawn. They drove to Villequier, where Victor Hugo's poem laments the drowning of his daughter. They spent hours admiring the spectacular view of the Normandy coast and the Aval cliffs.

And they went often to her place, a small but tastefully furnished apartment in an old building on the Avenue de Bosquet on the Left Bank. But she never visited his hotel or made the smallest concession to his regular life-style.

She tried cooking, but was not very good at it. He took over, performing small miracles with *omelettes, entrecotes, croque monsieurs*, even hamburgers. In fact it was his cooking that had put their relationship in clear perspective.

"God, the French," he complained bitterly one evening, as he sucked a burn blister on his index finger. "They can't grind beef. They puree it even if you plead with the butcher. Whatever you do, it tastes like wet mortar. Why the hell do we go through this cooking ritual every day anyway?" he asked, not altogether in jest. "We can eat well occasionally."

"I have to be a little different from the others, don't I?" she had answered petulantly. "Besides, I like eating what we cook."

"What *we*? What *we* eat together, *I* cook. You can't cook to save your life." His voice was harsher than he intended.

"I know you can pay for the best. You've made that boorishly obvious." She had been wounded and her voice was angry. "You prefer that life, don't you? Dinner at Lasserre and then Regine's, and then a fuck at the George V. You really don't want a normal relationship, do you? One with ordinary human moods and feelings. One that grows with time. No, you always want to buy a shortcut. You need six waiters hovering around, bowing, scraping and calling you 'sir' before you can have a good time."

Her cheeks were pink with anger. Her eyes brimmed with tears.

"I hate that part of you. You *are* Iranian. This is all an act, isn't it? Nothing means anything to you, especially women. You just buy them with your worthless money. I'm just a challenge. Someone you can't have that easily. Go on, then. Call Madame Claude. Get one of her whores. I'm not what you're used to."

In his reverie, Adel smiled as he downshifted the Lagonda's

automatic gears to negotiate the steep gradient of the final leg of the hill. He recalled how from that one small, almost inconsequential incident in Sam's kitchen, his whole life had changed.

He shifted the gear back to "Drive" as the road straightened out and remembered how he had stood absolutely still, frozen by her outburst. She had been wrong and yet she had been painfully right. Not since those blissful but infuriating times with Gina Mahmoudi had he really cared about a woman; and not since those carefree, illicit days with Jane Bennett had he felt such sheer excitement. Dear, loyal, romantic, secretive, screwed-up Jane, he thought. So anxious to love, yet so terrified of her husband and scandal.

Yes, Samira was different. It was such a different kind of love with her, the antithesis of all those feckless physical, relationships. It was honest and innocent and clean. She was a different kind of girl, too—fragile, unaffected, pure. She brought qualities he had buried in his efforts to impress the world. With her he was human again; he no longer posed, played a part. And she loved him, that was obvious. But she loved him honestly for what he was. She knew nothing of his past. All she cared about was the present.

Suddenly, in that one frozen moment, in a tiny crowded kitchen he had loved again. And for the first time since his schooldays, he had felt a strong urge to explain.

"Sam..." he said hesitantly, afraid to bare what he had kept hidden for so long. But the words were uncontrollable. A hidden, pent-up force he had never felt before seemed to blast them to the surface. "You're right."

He had told her about his past, about Gina and Natalie and the shell he hid behind. He told her about the glass-bubble society he lived in, the insecurity and alienation he felt in Iran and how, to survive, he had to adopt the characteristics of a chameleon. He told her about his business, the pressures, his relief when he spent time at the oil fields in the desert, away from the corruption and phoniness of Teheran.

But the pressure of the pent-up force had been unsatisfied. It had demanded more; it had demanded a full, total commitment.

"I love you, Sam. As much as I'm capable of loving, I love you."

She had looked at him, her eyes filled with sympathy and excitement. But she had held her look, contemplating her answer.

"I love you, too, Michael," she had replied at length. "But don't be that way with me. Don't be hard. You don't need it with me; you don't need to act. I love Michael Adel, not the money or the restaurants or the cars. They won't get me through the night. Only you will."

Adel turned the car off the Chemin de Collines, high above Cannes, into the graveled driveway of his home. Sam was the best thing that had ever happened to him, he thought, as the burly keeper stepped out of the gatehouse to open the wrought-iron gates. Adel went through the entrance and followed a driveway lined with pine trees that curved left. The house followed the ubiquitous Mediterranean form—white stucco, Moorish arches shading walkways under red-tile roofing. It was a large place, even by the Riviera's opulent standards.

At the far end of the building mist rose from the heated swimming pool, which extended into the house beneath a glass dome; a kind of solarium/hothouse crowded with brilliant potted plants: hibiscus, orchids, jasmine, gardenias and dwarf melons.

In front of the house lay a vast expanse of lawn. Adel passed the cascades of well-pruned roses, oleanders and bougainvillea that clung to the arch pillars and looked at the disciplined growth of yews and the exotic polus bushes that separated the main building from the garage.

To the left of the pool a barbecue pit squatted in the semi-darkness beneath the shade of the surrounding palms. It was Sam's enclave, a source of delicious charcoil-broiled aromas on summer evenings: chicken, beef, lamb and fish kebabs, even sweet corn for Natalie.

Behind the house, in a clear semicircle, stood a forest—mainly pines, but with hemlocks, imported cedars, several softshell pecans imported from Oklahoma and oaks from Limousin. Hidden from view, behind the thick foliage, was a paddock with a tack room where Sam and Natalie kept their horses, and a small gymnasium where he worked out daily.

But the *pièce de résistance* lay directly in front of the mansion. It was the breathtaking view of the Mediterranean, from Golfe Juan and Juan les Pins to the left, to Porte la Galère to the right.

Adel inspected it proudly as he walked toward the front door—even in bad weather it never lost its astonishing impact.

"Storm's getting worse, John," said Adel, entering the lobby.

John Usher was English and had been in Adel's employ for several years. Tall, balding, bespectacled, he was Adel's personal butler, as well as confidant and friend.

"You have a visitor, sir." Usher reached to take Adel's windbreaker. "A Mister Donald Anderson, an American gentle-man...."

Adel turned sharply, his eyes narrowing.

"He did say you were old friends, sir," said a surprised Usher, handing him Anderson's calling card.

Adel answered distantly as he studied the card.

"That's true enough, John," he said, running his fingers through his unruly hair. In addition to Anderson's name, the card carried an embossed golden seal of a spread eagle and the legend: THE UNITED STATES OF AMERICA, DEPARTMENT OF STATE, NEAR EAST SECTION.

CHAPTER 6

LONDON: FRIDAY, OCTOBER 19, 1979: 7:00 P.M.

The stunning girl with long jet black hair felt foolish and out of place. Never in her entire life had she considered looking incon-spicuous a difficult—or desirable—task to accomplish. Never, that was, until now. Moreover, hers was—as she was the first to ad-mit—only a half-hearted effort. Her expensive Fiorucci jeans, al-tered to perfection, and her exquisite mink windbreaker tailored by Chombert on the Rue de Faubourg Saint Honoré set her apart from the mundane commuter traffic heading home. Her suntan and immaculate coiffure only served to widen the gap between her and the throng battling its way through Knightsbridge Under-ground Station.

She glanced distastefully at her golden Piaget watch before aim-lessly picking out two more fashion magazines from the rack and dumping them on the growing pile beside the cash register of the newsstand. Thankfully, she thought as she plucked a crisp twenty-pound note from the wad in her crocodile bag, it was nearly seven o'clock.

She dropped the change carelessly in the bag, snapped the H-buckle closed and threaded her way against the heavy flow of traffic toward the decrepit telephone booths at the far side of the station.

What was she doing? she wondered as she studied the unhealthy yellow hue of the crowds flashing by her in drab, heavy winter clothing. Wasting her time—that's what she was doing. All this panic, all this talk of danger. Fake names, deadlines, flights across the world and not calling one's friends.

But this was the final straw. It was crazy. Secret long-distance calls. Had the old man's mind been affected by Leila's death? Or was it the opium....

Suddenly a heavy moving shoulder crashed into her side, momentarily paralyzing her arm and sending her stack of magazines tumbling to the floor. She turned angrily. But the culprit was long gone and the magazines lay scattered and smeared across the grimy surface of the floor.

She cursed and left them there, lengthening her stride toward the far wall. How many days? she wondered. How many days would she have to go through this tortuous routine?

The last few yards were relatively easy, the crowds decreasing as she gained distance from the escalators that descended down to the city's bowels. But on the right side of the three booths a group of scraggy Hari Krishnas stood milling about, chanting and extorting contributions from the passers-by. She pouted and ignored them, hurrying instead toward the sound of ringing that had suddenly erupted from the center telephone booth.

"Hallo... hallo."

"Yes, Father," replied the pretty girl, instantly recognizing his impatient voice, while still fumbling with the slippery receiver.

"I cannot talk for very long. We are going through the *ghosl* ceremony with your sister's body."

Gina Mahmoudi's heart sank as she visualized her sister's corpse being elaborately washed and wrapped in the sheetlike *kafan* according to Islamic tradition.

"I have managed to be alone for just a moment. So listen carefully, my darling."

"Why on earth didn't you use a coffin, father?"

"I begged them to give me a few last moments with Leila and this was the best way. Now, you must do as I tell you."

"But, really, father, you should have...."

"Listen," snapped Ali Mahmoudi in a frenzied whisper. "I have only a moment. They will be back soon to accompany me to her grave. The opportunity will be lost. And both our lives depend on you listening."

CHAPTER 7

CANNES: FRIDAY, OCTOBER 19, 1979: 9:00 P.M.

"That was delicious, Michael," said Don Anderson as he stood from the dining table. "Do you eat like this every night?"

Adel nodded at Usher. "Only when John here is hungry."

Usher smiled but said nothing as the two men went through the low, arched hallway separating the dining and sitting areas.

"How about a drink, Don?" offered Adel.

"Sure, why not?"

"Cognac?"

"Sounds great."

Adel pointed to a comfortable corner of the lavish living room. "Make yourself at home. I'll be right with you."

All evening it had been tense, thought Adel, as he went to an alcove that stood along one wall of the room. He opened the rustic wooden bar and poured two large snifters of Bas Armagnac. In spite of polite conversation, gossip about old friends and genial recollections of the past, including Anderson's account of his divorce, the atmosphere had not reflected their once deep friendship. On the contrary, it had suggested strain.

Well, Adel had thought, perhaps Anderson's divorce had left a bitter aftertaste. The end of his own affair with Gina had not been a divorce, but it had been a similar gut-wrenching experience. He had remembered the depths of his own depression then and he now gave his friend the benefit of the doubt.

Adel handed Anderson a brandy glass. "How long will you be

40

with us, Don?" he asked, placing the bottle on the glass table in front of his guest. "I hope it's not one of those all-American hit-and-run jobs."

"Afraid so. Two or three days at the most," replied Anderson. "But tell me, Michael, what do you make of the situation in Iran?"

Adel sat at one end of the couch, surprised by the abrupt change of topic. Perhaps Anderson was at last leading up to the purpose of his visit.

"I'm sure I feel the same way as you," he replied guardedly. "We both worked too long in that environment to believe the crap we're being fed. There's something missing that makes the whole thing... unbelievable. There's more to the Iranian story than we're being told."

Anderson shifted uneasily in the deep armchair. "You don't believe it was a straightforward, domestically motivated revolt, then?"

Adel studied his old friend: he had gained weight in the two years since he had left the U.S. Embassy in Iran, but the chubbiness only served to enhance his clean-cut boyish appearance. The blond hair was still cut short and combed tidily; the blue eyes retained their honesty, though the dark circles beneath them were new.

"I don't know what to believe, Don," he said. "It's not intellectual or fashionable to think conspiracy these days but there are too many unanswered questions, too many coincidences for my tastes. It just doesn't jibe."

Adel explained his doubts: his incredulity at the apparent ineptness of the CIA; the fumblings of the dreaded SAVAK, the CIA-created and -operated Iranian secret police; the fickleness of Iran's vaunted army; and the treachery of its two senior commanders, whose switching of sides guaranteed Khomeini's success. The case of one general seemed particularly bizarre—he had been the *de facto* controller of SAVAK, the Shah's right-hand man and childhood friend. Now he was setting up a new Islamic secret police for Khomeini.

Anderson remained silent as Adel continued talking of the nervousness of America's Arab allies in the Gulf and Middle East, how they were drawing lessons from American indifference to the fate of its friends.

Anderson grimaced and let out a long hiss of air.

"Yeah, the Iranian revolution has had a devastating effect. Unfortunately, a lot of people feel the way you do. The Saudis and Sadat in Egypt are very discouraged. They believe we let the Shah down too."

Adel sat forward in his chair. "They have every reason to be worried. It's going to get a lot worse out there. The whole Middle East is a powder keg and they've unleashed a lunatic, a nut who represents a violent god in an ignorant, backward part of the world. He's a time bomb, ticking away."

"You're exaggerating, Michael. Khomeini's bad. The Shah's gone—and I won't argue with you about the how or why of that. . . ."

"Why not, Don?" snapped Adel.

Anderson did not reply. He reached for the bottle of Bas Armagnac. It was late, he was tired and the worst part was still to come. The conversation had started off badly, he thought dejectedly. What he had hoped to avoid seemed impossible to do so now. He stood and stretched his aching body and strolled from the sitting area, past the hanging fireplace in the middle of the large room to the open verandah doors.

It had stopped raining and the night was clear and crisp. Below him lay Cannes and the glittering night lights of the Croisette, yet up here it was a serene, secluded Xanadu. Soon, he thought, it would be something quite different.

The thought jolted Anderson. He felt sorry for Adel. Here was a charming, carefree guy who worked hard and played harder. In the netherworld of Iranian big business he had acquired his riches honestly and with his integrity intact. His uncomplicated, almost childlike rules of right and wrong were appealing to Anderson's puritan streak. Besides, he thought, Adel's wealth had never changed him. He enjoyed spending rather than flaunting his money and he always attributed his wealth to luck, saying that making money in a corrupt society was neither something to be proud of nor much of an achievement. "It's not making money that's difficult," he had once said in a rare, open mood. "Making money with distinction is the hard part."

Anderson felt ill at ease as he returned to the room and looked at his friend. He doubted that Adel would believe his position. He wouldn't believe that he had no choice, that he was just a messenger. Usually he was a messenger who brought facts and figures, backgrounds and options, but now he was a messenger bearing something quite different. He was coming up in the world, he thought dejectedly.

"What do you know about the military equipment we have in Iran, Michael?" he asked bluntly as he sat again.

Adel set the magazine he was flicking through aside. "Not much," he shrugged, "except that some of the more sensitive stuff must have been removed." He was not about to question Anderson's change of subject; the man was obviously here for a purpose and he'd get to it in his own time.

"Exactly. All of it. All the sophisticated materiel at least has either been 'liberated' or destroyed. The most important items we had there were the F-14 Tomcat fighters. They're among the most sophisticated equipment we've got. They're the backbone of our tactical military capability. The Shah bought eighty of these fighters armed with another of our most sophisticated and sensitive items— the Phoenix missile. Toward the height of the unrest in Iran, these missiles, along with other sensitive equipment, were 'liberated' by trans-shipment to bases in Turkey and Israel. With them went all the software and technical manuals that were in Iran for training and maintenance purposes."

Where could all this be leading, Adel wondered.

"All, that is, but a commentary on the Phoenix missile system," Anderson said softly. "To be more specific, the tape of a verbal presentation of the manuals. Which is, needless to say, as valuable as the manuals themselves. The tapes contain everything there is, the essential information regarding the missile, on-board computers, over-the-horizon radar, digital-to-analog processors, the brains of the thing."

Adel let out a low whistle.

"You've guessed it, Mike. If these tapes fall into the hands of the Soviets, our security is screwed. Even more so if the data are added to the information gathered last year from the break-in of one of the subcontractor's offices in California. That compromised the engineering skills, so they already have the manufacturing know-how. If they get the information contained in the manuals it'll give them the entire thing, lock, stock and barrel. The manuals would give them step-by-step instructions to follow. And these tapes give them just about that."

Adel gave Anderson an irritated smile.

"That's about par for the course, isn't it?" he said, pressing a wall button. "Kind of completes the picture of incompetence the U.S. managed to paint in Iran."

"It was a mad scramble in those last few days, Mike. There was equipment scattered throughout the country—some had to be destroyed, some evacuated. In spite of the chaos, everything we knew about was successfully liberated. This set we knew nothing about. Not, that is, until a few days ago."

"Who made these tapes?"

"I don't know," said Anderson, shaking his head. "It's a major security leak. The immediate problem is..."

The sound of knocking interrupted him.

"Come in," said Adel.

It was Usher, bearing a coffee tray.

Anderson waited for the door to close before continuing.

"The immediate problem comes from the level of Soviet infiltration within the Khomeini movement. It seems that somewhere along the line, the Soviets recognized the magnitude of the revolutionary movement and were prepared for it. They've acted quickly and efficiently.

"The leftist infiltration of the Islamics is so widespread, we haven't yet been able to get a handle on it. The country is in total chaos; no law, no order, no administration; everything from the armed forces to private factories, from government ministries to political trials, from banks to the media, is run by small Islamic revolutionary committees, or, as the Iranians call them, *komitehs*. These organizations fall under the general umbrella of Ayatollah Khomeini's Islamic Revolutionary Council.

"It is here that the communists have moved quickly and effectively. They've infiltrated the key *komitehs* and have a stranglehold on the entire government apparatus. It's an intelligence nightmare; they've moled in deep. Sometimes they've done it in religious clothing; in others they've done it through the students and militants and so on. But they've done it well. They've gone in deep."

Anderson reached nervously for his glass and gulped a mouthful of brandy.

"If the revolution were just in the hands of a bunch of Khomeini fanatic ragheads, we'd be less worried. They'd never find the tapes and, if they did, they couldn't figure out their importance. But we're dealing with infiltration of the revolution by highly trained, radical left-wing elements. And that means Soviet access to those tapes."

Anderson stopped suddenly. His face was flushed, his brow sweating.

Three thousand miles was a long way to come and cry over spilt milk, thought Adel as he reached for his cigarettes on the side table. What was Anderson leading to? Why was he telling him all this?

"Michael, they want you to get those tapes out."

Adel snapped his head toward Anderson. But the statement was so unexpected, so remote from reality, that he sat stunned, unable to respond.

"You'll have good support."

Had Anderson drunk too much? Was this visit the symptom of some kind of breakdown? Was he serious?

"Your name has received the highest-level approval, Michael. A lot's riding on you."

Still, Adel could find nothing to say. He sat staring at his old friend.

"Meetings and briefings and orientation sessions have been set up for you over the next few days."

"Don, tell me I'm hallucinating," Adel said finally.

He lit a cigarette when Anderson did not respond.

"Why me? Why some private jerk with no experience? We must have operators trained to do this sort of thing. If we don't, certainly the Israelis do. Or the British. The Germans."

Anderson rubbed his sweaty hands on his trouser legs. He spoke in short, jerky bursts. "That's not possible. We can't use our own people. There's some sort of problem with it. I don't know what it is."

"Why the hell not? Is this another Carter administration brainstorm, holding back the specialists to give the amateurs a chance?"

Anderson shook his head. "Look, Michael. I don't know all there is to know about this thing. I only know what I've been told." He gestured helplessly with his hands. "Only thing I can think of is that the president doesn't want anything to tarnish the Camp David Agreement. He's pleased as a kitten with it. It's still too fresh and vulnerable."

"Marvelous."

Anderson looked at Adel and shrugged. "That's a personal opinion. It's not official or anything," he said. "Maybe it's because the Soviets are looking for a reason to cause additonal unrest in Iran and destabilize the region even further. But I don't know. I wasn't

45

told. I can only guess. In any event, that takes care of the U.S. and Israel. As for the West Germans, well, they rely too heavily on Iranian oil to get involved. In fact, they're anxious to establish good relations with the new government quickly. Same with the Brits. They have seventy thousand jobs dependent on auto sales to Iran. From what I've been told, all these countries are willing to help but none of them is willing to actually carry out the operations for us."

"Well, they're willing to do more than I am. I won't lift a finger. I'm not going in as some half-assed spy to get my neck chopped off. You'll have to find someone else."

"The assignment," said Anderson slowly and deliberately, avoiding Adel's eyes, "is of grave importance to us."

"Jesus Christ, Don!" snapped Adel. "Are you people nuts? I couldn't do it even if I wanted to, which I don't. I don't know a damn thing about this sort of thing."

Anderson said nothing.

"Do you people really believe you can sit around a mahogany table in the State Department and decide that a perfect stranger should go into the middle of a revolution and steal documents or tape recordings out from under the eyes of a bunch of raving maniacs?" Adel was almost shouting. "I mean, where do you people get these ideas from? You fuck up the entire area and then expect a rank amateur to risk his life to save your asses. Who the hell comes up with these ideas?"

"It's not the State Department," Anderson said quietly.

"CIA," snapped Adel, stubbing out his cigarette. "What the hell's the difference?"

"This is unofficial."

"What do you mean, 'unofficial'? Who is it, then?"

"I don't know, Michael. And I'm not authorized to discuss it."

Adel grimaced and lit another cigarette. "You're nuts, you know that? Crazy. You walk off the street and ask me to risk my life but you aren't authorized to tell me who I'm doing it for. You can't be serious, Don. And if you are, forget it."

Anderson looked away and sighed; a deep, troubled sigh.

"You have to do it, Michael," he said. "They have leverage."

"What the hell is leverage?"

"Your daughter. They'll use Natalie," Anderson said in an embarassed whisper.

The words stunned Adel as images of his daughter flashed before

46

his eyes. Instantly his body became paralyzed, his body cold and heavy.

"What do you mean, 'They'll use Natalie'? What has *she* got to do with this?" The words came out soft, frightened. It was the tone of a man who did not want to hear the answer.

"I don't really know, Michael. And again I'm not authorized to go into it. The colonel is going to take that up with you. Monday. Right here in Cannes."

CHAPTER 8

CANNES: SATURDAY, OCTOBER 20, 1979: 2:30 A.M.

It was almost two hours since Don Anderson had left and Michael Adel was still on the telephone, this time to the operator in the Bahamas.

"Please note the number for future use, sir." The lilting tones of the young West Indian woman caressed the transatlantic line. "The phone number of the Lyford Cay Club is 742710. Now what was the name of your party again, sir?"

"Case," Adel said impatiently. "John Alexander Case."

He lit a cigarette and tossed the match into a large ashtray already brimming with butt ends.

This was his third call, and he still didn't have any answers. Case, he thought, was his last and most reliable source. He stubbed out the cigarette and reached for the silver letter opener beside the phone.

He had to find out, he had to know where Bell stood, whom he represented. Was he still with the CIA? Or did he represent some private arms manufacturer worried about secrets carelessly left lying around? Was it a squeeze play to entrap him? Some crazy scheme of senile, demented or ex-spooks? Or what? Why?

None of it made sense.

He glanced at the picture of a smiling Natalie on his Adams

writing table. And what the hell were State Department officials doing running errands for retired spies anyway? Was it a bluff? Or did Colonel Grover Cleveland Bell still count for something?

In his government career Bell had been powerful. How powerful was not generally known. He was one of a handful of men whose names constantly cropped up on the sidelines, looming shadows on the perimeters of Washington's power structure. Edward Bennett Williams, John J. McCloy, Larry O'Brien. But the linkage with Bell's name was not business or law or even government work in the true sense. It was to the CIA—to the Covert Operations Staff of the Plans Directorate, the dirty tricks department. Vietnam, Watergate, Iran. Publicly Bell had emerged unscathed—as he always did—from his association with the disastrous American position in Iran. He had drifted quietly away, into apparent retirement or consultancy work. But the silence surrounding Bell was eerie. It had always puzzled Adel. No one else had escaped so quietly. Not President Carter, the secretary of state, the head of the Security Council, the ambassador to Iran, even the head of the Iran desk at the State Department—all had been raked over the coals. The media had had a field day. But not a single mention of Bell.

Why? And why were people so reluctant to talk about him now? A retired intelligence consultant?

It didn't make sense.

As soon as Anderson had left, Adel had singled out three people who could help him piece together the answers he needed. His call to Jake Holzstein at the Washington *Post*—an old classmate from Stanford, with whom he had kept in close touch—had begun with the usual banter. Holzstein's gossip about the Washington scene was prolific, indiscreet and punctuated by high-pitched giggles. But when Adel had casually slipped in Bell's name, Holzstein's tone changed perceptibly. It stiffened and the titters disappeared.

"He's around," said Holzstein brusquely.

"I heard he was doing consultancy work."

"Isn't everyone in Washington?"

"Who for, Jake?"

There was a silence before he answered. "Why Bell, Michael?"

"No reason in particular. He's the only old Iran hand I haven't heard about since the revolution."

"In the middle of the night, in the South of France, you're wondering about old Iran hands?"

"Why not?"

"Is everything all right?"

Every statement was a question. "Sure. Did you say he was retired?"

"I don't recall saying anything, Michael."

After they had hung up, Adel thought for a moment about Holzstein's sudden, uncharacteristic resistance to gossip. Mounting suspicion drove him on. He placed a call to Putney Chatsworth, who had retired two months ago to his native Charleston, South Carolina. Chatsworth was a first-class backgammon player or whom Adel had known well in Paris. They had spent many afternoons in the game room of the Travellers Club on the Champs-Elysées. Chatsworth's title was political counsellor at the American Embassy, but it was an open secret that he was the CIA station chief in Paris.

"Why, Michael, I didn't know the old colonel played backgammon," bellowed the southern voice, when Adel had asked after Bell. "I'm just an ole country boy these days, spendin' my time on the boards, if you see what I mean. What's eatin' you anyway, boy?"

"A friend of mine's been offered some work with Bell," he said, choosing a different approach, "and he was wondering...."

"And how's your cute little wife?"

The call had drawn another blank, increasing the tension. There was an inexplicable wall of silence surrounding Bell, even among men Adel had always considered friendly and talkative. The connection he was now waiting for was his ace, his last reliable card.

Adel had first met John Alexander Case in Iran after his appointment as chairman of Enerco. Case had come to pay his respects to the Shah and subsequently, as head of the world's largest energy company, his audiences were frequent. Often the work he had in the country filtered down to Adel at the National Iranian Oil Company. The discreet deference paid to this prince of commerce by governments American and foreign, was always reflected in the mannerisms of the people Adel saw him with—the nervous sheepishness of the Shah, the tense hand-wringing of the former CIA chief and ex-ambassador—the ingratiating respect of the ambassador. Even the indestructible Bell had always assumed a subservient manner in Case's presence.

Adel and Case had developed a rapport at their first meeting. Soon the relationship deepened and grew from one of avuncular

49

magnate and a bright young nephew to a more personal one; the transition had occurred at the very place Adel was now calling, the exclusive Lyford Cay Club. "You're the only one in the entire Iranian oil company it doesn't cost me to see," he had once said, half-jokingly. "And a pretty packet at that."

Case was a knowledgeable man, part of the inner sanctum of the American elite and a good friend. Adel knew he could rely on him.

The telephone line clicked.

"Lyford Cay Club. May I help you?"

"Mister Case, please. John Alexander Case."

"Mister Case is in the card room, sir. I'm afraid he's not to be disturbed for another two hours," the club operator replied without hesitation. "He requests all callers to call back then, sir."

"Look, this is an emergency," snapped Adel. "Tell him it's Michael Adel on the line from France and tell him it's urgent."

"Ah...one minute, please."

The phone clicked again.

Adel could picture the astonishment caused by his impertinence: the confused operator anxiously turning to the manager, who would nervously defer to Mrs. Case in their private villa, each unwilling to take responsibility for breaking one of their trustees' instructions. And he was sure Mrs. Case would overrule her husband.

In fact, he had a good relationship with all the family. His friendship with Shirley, their nineteen-year-old daughter, had started on the white couch the invalid Mrs. Case would probably be sitting on when the manager called.

As Adel waited, he recalled vividly the genteel luxury of the club, set apart from the poverty and squalor of Nassau and the garish Paradise Island. He recalled the Uncle Toms—gliding around the pool serving English dowagers, German landowners and "old money" from Boston, New York and Philadelphia—and the flashes of resentment and anger behind the masks of servility on those glistening black faces.

He remembered how, as a house guest of the Cases, Shirley had insisted on taking him to Paradise Island one evening when her parents had been invited to a formal affair. Strolling back along the narrow, rolling path to the bungalow in the early hours of the morning, she had suddenly dangled a small plastic bag of marijuana in front of her.

50

"Can you roll?" she had asked, smiling coyly.

"What makes you think I smoke?"

"This lump of hash was in your toilet case," she had shot back. He remembered how he had stopped in his tracks.

Before the night was out they had smoked several joints. In between they had gone for a midnight dip and then, wrapped in bathrobes embroidered with the Enerco arms, they had sat on the deep white couch overlooking the sloping white sand and the calm moonlit sea.

It was then that she had kissed him. Gently at first, stiffly, like a girl without experience. And then harder, with all the fervor of someone driven to cross the Rubicon of life.

The telephone clicked again and the worried voice of John Alexander Case came on the line.

"What is it, Michael?" he asked. "What's wrong?"

"Nothing that urgent, Mr. Case. I just need your guidance on something rather quickly."

"Thank goodness for that," Case said with a sigh of relief. "You had me worried there for a moment, Michael."

"Thank you for your concern, sir. I hope I didn't disturb your bridge game."

"Poker actually, Michael. In fact, your timing's superb. You just saved me from sitting patsy with two anemic pairs, so I'm doubly pleased to hear from you. Now what is it you need to know?"

Adel was uncertain what approach to take. "How are Mrs. Case and Shirley? Are they enjoying the sun with you?"

"Yes, Michael, they're both here and they're fine." The tone was laconic.

Adel chose the direct approach. "I need to know about Colonel Bell, sir. Is he still with the government?"

"Who?"

"Bell. Colonal Grover Cleveland Bell, sir. You remember, he used to be in Iran."

There was a moment's silence before Case answered. "You know, that's a good question. I don't really know, Michael. There's been so many changes in Washington lately that it looks like the Minnesota Vikings' offensive line."

"I know, sir," said Adel, with mounting anguish. He leaned forward on the desk and rubbed his temples. "But it's very important to me. I need to know if he's still with the government or if he's retired. Would it be possible for you to perhaps inquire on my behalf? You travel in the same circles."

Case hesitated again before speaking. "He's a fine man, Michael. That much I can tell you without checking. He's also the sort of man who will always be an insider. But as for checking, well, we're all going to be down here for the next two weeks and it's not the sort of thing to be discussed on the phone. What is it you need to know exactly?"

"Is he sanctioned, sir?"

"Grover Cleveland Bell," retorted Case with a raw edge to his voice, "doesn't fart in his sleep without covering his ass, Michael. I wouldn't get in a pissing match with him if I were you."

The rest was a blur. Adel had heard enough. The wall of silence was complete.

CHAPTER 9

PARIS: APRIL 1975

Air France flight 194 Teheran-Paris banked above the gleaming futuristic Charles de Gaulle Airport, shining in the sunlight of a clear, early spring morning.

Michael Adel set aside the *Herald Tribune* article speculating on the emergence of Senator Muskie as the most likely challenger to Gerald Ford in next year's presidential elections. Almost simultaneously, he felt a strange excitement at the thought of what lay ahead. What he had to do was unfortunate but it was also unavoidable and overdue. He reflected on his motives for the thousandth time but again dismissed the pangs of guilt; revenge was not the deciding factor. Gina Mahmoudi had nearly ruined him, simply for her own pleasure, but that was unimportant now. What mattered now was Natalie and her well-being.

He hadn't been in Paris for over a year, not since he had left his job at the oil company in Iran to go into private business. As he had expected, the 1973 oil price hikes had burst upon Iran like a giant Christmas cracker—every sector of the economy was in a state of dynamic boom. Fortunately the area he had chosen was the most expansive of them all and he was feverishly overworked. Engineering and construction jobs had poured in, with the oil field sites scattered over inaccessible areas of Iran. He had spent most of the last year commuting between his office in Teheran and the sites, working harder than he would have liked.

But now the company had taken shape and would run itself. He was freer and richer than he had a right to be. In the past eighteen months he had made over five million dollars and that was in the first year of operations, when capital outlay was at its peak. He knew the Iranian economy was out of control; the expansion was proceeding too quickly, without the necessary infrastructure to absorb or support it, and the pie was being shared by only a greedy handful. The economy would blow up sooner or later, but for now the future was promising. He was one of the privileged few. And his money was cared for with tender Swiss hospitality.

The Peugeot 504 taxi pulled up in the narrow access lane running parallel to Avenue George V; the minute road was crowded with huge limousines parked in front of the elegant Hotel George V and its sister hotel, the Prince de Galles. Adel stepped out in front of the George V and paid the taxi.

"*Bonjour*, Monsieur Adel. It's nice to see you again," said the dark-blue-uniformed doorman.

Adel had forgotten his name, but gave him a warm smile.

"*Merci*," he said as he lifted the slim black leather briefcase and the large aluminum case.

The doorman grabbed for the cases.

"That's okay. I'll take them myself," Adel said as he headed for the glass doors. He was unwilling to risk the contents at this late stage.

As an old client he was exempted from the formalities of registration at the reception desk. Monsieur Palli—and a crisp one-hundred-franc note—made sure that within minutes he was in the familiar brown and beige suite 633.

"Monsieur Palli, are the other two suites in order?" he asked the formally attired receptionist.

"Of course, monsieur," Palli responded with a ready, wide smile. "Will there be anything else, monsieur?" He backed toward the door, eager to peek at the denomination of the note in his hand.

"Thank you, no," said Adel, closing the door behind him.

Little had changed in these rooms during the past decade. The suite was small by comparison to others in the hotel, but Adel preferred it because of its relative isolation and quiet. The door opened into a small but well-designed sitting room. To the left was a larger-sized bedroom with a huge double bed. On each side of the bed were mirrors which accentuated the spacious cupboards and provided an elegant *belle époque* environment. At the foot of the bed stood an antique buffet-type chest of drawers. A TV, bar and sitting area in front of the bay windows overlooking the back courtyard served to complete the room.

The packages he had asked Usher to deliver were placed tidily on the bed; he was uncharacteristically excited. Quickly he made two phone calls, eager to move on to the work that lay ahead. The first call was to Catherine, Madame Claude's secretary, to confirm the evening's arrangements; the second to the sixth-floor maid to pick up his suits and shirts for ironing.

The camera assembly was not difficult. His equipment was the simplest and most efficient available and in addition to the main system, he had two backup systems to insure a fail-safe operation.

The primary system worked off two infrared lamps camouflaged as decorative lighting. One he placed on the chest of drawers in front of the bed, the other on the left side of the room; they would trigger the necessary light for the still photography. He hid the two tripod-mounted Nikon F2 photomic cameras in the closets on either side of the bed and positioned them at an angle covering the mattress.

The two cameras were loaded with infrared film in five-hundred-frame magazines. Both were motorized and attached to individual electronic timers; both were blimped to insure silence. The camera farther from the bed—about fourteen feet from the camera film plane—held an 85mm, f-18 Nikon lens. The second, about six feet from the center of the bed, was equipped with a 28mm Nikon f-2.8.

Adel carefully adjusted the tripod and locked it to provide firm support on the camera with the 85mm lens. He adjusted the split-image range finder on a sheet of white paper he placed on the bed.

Then he backed off the distance to the red dot on the lens barrel, situated for infrared focusing. He set the ASA rating on the dial, then set the lens aperture at f-5.6 and the speed at 1/125. He made similar adjustments to the second Nikon.

Finally, Adel set each remote timer individually to make an exposure every ten seconds.

The second system was a Sony video camera customized for him by a specialist firm in Amsterdam for fifteen thousand dollars; it was adapted to handle extremely high-speed film. He placed the video camera on a tripod and set the unit inside the left-hand closet. That provided a medium view of the pillows. He adjusted the tripod, focused and locked the tripod firmly.

The three hidden cameras covered the bed, one from the right, two from the left. He also clipped the microphone to the top of the video camera and adjusted the sound level to a predetermined "5".

For the next hour he wired the cameras and microphone to a small central control panel and placed the switch in the closet beside his shoes and the video recorder.

He ran the wires along the border of the cupboard and under the edge of the carpet past the radiator. A foot away, under the carpet, he found a small lump of hashish, presumably hidden for future use by a regular user of the room. Not to deprive the man of his pleasure, he replaced the brown lump and ran the wires along the carpet edge into the cupboard, where the central control lay.

The wiring completed, he rolled down the outside window shutters, pulled the curtains and doused the lights. In the darkness he pulled the highly sensitive film cassette from a lead container and placed it in the recorder. Then he plugged the central control unit, video cassette recorder and video camera into electrical outlets.

Next to the central toggle switch were three light-emitting diodes—LED—one for each system. He snapped the central switch and the LED glowed green.

Satisfied, he turned off the system and covered the video recorder with a heavy black-felt cloth.

He turned on the lights and glanced at his watch; it was 4:30 P.M. In four hours Gina Mahmoudi would knock on the door. He closed all the closet doors, except the three that held the camera. He left these slightly ajar to allow the necessary clearance for the lenses and attached to the three metal hinges of each cupboard door prism-shaped magnets that jammed the doors. He adjusted the magnets until he had the required openings.

Once the magnets were attached it was impossible to open or close the doors; they were more likely to splinter or crack before the magnetic fields were broken. The only way to neutralize them was to slide the powerful magnets rather than pulling at them.

Adel tested the system several times before he was completely satisfied. He slid the magnets off and on and opened and closed the doors. Everything was perfect.

The six-hour flight, the two hours of engineering and the nervous excitement had tired him. He picked up the telephone.

"Operator, I'd like a wake-up call at seven-thirty this evening," he said, lighting a cigarette.

"*Oui, Monsieur Adel. Dix-neuf heures trente,*" she repeated.

"Oh, and one at seven forty-five, to be certain," he added.

He lay back and took one last pull at the cigarette before crushing it in the porcelain ashtray on the night table. By this time tomorrow, he thought, his daughter Natalie would be out of the insane asylum her mother called home. He would have her and all this dirt would be over. It was unfortunate that it had to be this way, he thought, as he shaped the pillow into a comfortable position. He would have preferred a more civilized approach but Gina had made that impossible; she had spurned his offers of an amicable solution, and since they had never been married there were no courts to resort to. Anyway, he thought, taking a malicious pleasure in knowing that it was a humiliation Gina would never forget, it would all be over soon.

He relaxed and within minutes he was fast asleep.

CHAPTER
10

Gina Mahmoudi rolled over in her king-sized bed and glanced at her bedside clock. It was eight-thirty in the morning. An ungodly hour, she thought, as she tried to remember when she had last been up so early. Strangely, though, she felt vibrant and alert. She pressed two buttons simultaneously on the night table. The first smoothly parted the silk curtains. The second opened the window shutters.

Neither the curtains nor the shutters made much difference. It was a typical murky, rainy London day and it marred the handsome courtyard and park view of her town house on exclusive Montpelier Square. Although she rarely made use of the private park, she loved the view on balmy summer days. And it provided a perfect conversation piece, an ice breaker, at the start of her regular soirées.

She got out of bed and covered her slim, naked body with a white satin floor-length *robe de chambre*.

The private park, she thought in a rare mood of self-criticism, was typical of her attitude in life. She loved to be surrounded by beauty but there never was enough time to care for it, nurture it. She often thought of going out to the courtyard and pruning the flowers or whatever it was the others did, but she never seemed to get around to it. It was so much easier to have someone look after it. Every three months she would pay her dues and the beautiful well-kept lawns and flowers flourished. Actually, she didn't even pay herself; she would simply have Gerta, her Austrian housekeeper, take care of it; it was easier and more practical. Besides, pruning was hardly her idea of an enjoyable afternoon.

It was the same with Natalie. She was growing up and, in spite of her nurse, becoming much too demanding. She would have to go off to boarding school soon, but where? All the top girls' schools were too close to London; she would be home too often—almost every weekend—and then there were the long holidays. All the name schools in England seemed to be on holiday twelve months in the year, she thought. No, Switzerland was a better idea. She would have her lawyer look into the possibilities there.

Gina was well aware, and often sad, that she was not suited to motherhood. When Natalie was younger, it had been easier; she had given Gina enormous pleasure. She was a novelty, another part of herself, but as she grew older she was becoming an individual who needed too much attention and time. In fact, it was a full-time occupation, and Gina resented it. Not that Natalie was materially deprived; she had the best of everything that money could buy.

Gina loved her house. She hated sleeping in strange beds and although Natalie lived on an upper floor and was forbidden to enter Gina's sleeping quarters and observe the men Gina brought home, it was still a nuisance. Switzerland had excellent educational facilities and Natalie could acquire polish, learn languages and cosmopolitan ways there. Switzerland, she thought, would be ideal for everybody.

She picked up the phone and pressed the button marked "I."

"Gerta, I'm up and about," she said, cueing Gerta to deliver the morning coffee. Suddenly she was hungry.

"And two soft-boiled eggs and some toast," she added.

"That's better, madam, you should have breakfast every day. Coffee is not good for you," Gerta said with a heavy Austrian accent.

Gina smiled as she hung up. Dear Gerta, she thought, I'd be lost without her, even if she does repeat the same sentence every morning.

She walked into the bathroom and slipped off her gown. The shower was tingling and the thought of Adel and a whole week with him excited her. She caressed her body with the soap and thought of the last time she had been with him in Paris. It had been so long ago. He had picked up a girl at the François ler Discothèque and they had seduced her together. He had let her make love to the girl over and over, watching, smoking hashish and popping amyl nitrite for them at just the opportune moment to keep them at fever pitch. She shuddered as she recalled how,

58

when she was going down on the girl for the third time, he had picked the exact right moment to join in. How he suddenly stood up and entered her from behind. It had hurt, but she had loved it. It was quintessential pleasure.

Yes, she thought as she guided the soap to the intimate crevices of her body, she would enjoy the coming week with him and perhaps, this time, she could even hold on to him.

She added a dollop of the oily liquid soap to her index finger and massaged it into the opening, deploying her fingers around the upper edges and turning them with increasing speed and pressure. She thought of Michael and his body and focused the vibrating shower head. The excitement mounted. He was so good-looking with his wise, sad eyes, his wild curly hair and shy, wispy smile. His body was so beautifully proportioned too: six feet and one hundred and eighty pounds distributed over wide shoulders and narrow hips. She shuddered and her knees weakened as the passion exploded.

She stepped out of the shower glowing and grabbed a pink bathrobe. Insofar as she was capable of loving anyone unselfishly, she loved Adel. Perhaps it was because they had first met a lifetime ago in Iran when they were both children. They had grown up together, exploring the mysteries of adolescent love.

He had been an outstanding athlete, she pretty and spoiled. And she had been so proud to be his girl friend. He had been so kind and gentle, patient with her tantrums yet shyly dominant as teenage sexual awareness developed and bound them close together. He had always had a weakness for lame ducks; during the holidays he brought home lonely, sensitive boys for whom boarding school, with its inherent sadism, was sheer torture. She liked those qualities about him, his gentleness and understanding.

He had never changed, she thought. He was and always had been a survivor. But he was also a simple man whose success came from hard work, intelligence, perception and luck, rather than cunning, ruthlessness or corruption. And he knew her so well. He understood her selfish ways and forgave all until she goaded him beyond endurance. She wanted to see him suffer, to abandon his unquestioning acceptance—and he did. But at what cost? No one had ever replaced him though God knows there had been enough candidates.

The knock on the door was Gerta.

"Here we are, madam," she said, placing the green-and-white Wedgwood breakfast set on the table in front of the window. "And the mail," she added.

Gina, deep in thought, could not be bothered with another of Gerta's windy conversation.

Oh, she had got him back—when she had told him she was pregnant. But only until two months after Natalie was born. Under his care her pregnancy had been a healthy one—a little alcohol, no cigarettes. But it had not been the same. Sometimes she found him staring at her with a hard, bitter look. It frightened her; it was a quality she had never seen in him before and she knew she was responsible for it. The only thing that really worked—perhaps even better than before—was their sexual relationship. The gentleness and affection had dissipated. A violent, animal–like quality had replaced it. And for her it was even more enjoyable. But it didn't happen often. They saw each other less and less; and, more often than not, it was for Natalie's sake.

The telephone rang. Anyway, as long as she held on to Natalie, his precious little Natalie, she would have part of him.

"Hello, 584 2512." She never knew why she pretended privacy when half the town had her number.

"Hi," said a deep, mellow voice.

"Hello, Enrico darling," she said with feigned delight. "How was the Caribbean?"

"Boring without you, darling."

Count Enrico de Sapio was one of the current popular jet-set gigolos and one of her regular escorts. He was generously endowed but not sexually prolific. He served Gina as an agreeable companion on whose elegant arm she could appear at parties, discotheques, dinners, and he was not in the least possessive—indeed, he had acted as her pimp on a number of occasions when she had wanted a particularly delectable but inaccessible young man. For Gina, he was decoration for twenty-eight days a month and a stallion for two. It was an arrangement that suited them both.

"I'm dying to see you," he rasped.

"I am too, darling, but I'm off to New York today," she lied.

"What a pity, and I've been saving myself for you."

Gina thought for a minute. Perhaps she could fit him in before her flight to Paris. But the thought of Adel preempted the notion.

"Darling, you're adorable. I would simply love to see you, but my flight leaves at one and I have a million things to do. Save yourself for me, I'll be back next week," she said, putting a little sorrow in her voice.

"Oh, what a shame...." They chatted aimlessly for a few minutes. "So I'll see you when you get back, my love," he said, eager to be off the line. He was wise enough to know that in his line of work, retirement came early; time was mean.

"Bye, darling. Call me next week."

She put the phone down and realized that it could never work with Adel. She could never be faithful to one man and she really had no wish to be; there was too much variety in this world, and she wanted it all. On the other hand, she thought, there was no one quite like him.

"I'll always keep a part of him," she said out loud as she bit into the toast and marmalade and thought of her precious Natalie.

CHAPTER 11

CANNES: MONDAY, OCTOBER 22, 1979: 9:45 A.M.

The white stone pile of the Carlton Hotel blazed in the late October sunlight. The week-long cold spell had abated and suddenly the town was alive in the warmth of an Indian summer. Elderly couples swarmed along the ocean boulevard, admiring the natural and man-made beauty, while others sipped coffee in sidewalk cafes, bistros and *boîtes*. Still others browsed in the luxurious boutiques for something they didn't already have; in Cannes, need is not a prerequisite.

Outside Van Cleef and Arpel's a crowd hovered, gazing enviously at a priceless exhibition of crowns crafted over the years by that *maison* for kings and queens and other potentates.

Adel inched his Lagonda through the pedestrians, impatient with poky elderly winter residents. His mind ticked with nervous anticipation. Not only had his calls to three well-informed friends drawn a blank, but almost three days of incessant probing had proved equally fruitless. People scattered throughout the world balked at the first hint of involvement. At the first mention of Bell's name they shied away. People who otherwise were afraid of nothing; powerful, previously reliable, friends in positions to know. Government people, heads of companies, the media, intelligence operatives and even people on the far side of the law—all refused to talk about Colonel Grover Cleveland Bell.

At last Adel managed to reach the hotel's semicircular driveway and pull the car up between the white pillars of its awning.

"Now that we have nice weather you're not running," the doorman teased as he opened the car door and handed him a newspaper.

"Thanks, Jean." Adel rolled the paper and walked away quickly, leaving the plump figure surprised at this uncharacteristic abruptness.

In the east wing of the hotel, two floors above the patio bar area, a lace curtain ballooned out toward the pillared balustrade of a balcony. Colonel Grover Cleveland Bell's head appeared briefly, looking down.

The lobby was deathly quiet; the displays of O. J. Perrin, Van Cleef, Cartier and other fashionable shops sparkled, but there were few customers to appreciate their wares in the off season.

Adel walked briskly through the deserted lobby, ignoring the salutes from the idle hall porters. He entered the elevator and snapped the newspaper open. Every day the headlines screamed of the chaos in Iran. An old proverb came to mind: *They have sown the wind and they shall reap the whirlwind.* The day's front page confirmed that they were still planting.

What was worse, he thought, casting a look at the hallway sign that indicated suite 208 was to the left, he was getting caught up in it. And he was about to meet the man who had manipulated him into this no-win position.

He remembered Bell from Teheran as an affable acquaintance, whose sophisticated manner belied his reputation as a tough and ruthless operator. After his arrival in Iran following Watergate, his role as CIA supremo for central and southwest Asia was an open secret. Only the details of his operations were unknown, yet there were always strategic leaks. Propping up the Daoud Khan regime in Afghanistan; pulling the rug from under Mostafa Barzani's Kurdish revolt in Iraq; the Algiers accord between Iraq and Iran; monitoring Soviet missile launchers from the highly secret U.S. radar facility outside the northeastern Iranian market town of Behshahr; assassination of the Baluchi chieftain Amir Akbar Khan, whose graduation from opium smuggling to regional politics had proved inconvenient; financing the British aid program to the Sultan of Oman. Bell was even credited for manipulating congressional approval of AWAC sales to Iran, using his notorious "file card" system on legislators to insure a positive vote.

Adel knew Bell as a driven man whose commitment to furthering his "understanding" of American foreign policy interests knew no limits. Any state should be glad to have a Bell who could do its dirty work with such relentless energy. And one or two did.

As he raised his hand to the doorbell, Adel was aware that, for the first time in his life, he was genuinely frightened. He didn't have a card to play with. And Colonel Grover Cleveland Bell was hardly a man to be bluffed.

The door opened to reveal a tall, gangling man whose face had marked time since Adel had last seen him. At sixty, the colonel looked younger than his age. His flat yet hawkish face was crowned with thinning white hair, which was still brushed back with the aid of Vitalis.

"It's nice to see you again, Michael." The half smile on the left side of his face made a sharp contrast to the taut right cheek. The piercing eyes seemed to hang from arched brows. "Come in, come in."

Years of schooling at Switzerland's exclusive Le Rosey School, Harvard and the intelligence community had taught the colonel more than a fair share of social ease and *savoir-faire*. The veneer, however, could not quite mask the eyes and time had not been kind there. It had ploughed deep furrows that accentuated the coldness and cunning that lay behind the open, disfigured gaze.

"Please sit there, best chair in the house," the colonel said affably, pointing to a padded, highbacked Louis XIV armchair.

Adel looked at the corner Bell had chosen and his antennae vibrated. With people like Bell, every move, every phrase, was calculated. The chair was one of four in a circle around a marble table. It looked comfortable enough, but it faced the wall, leaving the large room out of sight. He chose instead the chair opposite, facing the room.

63

The colonel did not acknowlege the rebuff. He sat beside Adel, rubbing his palms together. A breeze carrying the smell of fresh sea air entered the room and blew the lace curtains of the bay windows toward him. Faint sounds of traffic filtered in from the beachfront below, all but drowning out the sounds of a distant campanile announcing the hour of ten.

"It's always a pleasure to see old friends," said Bell. "My years at the military mission in Iran are among the most memorable of my life. The friendships I developed there are a continuing source of pleasure to me." He paused and the two men studied each other. "Would you care for a drink?"

Adel shook his head. "No, thank you," he replied as he surveyed the room. One of the connecting doors of the suite was slightly ajar.

Bell looked at Adel, his smile unaffected. Behind the joviality Bell's mind ticked furiously; it scanned his memory of the psycho-graphic summary on Michael Adel which Operations Directorate had provided.

Fundamentally subject's makeup is reactive rather than active; a counterpuncher with lightning quick, shrewd, agile mind that relies on I.Q. of 153 and total confidence in both perceived self-image and physical prowess. Self-effacement is innate and should not be translated as self-doubt. Avoid open confrontation physical or psychological. Keep all contacts hostility-free or heavily weighted against subject.

Bell looked at Adel. "Very well. Very well," he smiled. "First let me say this." He stabbed the air with an index finger to induce confidence and sincerity. "I wanted our first meeting to be private, man to man, if you will. I didn't think it was necessary to drag in a bunch of bodies to sit around and discuss the details at this stage."

He looked Adel squarely in the eyes, not expecting an answer.

"You must realize, Michael, the circumstances in which we find ourselves are highly unusual and our options clearly limited. The danger to the United States is severe. In fact, this thing is poten-tially catastrophic for the entire free world."

Adel did not reply.

"Don Anderson tells me you're roughly familiar with what we have in mind."

"Yes," replied Adel. "About as familiar as you are with my re-action."

64

Hostility considered counterproductive to desired goals. This stimulus will meet with rejection. Barring subject's known weaknesses for wife and daughter (see attachment E) based on daughter's life history (see attachment C) only alternate mode of approach to stimulate willing cooperation and confidence is breakdown of subject's innate barriers of mistrust. Considered unfeasible within specified time frame.

Bell's features took on a paternal look. "Anderson also informs me you're a little disappointed by events in Iran."

"Bitter," said Adel, staring coldly.

"I beg your pardon?" Bell cocked an eyebrow and readied himself for the first thrust.

"Bitter. Bitter is a more accurate description of my feelings."

"Michael, that's a very natural response. The revolution in Iran was an unfortunate thing and it came at a particularly bad time for you. I know your construction business was doing extremely well. Why, your tax writeoffs must have been close to three point two million."

Adel was startled. That was the exact figure agreed to with his company's auditors in New York only twelve days ago.

"Not to mention your family's real estate holdings in Teheran and on the Caspian coast. But we all lost, Michael. Perhaps needlessly. The Shah was a good friend of mine, but unfortunately he was a bad listener. He wouldn't listen to me. In the last few years he wouldn't listen to anyone. He chose to ignore all the extraordinary problems that are by-products of rapid modernization programs. He simply went too fast and..." He lifted his hands in conclusion.

Adel nodded. "That's one way of looking at it."

Despite prescribed impactive mode of first contact, i.e., Anderson, second contact should appeal to subject's romantic makeup and simplistic view of the world and self-imposed adherence to strict but simple ethical standards.

"Michael," Bell continued in the same patronizing tone. "The fact that we need to call on you is the result of a buildup of an unusual set of circumstances. Rare circumstances. We analyzed the options closely before we found it necessary to select you. God only knows we would have preferred to use a professional operative, and not trouble you. But unfortunately that's not possible."

He paused and studied Adel before continuing. "I appreciate

the personal difficulty we are putting you to, but we have no choice. I assure you, we'll be indebted to you. I hope you never need to call on that debt but it's a good promissory note to hold on to."

Adel brushed invisible dust from the trousers of his khaki safari suit; it was a nervous action. "Tell me, colonel. How many promissory notes did the Shah have?"

"Yes," responded Bell promptly and without passion. "In retrospect perhaps we should have helped him a little more. But, as I said, it all got out of hand. Oh, I imagine there are plenty of conspiracy theorists around, especially among your Iranian friends," he added. "Only problem is, if there aren't any conspiracies, they invent some. The CIA subverted the Shah's government. Or the oil companies did it, or the State Department, or President Carter."

"You're right," said Adel in the same calm tones. "All sorts of silly rumors are around and it's not just among the Iranians. Even Alexander Haig and George Bush have joined the bandwagon." He gave his voice a sarcastic twist. "They've both suggested that General Huyser's role in Iran should be studied more closely. But I'm sure that's just campaign talk, aren't you?"

Bell uncrossed and then crossed his legs, exchanging the right with the left. "Well, they're wrong. Robert Huyser had nothing to do with any of this. The fact is, the Carter administration blew it. The clowns couldn't handle it, that's all. In retrospect, it's very clear that despite a buildup of crisis signals from very early on, when the actual revolution erupted in October of 1978, Washington was simply unprepared for it. The indications were there, they just blew it."

Adel played with the corner of his right eye. "You are an opponent of the conspiracy theory and an advocate of Murphy's Law, then."

Bell cocked his head. "How's that?"

"Well, you seem to be an expert on it," responded Adel. "Murphy claims that 'if anything can go wrong, it will.' And that's what you want the world to believe, isn't it? Forty thousand or so Americans lived in Iran, colonel. Scattered throughout the country, working in the most sensitive areas. We had at our disposal the SAVAK secret police, the CIA, the Defense Intelligence Agency, the armies, navies, air forces of both Iran and America. We had the friendly government intelligence agencies, the MI6, the Mossad, SDECE and so on. And you say Washington wasn't aware! It wasn't prepared!" He shook his head. "Well, the only thing you have going for you, colonel, is that no one gives a shit. That's all. But that doesn't mean anyone believes it either."

Despite U.S. citizenship, upbringing and education, subject by nature possesses complicated thought process that is suspicious and mistrusting. This should not be stimulated.

Bell returned Adel's cold glare and decided to test Operations' advice. His tone shifted dramatically.

"For whatever it's worth, that's what happened. I don't expect you to be convinced, or even swayed, by the logic of reality. After all, you are part Iranian."

"Whether you like it or not, colonel, I'm an American and that's exactly why I find it so unpalatable. Lying and stealing and extortion and kidnapping and murder are not part of the *American* ethic. Didn't Vietnam or Watergate teach you anything?"

Bell settled in his chair as he extended his legs in front of him and reflected on the impressive accuracy of Operations' report. The guy's acting true to form. He's a college kid who never grew up. Everything is black and white and conveniently simple. He's a romantic. And therefore, predictable.

"I'm surprised at you, Michael. Who said anything about kidnapping or murder or blackmail? That's not what we do. We're not gangsters, Michael."

"What the hell do you call 'leverage' then?"

Bell shook his head and smirked. "From what I hear about Gina, you're far better versed in that sort of thing than we are."

Adel was shaken. Did Bell know about the Gina scam at the George V four years ago? Of course he knew. Dirt was his profession.

"Let's have a drink, Michael." Bell slapped his knee and stood. "I have almost everything right here, but the room service is excellent if you'd prefer something more exotic."

"Scotch is fine," Adel said, his throat dry, his nerves edgy.

"Ice?"

"And water."

Bell walked to the marble-topped Empire console that stood against the wall beneath a Gobelin tapestry. Inside the potbelly of the console was a refrigerator and a well-stocked bar of miniature bottles. He poured a bottle in each glass, adding water and ice to one. He handed Adel his drink before sitting back in his chair.

"To success," he offered, raising the crystal tumbler.

"I have no interest in the success or failure of your operation, colonel."

"Michael, you know the critical nature of this issue to our country. As I shall explain, you are uniquely equipped to help us. You must look at this in..."

"Look, Colonel, I'm not your man," snapped Adel. "You need a professional, someone who's trained, willing. I'm not and if there's no blackmail, no leverage, no pressures on me or my family, then I'd just like to get up and leave."

"I see," Bell said calmly. He pulled in his long legs. "But, Michael, it's a question of degrees, isn't it?"

Adel tensed and waited. He lifted his glass and took a sip of whisky.

Only known effective stimulus available within required time span is threat to daughter or wife, Bell recalled.

He said, "We're not in a clear black-and-white situation. It's all a question of shades."

Beneath his tapered silk shirt Adel could feel the moisture building. "I'm not with you."

Bell looked at him and thought: It's time to jolt him again, to throw him off balance.

"It means, Adel," he said sharply, "That it's a question of ownership. I understand Natalie's mother is undergoing severe psychological strain as a result of your actions. And it would stand to reason that any court of law would find your deeds reprehensible, even criminal, perhaps."

So that was what the bastard had in mind. Using Natalie to tighten the screws again. The thought of Natalie being returned to Gina repelled him. Which is exactly what it was designed to do, he thought.

"Help yourself to another drink, Michael," Bell offered. He sat, his hands forming a steeple in front of his mouth.

Adel made himself a drink slowly, his mind desperately searching for a way out of this insanity.

"Let's settle this thing amicably, Michael. We're wasting valuable time. None of this has anything to do with the Phoenix."

"This may come as a surprise to you, but I couldn't give a damn about your missiles. I'm far more interested in my life. Besides, you should have thought about the possibility of compromise when you cashed the payment checks from the Shah. It's too late now; the missiles don't belong to us. The Iranians bought and paid for them. But that's something else that doesn't quite add up. Documents as sensitive as the Phoenix manuals were never available to Iranians. Not the military. Not the highest government officials. Not even the Shah. How the hell could tapes of a presentation of the manuals fall into the wrong hands?"

Bell smiled sheepishly and leaned forward. His left hand massaged the stiff side of his face. He thought: He's weakening. Back off a step or two. Leave him alone a minute. Let it take hold. Provide the fodder for chatter.

"You grossly underestimate the abilities of His Excellency Ali Mahmoudi."

"What does Mahmoudi have to do with this? He got what he wanted from the Shah by providing women for him," snapped Adel. "Pimping, it's called. And what a coincidence. He also happened to be the representative of just about every major American arms supplier in Iran."

Bell rose and walked to the bar. "Mahmoudi made the tapes," he said, pouring himself another straight whisky. "Somehow he got close to a meeting in which the manuals were being presented. At any rate he taped the meeting, presumably for blackmail purposes."

"How the hell could Mahmoudi put an entire presentation of the Phoenix missile system on a tape recorder?"

"Technically, it's quite feasible. He bugged the meeting with a little personal ploy. Planted a bug on one of the participants. There are evidently two Sony tapes, each with a sixty-minute recording capacity. That gives you two hours of recording time," Bell explained. "What Mahmoudi did was to first record the entire presentations on sixteen or seventeen miniature tapes and then transfer them all to two cassettes at very high speed. It's all gibberish if you hear them on a normal tape recorder. To make any sense out of them you need access to a machine that can slow them down to a crawl."

"Marvelous," said Adel disgustedly. "Where is Mahmoudi now?"

"Under our care," replied Bell.

Beneath Adel's shirt the perspiration began to flow freely. Under other circumstances it was called kidnapping.

Bell stuck a thin Davidoff cigar in his mouth and struck a book of matches. "I bring matches from back home wherever I go," he said. "I hate the damned wax-coated things they sell in Europe; they sputter and go out, or flare up. Lousy things," he said, grimacing. He inhaled a deep draught from the cigar and let the smoke leak out of his nostrils in wiggly streams.

"Michael, time is short. All this speculation isn't going to get us anywhere. There's a lot to be done and it has to be done quickly. The question can be..."

Adel shook his head firmly. "Forget it, Bell. And according to you there's nothing to force me."

"That's not what I said, Adel," Bell sighed. He stood and paced toward the open window, surveying the view of Port Canto and Les Iles Lérins that faced his suite. The distant campanile struck eleven.

"I said it's a question of degrees." He stood at the bay window, his back to the room. His voice was sharp, final. "And I'd like your cooperation."

"You're barking up the wrong tree, colonel; I'm not your man. I'm not trained for this sort of thing and I don't agree with it either."

Only known effective stimulus available within required time span is threat to daughter....

"You're all we have, and you'll do the job," Bell said.

"The hell I will."

Bell wheeled around toward Adel. "Call your house," he barked.

Adel squinted, his heart leaping suddenly. Anderson's warning echoed in his mind. *"Natalie! They'll use Natalie!"*

"What did you say?"

"I suggested that you call your house," Bell repeated, his voice flat, his eyes cold and piercing.

Adel's hands squeezed the arms of his chair as every muscle in his body stiffened.

"It's nothing serious," said Bell calmly. "Your wife and daughter should be experiencing minor car problems on the road to Juan-les-Pins. I think a call to your house would confirm my statement."

Adel's head pounded. His legs were suddenly very cold. He looked at the telephone, then back at Bell. Obediently he walked to the telephone and dialed.

"Adel residence," said Usher, after the third ring.

"Let... let me speak to Sam, John." He tried to control the unsteadiness in his voice.

"I'm afraid they're not home yet, sir. Madame just called. Seems the car broke down on Route Nationale Sept near Juan-les-Pins. I've sent the driver to pick them up. They should be back any minute now."

Adel's mind went blank. He was unable to think or speak.

Usher continued: "Rather unusual, sir. The car only just came back from the garage. I'll get onto them about it immediately."

Adel said nothing. He dropped his hand slowly and replaced the receiver. Then he turned to Bell. His voice came out a whisper.

"Leave them out of this, Bell. You touch them with your filth again and I swear I'll kill you...."

But even to his own ears the threat seemed hollow. The sparkle in Bell's eyes told him so.

CHAPTER 12

PARIS: APRIL 1975

At 8:30 in the evening Gina Mahmoudi closed the door of her suite behind her. As Michael Adel's note had instructed, she walked down from the seventh floor, glancing out of habit to check her makeup in the softly lit mirrors in the hallway. But it was a routine action; her mind was preoccupied by his unusual behavior; she could not understand why he had not met her at the airport, why they had separate suites. She shrugged off the questions as she descended the ornately sculptured wrought-iron back staircase. Maybe he had business to attend to, she thought. Even so, it was unlike him to invite people the first night they were together after so long. Her doubts faded as she reached for the doorbell.

At the sound of the chimes Adel closed the top button of his fitted white shirt and tightened the striped black and white tie that set off a conservatively cut black suit. He picked up the tall crystal tumbler of Glenlivet from the coffee table and walked toward the door. He felt remakably good; the anxiety had subsided, giving way to controlled excitement and determination.

"Hello, Gina," he said warmly, his heart missing a beat. He had forgotten how attractive she was.

The seductive dimpled smile on her face formed a pout as she rose on her toes. "Hello, darling," she purred.

Adel bent down and kissed her cheek. She was wearing the same Azzaro perfume and it produced a flood of bittersweet memories. He sensed the slight tremble in her body. He placed a hand on the small of her back and brushed her in.

"How are you?" he asked. "You look fabulous."

"Thank you." She dropped the white chinchilla draped around her shoulders on the back of a settee.

"First a drink," he said. "White wine still?"

She moved toward the Picasso lithograph on the beige, cloth-covered wall. "That would be lovely."

A bottle of Corton-Charlemagne 1969 lay in an ice bucket already opened. Alongside it, in the silver-plate bucket, were two others, unopened. It was a rich, spicy, lingering white Burgundy, aging magnificently. Not unlike Gina, he thought, as he poured the wine into a Baccarat crystal wine glass and handed it to her.

"It's been a long time. How've you been?" he asked.

"Oh, fine. Traveling a lot and keeping busy in general. I was in Beverly Hills in the spring and all I did was think of you, darling. I kept remembering how you love it and how nice it would have been if you were there. We never did go there together, did we?" she asked, then sat on the settee opposite him.

He shook his head. "No. We never did. I guess I like it because I grew up in the neighborhood," he said. He had attended Stanford, which was in the neighborhood as far as she was concerned; what was a mere thousand miles to Gina?

"How's Natalie?" he asked.

"She's fine. Growing and talking nonstop. She's such a happy child and so independent. Everywhere we go she's the center of attention. She's so pretty I envy her."

Adel felt a surge of anger. But he controlled it, careful not to let it reflect in his voice. "You know, it's been two years since I saw her."

"Oh, darling, we must arrange something. Perhaps you should come and have tea with her one day."

Two years now, thought Adel, feeling his determination mounting. For two years this was the sort of answer he'd been getting. Every civilized effort he'd made to establish a normal relationship with his daughter—to stop her lonely descent to insecurity—had failed in a jumble of flippancy and lies. And there was no legal tool to turn to. But soon, he thought. Soon it would end.

He was pleased to see Gina's glass already empty. He picked it up and refilled it halfway. Gina was a hard drinker but she was no fool; she must not think he was plying her.

"Lack of beauty has never been your problem," he said, holding out her drink. "You just take it too seriously."

She smiled and reached for her glass.

Yes, she was still a stunning woman, he thought as he sat back again and studied her closely. Her elegantly cut jet-black hair fell to just below her slim shoulders and her lips formed a permanent pout below sleepy eyes that were heavy-lidded and full of sensual promise. If it wasn't for the thin lines around her eyes, she could have been the innocent girl he had known so many years ago. Beneath the floating white chiffon dress, her slender, long-limbed figure showed not the slightest sign of aging. It retained its youthful hardness and her breasts pressed firm, invitingly and round, against the thin, almost transparent, material.

Yes, thought Adel, she was beautiful, but she was also used. Used so often, by so many, that she could well be declared a public playground.

"Might as well get over the free samples and start into the real portions," she said, walking to the bar and exchanging the empty wine glass for a tall crystal tumbler. "Who are your guests tonight?" she asked casually.

"Oh, I thought you'd enjoy a little bit of variety," Adel said suggestively.

She looked up at him and blushed as she discarded her shoes and curled up on the sofa, tucking her feet beneath her. At least one of her concerns was unfounded, she noted with relief.

"And what would you do if I said no?"

"Faint."

She laughed and came over to him. She knelt in front of him and kissed him on the lips, a long, tender kiss.

"You know I love you, don't you?" she purred.

She closed her eyes and moved her hands down his body, enjoying the feel of his chest beneath the zendaline cotton shirt. They moved down, past the silk of his trouser tops and then they stopped.

73

With practiced facility, she undid his zipper and then slowly, tantalizingly, felt for him. Like a mischievous child with a lollipop, she dipped her head and took him in, yet now her hooded eyes looked up at him—teasing, tempting eyes that promised so much.

Pleasure overwhelmed him as blood suffused his body. Gently at first and then harder he pressed her head, forcing himself deeper. She complied willingly. Slowly she lubricated him with saliva, wetting and forcing him deeper with each bow of her head. The tongue slowed, then quickened. Like a python, it twisted around his organ, covering it, engulfing it, catching every nerve and squeezing the life from it. He was visibly excited now, his heart beating faster, his body heat rising. . . .

Suddenly she stood, blushing red, moisture dampening her forehead. She lifted her skirt and, unencumbered by underwear, turned to sit on him, so he could enter her from behind, the way she had always liked it.

The doorbell, with its soft two-stroke chime, interrupted.

"Oh, shit," she said, dropping her skirt in mock anger. "I suppose we can't tell them to come back later?"

Adel smiled and stood up; with difficulty he zipped himself.

"Why?" he teased. "We can take up where we left off just as soon as the ice melts. Only you'll have more to play with," he said, turning his eyes suggestively.

Adel opened the door to reveal two extraordinarily beautiful young girls—a testament to the good taste of Madame Claude's organization. One was a brunette with shortish *flou* hair, cut just above the shoulders. Her large, almond-shaped eyes were accentuated by high cheekbones that hollowed out her cheeks, giving her a sleek animal quality. Tall and slim with full inviting lips, she was no more than twenty-three but carried an air of supreme confidence.

"*Bonsoir*," she said. "My name is Claudine and this is Barbara," she said, pointing to her blond friend.

Barbara looked even younger and, to judge from her appearance, was less experienced, but she was as tempting as Claudine. She had long fluffy hair that fell below her shoulders to the middle of her back. The skin that covered her delicate, doll-like features was smooth and unseasonably tanned, setting off her blue eyes and the blond hair.

The girls were elegantly and expensively dressed—the mark of the professional. Both wore mink coats of differing shades of brown which, when removed, revealed diaphanous evening dresses beneath. Nothing resembling underwear broke the smooth lines of their slinky yet tasteful clothes. They looked like fashionable, windswept animals of the night.

Almost immediately Gina had drinks in their hands. Then she poured on the charm to the more inexperienced and vulnerable Barbara.

Adel leaned back in his chair and surveyed the scene. The girls were relaxed and enjoying themselves and Gina was flourishing. She commanded the scene with ease and relish. Like a lioness stalking her prey she had little use for her mate.

The plan was going well—almost too well, thought Adel, feeling a sudden pang of anxiety. Would it work? Were the machines operating properly? The cupboards... He felt an urge for reassurance.

"Excuse me a minute," he said as he walked toward the bedroom. "I have to make a call." He locked the door behind him and rechecked the camera angles, the wiring, the magnets and the rest of the sensitive equipment. Everything was in order, functioning perfectly. But still he had a gnawing feeling of doubt.

He sat on the bed, pulled out the bedside drawer and took out the engraved Victorian silver cigarette case he had placed there in the afternoon. It was full of ready-made joints of the highest-quality hashish—acquired, rolled and delivered by Usher. Alongside it lay a green-and-white Limoges china pillbox.

The hashish would relax him. As for the girls, he thought, inspecting the cigarettes, it would break whatever ice was left and ease any inhibitions—if there still were any. He smiled, knowing that as far as breaking the ice was concerned, Gina had already made their thousand-dollar fees seem like mere icing on the cake.

He lit the thinnest, mildest joint and took in a deep breath. The bittersweet smell spread immediately throughout the room, the smoke billowing around the bedside lampshade. He took long, deep inhalations and held his breath.

For the tenth time he considered what he was about to do, for the tenth time he came to the same conclusion: he had no other choice. Gina marched to a different band. And its instruments did not include love or caring or compromise, even for their own daughter. And he wasn't going to let her be annihilated. He crushed the joint and determinedly headed for the door.

In the living room the three women sat talking and laughing

happily. Ordered for ten-thirty, two trollies stood in the center of the room, covered with an exquisite selection of canapés and several bottles of Dom Perignon 1955 champagne. The canapés ran from the conventional—*oeuf à la Russe, cocktail de crevettes,* smoked salmon, ham—to the more exotic *artichaut à la Tahiti, coeur de palmier Finlandaise* and stuffed tomatoes with curried prawns and tuna and anchovies. There was also a large crystal bowl decorated with gold-plated sea horses, standing over a matching gold-plated miniature bucket of crushed ice. It contained a mound of Iranian caviar surrounded by chopped onion, egg yolks and whites and parsley.

Gina had convinced the girls that they would be more comfortable without their evening dresses and both, like obedient schoolgirls, were now slumped down draped in cream-colored robes emblazoned with the hotel's coat of arms. Gina was in full cry.

"Caviar is good for you," she cried, scooping spoonfuls on to small side plates and adding the various spices, butter and toast. "The Iranians say it's an aphrodisiac and the Russians claim it gives you stamina. Either way it won't do us any harm."

The girls laughed, responding eagerly, and Adel marveled at Gina's authority.

"Here, this will help your appetites," he said, opening the cigarette case. "Leave the food for later."

The girls were delighted by this new diversion. Between the hashish, the wine, the food, the conversation, one sensual pleasure quickly followed another in an orgy of self-indulgence. It was nearly midnight before the foreplay subsided.

Adel opened the small china box and extracted a miniature golden spoon. He poured several spoonfuls of white powder on the dark marble tabletop and formed eight lines of cocaine with a matchbook.

Claudine lit up at the sight of the coke. "Ah...*J'adore ça,* I love that," she translated in that suggestive accent with which the French adapt to English. *"Il ne nous manquait que cela,"*—"That's all we were missing," she added as she inhaled two lines, one in each nostril, through a short straw.

"Ça c'est chouette," said Barbara, eagerly waiting her turn. "It's been ages since I've had any. Where did you get it?"

Gina picked up the china box from the table, annoyed that Adel had stolen her thunder by producing the ultimate in fashionable aphrodisiacs. As she did so, and before Barbara had a chance to inhale her lines, she brushed the white powder from the table with a flamboyant gesture that said she didn't give a damn what the powder cost.

Barbara was shocked and, from the look on her face, very disappointed. She stared at Gina questioningly.

"Come on," Gina commanded. "I'll show you how to use it properly." Her voice was soft and husky as she smiled and took Barbara's hand.

Adel immediately recognized the carrot and stick approach so often used by Gina. It was crucial, he thought, that the film record Gina's dominant role in the seduction scene. He didn't want some clever, high-priced lawyer claiming she had been drugged and coerced.

"Show us all," said Adel. He pulled Claudine from her chair and tugged her gently toward the bedroom.

Gina looked provocatively over her shoulder. "Join us."

Adel followed the three girls into the bedroom and immediately turned off the bedside lamp, pitching the room into darkness and camouflaging the cracks in the cupboard doors.

"Darling," complained Gina. "Give us a bit of light. We need to see what we're doing."

"Coming right up," he said, opening the bedroom door wider to allow light from the sitting room to filter through. He turned to see the faint outline of her white dress fall to the floor.

The two girls were already lying on the bed. Barbara had disrobed and lay naked on her right side, her head propped up by a pillow, leveraged further by her elbow. But for a minute triangle of glowing white skin and blonde hair between her legs, her body was a light coffee color, tanned by the Caribbean sun. Her eyes were dilated and yearning as she watched Gina step out of her dress. The hashish was taking hold, thought Adel, observing her fingers gently circling the small mound of white.

Claudine sat on the huge double bed, her back resting on the headboard, her arms hugging her legs, her lips suggestively sucking the smooth, shining flesh of her knee. Her robe was open at the front and her breasts, pressed against her thighs, were large and firm.

Gina caressed his face as she brushed past. "Join us!" she whispered, the alcohol and hashish slurring her words.

77

"You're stoned," he smiled.

She nodded toward the girls with her eyes. "So are they, my darling," she whispered, turning toward the bed.

Adel felt in his pocket for the miniature remote-control mechanism. He pressed the button that activated the equipment and immediately the invisible infrared glow encroached on the darkness. He looked at the cupboard doors to check that they were opened sufficiently to allow the cameras to record. When he saw no problem, he lit another joint and sat in the armchair at the foot of the bed. They don't need me, he said to himself. Which was just as well, since he had to keep out of the cameras' range.

Gina moved between the two girls and opened the china box. She tapped a generous portion of the rich white powder onto the patch of hair between her legs.

"Now try it," she tempted Barbara, in a deep, husky tone. "It's really much nicer this way."

Barbara went down on Gina and sniffed, deep inhalations that slowly became a desperate hunt. Like a terrier she pawed and licked and dug for the buried aphrodisiac with her tongue. The more she found, the more she sought, her sensual impulses fusing in uncontrollable animal desire.

Gina lay back in ecstasy, her hands guiding Barbara's head to the tender parts. Her eyes were devouring Claudine's buxom body, yet physically she ignored her. Instead she suddenly pulled Barbara's head away from her body in a violent, passionate movement.

It was a momentary action as she spread another generous dose of cocaine between her legs; this time she massaged the powder deep inside the opening. Barbara went wild with excitement. She went down again—deeper and with renewed vigor.

For the next fifteen minutes the two women clawed at each other; tongues flicking, lips devouring, fingers moving from one nerve center to another, a tangle of knotted arms and legs. As the burning passion grew, Gina turned furiously toward Claudine.

She collected a generous portion of the white powder on a moist index finger and gently penetrated it into Claudine. She knew the itching, tingling feeling it would create. She knew because she was experiencing it herself.

Almost immediately Claudine was burning inside and out. Soon she would yearn for something to alleviate the itch. Inside. Deep. To relax the aroused, burning nerves. And Gina provided the balm.

Her fingers dug into the wet opening, while her tongue cooled the outer edges.

The encounter was impassioned, yet tender and delicate. Intimate knowledge of their own bodies allowed the women to please one another in ways men could never comprehend, let alone master.

Eventually ecstasy took hold. Gina lay on her side while the two girls satisfied her. One soothed her from behind, the other nibbled at her vagina, stopping only to kiss each other passionately before exchanging roles on Gina's body. And she came. How many times Adel could not count, but she came. And came. Until finally, exhausted, the three girls slumped back in sweat and fatigue, knotted together in a tangle of arms and legs, sheets and pillows.

And Michael Adel had what he had come for.

He sat and forced himself to concentrate. He was physically and mentally excited; it had been a wildly sensual scene; he had been aroused to fever pitch but he had resisted the temptation. After five minutes of silence from the bed, he stood and opened the closet door discreetly and took out the leather briefcase before turning off the central switch. Then he collected the two Nikon cameras and placed them in the briefcase. With the video cassette he was more careful. Guarding against light, he withdrew the cassette, placed it in a lead container before putting that, too, in the briefcase.

"What are you doing, darling?" came the exhausted voice of Gina.

"I'll see you in the morning," he said softly. "There's two envelopes in the drawer beside you. Give one to each of the girls when you've finished with them."

Gina slowly pushed herself up on to her elbows. "But, darling, I thought..."

He bent over the limp, sweat-soaked body of Barbara and kissed Gina's damp cheek. "I'll see you in the morning," he said gently.

John Usher was consuming his third "Nino Special" in the newly decorated bar of the hotel, being suitably entertained by the drink's creator, when Adel entered the virtually deserted room. Three Arabs sat off in one corner talking loudly, the gutteral sound of their voices filling the large room as Adel approached the bar. Somewhere in the background Frank Sinatra fought a losing battle for attention. Adel handed Usher the briefcase and nodded at the head barman.

"How are you, Nino?"

"Fine, Monsieur Adel. Are you staying with us a few days this time?"

"I'm afraid not," he said, "I'm off in the morning."

He turned to Usher. "You won't get any sleep tonight, so take it easy with those, John," he said, pointing to the half-finished drink. "Everything okay?"

"Yes, sir."

"When can I have them?"

"They're waiting for them right now. They'll work on them through the night."

Adel nodded and was silent for a moment. "Okay. Bring them up to my room at nine in the morning, then," he said, "but be careful with them."

He turned to leave, then faced Usher. Almost bashfully he added, "Thank you, John."

As a rule Michael Adel was a late riser, but that morning, in a state of exhilaration, he forced himself to operate ahead of time. Neither the hotel operator nor Usher had disturbed him and it was early when he threw off the bed covers and stepped from the starched sheets. He looked around the room and noted, as he had last night, that Usher had set up the video cassette recorder and attached it to the television. He checked the closet for a fresh change of clothes and then bathed, dressed and ate breakfast in a leisurely and contented mood. He was almost finished with the *International Herald Tribune* and *Le Monde* when there was a knock on the door.

"Good morning, sir," said a tired and unkempt Usher.

Adel glanced at the briefcase in his hand. "How do they look, John?"

"I think you'll be satisfied, sir."

Adel nodded and took the briefcase. "Good." He moved toward the center of the room. "I'll be leaving for Cannes almost immediately, John. Why don't you stay over tonight and get some rest?"

"Thank you, sir. I think I will."

"And don't forget to take care of everything in both suites and Miss Mahmoudi's quarters too."

"I will, sir," said Usher.

The results of the photography were as good, if not better, than Adel had expected. The film and accompanying still photography gave a blow-by-blow account of the torrid love scene of the previous night. It showed every lurid detail and from three different angles, providing an incontestable document of a drug-induced orgy. Even more important, Adel was not implicated in either the stills or the movie.

As a work of art, Adel thought, the lighting was a little on the dark side. As an instrument of blackmail it was flawless. Gina's father could never absorb a scandal of the magnitude these pictures would arouse.

And Gina needed her father's money.

Gina Mahmoudi was awake and eating a croissant dripping with honey when Michael Adel entered.

"Good morning, darling," she said.

Adel gave her a nervous grin but said nothing. He placed the portable video recorder beside her breakfast tray and connected it to the television and a wall plug. As he set up the apparatus, he noted out of the corner of his eye the look of surprise and confusion on Gina's face.

"What *are* you doing?"

"You'll see in just a minute."

He loaded the cassette into the machine and then noticed a second cup on the breakfast tray.

"Is someone here?" he asked apprehensively, glancing toward the bedroom door.

"Yes, darling," Gina said with a mischievous grin. "Barbara was so tired I let her stay. She's still asleep."

Adel walked to the bedroom door and closed it. Barbara's presence was probably a blessing in disguise, he thought. Gina was less likely to cause a scene with her next door. He returned to sit opposite Gina and poured a cup of coffee.

"Gina, I'm going to take Natalie from you."

The carefree look of mischief on Gina's face evaporated.

"You're no mother for her and you know it. Your money provides her with food and shelter, but that's about all she gets from you. Like everything else in your life, she's just a toy, a gadget to play with.

81

"When I agreed to let you keep her, it was because I believed you would provide her with a better life. You convinced me that a mother's love is more important to a child than a father's and I was willing to go along with that. Looking back on it I should have known better." His voice was bitter now and a shade louder. "In your case I should have known better."

"That's not true, I..."

"Let me finish. The child's suffering and miserable. That's all there is to it. She never sees you except at parties when you show her off like a prize Pekinese. If it weren't for her nurse, you wouldn't know if she was dead or alive. There are men crawling in and out of that house like it was an army enlistment center. And you go on your merry way as if she doesn't exist. No love, no caring, no warmth, no responsibility. Hell, that's no home for her—it's a bloody brothel," he said angrily. "It's only a matter of time before it catches up with her, Gina. She needs a simple, orderly, secure upbringing."

Gina Mahmoudi stared at him in disbelief.

"Go fuck yourself. You self-righteous, pompous little trader. What gives you the right to lecture me about how I treat my daughter? My daughter..."

As she berated him Adel walked to the bedroom door and locked it. He wanted no interruptions. Then he walked to the small screen and pushed the start button.

Gina froze. She uttered no sound as the black-and-white picture flickered to life.

"I hope you get the general idea," Adel said calmly. "But if you miss anything, I can ask the concierge to send up a larger screen." He paused to watch the writhing ecstasy of the three women. "Not exactly a picture of motherhood, Gina."

The effect was devastating. Gina's voice, when it finally came, was trembling, barely audible. "You can have your fucking daughter, you bastard," she whispered, a gaunt expression on her face.

Adel turned to leave. There was nothing to stay for. Only the smell of victory lingered, and it was unbearably foul.

CHAPTER 13

Gina Mahmoudi was depressed and worried and a little frightened. It was an unfamiliar mix of feelings and she was ill equipped to handle it. It was a far cry from what she was used to, she thought, as she entered the hotel elevator on the penthouse floor. Nothing resembling a genuine problem had ever really entered her life before. Usually it was all pleasure; an endless round of lunches and dinners, shopping, coiffures and beautiful, interesting people. And marvelous places. Paris...Rome...Beverly Hills...Mykonos...Sardinia and, more recently, Aspen. She looked in the elevator mirror and admired her exotic features in the soft lighting. Then she moved closer and wiped the rouge on her cheeks a shade lighter.

The elevator came to a stop on the ground floor and she glided into the lobby. Think positive. You have things to do, she admonished herself. After four years Michael Adel had a lesson coming to him—the saving grace of this whole mess. And the lesson would start tonight.

"Good evening, Miss Mahmoudi. You look very smart," smiled the concierge as she passed his desk.

Gina opened her handbag and found a twenty pound note. "Thank you, Arturo," she said, slipping the note to him in her handshake.

She always looked after him. She didn't have to. After all, her father was the major shareholder in the Swiss holding company that owned this and twenty-seven other hotels across the world. But she liked Arturo and she needed him too often to rely on company loyalty. She had learned a long time ago that company loyalty was only skin deep. Personal loyalty, reinforced from time to time with financial remuneration, was far more dependable.

She smiled at Arturo and walked toward the marble entrance. She loved this hotel, she thought, casting her eyes over the sumptuous facilities. And someday it would be hers. On her twenty-first birthday her father had promised it to her.

Of course, he had told her to keep away from the Chelsea Towers and she had been alarmed when he had reiterated the command on the telephone last Friday. But now it all seemed a little unreal. Perhaps he was being overdramatic; he was getting old and senile and the opium had unhinged him. Leila's death was the final straw. Was it really murder? she wondered as she spotted her dark green Jaguar in the driveway. Knowing her sister she doubted it; the official version—an overdose—was more likely.

The uniformed chauffeur opened the rear door and she stepped in.

"Annabel's, Brian," she instructed, as she sat back on the black leather seat.

The Jaguar sped past the Regency splendor of Belgrave Square and the traffic maelstrom of Hyde Park Corner into the narrow streets of Mayfair. As it turned left, out of the hotel driveway, a shining black Ford Granada pulled into the traffic behind them, a hundred and fifty yards to the rear. Throughout the journey the distance between the two cars never varied.

In the blurry light of the Jaguar, Gina Mahmoudi glanced down at her white, low-cut Fendi dress. The slit on the right side ended high on her smooth, bare thigh. She slid her long leg out of the slit and was reassured that the dress was more than appropriate for the occasion.

As usual, Annabel's was crowded, boisterous and dark. The clientele was made up of two distinctly different groups—the rich and the beautiful. Traders who barter their assets in various forms of arrangements from wedding bands to one-night stands. But they do it with style and class, with an uncommon ability to use their gifts—to the hilt.

Gina Mahmoudi felt at home as she made her way through the packed floor. It had been some time since she had been seen out in London and she enjoyed her reentry into society.

"Don't make a spectacle of yourself," her father had said. But daddy always exaggerated. That's how he thought he could bend her. Poor daddy.

She stopped and said hello to numerous friends who dotted the tables and aisles. But she refused their invitations to stay; tonight she was determined not to be sidetracked.

At the bar she ordered a glass of white wine and scanned the darkness, occasionally blowing a kiss in the direction of a friendly face. If he was there she shouldn't have any difficulty spotting him, she thought. He was at least six inches taller than the average man and half as wide. Suddenly she was nervous again. What if she couldn't find him?

Her father had been adamant on the phone Friday evening. She was to contact the Iranian Islamic people in London immediately. It was all so bizarre. But then Daddy always knew what he was doing. He was always one step ahead. And what had clinched it was the opportunity to strike at Michael.

"As soon as you can, darling. It must be soon. Tell them about Adel and that I am sending him to our house in Teheran to steal our hidden land deeds, promissory notes, jewels and things. That's enough for them. Tell them I am sending Adel. Do not put it off, darling. You must tip them off right away. It is of paramount importance. If Adel is caught we have a future. If not..." He had stammered and changed course in mid-sentence. "I cannot talk too long. I must go. But do it, my dearest. Do it soon," he had said, hanging up abruptly.

She had needed no urging. At last she had an opportunity to get her daughter back. And what vengeance, what sweet vengeance, she would wreak on Michael Adel.

"Archie," she anxiously called the bartender above the loud Afro-Detroit beat, "have you seen Mr. Naderi tonight?" She was careful to seem relaxed, offering him an attractive smile.

"Ah, let's see," said the bartender, looking up at her while his hands continued to work furiously. He frowned as he tried to recall one face in two hundred.

Her heart skipped a beat as the bartender's expression remained blank.

"Oh, yes," he said finally, pointing to a dark corner. "I think he's in the back somewhere, Miss Mahmoudi."

"Thanks," she smiled, relieved.

She squeezed through the crowded floor as nonchalantly as she could and chose an area directly in his view. It had to be natural, she thought. She wanted him to approach her, as he always did, and she would have to be careful to act in character throughout

85

the night. True, they had slept together several times, but if there was anything she had learned about men, it was that they enjoyed the chase. The harder it was, the more they enjoyed it.

Except for that bastard Adel, she recalled with distaste.

She leaned against a column directly in Keyvan Naderi's view and thrust one leg through the long slit of her dress. Tonight she would give him what she knew he wanted.

God, she thought as her excitement mounted, Keyvan had never dreamed of tripping over the information she had. He had tried so hard, so cleverly, to uncover something about her father, what he was up to, where he was planning to settle, aimed at locating the assets he had taken out of Iran. But tonight she would present him with someone far more valuable. The information would surely please Keyvan's new paymasters. The old man had pointedly refused to tell her the details, only that Michael was involved and that he had to get caught. Despite her insistence he had refused to be more specific.

"I cannot talk for long, they have allowed me a few minutes of privacy with your sister before... before... Just do as I say and perhaps someday I'll explain everything to you. But for now, just do as I say."

She couldn't understand it. Why was there such a rush to pass on the information? Why was it so imperative for Adel to fail? Why was he to be trapped? Her father had always liked him. She didn't understand it. It was not like her father.

She shrugged aside the questions. After four years this was her chance to destroy Adel. The rest didn't matter.

Her father had meant her to go to the official representatives of the Islamic Revolutionary Government in London. But that would be clumsy, even dangerous. After all, she was supposed to be in hiding. The old man had forgotten that. Planting a leak through Keyvan would be far more effective. He would channel it straight to where it counted, without a middleman. And besides, how much more amusing to denounce Michael with another man inside her.

She watched Keyvan dominating the conversation at his table. When he stopped there was a roar of laughter. Another of the bastard's jokes, she thought, as the laughter subsided. The same old Keyvan, joking and living it up lavishly. The only difference in his life was his paymasters.

A year ago Keyvan Naderi had been a successful wheeler-dealer under the Shah's regime, close to the royal court and SAVAK. Now he was "unofficially" handling commercial transactions in Europe for the new regime. Unencumbered by principles or honor, he was raking in kickbacks and commissions. And in the process, to sweeten the pot for the new regime, he had become an informer, a stool pigeon who spied on old friends. A smooth ghoul who traded information for the right to sell rice, cheese and bullets at inflated prices.

Gina studied his handsome, if exaggerated, features as he talked and laughed with his cronies. What did Keyvan and the revolutionary Islamic regime have in common? His blatantly hedonistic ways were in sharp contrast to the spartan life-style of the Islamic movement. Perhaps Keyvan's favorite expression summed him up best: "Man cannot live on bread alone." And Keyvan made sure there was always more than bread on the table, no matter how it was obtained or from whom.

He had noticed her now and was feverishly trying to gain her attention. She turned toward the gyrating bodies on the dance floor. Let him work for it, at least, she thought.

A few moments passed before he approached her.

"Gina, dear, you're looking ravishing." His lips lightly caressed her cheek.

"Hello, darling," she said enthusiastically. "How are you?"

"Fed up, this refugee life is beginning to get to me."

"Why, darling? You have no problems."

"Well, now the Home Office is making it difficult for us to stay in England. Funny, isn't it? All our lives we were welcome wherever we went. We used to be rich Persians, running around blowing big money, subsidizing tourist industries. Now we're boat people, searching for a way to stay alive. Nobody wants to know us," he grumbled.

Gina smiled, but she wasn't fooled by him. Nonchalantly she surveyed the thrashing bodies on the dance floor.

"Don't worry about it so much, darling, perhaps the pendulum will swing back soon and you can stop being a yacht person." She smiled. "Come on, let's get a drink."

They spent the evening dancing, dining and gossiping. She spoke of her relationship with Michael Adel; she was still in love with him, he was a good father to Natalie, they were still close.

When they grew serious, they veered back and forth about Iran, each edging toward the subject for a specific purpose, then gliding away again, lest the other scent the trail.

By two-thirty in the morning the moment had arrived. Curled up in bed, relaxed and exhausted from the physical toll of love-making, Gina rolled over and kissed Keyvan Naderi on the palm of his right hand, holding and caressing it like a contented child.

"It was good," she purred. "You know you're very good, don't you?" She cuddled closer to him.

All night he had been joking with her and she had tantalized him with bits of gossip about her father and his exile friends. She knew that each dreg was being stored for later use.

Naderi turned in the darkness and felt the bedside table for his cigarettes.

"It's good to be with a friend when you're alone and worried," Gina mumbled.

"Why worried, Gina?" Naderi blew out a lungful of smoke.

"I'm afraid for Michael. He's going to Teheran. Ostensibly to wind up his company. But I heard my father talking to him on the phone last week. Saying something about going to my father's house in Teheran to get some of his valuables out." Might as well spice it up a little, she thought. "I just hope he's not mixed up in all this silly counterrevolutionary talk."

She sounded half-asleep, talking like a silly goose. But she knew Keyvan would sooner or later pick up on the lead.

And so he did. Was Michael going soon? How brave he was to be going to Iran for whatever reason. Could he, Keyvan, help in any way? Would he be staying long?

Gina provided appropriate monosyllabic responses to guide Keyvan along. Michael at her father's house. A safe. Some kind of rendezvous. Maybe it was just a dealer who wanted to make a quick black market buck on behalf of some *mullahs* for her father's priceless rugs. But she thought it had sounded much more serious. Her father was hardly in the rug league—however priceless.

"Shouldn't really be saying all this, should I?" she murmured.

The probing questions and muffled answers continued until she fell asleep. Keyvan lay on his back staring at the ceiling. Then he looked at his watch and quietly slid out of bed and dressed.

Through half-closed eyes Gina watched him tiptoe out of the room. When the door clicked shut she sat up with a huge grin. She felt mischievous and pleased with herself. After a minute she got up and hung the DO NOT DISTURB sign outside her door. Then she skipped back into bed, wiggled her feet under the covers and felt warm all over. Tonight, she thought, she would sleep restfully.

CHAPTER
14

LONDON: TUESDAY, OCTOBER 23, 1979: 4:00 A.M.

Keyvan Naderi turned right outside the hotel. The night was bitter; cold winds lashed the heavy rains and tore through his overcoat. He bent his head to protect his eyes and lengthened his stride to cover quickly the short distance to Sloane Street. He ignored the familiar surroundings; Gina's credibility and the bitter cold were enough to occupy his mind. The problem with Gina's information was that it was incomplete. He had tried to extract more from her but the dimwit didn't know the details. Her father's telephone conversation with Adel had little hard information. He shook his head disgustedly. She had the smallest details of the private lives of practically everyone in the jet set down pat. She knew exactly who was screwing whom on both sides of the Atlantic. But a plot to overthrow a government... that was too boring for her to listen to.

"Spacehead," he muttered. Besides, he thought, the Islamic people had assigned him to entrap her father. He wasn't so sure that Adel would interest them.

Halfway up the block his thoughts were suddenly interrupted. The door of a black car opened a few feet in front of him and Naderi had to swerve quickly to avoid a collision. He flashed around to see a man of massive proportions emerging from the car. He stood over six feet, with immense square shoulders on which a head seemingly with no neck was planted. The face was pitted with deep pore holes and a crooked mountain range of a nose separated two fierce, glaring eyes.

A shiver went through Naderi's body. He bent his head down and moved away quickly.

"Later, Wally," Naderi heard the man say with an American drawl. There followed the sound of a closing car door and footsteps that echoed on the wet pavement. Another shiver shook Naderi's body. He had never before seen such an animal.

At the intersection of Cadogan Place and Sloane Street, directly across from Coutts & Company, bankers to the rich, stood two red telephone booths. Naderi crossed the road on the zebra lines and closed the door of the booth behind him, thankful for the relative warmth. He slipped a ten-pence coin into place and dialed from memory.

"Come on, come on," he said out loud as he looked through the misting windows at the burly man heading toward the hotel entrance. Naderi's right hand, pressed to the metal coin drop button, trembled in the cold night air as he shuffled from one foot to the other.

Finally, a voice answered and Naderi pressed the coin into the slot. He stuffed his frozen hand into his coat pocket.

"'Allo," slurred a heavily accented voice.

"Mister Ambassador?" asked Naderi.

"Speaking." The voice was sleepy and distant.

"I have to see you right away."

"Now?" growled the ambassador. "It is nearly three o'clock in the morning."

"Yes, sir. But it's important. We cannot discuss it on the telephone. There are dangers lurking."

"Can it not wait until morning?"

"Not if you wish to reach the Imam's ear first."

The ambassador let out a heavy sigh. "Very well."

The burly man entered the deserted lobby and headed for the hall porter's desk.

"Fifteen forty-six," he said as he approached.

The elderly night porter squinted through thick spectacles and moved his hands along the bank of letter and key boxes.

"Ah, 'ere we are, sir," he said, pulling at a heavy buoy-shaped key ring. He read the man's name on the computer-typed slip on the box.

The burly man reached for the key.

"I need a wake-up at seven in the morning," he drawled.

"Not much sleep tonight, eh, Mister Taylor? You Americans 'ave so much..."

"Good night," the burly man said and headed toward the elevators.

On the fifteenth floor he turned toward the emergency staircase that twisted behind the elevator shafts. He walked up two flights of stairs to the seventeenth floor and followed the hallway signs to suite 1712-20.

Outside the door he looked up and down the empty corridor, then knelt on the plush brown carpet and opened his briefcase. He withdraw a Walther PPK and silencer and placed the case upright against the wall. He stood and screwed on the silencer.

He looked at the DO NOT DISTURB sign on the door and smiled as he pressed the buzzer. An appropriate epitaph, he thought.

He pressed the buzzer again and held it.

"Keyvan?" he heard Gina ask tentatively inside.

He coughed through his handkerchief.

"Keyvan? Is that you, Keyvan?" Her voice was more insistent.

His response came through the handkerchief. It was a mixture of grunt and yes, and it was enough.

The door opened.

The burly man showed no reaction to the look of terror on the naked woman's face. Instinctively he placed one foot inside the doorway and silently savored the scene. He had always enjoyed this moment. Her eyes were wide and fixed, her complexion gray and cold.

She took only one step backwards as her hands fell limply to her sides. She made no effort to hide her naked body.

The bullet hit her between the eyes. With barely a sound it scattered her midbrain and cerebellum on the lime-green sofa behind her.

The man stuck the gun in his belt, closed the door and picked up his briefcase. He took two steps down the hallway before stopping. He walked back and flicked the sign on the door to green: PLEASE MAKE UP THIS ROOM.

91

CHAPTER
15

"I don't know of a single authorized murder by any of our intelligence agencies. Killing is simply asinine and crude, a proof of failure. And in this business failure is unforgivable. It always comes back to haunt you," Bell had assured Adel.

"Allen Dulles once observed that assassination and murder are not part of the American character. I agree with him."

"So the Russians killed the Red Indians," Adel had replied, wondering how difficult it would be to convince Castro, Diem, Trujillo, Allende or Lumumba of Bell's sincerity.

Bell's lopsided gaze had turned a trifle cynical. "It's 1979, Michael, and the world's a sophisticated place. The state of the art permits us to be far more scientifically efficient than you give us credit for."

Adel shook off his thoughts, reminding himself that he had bigger and more immediate problems to worry about. In forty-five minutes he would be in Teheran. One thing at a time, he told himself. One thing at a time.

But his mind raced relentlessly. His thoughts had gnawed at him for five hours now, creating such tension that he could not sleep. He felt cramped, too, in the 707. There was no upstairs bar and no film to occupy the time. The Nice-Teheran run had lost its glamor; it no longer enjoyed the luxury of a jumbo liner and even this smaller jet was only half full.

Gradually his mind drifted back to Bell. He heard clearly the smack of the neatly folded document on Bell's desk.

"You just can't get round this, Michael," Bell had said, pushing the sheet of paper across. It was a *mandat d'arrêt*, a warrant for Adel's arrest from the French Ministry of Justice. The charges were blackmail and kidnapping.

"It's waiting to be served."

"It has no date," Adel had said disgustedly. "It's not valid."

"Technicality."

"I'll fight it."

"We have affidavits from Gina Mahmoudi, her father, her maid, Barbara, Claudine... Shall I go on? Michael, give me credit for having done my homework. We need those tapes. And you're our best bet."

"Enough to gamble with a kid's life."

"We're dealing with a national security issue, here. The normal ethical codes that regulate relations between human beings don't apply when problems are of this magnitude. These tapes are bigger than ethics. I will destroy you and your family to get your cooperation. And you have no course for appeal. This operation is sanctioned at the highest possible level. You have no other options available to you. You know that."

Adel did know. He had known for some time.

In Cannes, Bell had introduced him to Yuri Allon of the Mossad, who in three days had tried to teach him the art of clandestine operation and survival.

"He's a fine man, very experienced. He organized the raid on Entebbe so theoretically this should be a piece of cake for him," Bell had said before Allon's arrival.

The tone had been grudging, thought Adel, as he gazed out the plane's window. Why, he had never been able to detect. Perhaps the use of an Israeli agent had gone against the grain for a man who had spent his life with the CIA and the OSS. From the beginning of the agency he had, behind the scenes, contributed as much as anyone to making it the world's foremost intelligence network. He had headed military intelligence in Vietnam and Laos and had been a key member of the American intelligence community for over thirty-five years. Now his consulting company, or the agency, or whoever it was he was representing, was turning to an operative from an upstart client state for assistance, perhaps because of the recent spate of U.S. intelligence flops. It rankled and because of Bell's obvious discomfort, Adel had suddenly detected something human in the colonel.

"So you want to limit the risks and use proven sources?" Adel had asked.

Bell had puffed out a lungful of air. "If you're referring to the CIA, they have nothing to do with this. As I told you, this is being handled privately, through me."

"Of course it is, colonel. Of course it is." He was determined to play out the game if that's what Bell wanted.

On the first day of training with the imposing Allon, Bell had showed up for a final briefing. He had drawn him aside to talk privately. "I'll inform one man at the embassy in Teheran to put at your disposal anything you may require. However, this will be on a private basis. We will officially deny any connection should you be unsuccessful. You understand that, don't you?"

"I thought you said this thing was unofficial, colonel."

"Your contact in Teheran will be George Clark, he's in the economic section of the embassy. His code name will be 'Khan'. Whenever you contact him, use that name at the beginning of the conversation and he'll trigger a scrambler. After that you can talk freely. He's also the man who is arranging the delivery of the equipment you need to your house in Teheran. Probably in the form of a suitcase. It will be delivered two days after your arrival.

"It would probably be more desirable to work out the operational details with Allon and . . . and Gleeson at your own convenience. That's the man I'll send down to assist you: Jim Gleeson. He's an excellent strategist. I recommend him highly.

"You're not given to suggestions, Michael, but I'd like to offer you a couple. This matter regarding Clark—I suggest you keep it to yourself. There's no need to mention it to either Gleeson or Allon. There's no point in anyone except you being aware of the various components that make up the whole. It provides you with a secondary escape channel if anything goes wrong. In this line of business, options are what keep you alive."

Adel had been silent for a long moment. "Options are what we all strive for, aren't they? I mean, you take a man's options away and you control him, don't you, colonel?"

Bell had ignored the question. "The second thing is that Allon must not know what specifically it is you are going in for. He's a good man—probably as good as they come—and he can be helpful to you, but I don't want him knowing about the tapes. Under no circumstances must you mention them or what they contain to him."

"Why not?"

"Because those are your instructions."

The past gave way to the present as the public address system came alive. "Ladies and gentlemen, we've started our descent toward Teheran's Mehrabad Airport. Please fasten your seat belts and make sure your seat is..."

Adel moved his seat to the vertical position, extinguished his cigarette and turned toward the window. In a few minutes, the lights of the provincial towns of Ghasvin and Karadj would appear and then the sprawling city.

Teheran's Mehrabad Airport had not changed; it retained its prison-like architecture and ambiance. A twelve-foot-high barbed-wire fence surrounded the outer perimeters of the vast compound that acted as the country's main civil and military airport. From guard posts and watchtowers beamed searchlights keeping a constant vigil over every inch of the complex. Armored cars dotted the barren landscape, ready to welcome arriving passengers. And an asphalt apron, large enough to hold ten of Xerxes' battalions or stage a royal ceremonial for the Shah, stretched away from the administration buildings.

The main terminal itself was still under construction; it seemed it had always been under construction. The roof had caved in under the weight of an unprecedented snowfall in 1974, killing over one hundred people, and still it was under repair. The arrival lounge now was a "temporary" expedient, off a considerable distance to the right of the main building, and it was ill equipped to handle even the lightest off-season load, let alone revolutionary turmoil.

Adel was the first of the first-class passengers to disembark into the cold, drizzling night. He stepped on the rickety, open ramp and turned up the collar of his black leather windbreaker to ward off the rain. He noted the informal garb of the guards who waited at the foot of the stairs—fatigue jackets, bell-bottom jeans and Che Guevara chic.

They carried their weapons casually—Kalashnikovs, M-3s, Uzi submachine guns, M-16s. Hand grenades hung on them like strange fruit, and knives and bayonets dangled from their belts. Their pockets bulged and their chests were crossed with bandoliers of bullets. None of the group wore boots, Adel noticed as he descended. Clearly they were unaccustomed to wearing footgear of any variety. Like the people of the bazaar and the rural areas they were only too happy to affect the Western way, but lack of familiarity undermined their pretensions. And so they improvised; they wore shoes with the backs crushed downwards and inwards, flip-flopping and dragging as they walked on the asphalt surface.

It took ten minutes before the last passenger descended. They stood waiting and silent in the falling rain, outnumbered and encircled by what looked like an Islamic version of Mexican bandits. To Adel they were all too readily recognizable; they were the *pasdaran* militiamen, Ayatollah Khomeini's chosen forces of the Lord.

Adel saw the revolutionary militiamen as little more than a fragmented street gang. Their average age was twenty-two or twenty-three. They lacked discipline, efficiency, cohesiveness, but they swaggered with an arrogance that would have been absurd had it not appeared so menacing, so uncontrolled. They stood, cigarettes dangling, enjoying their revolutionary roles: talking and laughing, carelessly swinging their rifles like phallic symbols.

"*Autobus nist. Bayad piyadeh berin,*" shouted one of the militiamen in Farsi. He appeared to be the mob's leader.

"What did he say? What do we do?" asked an elderly European gentleman.

"There's no bus. We have to walk," Adel interpreted.

"*Yallah,* move," ordered another militiaman, swinging his Uzi in the direction of the terminal.

"My two children and these bags—can you help me? I can't make it with all of this." A young, well-dressed Iranian woman pointed to her unwieldy hand luggage.

"We can't help the passengers," shouted the leader. "It's forbidden. Get one of the others to help you. Besides, you should have thought about it when you bought all that expensive stuff in Europe. Did you steal from the people to pay for it? Or did you get it the usual way?" He pointed between his legs and cackled.

Adel felt his blood pressure rise as the soldiers echoed the man's raucous laughter. Instinctively he stepped toward the woman but a distant voice pulled him back.

"*Blend into the background,*" the Israeli agent had said. "*Never draw attention to yourself. Never.*"

He stopped as the elderly European moved apprehensively toward the young woman.

"I'm not carrying anything. May I help you?" he offered.

"Thank you. You're very kind," she said in English, relieved. She gripped the hand of her elder child, and pressed the infant to her chest. Even in the pale light her face was pink with embarrassment. The man picked up her two canvas bags and a large package and together they trailed the other passengers, towards the building.

Inside the terminal the security measures were even more menacing. The adolescent guards now outnumbered the passengers by five to one. There was a cacophony of conflicting instructions; passengers were ordered first one way, then another, and always at the end of a gun barrel. There was neither logic nor reason to the instructions, only a sense of competition within a leaderless rabble.

Adel felt both apprehension and reassurance. The air of violence was awesome, but organization and training were nonexistent. He had to blend, disappear into the chaos, hit and run.

At last the line advanced and Adel stood before an unshaven immigration clerk.

"Passport," the official grunted.

Adel held out the document and the man snatched it from his hand.

"Saleh... Saleh," the official mumbled under his breath as he thumbed the thick book. He stank of onions and sweat.

"Saleh... Saleh... Reza," he repeated.

He closed the book with a thump and picked up three dirt-stained sheets of paper, studying them carefully. Then he turned his attention to the burgundy Iranian passport again. It was one of the old variety now being replaced by a new Islamic version.

Islamic hit list, thought Adel uneasily.

"Hmm," the clerk mumbled. "Height one point eighty-three meters. Weight eighty-two kilos," he said, looking up at Adel again. He flipped a few pages. "Businessman. Passport issued in London on February fifteenth, 1976. Valid until February fifteenth, 1980. Okay."

He stamped the passport, pushed it carelessly across the Formica counter that separated them and turned to the next passenger. Adel moved on, relieved that the first formality was over.

There was another long wait for the luggage. For the fifth time Adel walked to an ashtray ten feet away, flicked the ash and walked back. He did not do it out of any fastidious habit—the floor was filthy—but it calmed him, helped curb his impatience. It also gave

97

him an opportunity to amble around and size up his surroundings.

As he turned to walk back, he noticed off in the far corner an island of composure in the sea of chaos. A group of militiamen surrounded a large, rugged man of fair complexion. His powerful arms were folded across his chest, one hand occasionally moving to draw on a cigarette. His skin tone, hair and blue eyes branded him Teutonic. From a distance the man seemed to speak authoritatively and with few words. He was clearly respected by the darker-complexioned militiamen, who listened intently.

Adel looked away and edged into the crowd; there was nothing to gain from standing and staring. But it was a disconcerting sight; how many blue-eyed, blond Iranians were there?

With a screech the luggage belt jerked to movement and Adel changed direction. After a short wait he collected his luggage.

The young customs girl was wearing the latest Islamic fashion— a *char-ghad*, a cumbersome Islamic scarf modestly hiding the hair, but leaving visible the sight of two thick, bushy eyebrows that almost joined together over the nose. She looked at him and smiled. After a cursory inspection of his luggage she stamped his passport and smiled again, this time raising an eyebrow suggestively. Adel smiled back in gratitude.

Khomeini's Islamic honesty and the country's revolutionary principles had made the taxi fares a negotiable item and the result was a fourfold increase. Given the lateness of the hour and his eagerness to get off the streets and into the sanctuary of his home, Adel was in no mood to engage in the Iranian sport of *chuneh*, haggling. It was eleven-thirty, he was tired and, he realized, unnerved by the sight of the blond man at the airport. He had looked distinctly professional, and dangerous.

Adel handed his suitcase to the first driver who approached: a short, stocky, mustached man wearing a three-day stubble and tight pants that were two sizes too large in the seat.

"Dezashib," he told the driver, indicating a suburb on the northeastern tip of the capital.

The man lit up at his good fortune; it was the most profitable route in the city.

"You live there?" asked the driver, throwing the small suitcase on the front seat.

"No. I'm picking up a friend's car," Adel lied.

"Nice friend lending you a car these days. A man can't depend on his own family, let alone a friend."

The cab moved out. Adel did not want to stretch the conversation; he had a thirty-minute drive ahead of him and he wanted to observe the changes, get the feel, the mood of the town. But the driver was in a gregarious mood as he swung the ancient Hillman onto the freeway heading for Shahyad Square, now Freedom Square.

"You been away long?" the driver asked.

"About a year."

"That's a long time. Why? Do you live abroad?"

"Yes," said Adel, "My wife is foreign, and I've lived in her country since we were married." At least half true, he thought.

"Things have changed here in the last year," said the driver cautiously.

"For the better, I'm sure."

"Certainly, certainly." The answer came too quickly. "*Agha* looks after everything. Everything will be better soon."

Adel recognized the word Agha as a term of endearment for Ayatollah Khomeini, now called the Master. The Shah's nickname was *Ra'is*, the Boss, when he had ruled the country.

"Too many spies here," the driver hazarded. "I don't know where they come from. I mean, where were they before? If *Agha* doesn't control these kids soon, there won't be anything left."

Adel searched the driver's eyes in the rearview mirror. Was the man asking provocative questions or was he just making conversation? Was he probing? Or was he simply an opponent of the regime, tentatively feeling out a fellow rebel?

He couldn't tell and there was no point encouraging the conversation. As the driver went on talking Adel turned his attention to the scenes speeding outside. The first thing that caught his eye was the inordinate number of *mullahs* who filled the streets. Every second pedestrian seemed to be wearing the turban, gown and sandals of the new elite. The women were all draped in *chadors;* it took a breeze to reveal blue jeans, high heels and human shapes that were now taboo. The scattered groups of young men were all heavily armed. Some huddled around oil drums—makeshift cauldrons—from which orange flames of heat danced. Rubbish littered the street, left by the rent-a-mobs on their daily protest marches against imperialism, colonialism, whateverism. The walls were blackboards of revolutionary slogans, the graffiti preaching murder: *Death to the Shah. Death to Carter. Death to Russia. Death to the Army. Death to Bakhtiar. Death to the U.S. Death to SAVAK.*

Death to Sadat. Death to Israel. Under one slogan a wit had added in large red letters: *Make sure you don't forget anyone.*

Adel gazed around. The occasional minaret broke the contours of the shabby, mud-brick, square-shaped houses, dwarfed by high-rise buildings and the shadows of the mountains to the north. The roadside was crammed with hawkers from whose carts a hundred tempting scents filled the air. Lamb kebabs, hot steamed beetroot, grilled kidneys, marinated walnuts, incense. Afghan and Baluchi tribesmen with long trailing turbans offered medicinal herbs while others competed to sell a variety of spiced stews from copper vats.

The driver's voice penetrated his thoughts. "I don't understand something. The Shah told us he was guided in his ways by Allah. Mr. Khomeini claims Allah leads him in his judgments. Then how come they don't agree? If you ask me, Allah talks a lot. And no one's listening to what he has to say."

Maybe the man is simply looking for a decent tip, thought Adel.

"Allah is mysterious in his ways," he replied, knowing the cliché would be wasted on the driver as he drifted off into his own thoughts again. The schedule Gleeson had set entailed too much risk. If he followed it without protecting himself, it would provide Bell with what he wanted—a reliable timetable to follow, and there was too much needless risk in that. If Bell was to be a danger, it would be after he had the tapes, not before. And there was no point in making it easy for him by giving him a hand-picked time and place.

Then again, he thought, perhaps Bell and Gleeson were being straight. Maybe all they wanted were the tapes and he was letting his suspicions get the better of him. Maybe they knew something he didn't, something that made the schedule essential to follow. They had insisted that timing was crucial to the plan.

Why then had Yuri Allon been so hesitant? He had never outwardly disagreed with them, yet that in itself was another disquieting factor. Allon was by nature an undiplomatic man, direct and to the point. He didn't falter or hang back in any other instance. But here, even to the end, Allon had been hesitant and reserved, insisting only that the other ingredients of the operation were more important to a successful outcome than the timing and should be given priority.

"It'll all come together at the airport," the Israeli had warned. "That's the critical juncture."

"What about the schedule? What if there's a forced play on that?"

"Concentrate on the airport," Allon had said. "The run of the play there on your way out is what's going to buy you retirement. And it's not going to be easy. Build yourself up to that point and remember it may be painful. How painful will depend on how good an actor you are, how well you improvise. You must make sure they believe two things: your story and your act."

"And the timing?"

The Israeli operative had been silent for a long moment, his hard, lined, sunburned face contemplative yet strangely sympathetic.

"Planning is the prerogative of generals and you're not even a soldier. These things have a way of changing in the field, so concentrate on your own problems. Worry about surviving."

Adel cursed under his breath in frustration. Right now all he needed from them was the suitcase containing the equipment. And the onus was on them; they were to deliver it at the house in the next few days. For the time being that was all he needed from them. He would decide later what he was going to do with Bell. One thing, though, was for sure. He was not going to part with those tapes in Iran; no damned way he would turn over the tapes to Bell or his people before he was safely out. It would be in London, on his own schedule, when he chose. And he didn't plan on walking into their arms at the bottom of the ramp at Heathrow. He would have to think of a way to insure himself. But what? How could he cover himself? Whom could he trust?

"Where in Dezashib is your friend's house?" asked the driver as the taxi pulled up before the tattered doors of the small mosque in the center of Dazashib's seventy-five-yard village strip. The building was daubed with banners bearing Islam's message. Quotes from the Koran. Slogans from Khomeini. And the never-ending list of enemies to be exterminated in the name of God.

On one wall large red letters proclaimed:

"America is incapable—Imam Khomeini."

"Russia is incapable—Imam Khomeini."

"England is incapable—Imam Khomeini."

"Israel is incapable—Imam Khomeini."

Beneath it someone with a sense of humor—and much courage—had written:

"Khomeini is incapable—Mrs. Khomeini."

Adel looked past the storefronts to the darkness beyond. "An-

101

other two hundred meters or so, up by the old Alam crossroads. I don't know what the new name is," he said.

Adel was generous with the driver, but not too generous.

"Blend into the background," Allon had said. *"Try to be like a bad commercial. You don't want to be remembered."*

"Shall I wait for you? Your friend may be out, or the electricity may be off, and he won't hear the bell. We've been having power failures as usual."

Adel looked back at the lights on the village strip. "The electricity seems to be working tonight and I'm sure he's waiting for me. You're very kind just the same."

He ducked into a narrow alley off the crossroads and waited in the darkness as the taxi made a U-turn. There was still another mile to walk to his parents' house, but he waited to gain distance between himself and the cab.

"Nothing should be traceable to you. Everything about you must be hazy. If you travel about town, never use one car. Change vehicles often. Never take a direct route. Always keep an eye in the back of your head," Allon had instructed. *"That's where it comes from—the back."*

Once the taillights had disappeared, Adel started down the decline that was the beginning of Farmanieh Avenue, two miles from the Shah's former palace in Niavaran. A year ago this had been a wealthy suburb, alive with the hospitality Iranians were once famous for. Flashy cars used to fill the streets and bands, with their mélange of Persian and western beats, contributed a rowdy tone to the glittering parties that vied for attention at almost every other door.

He glanced at his watch; it was a little after midnight and the place was now a cemetery. The streets were deserted; not a light broke the blackness. Fear and insecurity had driven the inhabitants to seek refuge behind the protection of brick walls and darkness.

Walking briskly, Adel reached his parents' house in less than fifteen minutes. Except for a speeding powder-blue Mercedes-Benz minibus, he saw no other sign of life. Across from his parents' old house the once flamboyant Argentine Embassy stood derelict and feless. Inside the compound scattered lights gave off a pale orange glow, while outside two listless policemen slouched on either side of the wrought-iron gates. They looked at him casually, uninterested and demoralized.

Adel stood quietly before the door of his parents' house, feeling in his pocket for the key. The century-old arched wooden door of his parents' house, with its decorative carvings from the Qajar era, stood high and wide enough for a truck to pass through, and was also thick enough to stop one. A Judas gate to the right of the main gate allowed people to pass in and out. Affixed to it were two heavy circular door knockers made of brass. Now obsolete, they had once served an essential social function. The larger one was always mounted higher—out of reach for female callers—and its sound, Adel recalled, was deeper than the smaller one. The two knockers were used to announce an arrival and to indicate the gender of the visitor, and thereby indicate whether a maid or manservant should be dispatched to welcome the arrival.

Adel's lips widened as he touched the antique brass in fond memory.

Originally the house had been a summer country estate, sprawling at the base of the soaring Alborz Mountains. Built in 1870, it had been a half-day ride from Teheran, an oasis comfortably remote from the scorching heat of the city, where his forefathers had spent summer days in cool comfort and luxury. In those days a private army protected them from roving bans of marauders; the massive gate was one of three that connected the twelve-foot-high walls surrounding the private park. Now the oasis lay neglected and empty, the last of the family wealth. The remainder had been nationalized by the Shah, or sold off piecemeal by family members in need of ready cash.

Adel fit his key into the sturdy lock on the Judas door. It squeaked but opened easily. The grounds rose in the darkness toward a majestic building that sat atop an earthen mound overlooking the estate. An umbrella of century-old walnut trees, strategically planted for their grace and cool shade, offered sanctuary from the pitiless summer sun, while a jungle of citrus trees, ragged from lack of pruning, bulked in the darkness, cutting off a clear view of the mansion. A fresh mountain spring meandered through one corner of the grounds, the sound of flowing water audible on dark, still nights.

A flood of memories filled his mind. There had been so many wonderful days and nights spent here. The warmth of his grandparents, his brother Mark, the love of his parents, the glamorous parties during his summer holidays from England, his first experience with sex. And Gina.

He walked toward the building, remembering exactly where the trapdoor that led to the *qanat* tunnel was: at the end of the garden, to the right of the main gate. It had been his childhood hideaway when playing hide-and-seek with Mark. Occasionally the boys would pretend they were ancient Persians digging the narrow tunnel when the subterranean irrigation system was first developed three thousand years ago. In the hot, dry summers they loved to splash their faces with the cool water which flowed underground from the mountains to the parched plains. And they would take refuge from the scorching sun in the *abanbar* reservoir that stored the water. Every rural dwelling—and the Adel mansion was rural when it was first built nearly one hundred twenty years ago—was connected to the *qanat* system. The underground network and *abanbars* meant that no water, so precious in this arid country, was lost to evaporation. The Adel *abanbar*, like so many others, had been a mine of hidden childhood secrets. Even now in the darkness it would present no challenge.

Adel lay down on the damp ground beside the steel trapdoor and pulled it open. He stretched his arm into the pit and felt sticky cobwebs, the coarse concrete of the wall, and found the light switch. He clicked it, but nothing happened; time had taken its toll; it had been years since anyone had entered this obsolete underground reservoir.

"Just one more time," he whispered in the darkness, smelling the familiar dankness. "Hide me just one more time," he repeated, and closed the heavy door.

Only this time, he told himself, it was no childhood game.

Adel stepped back from the trapdoor and headed up the driveway toward the mansion. A soft yellow light glowed warmly in the kitchen window, setting off the dark, sprawling mass. As he drew closer, memories of happier days flowed through him; days when for one brief moment in its long and uncivilized history the country had flourished. But the gravest error of all had been committed. Stability had been taken for granted.

In the distance gunfire shattered the night and sent a shiver of cold through him; the deadly sound strengthened his determination. He quickened his stride and made his way through the jasmine bushes to the window over the large kitchen sink.

Inside, a woman in her seventies sat in a rocking chair, wrapped in a shawl, a head scarf covering her once hennaed hair. She was waging war with her knitting, each stitch a victory over failing eyes and trembling hands. For a brief moment, time stood still. She had not changed her habits in over thirty years.

He tapped on the door and called her name.

"Mariam."

She heard but did not seem to recognize his voice. Fearlessly, she opened the door and then, squinting, she recognized him. Tears welled in her eyes and an enchanting smile spread across her wrinkled face. Adel looked at her lovingly. She had always been a small, slender woman but with age she seemed bent under the weight of the years.

"I never thought I'd see you again," she said incredulously, the tears falling down her cheeks as she held out her arms in welcome.

He gathered her in, holding her fragile body in a gentle bear hug. Mariam had been with them for over fifty years now, starting in her early teens as a cleaning maid and staying on through three generations of Adels.

He held her closer, the scent of her body familiar and comforting. He closed his eyes and remembered. She had been the one who had raised them, him and his brother, Mark.

Michael suddenly remembered with a pang of regret how close he and Mark had been as youngsters; and indeed still were, although time and work commitments insured that they saw each other less often now. Mark was always traveling and incommunicado for long periods on business. Hardly surprising that he had never married, Michael thought.

Mariam, however, had allowed no one to spoil them when they were young. The fact that both boys had grown up so well adjusted was due to her common sense and wise discipline.

Other members of the staff had left seeking wealth and fame in Khomeini's "revolution of the disinherited." Some had even tried to blackmail the family through the *komitehs*—the revolutionary committees which had taken their name from the foreign word. The *komitehs* had been set up in each neighborhood to purge the "sins" of the Shah's regime—and to make a little money on the side. And Khomeini himself had given them their frame of reference: anyone found guilty of "corruption on earth and crimes against God" was punishable. And under the new Islamic law there were only two sentences: confiscation of property and death.

This fragile woman whom he held in his arms had defended and protected the family property so far.

"You can't get rid of me that easily," he joked, stepping back to look at her.

But immediately she started, "Are you hungry? You must be starved. I have cold cucumber and yogurt soup and I'll heat up some *dolmehs*. I've got stuffed aubergines, stuffed peppers and stuffed tomatoes. That should be enough, no?"

Knowing the pleasure it gave her, he let her fuss over him.

"Do you have any whisky, or did they confiscate it?"

"*Goosaleh-ha*. The goats! Of course I've got some. Nobody's taking anything out of this house."

She disappeared into the larder and reappeared with a bottle of Johnny Walker Black Label.

"Don't worry about alcohol. We've got a basement full," she said, pouring a healthy ration into a glass and adding ice. She set it in front of him with a tumbler of tap water, then began to prepare the meal.

He raised the glass to toast her.

Her chatter continued for two hours. She reminisced about the past and then, with a sadness tinged by bitterness, recounted life in Khomeini's Iran. Her isolation. The hate. The killings. The fear. The inflation. The shortages, especially of heating oil. The hooligans who ran the revolutionary committees. Visits to her few surviving friends. A sharp-minded, sharp-tongued assessment of "the situation in this place today," as she put it.

"There's even a revolutionary office, a *komiteh*, down the road in Mr. Mahmoudi's old house."

"Oh," he said nonchalantly, his heartbeat quickening. "What do they do there?"

"Nothing but bother people. In the day it looks like a university; young hooligans flock there and sit around trying to figure out how to steal from people. They're always holding court, arresting people and shooting them without a trial. Then they steal their belongings. Do you remember Mansour, the young barber down the road? They arrested and shot his father and brother two months ago. Just for being soldiers in the Royal Guard. Now they want to grab Mansour's shop and put him out of business. All of this in the name of Islam and God." Her tone was scathing.

"And at night?" he asked.

"Some guards are left there at night. They sit around smoking opium and drinking the alcohol they steal from people's homes or restaurants. They hang around the front gate and watch cars go by, stopping and searching them for no reason at all whenever they get bored." She shook her head angrily.

Adel nodded. "How many of them are there at night?"

Mariam looked at him closely.

"Michael!" she exclaimed. "You're up to something."

"No," he said, "just curious."

She looked at him in disbelief. "Do you think you can fool me?" she asked, a conspiratorial smile on her face. "I know you too well, Michael. What is it? Why do you want to know all this?"

He took her fragile hand and looked into her eyes somberly. "Mariam, this is important. Very important. No one must know I'm here. I don't want you to buy extra food—no bread, milk, eggs, anything. Nothing must be done to suggest an extra person. There's something I have to do, but I can't tell you any more than that. I have to come and go, and I don't want anyone knowing about it. Okay?"

She eyed him carefully. "You're not trying to save the world again, are you?"

"No. Just survive in it."

"You're a good boy, Michael," she said. "You always were."

She removed her hand from his and spoke in a more serious tone.

"There are about six or seven of them as far as I know. But by about two or three in the morning most of them pass out from drugs and alcohol. They've kept Mr. Mahmoudi's old servant, Hossein. Sometimes they even bring young girls there. I can find out more tomorrow when I . . . ."

"No," snapped Adel. "That's exactly what I mean, Mariam. I don't want you doing anything. There's nothing you can do—except make things worse."

The old woman searched his eyes.

"All right then, I will do nothing," she said.

"This is serious, Mariam. And dangerous." To drive the point home he feigned irritation and cut the evening short. "I need a shower and some sleep. Which room shall I use?"

"Use your own, of course," said the old woman, hurt by his abruptness. "The room is all ready; in fact, the whole house is ready. It always is. Perhaps someday we'll all live here together again. Like in the old days. All the family together."

107

"Perhaps someday," he said, knowing it was unlikely to happen in her lifetime.

The old woman sighed. "I'll just make up the bed while you take a shower."

They walked together to the second-floor landing.

Suddenly the old lady exclaimed, "Oh, my! I almost forgot. Some man brought a case, a package for you this afternoon. I told him you weren't here but he insisted. He told me to give it to you the next time you came. I should have known, shouldn't I? I mean, I should have known then," she mumbled to herself. "Anyway, let me bring it up. You go ahead and have your bath."

Adel watched her descend the staircase. He wondered how much of what she had told him was real, how much the product of her outraged disapproval.

He wondered, too, why the suitcase had been delivered ahead of schedule.

CHAPTER 16

TEHERAN: SUNDAY, OCTOBER 28, 1979: 4:00 A.M.

The shower had relaxed him, but still sleep would not come. Images of Samira and Natalie and fear of what lay ahead played havoc with his mind. He looked at his watch for the tenth time; it was four in the morning. He cursed and turned onto his stomach, but it was useless.

"Damn," he said. He turned on the bedside lamp and lit a cigarette.

It was impossible not to think of Samira and Natalie. It was fear, but it was more than that. It was not death or danger so much that terrified him but the gnawing thought that he might never see them again; it filled him with deep insecurity and sadness. Yet he was powerless to react in any rational way; there simply was no alternative.

He threw off the blankets and took up his briefcase from the coffee table in front of the fireplace. He walked back and spread its contents on the bed. There was an Ingram M-10 LISP (Lightweight Individual Special Purpose) machine pistol with a noise suppressor, night scope and three clips of ammunition; a magnetic torch; a gas mask with activated carbon canister to offset methane or other gases in the tunnel; a Walther PPK pistol with two boxes of special .45 caliber bullets; fifty feet of nylon rope; a miniature rubber suction pump; touch-sensitive black leather gloves; a six-inch knife in a holster to go on his belt; a stainless steel pry bar; a U.S. Army collapsible shovel to dig through obstructions in the antiquated *qanat* tunnel; and four Israeli grenades insulated in plastic blister packs.

The grenades resembled turquoise-colored stones, exactly like the ornaments decorating a hippie's belt and similarly designed to fit his belt buckle.

The suitcase also contained two false passports. He studied them and admired the quality. At the bottom of the case he found a sealed plastic packet holding $5,000 in U.S. currency. It was uncomfortably thick; he wished they'd used larger notes, fewer tens and twenties.

Adel picked up the Ingram and looked at it. It was clean and ready for use but he stripped it and checked the firing mechanism. It was an amazing machine, he thought, recalling Allon's words.

"This miniature submachine gun is a deadly, sophisticated firearm. It is American-made and capable of firing up to twelve hundred rounds per minute at an effective range of two hundred and fifty to three hundred yards. With attachments it is accurate enough for a sniper. It is the deadliest weapon on the market for your purposes. Some of us had them at Entebbe.

"The Sionics silencer virtually negates any sound, and it reduces the barrel vibration, thereby increasing your accuracy. One other advantage is its sonic boom; because these bullets move faster than sound, your target will only hear the sound as it leaves him, as it goes away from him. Consequently he will misinterpret the direction from which the bullet was fired. If you miss him, his first reaction will be to move toward you, thinking the shot came from the other direction.

109

"The Starlight scope, of course, will come in handy. It'll give you night vision of remarkable clarity."

Carefully Adel set the compact machine pistol aside and extracted a grenade from its protective package. He checked the magnetic clip and fastened it to the belt of his jeans; it held firmly but came away easily when tugged. He rewrapped the grenade in its protective package and then stored everything in the small case, placing it on the top shelf of the closet behind some old sweaters, out of harm's way and Mariam's reach.

He gathered up a two-week-old *Etella'at* newspaper and walked over to the fireplace. He lit the paper with his lighter, making sure the fire was healthy before tearing the pages from his passport, in the name of Reza Saleh, and tossing them into the blaze. After the document turned into a mass of charcoal he used the poker to break up and scatter the ashes.

He glanced at his watch; it was nearly five in the morning. He crawled back into bed and turned off the bedside lamp. His body ached with fatigue, but still his brain would not stop.

He had spent a lot of time during the past week with Natalie and Sam; every minute he could get away from Allon and Gleeson and the briefings about the mission, the psychology of an operative, the equipment he was being trained to use. It had been precious time, filled with meaning and deep affection, yet tinged with shadows of finality.

In the darkness he reached for the cigarettes on the bedside table. He lit one and tried to forget his loneliness, his sorrow. But is was useless. Lying in bed three thousand miles away from Sam, he realized how much he loved her.

Only now, when time was running out, perhaps never to return.

He got out of bed and stood by the window. He parted the curtains and looked down at the gardens sweeping away into the darkness. But he couldn't get Sam out of his mind.

She was such a delicate person, yet sensible and strong. So balanced, so comfortable with life, and undaunted by its temptations. How powerful her love was. And how much she had taught him, and how much he needed, and cared for, her.

A new thought wracked him: If he were to die, would she find another man? What sort of man? Suddenly he remembered another girl he had once known and cared about, someone whose name kept crossing his mind during the past few days. He thought of

Jane Bennett and the agony she had suffered after her first husband died of cancer. The degradation and pain she had endured in her search to find a substitute. The suicide attempts, the hospitals, the humiliations. Would that happen to Sam? Would she be engulfed in the same inferno of torment? He ached inside, overwhelmed by jealousy. But it was also reality. It would happen. Perhaps in a year, maybe two, but it would happen. Sam was too beautiful, too alive, to wilt. She would be sought and courted and finally won. It was the rule of life, the law of nature.

And what would happen to Natalie? he asked himself. His precious Natalie, his flesh and blood. But it was only a momentary concern; he knew why Samira dominated his thoughts: he had little to worry about with Natalie. Except for his love, she would miss nothing. Sam would take care of her completely. Of that he was certain.

But who would care for Sam?

CHAPTER 17

TEHERAN: SUNDAY, OCTOBER 28, 1979

The rattling of Mariam's pots and pans through the open kitchen door grew louder as he descended the staircase. When he entered the kitchen she greeted him with a buoyant smile.

"Did you sleep well?"

"Not a wink," he grumbled.

"That's not new. You never could sleep the first night back from abroad. Take a nap this afternoon."

"Good idea."

"Sit down and I'll get you some breakfast."

He did as he was told.

"Did you know he's not an Iranian?"

"Who's not?" he asked, taken aback.

"Khomeini of course. He's Indian."

He reached over and moved the old-fashioned, charcoal-fired brass samovar closer, careful to keep the delicate balance of the china teapot on top of it.

"East or West?" he asked with a smile as he poured an *estekan* of tea.

"East or West what?"

"East or West Indian?"

She shot him a peeved look. "Don't try to provoke me. He's an Indian and that's all there is to it. And he's illiterate."

"You mean Khomeini can't read or write?" He turned the tap of the samovar to dilute the rich, strong tea with boiling water, then dropped three lumps of sugar into the glass to saturate it. "I thought Khomeini was a student of Plato."

"I suppose Mr. Plato is one of those Indian gurus," she retorted. "If Khomeini was literate he wouldn't be such a liar about the Koran. All that nasty business he wrote about God. It's shocking. Did you read it?"

"Ummm," he replied, biting into a piece of hot, unleavened *barbari* bread and recalling Khomeini's rules to guide devout Muslims in proper piety: rules ranging from shaking the last few drops from one's penis, to the detailed procedures and acceptable circumstances under which one could engage in sexual intercourse with one's camel. Or one's favorite ewe. Or one's favorite youth. Or how a man could divorce his wife by merely stating so, without any obligations to her or his children.

"So don't tell me the man's literate," she said.

She shuffled back from the refrigerator and placed butter, goat cheese and honey in front of him. Then she brought a bowl of fruit and a plate covered with sprigs of fresh rosemary, mint and other herbs. The Iranian breakfast brought a rush of family memories from his childhood.

"Do you know what they say about him?" she asked, as she sat opposite.

"Well, I've heard a few things they call him." He added a generous portion of butter and salty cheese to the bread and bit into the open sandwich, adding seedless Askari grapes for contrasting flavor.

"They say if you lift his beard, you'll find 'Made in England' printed underneath."

112

She cackled and he joined in. Then he washed down the sweet jasmine-scented tea which had acquired a whiff of charcoal from the samovar; the contrasting flavors of creamy butter, brittle bread, salty cheese and sweet tea were delicious.

The British were not well loved by Iranians—respected for their cunning but not trusted. For the last hundred years the popular lore was that they were always behind all of Iran's woes. In the nineteenth century the tacit alliance between the British Legation in Teheran and the clergy was well documented. Now the British were obviously up to their old tricks again. After all, what other explanation was there for the BBC's Persian broadcasts during the revolution? Clearly it was the British who wanted Khomeini to come to power.

Popular lore was irrepressible, Adel thought, especially with sages like Mariam stoking things up from time to time.

The old lady said: "No religion preaches hate and revenge and murder, especially not Islam. Islam is a beautiful and kind religion, full of forgiving and love. This fool, Khomeini, slanders it."

"Do you know how many crimes have been committed in the name of God?" Adel asked.

"Yes, and that's exactly what he and his sponsors are doing right now—Khomeini, I mean."

"That was delicious, Mariam," Adel said, nodding at the food. "I'd forgotten how good your breakfasts are."

Momentarily she seemed to forget her worries and suppressing a smile of pleasure she removed his empty plate.

The rest of the morning passed slowly as he went over his plans. Mercifully, the anxiety and pessimism of the night before had faded, allowing him to relapse into a long afternoon siesta, several hours long. He woke refreshed. With little else to occupy him, he decided to scout Mahmoudi's house and its surroundings.

If things went well, it might provide answers to the two critical questions Bell and the briefings with Gleeson and Allon had left unanswered: How many guards protected the grounds and where they were posted?

Several times during the afternoon he passed the old mansion, which was now the district revolutionary office that attended to the grievances of local constituents; each time on the pretense of purchasing something from the neighborhood shops beyond. But the answers eluded him; it became increasingly clear that without actually entering the premises he would never get them. For a moment he thought of joining the queue of pleaders and petitioners that formed at the gateway to the *komiteh* center. But it was not moving; those seeking the attention of the authorities stood and huddled in a sullen line.

By five o'clock he had managed only to confirm the outdoor count—six heavily armed militiamen in paramilitary fatigues, lounging near the front gateway, occasionally leaving it to wander aimlessly along the wall.

On the three other sides of the estate the militiamen were posted at the midpoint of the walls. These guards did not move from their posts. Their view was unobstructed and the traffic on the side streets was light and easily monitored. So how many more guards were inside the grounds? And where?

When he returned to the house, a worried Mariam was waiting for him.

"Well, I'm glad to see you back."

He smiled at her and poured himself a large whisky.

"You worry too easily," he teased as he sat at the kitchen table and looked up at her. She had always been a devoted woman, he thought. So kind, unselfish, loving. She had been a second mother to him and Mark. Loving them and guiding them through life as if they were her own. And she was suffering now, her life a shambles in the wake of the revolution.

"Mariam, when this thing is over, I want you to come and live with us in France. There's nothing left for you here and you belong with us. We all miss you."

She shook her head wistfully. "No, Michael, this is where I belong. This is my house, my country. This is where I want to die, not among foreigners."

Slowly she shuffled over and kissed him.

"Besides, who's going to look after this place if I go?"

CHAPTER 18

Adel heard thunder and cursed. As he walked down the gravel driveway a steady wind was picking up in force and intensity. Overhead, the cumulus clouds hung low, blocking the full moon and making the stormy night black and ominous.

The darkness was a godsend, but rain would force the guards to seek shelter inside the house. And that could prove hazardous.

He looked at the storm clouds again. Perhaps he could get in and out of the house before the downpour, he thought, as he glanced at his watch; it was nearly one-thirty in the morning. Getting through the *qanat* tunnel should take about forty-five to sixty minutes, Yuri Allon had estimated. Once he had the tapes, if he got that far, the rain would help. If, that was, the *qanat* was clear. These old irrigation tunnels criss-crossing the country were usually constructed in soft alluvial soil and were notoriously susceptible to cave-ins. They had been obsolete now for over fifteen years, ever since the new city water supply had been installed to replace the antiquated system that carried water from mountain streams to the city.

He took a last drag on his cigarette and crushed it beneath his dark blue sneakers. Holding the oversized briefcase, he dropped down into the underground reservoir that led to the *qanat*. The room smelled stale and musty and his body stiffened as his face brushed against the sticky spider trails.

The only noise in the pitch darkness was the steady pit-a-pat of dripping water. He turned on the flashlight and pressed its magnet to the metal ladder. In the dim light he opened the briefcase and began to activate its contents. Carefully he unwrapped and attached

115

the grenades, first rechecking that their primers were secure, then grouping them near his belt buckle, two on either side, in their allotted slots.

He picked up his Ingram. Marveling again at its seven-pound weight, he attached the Sionics noise suppressor to the nozzle and inserted a clip. Then he attached the Starlight night scope and slung the almost weightless machine pistol by a thin strap over his shoulder. The two extra clips went into their pouch on a second belt made of webbing that tied more loosely around his hips. He bound one end of the nylon cord to the belt loop near the front of his jeans and secured the pry bar, collapsible shovel and rubber suction pump in their allotted pockets. He put on the gas mask but it was cumbersome and uncomfortable and it added to the feeling of claustrophobia. He removed it and put it back in the case.

Dousing the light, he climbed the ladder and placed the brief-case—containing now the money, the passports, the gas mask, the Walther PPK and one box of ammunition—at the entrance to the reservoir, behind the clump of roses that hid the trapdoor.

In the dark he descended into the reservoir again. As he entered the narrow tunnel he was surprised at his own coolness. There was no feeling: no fear, no consternation, not even foreboding. He had no idea what lay ahead or whether he was capable of handling it. He didn't care if what he was doing was right or wrong, or even if there was an alternative. It was too late for all of that now. All he felt was a strong urge to survive. To live to see his family again; to live his own life.

It was cramped; the tunnel was barely more than half a meter high and the fit was almost too snug. The ammunition clips attached to his belt scraped the *qanat* walls as he crawled and he prayed that the tunnel did not narrow up ahead. The earth was also a problem; it was soft sand and the knees of his jeans were soon wet and soiled, with the tiny stones biting into his flesh.

Gradually the air began to thin and rapidly became foul. The farther he progressed, the worse the sickening odor and its debilitating effects. Soon it was unbearable.

He cursed himself for having left the gas mask behind, and stopped to construct a makeshift filter around his nose and mouth from a handkerchief. Then he crawled on, faster. He had no choice; it would take too long to go back.

He pushed himself forward, torch in hand, his back occasionally brushing the roof of the tunnel, the nauseous stench making him light-headed and faint. Like a wounded animal he crawled and scraped to escape the pain that seared his lungs; he pulled and pushed his body to escape the gases that had ignited an uncontrollable fit of coughing. He felt himself weakening into semiconsciousness, listlessness. He forced himself on, refusing to be seduced, pushing himself, remembering the reward at the other end. The prize of Sam and Natalie.

Then the air started to improve; oxygen filtered through to soothe his burning lungs and bring his mind back in balance.

He had arrived at the first reservoir; he was at his neighbor's house, the one that separated his own and Mahmoudi's. He sat on the floor, muffling his coughs and panting, but at least breathing fresher, cleaner air. If everything went right, he thought, as the fire in his chest subsided, the next reservoir would be Mahmoudi's house. He was halfway there. He stood and stretched in the generous space, his neck and back aching, his knees scuffed and sore. There was nothing he could do to relieve them. They would be bleeding before the night was over.

He crawled back into the tunnel and pressed on. In the torchlight he noted that the wooden ceiling had completely rotted. The cypress columns had decayed but miraculously they held. His luck had improved: the tunnel was not only clear of cave-ins but there were no gases either. Fifteen minutes later he entered the reservoir at Mahmoudi's house.

He stood and leaned for a moment on the cold damp wall and caught his breath. He rolled his neck and forced it back as far as he could and then forward. It ached and the massaging exercise relaxed the cramped muscles. The flashlight showed a trace of blood on one knee; he could feel the rawness of the other.

He stuck the magnetic flashlight, its light pointing downwards, close to the center of the metal ladder, and brushed the earth from his clothing. Then he sat on the damp concrete floor of the reservoir and lit a cigarette, inhaling deeply and savoring the brief rest.

After a few minutes he stood and crushed out the cigarette before bending to pick up the butt.

"Leave no trace of your route. No clues whatsoever. Protect it. If they find your route, they'll find your house—and then you. Remember, you have several days before you leave Iran. They'll

117

be looking for you in that period, so protect your route."

He placed the butt in his pocket and climbed the ladder slowly, his heart beating faster, the adrenaline flowing through his body. Carefully he pushed at the trapdoor. It did not budge. He pushed harder. Perhaps it was locked, he thought, his heart beating still faster.

"Shit!" he whispered as he descended.

At the bottom Adel freed the flashlight from the metal rung and climbed back to the door. It wasn't locked; time and lack of use had welded door and frame. He stuck the torch to the ladder and unpacked the pry bar. Carefully he inserted its sharpened edge between the metal door and the frame. He turned the flashlight off and applied pressure, levering the bar downwards. Still the door would not budge. He pried harder, pulling down violently with his shoulder.

Abruptly it gave.

A thunderous crash split the night's silence as the metal door smashed against the marble surface surrounding the swimming pool. Instinctively he grabbed the door handle and closed it above his head. He scrambled down the ladder, missing several of the rungs in his haste and bruising his left shin. At the bottom, he dived into the tunnel.

His heart beat furiously as he lay there, his ribs pressed against the damp earth. Great, he thought, as he grabbed the Ingram, cocked it and flicked the lever to automatic, the whole neighborhood had probably heard the explosion.

He waited, the Ingram at the ready, frightened and uncertain as to what to expect. Nothing happened. He listened; not a sound.

Twenty minutes passed before he felt confident enough to leave his hiding place. Thank God for the thunder, he thought as he slid out of the tunnel into the reservoir, his eyes fixed on the trapdoor above. He climbed the ladder again and carefully opened the trapdoor. Through the slit he squinted into the dark pool area that separated him from the building. Then he scanned the rest of the large grounds.

Stoned or drunk, he thought. They have to be. If they didn't hear that, they wouldn't hear anything. Perhaps it was a good omen.

The Olympic-sized swimming pool was twenty-five to thirty yards from the front of the mansion. Massive colonnades opened onto the building and in the center stood a white door embossed with gold carvings. He opened the trapdoor wider for a better look. The ornate door was ajar and light spilled onto the patio. He swallowed and opened the trapdoor all the way, resting it on the marble poolside surface. He could see in every direction now as he heard the thunder closing in and smelled rain.

To his right he observed two guards in the gatehouse, a hundred and fifty yards away, down a gentle incline. The men were smoking, talking and laughing, oblivious to danger.

He looked left and saw the mansion.

"Unless you have to do otherwise, move slowly. Watch and wait. Look for movement. Check the shadows, check the trees, check the building and its windows. It could come from anywhere. Your natural reaction will be to move quickly, to get it over with and get out. Don't. Move slowly. Make certain you've seen everything there is to see before you move from the safety of that tunnel."

He checked the gatehouse again. For the moment the two men presented no threat. They were too far away, too occupied in conversation.

The wind rose, setting up a chatter in the birch trees covering the lawns and flower gardens that surrounded him on all sides; lightning cut a jagged scar in the black sky. He counted the seconds. A sharp thunderclap arrived in under ten—eight or ten miles if I have the right lightning and the right wind speed, he thought. Eight or ten minutes before the storm would pass directly overhead.

He turned his attention to the house, ablaze with light. He watched and waited for more than ten minutes. Except for a blur of movement on the second floor, where the rising wind tugged at the curtain of an open window, there was no sign of life.

He glanced at his watch: 03:11:25—an ungodly hour, he hoped, for Muslims committed to *namaz*, prayers at sunrise.

More lightning was followed by pelting rain; the roar of thunder was loud and almost overhead; the storm was drawing near.

He jerked himself out of the pit and ran, ignoring the heavy rain and holding the Ingram loosely to his right, ready. He darted toward the shadows of the nearest rose bush and he threw himself at the base, twisting and rolling into its foliage. Immediately he positioned himself and lay still.

There was no sign of life, only vapor from his own breath and the loud, heavy pounding of his ribcage.

119

He waited. Still there was no movement. Cautiously he started crawling toward the building, the grass and mud drenching and caking his clothes.

"Blend into the darkness as much as you can," the Israeli had said. *"In the darkness there is the unknown. In the unknown there is fear."*

He moved to the steps below the main doors and lay still. There was no sound except rain, no movement except wind.

"Use the setting. Anything that distracts, even momentarily, is your friend."

It seemed like a long time, but when it came, it came suddenly. A streak of light accompanied by a thundering crash momentarily illuminated the entire compound. Fleetingly it was day. Abruptly it was dark.

Adel moved rapidly. He dashed to the porch and hugged the door, holding the Ingram at waist level. Another ear-splitting thunderclap and a blaze of light lit up the garden, followed by yet another shattering explosion. He saw no movement in the brief white glare but knew the storm was now directly overhead.

"Now or never," he told himself.

He grabbed the ornate door latch and pushed lightly. The door gave and he followed it, crouching low as instructed, dashing across the vaguely familiar dark parquet tile floor and kneeling on one knee, his back against the wall, the gun ready.

He waited, but again there was no sign of life.

He knew the house well. The eight glazed mahogany doors in the lobby were in a perfect circle. On the left, a twisting semicircular glass, gold and chrome-plated stairway led to the second floor. Above this, and extending nearly four floors, a hand-painted sky, complete with cirrus clouds, formed a massive dome.

Was it a replica of some rococo mansion? A bizarre vison of the White House? Or simply Mahmoudi's opium-inspired mausoleum; the son of a Kerman pistachio peasant farmer's legacy to his own magnificence?

What it was was a bordello, thought Adel as he glanced at the serene summer sky painted above. A ten-million-dollar bordello built by Mahmoudi to accommodate the Shah's extramarital activities. The Shah's women had been provided by Mahmoudi, usually buxom blondes of tender age and expensive tastes. In return, Mahmoudi would arrange the purchase of nuclear reactors, computers, F-14 fighters, arms—by royal decree.

Adel walked to the first door on the right, the entrance to Mahmoudi's private study. He opened the door and slipped into the dark room and stood there with his back to the door, sweat pouring from his body but his ears alert, sensitive to any sound. His luck was holding; there was none.

He flashed the torch briefly to memorize the shape of the room and obstacles—chairs, lights, tables. The gaudy room was a jungle of ostentatious furniture and paintings. There were too many antique tables, chairs, statues and busts. It looked like the storeroom of a provincial French theatrical company.

In the darkness Adel walked to the inlaid Empire desk; it sat on a small silk Isfahan rug that slid easily and conveniently when pushed. He flashed the torch on the bare wooden surface, looking for the removable parquet tile above the floor safe. A seam of dirt outlined the two-foot-square panel; he lifted it out with the miniature chrome-rubber suction pump and set it aside.

He paused again to listen, but the heavy rainfall drowned out all other sound. He flashed the torch at the three chrome knobs of the safe and spun them to zero. Beneath him, as he knelt, a puddle of water formed on the dark parquet surface. His leather gloves were wet and heavy, slippery and insensitive to the touch.

Dial three—turn left once to two.

Dial one—turn right twice to five.

Dial two—turn right once to three.

He pulled the handle and the heavy steel door swung open.

The safe was jammed to the brim. He dug in, pulling out the contents—jewels, packages of Krugerrands, documents, opium pellets, glass tubes of white powder—and laid them in a growing pile, ready to be swept back. Near the bottom he found a burgundy-colored drawstring leather tobacco pouch; inside were two Sony cassette tapes.

He stuck one tape in each knee-length sock and quickly brushed the pouch and pile of discarded valuables back into the safe. He closed the metal door, spun the knobs and replaced the parquet cover.

Abruptly the room was filled with light. For a split second he prayed it was lightning, but a voice behind cut off his prayers.

"If you move you're dead." It was a deep, heavy voice.

Adel froze on his hands and knees.

"The passport says Saleh, but I believe Adel is the name," the guttural voice said.

121

Adel was gripped with fear as he heard feet move to his rear.

"Very carefully slide the machine pistol backward," the voice instructed.

He did as he was told; the Ingram skidded along the floor, scratching the dark wooden surface.

"Good. Now stand up and put your hands and arms around your neck.... No! Higher!"

Adel was petrified; a massive weight pressed against his chest, making it difficult to breathe. Icy needles pricked his body.

"Good."

The man spoke English but the accent was indefinable. It was neither British nor Iranian English. Hands moved roughly down his body, removing his equipment. They were thorough in their search and the tapes did not escape them.

"Now you are permitted to turn around, but keep your arms where they are."

Adel turned to face three men. Two stood twenty feet away near the glazed mahogany door, confronting him with leveled G-3 rifles and menacing looks. They were obviously militiamen, slovenly and ill at ease. The third man made Adel shudder. Instantly he recognized him. Impressively in command, the man raised his rump to sit on the desk. He was relaxed and confident as he shuffled the two cassettes in one massive hand.

Adel's knees seemed suddenly rubbery and weak. It was the man at the airport. The tall, blond, foreign-looking one in the customs hall. And he looked even more intimidating at close range.

"We've been expecting you, Mister Adel," he said, his guttural accent making the words even more threatening. "Our brothers in London could not tell us precisely when you would arrive. But we knew that you would come to this house." He stopped. "Put your arms down slowly," he instructed.

How the hell could he know I was coming?

"To be honest, we were told to expect you some days earlier. But that is all unimportant now that you are here. What have you come to steal—these tapes, Mister Adel?" The huge man fondled the plastic boxes. "And what are on these tapes? Please, quickly and honestly, is this what you have come to steal? It would be foolish to lie, Mister Adel. And so much a waste of time."

Adel knew he had only one chance left—the turquoise studded Israeli grenades decorating his belt. With his hands down he had a chance. Not much of one, but nevertheless, something. He hooked his right thumb above the belt buckle, his splayed fingers extending down to the grenades at the front.

"Okay," he said, shrugging his shoulders. It wasn't going to be easy to fool this man and he decided not to try. "I . . . I haven't heard them myself," he stammered, "but they contain information regarding a weapons system." He needed time. He had to freeze the action and hold their attention.

"What weapons system?"

"Ballistic missiles. Something called a Phoenix missile. These tapes carry information about the Hughes guidance system, on-board computers, digital to analog micro-processors, over-the-horizon radar. That sort of thing."

He felt no loyalty to Bell or to the U.S. government. Not right now anyway. He had developed a more immediate concern: two G-3 rifles pointing directly at him and an Uzi submachine gun waving in his vicinity.

The blonde shook his head and grinned.

"That does not seem possible. How does one place printed matter—and such a large amount as you say—on a cassette tape? And only two of them. No, it does not wash, as you Americans say."

"Well, that's what I was told. I haven't heard them."

"All of that material?" asked the blond man. "And on only two cassette tapes, Mr. Adel. Do you take us for fools?"

"No. It's sixteen or seventeen tapes recorded at high speed onto two," said Adel, repeating Bell's words. But the explanation sounded as hollow as when he himself had first heard it. "That's what I was told," he added.

"You took nothing else from in there?" the blond man asked, pointing to the safe with his foot.

"Nothing."

"No jewels?"

"No."

"No documents?"

"No. You saw when you searched me."

Slowly the blond man sauntered back across the room again, his head bent down, contemplating the tapes in his hand and the priceless carpet beneath his feet. He pulled up only inches away from Adel and raised his head. For a long moment he stood silently, his hard, cold blue eyes boring into Adel, studying him, gauging

123

him, weighing him. "We are going to have a long conversation, you and I," he said turning to walk away. But suddenly he reeled back and the palm of his hand slammed into Adel's face. "And I plan to enjoy our conversation."

Adel rubbed his throbbing cheek and watched as the blond man walked purposefully to the door and opened it. "*Ahmad, baatchehara sedakon!*" he shouted, summoning "the guys."

The accent was guttural, even in Persian, thought Adel. Perhaps he was Eastern European. But no. It was not that sort of accent. It was more... Then it hit him. The man was an Arab. And suddenly he remembered Allon's words.

"There is every reason to believe the real power in Iran lies in the hands of Khomeini's PLO advisors. These people are running the show. And they are good. Experienced professionals. If you run into them, be careful. They're merciless."

"Now, Mister Adel, come here and face the wall." The man clamped Adel's biceps in a powerful grip.

He's blond; Arabs aren't usually blond, thought Adel as his limp body was towed toward the wall.

"Good. Put your hands up against the wall... high... up there." He pointed above Adel's head. "Very good. Now, don't move until you are told to do so. I will ask you one more time. What did you come to steal and what is the number of the safe?"

Adel hesitated and felt his stomach sink. But of course there were blond Arabs—Crusader seed. The son of a bitch was probably planted in Palestine by some horny German peasant seven hundred years ago.

But now, with his hands above his head, he had missed his chance; the grenades were out of reach.

"I told you what I know. They contain highly classified information about the Phoenix missile," he repeated, playing for time. "As for the safe combination, it's..."

The man wrote the numbers down.

"Any distraction is your friend." But what distraction? There was no distraction. Only two guns trained on his head and a man called Ahmad on his way with a bunch of goons.

"You may put down your arms while we wait for Ahmad, but do not turn. There is no desire to make you uncomfortable. Not yet anyway," the Arab taunted.

Adel cautiously moved his hand toward his belt buckle. It was his last chance. He removed one of the grenades with his trembling right hand and gripped it tightly in his sweaty fist. Then he removed another.

"Thank you," he said. His body protected his movements as he pulled out the miniature primer pins.

"*Any distraction is your friend.*"

"Now, Mr. Adel, for the last..."

Adel heard the door open and the mercenary stop in midsentence; the man called Ahmad had arrived. It was a meager distraction, but it was all he had.

He flung the grenades behind him and threw himself to the floor.

"Look out!" shouted one of the militiamen in Farsi before pandemonium shook the room. A burst of machine gun fire raked the enclosure and a stream of bullets tore at the wall, inches above Adel's falling, rolling body. An instant later the two grenades exploded simultaneously and a cacophony of additional sounds erupted. Screams and shouts. Breaking glass. A blast of air smashed a chair across his back and the sizzle of flying metal tore into his left leg, crushing the limb against the wall.

And then darkness and the smell of smoke.

Darkness and silence engulfed him. He was stunned, half conscious. He tried to move, but momentarily blacked out from the pain in his calf. He lifted his head but could see nothing in the pitch blackness. He moved his right hand down to feel his wound. His trousers were torn and blood oozed from his flesh. He lay back, exhausted and faint, knowing he had to move, knowing he didn't have the time to rest. He forced himself up onto his hands and dragged himself crawling among the tangled bodies of the blond Arab and the guards, peering into the darkness for his gun. Near the door smoke rose from a growing fire.

He pushed forward, knowing that help was on the way; any second now the door would open and a flood of them would arrive. He heard a groan in the darkness and the sounds of distant shouting. They were coming. He crawled nearer the doorway where the blond man had stood. Nothing but mangled bodies. *The tapes! He had to find the tapes!* And where was his gun?

He was panicking now, brushing the floor in wide circles with his hands. The guards from the gatehouse would be here any second and God knew how many more from inside the mansion. He was desperate. *The tapes. The tapes. The gun.*

The fire was spreading quickly, the flames growing in fury. Suddenly, in the flickering light, he saw the gun and the belt with the ammunition pouch. He pushed himself upright and lunged for the automatic. He landed short; his left leg buckled beneath him, driving the power from his dive and knocking the wind out of him. He buried his face in his hands in pain.

The shouting was growing closer. He had no time to rest. He forced himself up again and crawled forward to the gun. There were only seconds left. He had to get out of there—into the garden—into the tunnel. To hell with the tapes.

He crawled toward the shattered windows. Two guards were running toward the house about a hundred yards away. He waited for them to draw closer.

Rain poured, but the lightning and thunder were a distant rumble as he flicked the lever from automatic to single and focused the night scope on the closer of the two figures. Through the visor, night became a green day.

The shot was soundless, exuding only a hiss of air that caught the first of the runners in the chest. The slug tore a hole the size of a tennis ball through him. The second man stopped when his comrade fell, unable to comprehend why he had stumbled. He never found out. He died standing there, looking at his friend's contorted body. Another hiss of air ripped him apart. For them, the revolution was over. They were *shahids*, martyrs.

Adel crawled back toward the door, praying he could find the tapes, praying they had not been destroyed in the explosion or fire. Frantically he pawed the wooden surface in semicircular arcs. Still he couldn't find them.

The fire was spreading and smoke filled the room. There was the sound of running feet from above.

Suddenly, he remembered. *The pocket. The blond man had put the tapes in his pocket.*

The body was bent and crushed against the left-hand wall, a mass of blood and oozing flesh. All that remained of his legs were two stubs of differing lengths.

Adel fumbled through his denim jacket pocket. He could feel the sharp edges of the plastic boxes through the heavy material but he couldn't find the pocket openings. He ripped at the cloth desperately; on the second heave the material gave. He grabbed the two tapes and crawled toward the door.

At the doorway he steadied himself against the wall and pulled himself up. He was weakening quickly. His head spun and his eyes went in and out of focus. He staggered through the lobby, using the wall as a crutch. His left leg was in agony and his head pounded with pain. He longed to rest, to let oblivion take over.

At the edge of the patio, his leg buckled again and he fell in a heap on the soaking earth. But he forced himself to keep moving, knowing it was his only chance of survival. He grabbed at the grass, digging his fingers deep into the mud and pulling himself toward the sanctuary of the nearest bush.

"Keep moving. Keep moving," he urged himself. He crawled on, his leg numb now, his pain receding into half consciousness. He wanted to sleep; more than anything else in the world he wanted to sleep.

He stopped and looked behind at the mansion. It was a blurred mass of flashlights. The power had been knocked out and now mobile lights blazed in haphazard circles like fireflies, sweeping across the garden. He had to move those last few yards to the tunnel. He clawed at the mud frantically.

"Don't leave any trace of your route," Yuri had urged him.

He opened the tunnel door and slid down the ladder. He had to close the door...otherwise they would know...they would trace him. He summoned his last ounce of energy and closed the heavy steel sheet before falling into a heap at the bottom of the tunnel.

CHAPTER
19

MONDAY, OCTOBER 29: MORNING

His eyes would not focus, but somehow his senses registered a strange familiarity with his surroundings. Through the haze of semi-consciousness he could distinguish friendly objects. A familiar painting here drawn curtains he had known there, furniture he

could recognize anywhere. Gradually the pieces formed the out-
lines of a blurred shape and the shape took on a meaning. He was
in his own bedroom.

But how long had he been there? And how did he get there?
The darkness provided no clues. He raised his head from the pillow
to check the antique clock on the mantelpiece of his own bedroom.
The hands merged in and out of focus. He squinted, forcing his
eyes to absorb them; it read eleven-fifteen. But was it day or night?
Either way, he thought as he slumped back, miraculously they had
not come for him. Not yet anyway.

He was weak and his body ached. He wanted to sleep, but his
mind raced. How did he get to safety? He remembered only the
struggle to stay conscious in the tunnel.

The tapes. Where were the tapes? He lifted his head and looked
around the room. He could not see them. Through the haze he
scanned the room, frantically. Still they were nowhere to be seen.
His clothes! Where was his gun? There was no sign of either. He
pushed back the bedcovers. Stiff, aching, the leg throbbing, he
pushed himself upwards.

He started to move from the bed. Pain stabbed his left leg and
anchored him to the floor. It spread throughout his body. He was
dizzy and sweating profusely.

"Mariam!" he cried.

"Get back into bed, I'm coming."

Even through the open door her voice was distant and muffled.

He stood on his right leg, clinging to the chest of drawers and
the chair, fighting the lightness in his head, pushing back the urge
to collapse. It seemed an eternity before Mariam appeared in the
doorway.

"Where're the tapes?" he croaked, his throat burning.

"They're safely tucked away. Now get back into bed."

A wave of relief swept over him.

Only then did he notice the heavy bandage tied around his calf.
But he asked no questions; he didn't care. He sat on the bed, the
urge to rest overwhelming.

"I don't think it's very serious, but the cut is deep and you've
lost a lot of blood," Mariam said as she set a tray down beside him.
"There may be something in there, too. I can't tell. At my age you
can't rely on your eyes."

"How did I get here?" he asked, glancing at the traditional Iranian *ash,* thick vegetable and yogurt soup with meatballs.

"I don't know how you got to the kitchen door. You were in such a mess. You were absolutely soaked to the skin and covered in mud. Blood was everywhere. Your left leg was caked in it. I had quite a time getting that gun away from you too. You wouldn't let go of it. But I did and then I got Mansour from down the road —the boy I told you about—to help me get you up the stairs."

He nodded; she had had no choice but to get help to move him. "Are you sure he's safe?" he asked nervously.

She gave him a reproachful look and instantly he knew it was a foolish question.

"Where's the gun?" His hand shook as he spooned the hot soup.

"I threw it down the well," she said, her lips tight. "I also found a suitcase in the rose bush by the *qanat.* That's in the closet." She pointed to a wardrobe as she sat on the chair next to the bed.

"I couldn't sleep last night," she continued, "there was so much commotion. Shooting and thunder and lightning and I don't know what. When I went to buy the morning bread I found you—well, you fell through the kitchen door, to be more precise."

She shook her head in disapproval.

"Where are the tapes?"

"Where you used to hide all your secrets. On the ledge in the chimney."

Adel looked at her and smiled weakly. "Come here," he said.

The old woman straightened her back as she stood and shuffled to his bed. Adel pulled her down and kissed her.

"Thank you," he whispered.

"That's all very well," she scoffed, shuffling away from his reach. "But what are we going to do about that leg?"

"How bad is it?"

"Bad enough to need a doctor. And if you don't call one, I will," she said firmly.

"Okay. But let me eat something first."

The aroma of the steaming soup was welcome but he also needed time to think.

"There's an awful clamor out on the street by old Mr. Mahmoudi's house," she warned him.

Adel stopped eating and looked at her.

"No one knows what happened; someone broke in and killed several guards and then disappeared. They think it was the Forghan group, the anti-Khomeini terrorists. One of the guards is still alive, but he's in very bad condition. He'll probably die, according to Mansour. He's a foreigner, an Arab, I think. He's lost both his legs. White as paper, Mansour said. They took him to hospital."

Adel pushed the tray away. Damn, he thought, the son of a bitch was alive. Why hadn't he been more careful? Why hadn't he made sure?

"Mariam," he said, as he carefully unwound the bandage. "I stink. I need a shower. Then we'll see what we can do about a doctor."

"You can't take a shower!" she said indignantly. "The most you can do is take a bath and then only if you keep that left leg hanging over the tub. You have to keep it clean and dry."

"Whatever you say."

CHAPTER 20

LATER, THE SAME MORNING

He spent a long time soaking in the tub, letting the aches and bruises dissolve in the hot water, thinking about his next move. The calf wound was long and deep and Mariam's fear was well founded; there was something in it, a foreign object, probably a piece of metal. He couldn't risk leaving it there for long. The shrapnel together with the slime and dirt from the stagnant *qanat* would cause infection; it needed immediate attention. Especially when he thought of the days ahead.

As he lay there, his left leg resting on the rim of the old tub and the cushioned stool beside it, Adel remembered the blond Arab. If he recovered he would point the finger squarely at him. If he hadn't already . . .

They had been waiting for him in there. They had known he was coming. But how? Somehow there had been a leak.

130

Adel pulled the plug and gingerly lowered his leg to the floor, using his arms to push himself out of the tub. He had to get out of Teheran quickly. Before they came after him.

In the bedroom he used the telephone, dialing from memory 8-2-0-0-9-1.

A voice answered after the second ring.

"*Sefarate Amrica*, United States Embassy," it said in Farsi and English.

"Extension 2184, please," Adel replied in English.

"Connecting you."

A hearty male voice answered after several connecting clicks. "Economic section."

"Khan!" said Adel as he had been instructed.

"I beg your pardon."

"Khan!" he repeated, a flutter of doubt running through him.

The voice responded without hesitation. "One minute, please."

The phone clicked. Moments later it clicked again.

"Hello." It was the same voice.

"Hello."

"It's okay. We can talk now. This line is sterile," said George Clark, economic counsellor, American Embassy, Teheran. Alias Khan.

"I need a doctor," said Adel.

"Where are you?" snapped Clark. "You were supposed to contact me yesterday." His tone was abrupt.

"You know exactly where I am. I didn't call yesterday because I had nothing to say. Now I do. I need a doctor," Adel repeated, confident that as long as he had the tapes they needed him.

There was a moment's hesitation before Clark replied.

"Very well, but your area is overrun with revolutionary guards and militia. It may take us a little time to set up a watertight reason for being there. We have to take security precautions—for our own sake, as much as yours. Let's say between three and four o'clock this afternoon."

Adel hung up but Khan's words lingered. "Your area is overrun with revolutionary guards and militia."

The embassy was monitoring him.

131

CHAPTER
21

"I think it looks worse than it is," the embassy doctor said. He was over six feet tall, with an egg-shaped body topped by a large shining head of the same shape. He camouflaged his torso with a gray herringbone suit, white shirt and dark blue tie.

George Clark, alias Khan, remained silent, watching from the leather couch to the left of the bed, squinting his gray eyes.

"The only point of immediate concern is that thing in there," the doctor said, squeezing the wound.

"Damn it, take it easy!" Adel winced.

The doctor ignored Adel's pain and pulled the flesh apart for a better look.

"Have that removed as soon as you get to London, presuming of course, you're leaving right away. Otherwise, among other things infection could be a problem: gangrene and so on. All I can do is clean it up, close the wound and give you an antibiotic shot. You allergic to penicillin?"

"Not as far as I know."

"Fine. There may be some bone damage, too. It doesn't look like it, but I can't really tell without X-rays. Just to be on the safe side, I'll put a cast on."

Adel was silent.

"That's about all I can do." The doctor moved away from the bed to sit beside Clark.

Adel thought quickly. The days ahead were uncertain. It was not as if he were flying first class to England and checking into the London Clinic for a month. Just staying alive was going to be a problem.

132

"That should do it until you get to London," said Clark, breaking the silence.

"There's no guarantee I'll be in London or any other civilized corner of the earth that soon. Why can't we do it right here and now? As you say, it's not that serious." He observed the two men closely.

Clark brushed his blond crew cut with elegantly long fingers and stood. He ignored the doctor's uncertain glances as he moved toward the bed.

"You were instructed to follow an itinerary," he said. "And you didn't. Everything's been screwed up already." He was standing above Adel's bed now, looking down. "You need hospital care and attention after an operation of this kind. It's not that easy," he said, snapping his fingers.

Adel smiled, but did not feel pleased.

"As a code name, Khan is perfect for you," he said, looking into Clark's eyes. "It means gentleman in Farsi and no one's ever going to suspect you of being one."

He turned to the doctor. "What can you do with a local anesthetic?"

The doctor looked at Clark for guidance.

"Put it this way," said Adel, turning back to Clark. "If you want the tapes, I'm not going anywhere with this leg. And I sure as hell don't intend to turn them over until I get out of here. And in one piece." His stare was fixed and cold.

Clark and the doctor exchanged glances before Clark nodded.

"I'm only thinking of you," the doctor said uncertainly. "This sort of procedure requires more than we have here. If I'd known, I'd have brought something. God knows what," he said, shrugging his shoulders. Then he pointed to the leg. "And I can't guarantee this will be painless."

"I'll risk it, replied Adel tartly. "But just make sure it's a simple anesthetic."

The doctor rolled up his shirt-sleeves, wearing an aggrieved expression, while Clark stared back at Adel, his eyes fixed and curious.

"I'll need a few simple things, like boiling water, lots of it, and ..."

133

CHAPTER 22

With the help of morphine the operation had been painless, but the side effects had brought uncontrollable lethargy. All evening he had been in and out of a stupor.

His mind was light and foggy, but a sense of weightlessness and immobility had crippled him. Something in the back of his mind kept stressing the importance of time, forcing him back to consciousness. But each time the morphine drove him back into darkness. And each time the pain advanced the lightness retreated, and he awoke. But then the pain receded and the darkness took hold again. All the while he remained paralyzed, unable to move.

It was close to 9 P.M. before Adel could summon the energy to push his shoulders upward to rest on the headboard. It was late, and he had so much to do. He couldn't afford to lose time. He pushed upward again but his arms were rubbery and refused to respond.

"Two days," the doctor had said. "You'll be able to move about in two days."

He needed those two days. Bell wouldn't be expecting him before then. Besides, one of the days would be lost getting out of Teheran, and that would give him a lead of only twenty-four hours. With one foot in a cast, twenty-four hours was not a lot. He had to move.

His mouth tasted like the *qanat* and his stomach was queasy. He poured a glass of water from the bedside jug. Slowly he moved the glass to his mouth and sipped the ice water. It cooled his throat and stomach and helped to gradually clear his head.

He picked up the phone and dropped it on the bed. Wearily, he dialed Mariam's room. There was no answer.

"God damn it," he croaked, his throat sore and dry again, more disappointed than angry. She had probably gone out to buy bread or something, he thought.

On the night table, beside the jug, he saw an unfamiliar bottle. Pills—painkillers. The doctor must have left them. He took two of the capsules and lay back.

To the right of the table he saw a pair of metal crutches. Immediately he recognized them—mementoes of his athletic days. Mariam must have found them in some dark corner of the cellar.

The pain was bearable now after the pills. But the grogginess was still there; it came and went and affected his vision. He had to overcome it. He couldn't afford to wait for it to pass naturally. It would take too long.

He raised himself again and rested on the headboard; it wasn't as bad as before—a little strength had returned to his arms. Carefully he put his right leg to the floor. Then the left one, heavy with the new cast. He used the crutches to get to the bathroom, step by step, resting frequently to gather strength and for the dizzy spells to pass. In the bathroom he drew cold water and doused his head until his mind cleared. Gradually he felt strength returning to his body.

He dressed with a struggle; the left trouser leg was barely large enough to accommodate the cast. From now on, he told himself, the trousers stay on.

He felt the first signs of recovery, pangs of hunger. Downstairs he would grab something light to eat.

The ground floor was in darkness as he stepped onto the first-floor landing. He switched on the hallway light and started down the stairs. Then he limped toward the kitchen and reached for the light, which hung by a cord in the center of the room. As he moved toward it, his foot caught on something in the middle of the kitchen floor and he went sprawling to the ground.

Pain shot up to his head as he rolled in agony, clinging to the hard cast for comfort. The pain was excruciating and he lay holding his left thigh and waiting for it to recede. He forced himself to his feet and fumbled in the darkness for the light switch.

He turned on the light and looked for his crutches. But suddenly they were unimportant.

Mariam lay face down on the floor. Dead.

He stared at her warped body uncomprehendingly, dumbfounded

135

by her stillness, afraid to touch her but overpowered by the contorted position of her body. At last he sat beside her and slowly turned her on her back. Her soft, aged skin felt cold, her eyes were fixed and lifeless. Tears welled in him but he fought them as he straightened her limbs and smoothed her white print dress.

Then he leaned back on the table leg, exhausted and dizzy. He was unable to function, unwilling to leave her side.

Suddenly the numbness disappeared; something was out of place, out of character.

The sleeve of her left arm had been rolled up. Why? She never did that. It was one of her phobias; undignified, she would always say.

He turned her arm; two needle marks punctured the inside of her right elbow. Two tiny streams meandered down the pale, wrinkled skin of her inner forearm.

Adel felt sick. His stomach churned with anger and disgust. They had killed her. To find the tapes, they had killed her. *The tapes,* he suddenly remembered. Had she talked?

He jerked himself upwards, ignoring the pain, half dragging, half running. Forgetting the pain. Forgetting the cast. Using the staircase and the walls for support.

He raced into the bedroom to the fireplace, feeling inside, reaching up into the chimney and tearing the loose brick from its slot. His heart pounded furiously. If she had talked, if they had found the tapes, he too was dead. Now. Right here. He would never make it out of Iran. Never make it to London. He would never be safe from Bell.

Then he felt the plastic boxes and ripped them from their hiding place. Blood and dirt were still caked on the plastic covers.

She hadn't talked. That's why she had died; they had given her too much. A seventy-year-old woman had died from an overdose of truth serum.

Khan had guessed. He had put it together. If anyone knew where the tapes were it had to be Mariam. And he had killed her. But why? Dear God, why? They had him by the balls—he had to turn the tapes over. Why kill her? Why kill a defenseless old lady?

Tears welled up again but this time he could not fight them. He sat down and sobbed, crying for a woman who had been as good as a mother to him.

Eventually the anger and sorrow subsided and a new determi-

136

nation took hold. The leg ached again, a dull throbbing pain, and he knew he had damaged it. Perhaps he had strained it or ripped the stitching in the fall or the rush upstairs. But it was a distant pain; all he could feel was hate.

He limped to the bed, picked up the telephone and dialed 6-4-3-0-1-3.

It was busy. He tried the second number: 6-4-3-0-1-4. That, too, was busy. He dialed again and again, frustrated and angry, until he finally got through.

"Hello," a bored male voice responded.

"Mehrabad Airport?" he asked.

"Yeah," replied the voice gruffly.

"Revolutionary committee, please."

There was a click, followed shortly by another.

"It's busy."

"I'll wait," Adel said.

"Hello," the phone came alive with a rough, abrasive voice.

"Hello," he tried to sound hesitant. "Is that the airport *komiteh?*"

"Yeah," the voice growled.

"I'd like to report a crime that's due to be committed at the airport tomorrow."

The voice picked up interest. "What crime?"

"There's a passenger booked on Swissair leaving at seven in the morning for Damascus and Geneva." He did not offer the flight number. Detail, to Iranians, was always suspicious. They preferred to think in *ousouli*, general terms.

"He's got a cast on his leg. There's nothing wrong with his leg. It's full of jewelry. Jewelry he wants to smuggle out of the country."

"Who is the man?" asked the voice. "What's his name?"

Adel said nothing.

"Hello. Hello!" The voice was eager now.

"Hello," said Adel.

"Who is he?"

"A traitor. A bastard who wants to steal our country's wealth."

That should do it, thought Adel. He hung up.

He thought a moment, then picked up the phone again and dialed 8-9-0-6-0-6.

"Hello."

"I'd like a taxi at five in the morning."

"Destination?" asked the man.

137

"Mehrabad Airport."

"Address?"

Adel gave it. "Okay. We'll have one there."

"I have a plane to catch. Please make sure he's here at five," Adel said. In Iran, time, like detail, was only approximate.

"Don't worry, mister, he'll be there."

Adel spent the remainder of the night burying Mariam beneath the elegant walnut trees beside the pool. She had always loved that part of the garden where the trees offered protection from the merciless summer sun.

Many years ago, when he and Mark had been children, she had made them play there in the cool grass tract, out of harm's way. Always under her watchful, protective eye. Even in death she had kept her vigil.

The earth was still damp and soft from the rainfall and recollections of Mariam and his childhood were so vivid that the task went by quickly. Tears flowed down his face and he sat there looking at her for a long time before he covered her for the last time. Finally he kissed her before laying her light body in the shallow grave, then covered her with a sheet; it was the only protection he could offer her from the ravages of time.

CHAPTER 23

TUESDAY, OCTOBER 30, 1979: 5:30 A.M.
MEHRABAD AIRPORT, TEHERAN

The yellow taxi, an obsolete Rambler assembled in Iran, inched ahead to a stop half a mile from the "temporary" international terminal at Mehrabad Airport.

While the yellow glare of the lighting fought the darkness of a cloudy winter morning, hundreds of people pushed and shoved through the tangle of vehicles that had been brought to a knotted standstill. The confusion, born of the inadequate and badly designed facilities, was exacerbated by a horde of officials, who perplexed the anxious passengers with bewildering instructions which were often at cross purposes.

Inside the building, the nervous travelers were overburdened with luggage—Persian rugs and silverware, antiques, jewelry and other valuables that might provide them with a new life. They were middle-class people leaving the uncertainty of Iran behind them.

A section of the crowd pushed battered lime-yellow wire carts, stacked with mountains of luggage—suitcases, boxes, cartons, trunks. Carts, like everything else in the shattered economy, were in short supply. The travelers pulled and pushed their possessions, sweating and cursing. Women, children and the elderly were forced to help their menfolk, carrying or pulling more than seemed possible for the old, the young, the weak.

Adel entered the building and threaded his way through the disarray. In the confusion he was careful to protect his damaged leg from further injury, but each yard was a physical chore; the hall was packed with nervous, disappointed people.

"What do you mean the plane won't be coming?" he heard one lady sob as he approached the Pan American counter.

"Why the hell not?" said another. The man's tone was hostile.

"You sold the damned tickets, didn't you?" someone else shouted.

Adel glanced at the airline official trying to placate the desperate passengers. He was frustrated, too, unable to provide answers. His hands, his voice, his facial gestures, pleaded for understanding.

Adel sympathized with him as he moved past, but he identified more closely with the frustrations of the passengers. They were scared; frightened of the new Islam that preached vengeance and death.

It was the same at the British Airways counter.

"At least you could have called to let us know," said one man.

"We came all the way from Chemran," moaned a middle-aged woman.

"Can you get us on another flight?" asked a young man.

Adel passed through the throng toward the Swissair counter. One man he passed was explaining to his family why he had been turned back.

"It...it...must be a mistake," he stuttered to an elderly woman, using his hands and shoulders more than his voice. "He...he...said I was on some...some list." The man's face was ashen and moist.

The elderly woman, presumably his wife, burst into a loud wail.

Flights had been canceled, arriving planes were overbooked, passengers were being turned back by three different forces—the *pasdaran* militiamen, the police and immigration officials. Each force worked separately, bullying and competing to apply its own brand of authority.

The melee at the Swissair first-class counter seemed somehow less chaotic than the others and Adel was thankful for it. His optimism, however, quickly turned sour.

What if they don't spot me? What if they miss me and let me through?

With his wooden cane he hobbled to the end of the line. He was sure they were expecting him; it was only a matter of time before they singled him out. Besides, if it went that far, he would have to cause a scene. He would have to draw attention to himself.

Though the queue was short, its progress was slow and irritating. He was tired; to the marrow of his bones he was tired. He felt grubby and dirty; he hadn't shaved in days and the clothes he had found in the house were ill fitting and uncomfortable. The slacks barely fitted around the cast. The leg pain was dull and bearable; the painkillers were doing their job. But the overall effect of all the pain and violence, of his brief stay in Iran, was beginning to take hold. The stench of cordite and death, the lack of sleep, the aching leg. And Mariam....

And it was not over yet. There was still another day.

Suddenly his thoughts were interrupted. There was a frenzy of activity; concentric circles closed in on a given point, bringing with them the shock waves of fear and panic among the crowds. The circles closed in, converging almost instantaneously. Bodies flailed to gain distance in the pandemonium. Luggage carts were pushed and upturned. Sounds of panic filled the air. There were screams and shouts, tears and cries. Instinctively he wanted to move away, to seek cover. Instinctively, he had forgotten.

"Put your hands on your head," a harsh voice rasped.

He was surprised by the size of the arresting party. At least thirty young men surrounded him at a distance of ten to fifteen yards. Kneeling, crouching and standing, they held an assortment of arms and they were all aimed at him. Adel followed their instructions, holding his briefcase in one hand, his cane in the other for effect.

One of the group, a young man dressed in a commando uniform, swaggered forward, carrying an Uzi submachine gun. He had a crop of uncombed wavy black hair; a three-day growth of stubble enchanced the image of Iran's post-revolutionary guardians.

He nodded to Adel to follow. As he did so, several uniformed police arrived running, their Colts drawn, ready.

"Do you need help?" asked a tall, thin police captain who sported an Errol Flynn moustache.

The young revolutionry guard sneered at him.

"Late as usual," he said, pushing Adel toward the center of the building.

Adel was taken through several low-ceilinged corridors and seated on a wooden chair in a small, fly-infested room. It was situated, Adel had noted, somewhere near the feeder ramp of one of the luggage belts behind the arrivals lounge.

"You are a thief," said the militiaman who had guided him. "What's your name?" he demanded.

"Me?" asked Adel, incredulously.

"I'm talking to you, right?" the militiaman sneered.

"Yes. Yes, you are. I'm sorry. You're the brave guardians of our revolution, but I am not a thief," he said, his voice appropriately servile as his eyes scanned the packed room.

"What is your name?"

"Shariat. Mohammed Shariat."

"Your passport," the man demanded, extending a hand.

Adel opened his briefcase and gave it to him.

"What's in that cast?" The militiaman pointed his Uzi at Adel's leg.

"The cast?" said Adel, exaggerating his surprise.

"Yes, the cast." The militiaman passed his machine gun to one of his cronies. "The cast," he mocked as he thumbed through the passport.

Adel hesitated. "Nothing."

"I am only going to ask you once."

"Nothing." Again Adel's tone registered surprise. "Why?" he asked.

The the militiaman glowered.

"It is I who will ask the questions."

"Yes, but you're accusing me of something. What? I'm not sure. But you have no right to treat innocent people this way," replied Adel with rising indignation.

The backhanded blow caught him between his mouth and right eye. Instinctively he grasped his face with his right hand; a trickle of blood flowed from the corner of his mouth.

"I don't know what you're talking about," he moaned. "I've got a badly injured leg. That's all. I am . . . was . . . going to Geneva to see a specialist," he said, surreptitiously glancing at his watch. There was still fifteen minutes before departure time. He had to be careful. He had to stretch out this scene to cover the possibility of any delay in take-off. "Do you know how hard it is to get an appointment with Doctor Lucien? I don't know what you're talking about. What could be in the cast?" he whined, dabbing at the blood trickling from his mouth.

The militiaman pointed to one of his subordinates.

"Cut the cast off," he ordered.

The subordinate took a pair of stained scissors from the desk drawer and approached Adel.

"Are you mad? What in God's name do you intend to do?" cried Adel as he recoiled.

"Hold him still," ordered the leader, pointing to two militiamen. The men grabbed Adel's arms and shoulders and anchored him to his chair while the man with the scissors attacked the plaster.

Adel writhed in pain but it had little effect. The man half cut and half pulled at the white, powdery plaster of Paris with little regard to his agony, feigned or real.

It was painful, but it was not as painful as Adel made it look . . . and sound. Halfway through the ordeal he asked for water to use up additional time. Fearing an unconscious prisoner, they provided him with a glass of tepid water. As he drank it he heard the rumble of a departing plane.

Five minutes later the surgery was over; the cast had been cut.

"There's nothing here," said the astonished man as he held the soiled cast.

"That's impossible," replied the leader, the man who had hit him. "Let me see." He grabbed the cast.

It was dirty, more so inside than out. The activity of the past night had opened the wound again and dried blood caked the inner wall. Dirt and mud had also gathered inside the opening around his toes. But there were no jewels.

"Wrong man," said one of the militiamen as he marched from the room. "What an *olagh*," an ass, he shrugged in disgust.

"Typical Hossein," said another, following him.

There were more sardonic comments as one by one the men drifted from the room.

"It could be in the plaster itself," said Hossein Mikhchi to one of the handful that remained.

His suggestion was met with rolling eyes and barely suppressed grins.

"*Khoddah yeh aghli beh to beddeh, yeh pouli beh man.* God give you a brain and me some money," said the man Hossein had addressed as he, too, turned and left the room.

"Now what?" asked one of his two remaining subordinates.

Hossein Mikhchi was visibly perturbed, his confidence shaken. He seemed as distressed by the physical inconvenience he had caused the cripple as the loss of face before his peers.

"I'll never make it to Geneva in time," said Adel writhing in pain. "I've missed the flight and the planes are booked solid out of here. My appointment is for tomorrow afternoon. There's no way I'll make it." He buried his head in his hands.

Hossein was embarrassed; he waved his hands to signal silence, and adopted a subservient air.

"Don't worry, sir, I'll get you there. Just keep quiet, I'll get you there somehow," he repeated before slamming the door behind him. Two guards remained behind.

"You people do more damage to this beautiful revolution than all the SAVAK agents around. If only Imam Khomeini knew the pain you cause people. How you alienate his followers and give him a bad name," said Adel, careful to use the words of the Imam himself.

The two men looked at each other.

"I want your names. All of you," said Adel, building his feigned anger. "This isn't right. This is not why we threw out the Shah and make no mistake, I'm going to make sure the Imam hears about this incident. Sadegh Ghotbzadeh is my cousin and I will tell him."

The two men looked at each other again, suddenly worried. The threat of the incident reaching one of Khomeini's right-hand men was enough to put the fear of God into any man, militiaman or not.

"Look...ah, your excellency, we will put you on the plane tomorrow, there's no need to make a fuss. What's an extra day?

This was a mistake. Really it was. Some *jakesh,* pimp, called us and said you were smuggling jewelry out in your cast. We really didn't mean to harm your honor," said one of the two men, a short, bald man with a large potbelly. "If we can all keep quiet about this mistake, we'll get you on the plane first thing tomorrow morning."

"Fine. Fine. Just get me to Geneva," said Adel. "You can see that I'm in pain and need medical treatment."

The plump militiaman left the room. Moments later he reappeared.

"May I have your ticket, sir?"

"It's in my briefcase."

The man opened the briefcase, took out the blue-and-white Swissair ticket and left the room, the door shaking the thin wall dividers as it slammed shut.

Adel smiled inwardly. It was working. It was going as he planned.

Ten or fifteen minutes passed before a murmur of conversation stirred outside the room. The door opened a few inches, only to close. Then it opened again, about halfway. Then it closed.

Adel grew nervous. What the hell were they discussing? The voices were distant, soft and distorted. It was unlikely that they had seen through his ploy. But what was it then? Whatever it was they were discussing concerned him, what to do with him. He had to stop it. He had to decide for them.

He let out a bellow of pain and grabbed his leg with both hands, pulling apart the wound. Immediately blood poured out.

The door banged open. "Keep quiet," Hossein shouted.

"For God's sake let me out of here. I'm bleeding. Let me get to a doctor." Adel rolled his head in pain as the blood oozed from the cut. "The pain is unbearable."

"Your excellency, I've got you on the same flight tomorrow morning," said Hossein Mikhchi nervously, distressed at the sight of the blood. "I'm sorry for what happened here today; it was a mistake. But I'm going to make it up to you. Tomorrow morning when you come to the airport, we'll speed everything up for you. We'll get you on the plane first. You won't have to go through all the formalities."

He sniffled and turned to his colleagues. "I'd like to talk to this gentleman alone."

He was obviously the leader, but only barely; the others shuffled out grudgingly. Hossein waited until they were alone, then walked

144

to the door, making certain it was firmly closed before moving toward Adel. He stroked his stubble nervously.

"I am willing to assist you on one condition," he said, keeping his voice low. "That this episode goes no further than this room. If it does," he paused, "we will meet again.

"I'll explain why. The problem we face is that the revolution is young. There are many who are traitors to the cause. Some of these heathens are members of the ex-Shah's secret police, and they look for—sometimes invent—ways to make the *pasdaran* militiamen look bad."

He smirked. "It would be a shame if this reached their ears. That is, it would be a shame for you, because I'll place a kilo of heroin in your suitcase and shoot your excellency in the balls for being a pusher. You follow?"

Adel shivered; he had no reason to doubt the man. Every day innocent people were being framed and shot as drug peddlers; it had become standard procedure.

"We understand each other," said Adel, trying to sound aloof.

Hossein stood and looked down at him, his hands on his hips.

"I am sure it is the word of a gentleman. Otherwise you won't enjoy our next meeting."

CHAPTER 24

TEHERAN: TUESDAY, OCTOBER 30: NOON

"*Pesaram*, my son, it has been over twenty-four hours since we put this man under your care and still he has not recovered consciousness. It is a matter of great urgency for the revolution and even to the Imam himself that we learn what came to pass in this satanic plot. We must learn what is behind this attack on God's government. Can you do nothing to wake him?"

The doctor looked at the *mullah*, the Islamic priest, listening intently, but fighting a losing battle to suppress the nausea brought about by the man's odor. The short, fat man wore thick round eyeglasses that magnified his protruding eyes and affected a wide grin that belied his severity. His *aba,* the loose dark brown outer cloak, was soiled and dirty; two dark stains extended beneath his armpits and the front was a polka dot print of uneven design and colors. The residue of the past month's food intake, thought the doctor. His *amameh,* turban, had once been white. But that had been some time ago. Now various shades dulled it grayish yellow and he wore it as he wore his grin, crooked and offensively. Strands of oily, unwashed hair fell unevenly to his forehead.

The doctor was not taken in by the holy man's amicable smile. On the contrary, he was aware of the man's reputation as the Hanging Judge. Every day for the past year an average of twenty people had been executed; twenty people whose trials consisted of a single judge, jury, defense and prosecution, and that man was now sitting in front of him, smiling.

The doctor, like most of his colleagues, was also aware of the man's medical record. In his vocation, rumors spread quickly. The word had made the rounds at the beginning of the revolution that the judge was a lunatic; a psychotic who had spent seven years in an asylum for his insatiable and uncontrollable obsession to strangle cats and dogs. But that had been before the Islamic revolution. He had been a psychopath then. Now he was minister of justice.

"Your excellency," said the doctor with deference. "The patient has lost both legs and his left arm. He has lost more than half the blood in his body. We have operated on him twice in the past twenty-four hours. He is weak and close to death; he must be given time to recover."

"Doctor," the *mullah* said patronizingly, "is there nothing you can do to speed his recovery—even if it is only temporary? He has no reason to live. He is a cripple; a lion cannot survive in the jungle on three legs.

"To relieve a cripple is an act of mercy; it avoids much agony and pain. Even many of your medical brothers have blessed the practice. Is it not possible with all you have so painstakingly learned in your studies in America to give him something to make him conscious, if only for a moment? There are things we must learn, and only he can provide the answers.

"Many have died in this just cause, my son. What is one more life compared with our high goals of an Islamic Republic? God will smile on you and so will I."

Dr. Bahman Chirazi looked at the religious man incredulously. It went against every grain in his body, was antithetical to everything he had learned, contrary to all he cherished: the sanctity and value of human life, the moral obligation of his profession, the meaning of ethics.

"Does the Holy Book not compel us, your excellency, to minister unto the sick and prolong their life?"

The *mullah* arched his thick, oily eyebrows, his eyes blazing.

Chirazi's fear mounted: his heart raced and his stomach churned. Then, suddenly, the *mullah's* smile returned.

"The good book has many interpretations, my son," said the priest. "It is the overall message that is important for you to understand and that is the establishment of an Islamic Republic—the establishment of God's government through God's own emissaries—of whom I am one. Nothing must stand in its way. Nothing," he shouted, "is too high a price to pay."

Chirazi looked at the priest's bulging eyes. What the madman was suggesting was murder!

Beneath the desk top he rubbed his sweaty palms together and tried a different approach.

"Your excellency, there are a few drugs we could use, but at this stage they're simply too dangerous. They might cause side effects that could kill the patient by inducing a coma or damaging recovery in any number of ways. Getting this vital information would be impossible if that were to happen. Be patient, your excellency. We must be careful not to lose him before we gain the knowledge you need."

The *mullah's* eyes were distant and glazed. His face wore a foolish grin.

"Very well, my son..." With his words the grin faded and his complexion turned bright red. Chirazi recognized the symptoms: the man was on the verge of another fit. Then, abruptly, the color faded and the *mullah* stood to his full height of five feet.

"Tonight. I'll be back tonight at ten o'clock. Have him ready then. And you be here too," he snapped, as he turned and stomped out of Chirazi's office. As the man disappeared round the corner, half a dozen heavily armed militiamen formed a protective circle around him and escorted him out.

Chirazi closed his eyes in anticipation of their next meeting.

147

CHAPTER
25

Michael Adel watched from the ground-floor library overlooking the driveway when the two men arrived exactly on schedule at five-thirty. As they drew steadily closer in the fading light he could feel his anger mounting.

"Stay cool," he told himself. "It won't be long now."

But it was hard to do. His mind ran a picture of an old woman lying contorted and dead, her skirt riding high above her waist, uncovering spindly legs that could barely hold her own weight, let alone put up a defense.

He watched the two men draw closer. He watched and hated.

"You'll have to forgive me," he said after greeting them. The men looked stiff and uneasy.

"I can offer you tea or, if you prefer, drinks. I'm afraid I have no help in the house and a poor excuse for a leg, so you'll have to put up with a dirty kitchen," he said as he led them through the corridor. "My luck. In all this mess, my maid passed away last night. Heart attack, I think, but I couldn't exactly call a doctor."

The doctor glanced at George Clark, who made no response.

Suddenly the doctor noticed his leg.

"Where in heaven's name is your cast?" he asked incredulously.

"Oh, that's a long story," replied Adel. He limped through the pantry into the kitchen, followed by the two men.

"My God, let me look at it," said the doctor with genuine concern.

"Plenty of time for that. Make yourselves at home while I get some ice out."

"Let me see it," the doctor insisted, bending to touch it.

"All in good time," Adel repeated, making light of his discomfort.

148

He took ice from the refrigerator and glanced through the clear glass of the vegetable compartment. The Walther PPK lay cocked and ready.

"Actually, that's why I asked you here. The leg's a mess, I'm afraid."

"What the hell happened? What did you do?"

Adel sat down, relieved to take the weight off his aching limb. "I ran into a man who didn't like me."

He poured three glasses of whisky on the rocks. "There's no soda in the house but help yourselves to water," he said, pushing the pitcher closer to the two men.

The doctor opened his satchel, then busied himself with the messy wound, mumbling while Adel recounted an abridged version of the airport incident. George Clark said nothing; he sipped his drink and stared blankly at Adel.

"Make it a bit large, doctor. There's a lot I've got to get in there this time," said Adel, pointing to his lower thigh.

Clark nibbled at the dead skin around a fingernail. "You're not leaving without our knowing?" he asked.

The time was approaching, thought Adel with pleasure. He looked back at Clark coldly, confident that he was powerless; as long as the tapes were out of his reach he was impotent.

"Where does it say I have to let you know what I'm doing?" Adel said coldly.

Clark shifted in his seat.

"That should do it," said the doctor, patting the new cast.

"How long before it comes off?"

"You must have been a premature baby, Adel. Give the damned thing a chance to heal. There may even be a nick on the bone for all I know. Just remember to get it attended to properly as soon as you reach London."

"If I live that long," countered Adel, his eyes turning back to Clark. "That feels a whole lot better," he said, standing up and measuring the cast for size. "Now let me refresh your drinks."

Adel opened the refrigerator and felt the cold stab of gunmetal in his palm. He turned swiftly.

"Get up, you bastards."

The look on the two men's faces was distinctly different yet remarkably the same. Shock. Surprise. But training and experience made the difference. The doctor was stupefied with fright. His eyes

149

glared, wide and unbelieving, his mouth gaped, his lips quivered. Slowly, as if time was not a rapidly depleting resource, he lifted his hands toward his shoulders and shielded his chest with his open palms.

Clark reacted differently. His eyes reflected his fear only momentarily. Then they narrowed, a man calculating, looking for solutions. His body turned, ready, while his fingers curled into a ball.

"Out that door," said Adel, pointing.

Neither man replied; they moved toward the opening.

There wasn't far to go. Behind the kitchen, thirty yards in the back courtyard, lay the mansion's sewer: a deep well that soaked up the refuse, sucking it deep into the earth's crust.

"Your grave is a sewer and it's too goddamned good for you, you motherfuckers!" he said, forcing the men at gunpoint toward the large wooden door covering the well. "She was over seventy years old and you killed her. Why? Why, you bastards? The tapes were safe. You knew I had to turn them over to you sooner or later. I had no choice. Why did you kill her?" His anger rose as images of Mariam's lifeless body ran before his eyes.

"I . . . I told him she couldn't stand a second dose. He forced me to. . . ." The doctor's voice quivered as he stepped toward Adel.

The roar of the gun cut him short. The bullet smacked him three inches above the left ribcage, tearing his heart out and blasting him backwards on the damp grass.

"And now you, Khan. The man who would be tough."

Clark's eyes were saucers of fear as he turned back from the doctor's still body. His color was deathly white. Reality had replaced his search for a solution, for a mistake. Slowly he dropped his hands from above his head. He knew it didn't make a difference anymore. He knew he was about to die. A second roar from Adel's gun ripped George Clark's heart to shreds.

Adel slowly lowered his right hand and dropped the gun. He was drained, spent and suddenly very lonely. But he looked at the two dead men on the ground, and knew it wasn't over.

Slowly he walked past the two crumpled figures, opened the door to the artesian well and moved back to the heap that had been George Clark. Grasping the corpse up by the armpits, he dragged it, half off, half on the ground. He heaved and pulled, his leg throbbing with pain, and twisted the final yard to pitch the body into the bottomless well.

The doctor's body was heavier, more unwieldly. Adel had neither the strength nor the will to lift it. He sat on the ground and dragged it, inch by inch, digging his foot deep into the ground to gain leverage. The distance was only five yards, but the load was awkward and heavy. Adel heaved the great egg-shaped cadaver toward its grave, each twist sending a streak of agony through his leg.

He lay back a minute, then with renewed energy dragged himself up and twisted and pushed the corpse until finally it disappeared down the shaft.

It was over, he told himself as he lay back, gazing into the darkness of the turbulent night sky. It was over. Forever. He could not spend another night in this house.

He raised himself up and limped toward the house. Inside he called for a taxi immediately and while he waited for it to arrive, he packed his suitcase, including the passport and ticket he had used that morning. He stuffed the two tapes, the money and two additional passports—his own and another alias's—into the cast. In spite of the extra room the doctor had allowed, they pressed against his flesh painfully. He adjusted them to the most comfortable position he could find and then limped down the long gravel driveway. At the gate he turned to take one final look at his family home.

CHAPTER
26

MELLI HOSPITAL, TEHERAN: TUESDAY, OCTOBER 30:
10 P.M.

Melli Hospital is situated in the heart of Teheran, just south of the main east-west commercial thoroughfare of the old Shah Reza Avenue, now renamed Avenue of the Revolution. It is surrounded by a mélange of historic and modern architecture, harboring within its mosaic a mixture of ornate, artistic Persian architecture and the cold, impersonal lines of contemporary buildings.

The hospital's driveway is narrow and threads between two bank buildings—Bank Melli, the government-owned commercial bank, and Bank Markazi, the nation's central bank. Once behind these massive structures, the road opens onto stunning floral gardens. It also passes within a stone's throw of the fortress that houses the priceless treasures of the Empire of Iran; the treasures liberated in 1739 by a victorious Nadir Shah who, in one daring swoop, relieved India of the wealth it had amassed over three hundred and fifty years.

Shortly after ten o'clock a silver-blue Mercedes-Benz 600—one of a fleet formerly used for ferrying members of the Imperial household—screeched off Ferdowsi Avenue, escorted by four olive green Range Rovers filled with militiamen. The fleet of cars sped between the two bank buildings, leaving behind a trail of spattered mud and water.

Ayatollah Sadegh Khalkhali did not like being late, especially when he had given his word. A man's word was important if he was to be respected. It should be taken seriously and obeyed. Yes, that was it, he thought. The key to success was to be taken seriously. He was taken seriously now; no one took him lightly anymore. No one joked about him. Oh, there were still rumors about his affinity for blood, how he strangled cats and dogs for enjoyment. But they were taken out of context, voiced by jealousy and spite.

He didn't necessarily like blood, but he was not frightened by it either. The important thing was the use of punishment and discipline to establish an acceptable social order in which right and wrong, good and bad, justice, equality, were based upon the rules of Allah.

His enemies—and they were all the Shah's agents, his enemies—refused to understand that. They were jealous and frightened. Ah...and why were they frightened? he asked himself. Because he spoke the words of the Holy Book and punished as the Holy Book prescribed. But the Shah's agents were *kafar*. Even those godless leftists and communists—some posing as Islamic—were the Shah's agents. They were infidels, nonbelievers, and they feared him. They knew he was a man of his word. They knew he would kill every one of them.

He looked out the window as the floodlight landscape of a rose-studded park sped by.

"Where are we?" he barked.

The driver cleared his throat. "Just entering the hospital's gardens, Holy One."

"Looks like Hamadan," Khalkhali replied, recalling his home town in west Iran. It was not really his hometown. He had been born in Khalkhal in Azerbaijan province in the north of Iran—hence his family name—but his family had moved to Hamadan while he was still an infant and that was where he considered home. He pictured the city's beautiful snowcapped mountains and its rich green, arable pastures. It was not like this acrid hellhole of a capital the Shah had built. Hamadan was rich in history and culture: the inspiring mausoleum built in tribute to the twelfth-century Persian philosopher-physician Avicenna, the intricate, traditional patterns of the priceless handmade carpets, the beautiful medieval Korans housed in the library of the mosque.

And his home—he remembered that well too; his gray, wrinkled, loving mother who had been forced by his father to sign the warrant to commit him to the mental asylum.

As always the thought of his father jarred. He had been like the others, stupid and ignorant and brainwashed by the Shah's propaganda.

The old man had never understood Islam. What good was industry when women had lost their shame, walking the streets virtually bare-breasted, with legs exposed? When Western materialism was destroying traditional family life and devotion to God?

Khalkhali felt the old feeling returning; whenever he thought of his father it recurred. His head throbbed—that was the most prominent sensation—but he also felt a sudden, almost unbearable heat engulf his body, and an extraordinary tension build within him. He had first had this feeling at eighteen, or was it nineteen? It had been followed by a full-scale depression, uncontrollable and irrepressible. For a while he began to believe that perhaps his father was right, perhaps he was not normal.

The dejection had lasted for months before finally he had turned for guidance to the house of the Lord.

It was, as luck would have it, the best decision he had ever made. The wise man had dismissed his concern with the wave of a hand and a knowing smile. "It is, my son, a normal occurrence in men of unusual intelligence," the Holy Man had said. "The sign of depth of character, of intense commitment." Khalkhali smiled as he recalled the happiness he had felt that night as he left the

Holy Man's modest residence. No, he was not insane, he was a man of unusual intelligence.

The limousine swept up to the main entrance of the hospital. Khalkhali stepped from the vehicle and strode toward the building. He did not knock as he entered Dr. Chirazi's seventh-floor office.

"Good evening, my son," he greeted him as he burst in. "I pray the patient is prepared."

"There...there's been little change in his progress," Chirazi stammered, taken aback by the sudden entrance.

"Ah, but we will proceed, will we not, doctor?" Khalkhali rubbed his hands enthusiastically. "Time is short, my son."

"Your excellency, I'm concerned that the shock of trying to revive him—even temporarily—will kill him," Chirazi ventured.

Khalkhali dismissed his concern with the wave of a hand. "Then that is the will of God. You need not concern yourself with such matters. All that is required of you is to revive him long enough for me to learn what happened in that house. What happens after that is unimportant."

Chirazi hesitated. "In my profession, your excellency, there are certain technical requirements that have to be fulfilled before I can do such a thing."

Khalkhali glanced at his watch. "Such as?" he snapped.

"I need the approval of one of his family, his next of kin, someone. I cannot take such a responsibility upon myself. It's unethical and illegal."

"I am the law," bellowed Khalkhali, feeling the same intense heat spreading through his body. "Do not speak to me of law. I decide here what is or what is not against the law." He poked his chest vigorously with his stubby index finger. "I will sign the paper you need. Give it to me," he snapped, reaching across Chirazi's desk.

Chirazi looked up at the priest. The bulging, maniacal eyes stared fixed and unblinking. His face was suffused with blood, the outstretched hand quivering in anger.

Chirazi knew there was no choice; the man was uncontrollable. He lowered his head and held out the standard waiver-of-responsibility form.

Salim Jabeh knew he was in the twilight of his life. He knew because he had seen it so often before. For the past ten years that

154

was all he had seen; pain and death and sorrow and hurt. But now, from up close, there was a peculiarly satisfying sensation about it. A feeling of contentment, of calm. There was no more that he could do in his life. He had achieved his aim; he had dealt a blow of immense magnitude to his enemies and he did not mind dying now.

Strangely his mind seemed separated from his body. It was alive, clear, sharp, while his body lay comatose. Even the smallest detail of his life flashed before his eyes. And yet his limbs refused to obey the simplest order. He did not try to fool himself. He knew why. He had seen too much not to know. His right hand was all that remained.

In fact, he had been lucky to last so long. The others in his training unit had long since departed. All of them killed or injured or imprisoned on different missions; mostly against Israel, but some against Israel's benefactor, America, or one of its surrogates.

The thought of the United States brought contentment. He had dealt them a blow they would not soon forget. A blow, he hoped, that would be the first of many against the imperialists.

In his last moments Salim recalled the details of memories too unbearable to contemplate in the past. His mother and father blown apart by an Israeli bomb, their bodies scattered in irrecoverable, charred pieces. The confiscation of his home, indeed the confiscation of his country. The poverty of his two sisters driven from Palestine to a refugee camp in Jordan; their new and permanent home a tattered tent from which there was no hope of escape. The sorrow, the frustration and finally the hate that drove him to revenge. The long and arduous training, the meaningless missions for the PLO and finally their first major success—Vienna and Carlos. Together they had kidnapped the OPEC ministers. Carlos had received most of the publicity, but Salim Jabeh had done his part and done it well. So well, in fact, that he had been transferred to the organization's most ambitious project—the mission to topple America's pet bulldog—the Shah of Iran.

Now that too had been a success; America's bulwark in the Middle East had been crushed. Only Israel and Anwar Sadat were left. He would miss the assassination of that traitor. He would miss the establishment of a free, sovereign and secular Palestine.

The Arabs had expected so much from the Americans. But they had turned their backs on the Arabs in their hour of need. They had sold the Arabs out to the Jews. They had taken Salim's country lock, stock and barrel, and given it to the Zionists. And now, too late, America, that nation of merchants, had finally realized that sometimes the price of betrayal was high.

The day was not far off when the Arab nations would unite and not a drop of oil would flow to that nation of salesmen. Then let us see what that industrial might is all about, he thought.

There was only one difference between the Russians and the Americans: the Russians knew they were bastards and their regime acted accordingly. Americans...ah, the Americans, he thought. They called themselves the good guys, people who believed in liberty and freedom, equality and justice and human rights. But that was only an image created to fool. In reality, they lived, breathed, understood and cared about only one thing—money. Profits and bottom lines, cost efficiency and benefits, acceptable returns on investment and balance of payments. They were a nation who understood quantity, but never quality. They had no values, no ethics, no culture, no principles. He had been taught all this in the education classes of the refugee camps in which he had grown up. And life had borne out his teachers.

What a great picture that was, he told himself. The picture of Vietnam with America defeated and on the retreat; a burly American soldier punching his former Vietnamese ally from the rungs of an airborne helicopter. That was America. Oh, how he'd love to see their faces in Washington now. And the Shah's face. To ask him what he thinks of the Palestinian cause now. To ask him what he thinks of America—his dear ally America—now.

His reminiscences were suddenly interrupted. Distantly he heard a voice.

"Salim."

There, he heard it again.

"Salim, my son."

He tried to stir, but his body spurned his instructions. His brain was active and alive but his eyes refused to focus. He tried more diligently; the lenses seemed mismatched, they zoomed and retracted in a blur. Only a semblance of movement, of life, filtered through.

"Salim...Salim. You must answer me. It is very important."

He mustered all his strength and moved his lips, hoping a sound would emerge.

156

CHAPTER
27

MEHREBAD AIRPORT, TEHERAN:
TUESDAY, OCTOBER 30: MIDNIGHT

"He's here," said the young militiaman.

"Who?" asked Hossein Mikhchi indifferently as he flicked the pages of the daily circulated list of "Enemies of God."

"The man with the bad leg."

Hossein Mikhchi looked up from his papers casually, his eyes distant and bored. "He's early, isn't he? It's only just after midnight. His flight doesn't leave for another seven hours."

"Yes, and he looks in poor shape," replied the militiaman.

"Where is he?"

"Sitting in the corner near the Swissair counter."

"*Khodah margesh bedeh*," cursed Hossein. "That's right next to the police office, isn't it? They'd just love to cause another scandal about us."

He walked to the window and dislodged a piece of jagged glass from the broken pane.

"What time does the plane arrive?" he asked.

"No idea," shrugged the militiaman.

Hossein looked at Samad Nafti. He thought: the man's useless, but at least he's trustworthy. He has no ambition and is therefore unlikely to pull a fast one. He thinks small and all he wants is to move his wife and daughter from his desert village in Khuzestan to Teheran. He had spoken to Hossein about applying for housing in one of the Shah's old army camps. Of course Hossein could do nothing to help but he had promised the man a house. And he knew that he was Samad's only "contact." So Samad would do as he was told.

"Samad, find out exactly what time the plane lands. Then get

157

one of the Swissair officials and check this man on right away. The minute the plane lands, get him on board out of harm's way. In the meantime, keep him out of sight. Check to see which of the offices are empty and hide him in it. Whatever happens I don't want him limping about the place. With his connections he may run into someone and blab his mouth off and we don't need that. Most of all, don't let the police get hold of him. Those bastards can't be trusted; they're all monarchists."

Samad looked at Hossein. He knew that what they were talking about had nothing to do with the revolution or untrustworthy police. It had to do with Hossein's mistake yesterday and his fear of it being reported.

But he didn't care; he had nothing to lose.

"No problem," he said. "With your permission, it might be wiser to keep him out of this building altogether. Maybe one of the empty private plane hangars would be the best place. They're very safe; no one ever goes into them."

Hossein studied Samad's rough, weatherbeaten face. Perhaps the boy wasn't as stupid as he looked. The hangars were an excellent hiding place and only a stone's throw from where the Swissair flight boarded.

"Use the Pars Air hangar. That's the closest and it's deserted."

Samad Nafti nodded.

"Oh, and Samad," Hossein added, "keep this to yourself. There's no need to tell anyone about it. Not even the rest of the boys. Just get him out of here; make sure he leaves. If anyone asks any questions refer them to me. *Fa'midi*, got that?"

"Yes, sir," smiled Samad.

For the first time in days Michael Adel relaxed. He was warm and comfortable and, he assured himself, relatively safe. The concrete hangar was well equipped; it had bunk beds, a functioning shower, toilet facilities and a small kitchen. What he needed now was a stiff drink. And suddenly he recalled the words of Nat King Cole: "As a rule, man's a fool. When it's hot, he likes it cool. When it's cool, he likes it hot. Always wanting what he has not." He suppressed his thirst and thought instead about the streak of luck he was riding.

Samad Nafti, Adel had discovered, after only a few minutes of conversation, was not a devoted revolutionary; in fact, he was hardly a revolutionary at all. Like the majority of his countrymen he was an opportunist. To him the revolution was merely a propitious event which, if used intelligently, offered a golden, once-only opportunity for a leg up in life. He could climb from laborer's son to whatever level his cunning—and fortune—would carry him. And Samad was well equipped to handle it. Subservience, or the ability to play the role, was the essential quality, and he had combined this basic ingredient with disarming wit and an agile if uneducated mind.

But to Adel, Samad Nafti was a likeable fellow. Twice he had apologized profusely for "any pain or inconvenience my colleageus caused your leg yesterday." He had taken him through immigration and other checkpoints speedily. Along the way he had stopped and picked up a backgammon set and commandeered a jeep to facilitate, and presumably spare Adel, the long and painful walk to the hangar.

Adel was genuinely grateful; it had been an agonizing twelve days, from the moment Anderson had appeared in Cannes. Twelve unimaginable days, of which the last three had been unbearable. But it was nearly over now, he told himself. This was the end of it. Three more hours and he'd be out of this madhouse, tapes and all.

His optimism, however, was short-lived; the thought of the tapes reminded him of Bell.

By now the American Embassy in Iran would be concerned about the disappearance of two of their staff. They would have automatically linked their absence to him. The two men would have logged their visit to his house; departure time, mode of travel, destination and estimated duration of visit were routine procedure. By now the responsible embassy officials would have informed their department heads, who would have communicated with Bell, who in turn would have alerted half of Europe to be on the lookout for him.

And he wasn't ready to see Bell yet. No, he had to insure himself before he did that. He contemplated his options; he had a choice: either he could change flights during the stopover in Damascus, or he could go on to Geneva. The difference being...

The door of the pilot's quarters burst open, shattering his thoughts. Adel turned, startled by the outburst.

Abruptly his heart skipped a beat as his body tensed. A wild-eyed Hossein glared at him from a distance of three yards. He towered above Adel, hands on hips, eyes darting.

Adel considered trying to break the tension but thought better

159

of it. From the little he had learned about Hossein, he was an intimidator; an arrogant, brazen street tough who would bludgeon his target into submission if he sensed weakness.

"Passport," snapped Hossein. Gone was the forced politeness.

Adel felt his nerves pinch as he fidgeted with his briefcase. What the hell could have gone wrong?

Hossein Mikhchi went through the plastic-coated booklet page by page, scrutinizing the various identifying marks. The document Adel was now using was one of the new, post-revolutionary variety, dark brown with gold bordering. Stamped on the cover in gold were the words GOVERNMENT OF THE ISLAMIC REPUBLIC OF IRAN PASSPORT, in Farsi, French and English.

Adel was not worried about the document's authenticity; he had inspected it carefully. What unnerved him was the possibility of another interrogation, perhaps even a body search. This time the tapes were on him. There would be no escape. He eyed Hossein, then glanced over at Samad's Uzi lying on the counter several feet away.

The blond man. It had to be the blond man, thought Adel, a sickening feeling in his throat. He had recovered and talked.

Hossein Mikhchi clutched the passport as he nervously knotted his hands together; one by one he cracked his fingers. After some hesitation he turned, crossed over to Samad and whispered in his ear. Then he tucked Adel's passport into Samad's breast pocket, shot a look at Adel and strutted out of the room, slamming the door behind him.

"It's chaos," said Samad Nafti, raising his hands in helplessness. "Every day there's a crisis."

"What's going on?" asked Adel in an unnaturally calm voice.

"Seems a man blew up one of the *komitehs* in the north of town and killed half the *pasdaran* in the building before making off with something or other. Today he's the hot item, everybody's looking for him. The only problem is, they don't know who he is, or what he looks like. All they know is his name."

"What is his name?"

"Adel."

Michael Adel cursed himself again for not having followed Allon's instructions exactly: *"If there is any doubt, just remember, it's you or them. Don't leave anything to luck. Kill if necessary but don't leave an iota to chance, not an atom. You'll regret it; it'll come back at you. It always does."*

"So why is your friend Hossein so mad?"

"He just wants you out of here. I'm supposed to get you on the plane during the *namaz*, morning prayers, when there are fewer people around. With the increased security now because of this character Adel, Hossein's worried you'll be discovered. He doesn't want to have to explain ripping a cast off an invalid."

CHAPTER 28

TEHERAN—SOUTHSIDE:
WEDNESDAY, OCTOBER 31, 1979: 5:00 A.M.

The bright winter sun had started to cast long shadows on the capital's deserted streets when the two young militiamen arrived at Ayatollah Sadegh Khalkhali's modest residence near the railroad tracks. Once this area with its coppersmiths, spice merchants and rug dealers had been the hub of the metropolis. But that was before the well-to-do had migrated northward, toward the cool Alborz Mountains. Now it was a sprawl of tumbling mud-brick dwellings, dilapidated tea houses and fruit and vegetable stalls.

The trip from the northern tip of the sprawling city to the south-side took the two men over an hour. Figuratively they went back in time, two centuries to a medieval squalor the more fortunate northern inhabitants of the city had long since forgotten.

They had made the trip separately, from different starting points, but they arrived at the heavily armed building within minutes of each other.

The familiarity of the Iranian guards did not exempt either from a thorough search; the Ayatollah's Palestinian "advisors," even after years of close cooperation with their Iranian brothers, insisted on the formalities.

After passing inspection they were shown into a drab room with only a single piece of furniture. Its main feature was a cheap *gash-*

ghai tribal rug in an orange, brown and red design. On the dilapidated table in its center stood a chipped, smoked-glass ashtray
with the inscription ROYAL TEHERAN HILTON.

The men were informed that they had been excused *namaz* by
the Holy Man himself and were left in the musty room to await
his pleasure. They sat on the floor, thankful for a few moments'
rest; they had not slept for close to thirty-six hours and the prospect
was not promising. At times like this, when the Holy Man showed
abnormal energy, he expected the same from his disciples, or even
more.

Shortly after 5:30 A.M. their brief rest ended. The Ayatollah's
new adjutant, a former comrade-in-arms who for the past six weeks
had been withdrawn from the troubled streets to the more pleasant
atmosphere of his uncle's office, opened the door and aroused them.

"*Baradarha,* brothers, he is ready for you," he smiled grandly.
Without further word the Ayatollah's nephew showed them through
the corridor and into the Holy Man's office.

The large room was, like the rest of the house, sparsely decorated. A huge, recently liberated antique Kashan silk carpet covered the entire floor. At the far end of the room, the Holy Man
sat cross-legged on the floor; opposite him rested three tall, fair-
haired men, obviously Westerners. Their legs, unaccustomed to
lengthy periods in the semi-lotus position, seemed tangled and
uncomfortable. It was a far cry from the plush facilities of their
European news bureaus.

"...therefore is not necessary to try criminal. Once criminal's
identity has been established, he should be taken out and executed," Khalkhali said in English heavily laced with a Favsi accent.

The two militiamen stood hesitantly near the door while the
Holy Man spoke.

One of the journalists asked, "But what if there's a mistake?
What if an innocent man is executed? A case of, say, mistaken
identity? It's more likely, you must admit, your worship, without
proper safeguards to establish guilt."

"No matter," the Holy Man said earnestly. "That is of no con-
sequence. In such case victim is blessed. He will go straight to
heaven."

Khalkhali looked at the two militiamen. He waved permission
for them to enter, indicating a corner of the room for them to
occupy.

"This won't take long," he said to them in Farsi before turning back to the foreign correspondents.

"My friends call me 'Wrath of God,' my enemies 'Cat Killer,' but both groups respect me, gentlemen. I do not care what they call me. I have duty to fulfill. To put it in—how you say?—a nut peel, I have most difficult yet gratifying job. I am Iran's Islamic Revolutionary Court. It is heavy burden to carry, but vengeance is religious duty and I am determined to rid Iran, and indeed world, of those guilty of 'corruption on earth.' Those so far executed can be likened to Nazi war criminals. They have done evil and incurred the wrath of God. Like Nazis, they have been justly punished. Your nations authorized Nuremberg trials, gentlemen, so you understand evil, do you not?"

He did not wait for a reply.

"All of this is simply first phase; we have only just started to cleanse. We will export this purification and spread the word of God to entire world, even to your countries, gentlemen," he said, waving his hand in an arc to include the three men.

"But for time being," he said slapping his knee, "you will appreciate that there is much to be done right here; much that I must attend to. Regretfully, we must terminate this meeting. Hopefully we meet again in very near future to continue these thoughts. Perhaps, even, we will meet in your countries," he said, bursting into a cackle. "But if that is to be the case you must accustom yourself to working these early hours of day, gentlemen. You all look exhausted." He bellowed with laughter.

The journalists stood up eagerly. Under the circumstances, there seemed to be no appropriate final question to ask.

Once the door had closed Khalkhali turned to the two men and motioned them closer. His expression turned businesslike and somber.

"Mehdi, what did you find at the airport?" He motioned the man to sit before him on the carpet.

He needed a crisis to show Imam Khomeini his worth once again. His enemies had influenced Khomeini against him recently, telling the Imam lies about his unpopularity, his insanity, his exaggerations. He prayed for a positive response.

"Nothing suspicious. Nothing worth mentioning."

"Well, mention it anyway."

"Ah...well...the man out there—a Hossein Mikhchi—is most

163

uncooperative. I don't think he wishes to be connected to our brotherhood. He's arrogant and difficult. I think he's a communist."

Khalkhali smiled. "His time will come. Very soon now, it will come," he said turning to the second man.

"You... Farhad. Did you get the file?"

"Yes, sir," the young man replied, placing a blue plastic folder on the coffee table in front of the ayatollah.

Khalkhali took the file and opened it. Holding the papers close to his eyes he squinted through thick, curved spectacles.

Farhad Samandar stuttered, unsure of himself. "After... after I collected the file I... I went over to the Farmanieh Komiteh head-quarters to take a look for myself. I inquired around and found something interesting, sir."

"Well?" said Khalkhali, his eyes still scanning the file.

"This man... his house is only one away from the *komiteh* head-quarters, sir."

Khalkhali looked up abruptly.

"And?"

"Well, I went to his house, Holy One; it was full of blood, especially near the *qanat* entrance. I also found a gun near a well and, from the smell of it, it's been fired recently."

"Good. Good," said Khalkhali. "That's very good."

Samandar took a photograph from his pocket.

"This may prove useful too, sir. It's a picture of Adel. It's signed here," Samandar said, pointing to the inscription: 'To my beloved parents. Michael.'"

Khalkhali looked at the photograph intently.

"One other thing, sir," Samandar interrupted.

"What, my son?"

"There's an American Embassy car parked near the house, in an alley. At least I think it's an American Embassy car; it looks exactly like the ones they use. The black four-door sedan type with no hubcaps or white walls. Only the Americans use those."

"Does it have diplomatic plates?"

"Yes, but I haven't been able to gain access to the vehicle reg-istration office. They don't open till eight."

Khalkhali nodded and smiled contentedly. He had found the crisis he needed. Spies sent into Iran, secret tapes stolen from a *komiteh* headquarters, killings. And now an American Embassy car in the neighborhood. Yes, with a little embellishment, this would do very well. As a conspiracy it would do very well indeed.

He pushed the photograph toward Mehdi.

"Have this circulated right away. I want this picture in every air terminal, train station and border crossing in the next twelve hours. I want it stuck on every wall, in every shop, in every government building of every town and village in the country. I want this man caught and brought to me immediately. You can leave right away and drop everything else you're doing. This is of utmost importance."

Mehdi left the room quickly. Khalkhali turned to Samandar.

"What do you think the next step is?"

"I'd like to search his house. I think we might find some interesting things in there."

"Yes...yes," Khalkhali answered distantly, preoccupied with planning what and when to tell the Imam to make his case most effective.

"I would also suggest we learn more about that car parked in the alley. We should contact the American Embassy to learn more...."

Khalkhali snapped out his thoughts.

"Samandar, I'm putting you in charge of this. Search the house. Find out whatever you can. Here," he threw the SAVAMA secret police file in front of his deputy, "read this and find him. Get those tapes. I must inform the Imam himself of an American plot against our revolution." He stood up.

"In the meantime I don't want anyone to know about this. Not the prime minister nor Bani-Sadr nor Yazdi nor Ghotbzadeh. Especially not Defense Minister Chamran or General Fardoust. Keep it to yourselves; discuss it only with me. Some of these men are foreign agents."

CHAPTER 29

The whirr of the DC-8 engines blasted through the open hatch as the pilot once again revved the engines. Over and over he had gunned the motors in an attempt to stop the needless last-minute inspection the *pasdaran* militiamen were conducting. It was seven-twenty; already the flight was half an hour late, and it went against the methodical grain of the Swiss pilot. There was no discernible reason for the harassment either; the passengers had already undergone thorough searches prior to boarding and still the scraggy militiamen walked up and down the aisle, brandishing their firearms. The engines calmed to idle again; waste, too, was reprehensible to the Swiss.

Michael Adel sat in a window seat in the front row of the first-class cabin. He tried to hide his anxiety, watching the flow of traffic on the tarmac; each arriving vehicle brought fresh tension, each parting one a measure of relief. He moved his unwieldly cast to a more comfortable position and glanced at the elderly man sitting beside him. Mercifully he did not appear to be the talkative type; and Adel turned away to the oval window as the whine of the high-pitched engines picked up again. Relax, he told himself. Just a few more minutes and it will all be over.

To occupy his mind, and block out the pain in his leg, Adel stared beyond the airport into the distance.

It was a cloudless, bright winter morning; the sun bounced off the snowcapped Alborz Mountains, giving the long rugged range a shimmering coat of majestic authority. On the horizon to the east stood Mount Damavand, awesome in its beauty and size, lonely in its solitude.

"Mister Adel."

Adel snapped his head toward the old man. But he was gone. In his seat sat Samad Nafti, a 9mm Browning partially concealed beneath his olive denim jacket.

"Mister Adel. That's your *real* name, isn't it?"

Adel did not answer. His heart thumped in his ribcage.

"A few minutes ago a jeep brought this to the plane." Samad stuffed a folded piece of paper in Adel's lap. "That's you, isn't it?"

Adel's hands trembled as he unfolded the paper. It was an old picture taken in Huntington Beach, California, in 1963; it had sat on his father's desk at the house, a gift to his parents on his twentieth birthday. They knew everything; who he was, how he had broken into Mahmoudi's house, the tapes, everything.

Samad's voice interrupted. "The poster you have in your hand is part of the first batch to be distributed. In a few hours there'll be more pictures of you plastered to the walls than Imam Khomeini's, if that's possible. There'll be no way out for you."

Adel bit his lip and nodded. He tried to think but his mind refused to function. He barely heard the young man's words as wild ideas raced through his head, only to be dismissed. He was cornered on the plane and there was nothing he could do about it.

Abruptly the man's words broke through the nightmare.

"But I'm willing to make a deal with you, Mister Adel."

Adel nodded again but avoided Samad's eyes. He shrugged his shoulders. It was easier than talking and it bought time.

Samad looked around the plane, then bent toward Adel. "These people are never going to last," he whispered. "Sooner or later their time will come. If we're lucky the Americans or English will do it. If not, the Russians will."

Samad stopped as a militiaman went by. He looked up at his comrade and smiled casually. "I'll be right with you," he said.

He waited for the man to gain distance. "It cannot last very long like this," he said, turning back to Adel. "It's a mess." He stopped, waiting for a reaction.

Adel nodded, a nervous smile forming at his lips.

"It's a simple deal, Mister Adel," said Samad. "You look after me when the country returns to civilized government, when people like you return. You look after me then. Tell them I worked with this mob but that I never killed or hurt anyone. You look after me then and you're free to go now."

Adel looked away from Samad. He couldn't believe it . . . the man was letting him go. Offering him his life on a half-assed promise of future help.

"That and ten thousand dollars cash."

Adel stared at Samad. It made more sense now. Even though he didn't have the ten thousand, he felt at ease; he was on familiar ground; he knew the figure was negotiable.

"I don't have that much money," he said.

Samad Nafti looked at him, his expression cold and hard. "How much do you have?"

"Five thousand. I can give you four thousand," Adel said, leaving a little for Samad to haggle over, in Iranian fashion.

Samad held his hard expression for a moment. Then he grinned, "I suppose you need a little pocket money. Make it four thousand five hundred and you owe me the rest."

Adel hid his relief. "What about the others?" he said, motioning down the aisle at the militiamen.

"Leave that to me," said Samad confidently.

Adel hesitated a moment. "I have to use the lavatory to get to it."

"Okay, but hurry," said Samad nervously glancing down the aisle.

Adel tried to stand but Samad's powerful arm held him back.

"If you have any ideas, take a good look around you," he whispered. "You don't stand a chance."

Adel had no ideas; he returned quickly from the lavatory and as he sat he passed a bulky envelope to Samad.

"I hope it's all there." Samad measured the weight of the envelope. He looked at Adel and began to open it.

His action was cut short by two approaching militiamen.

"Your passport," said one as he drew closer.

Adel felt in the breast pocket of his windbreaker but again Samad stopped him.

"This gentleman is all right."

"We have instructions to inspect everyone's passport and hand luggage. Your passport, please," insisted one of the militiamen.

"Why?" asked Samad. "They've been searched ten times."

"Orders," the militiaman shrugged.

"Come here." Samad motioned the two men closer.

The militiamen huddled closer and Samad whispered. Suddenly

they seemed to wilt. Their eyes darted, flustered. The whispered conversation continued.

Adel felt a rush of sweat on his body as the debate ran on.

"I'm sure his excellency understands," said Samad, raising his voice at last. He turned toward Adel, his face suggesting relief as his eyes urged Adel to put their minds to rest.

"No problem, brothers," Adel said. He cleared his throat and smiled casually. "It's good to see men of your caliber, your dedication."

The two men smiled back and gave the traditional Iranian bow of servility.

Samad watched them move down the plane. He looked at Adel, a wide grin covering his face.

"I told them you were one of Khomeini's relatives on a delicate mission to Europe," he said, pleased with himself. "I don't know what you've done and I don't want to know. Maybe you deserve to die, maybe you don't. But it doesn't make any difference here. They kill you first and then ask questions."

Adel looked at the luggage rack above his head. Then he turned toward Samad, relief surging through him.

"What about you? What will they do to you when they find out?" he asked.

"I have my orders. They're to get you out of here without any more problems. And that's what I'm doing."

He looked up and down the aisle, then back at Adel. For a brief moment their eyes were locked on each other before a small, almost imperceptible smile appeared at the corners of Samad's hard mouth. Then suddenly he was gone.

Five minutes later the plane was airborne.

CHAPTER
30

If there is one airport in the world built for inconvenience, it is London's Heathrow Airport, thought Adel, as he limped painfully down the drab and endless corridors to the terminal building. He anticipated with dread the long delays at Immigration and Customs, and glumly predicted that his Iranian passport would cause additional aggravations. But he forced himself on, thinking of Sam and Natalie, and how close he was to them. He told himself, too, that good luck was not everlasting that it came and went in cycles. And his had lasted a long time now.

It had lasted through Damascus, where he had changed planes, choosing to continue his trip with a new identity and on a different flight. To offset the computers that spun out their information to every intelligence agency in the world, he had ignored his booking through to Geneva. He had simply stood up and left the aircraft with the other departing passengers.

The Swissair flight had arrived in Damascus at eight in the morning, nine-thirty Teheran time, six o'clock London time. In a foul-smelling cubicle in the men's room of the terminal, he had discarded the Iranian passport in the name of Mohammed Shariat, first smudging the name from the document with soap and water, then using a razor blade to cut out the identification numbers.

He had stuck the document behind a row of books in a bookshop next to the lavatories. It was not important if the document was found, as long as it was not in the next few days. Considering the unappetizing selection of English and French books and a clientele of mainly Soviet advisors and Islamic priests, book sales were hardly flourishing. The document was unlikely to be detected for sometime.

170

He had checked out of the small airport on his American passport, then returned to catch British Airways flight 232 leaving for London at nine-thirty, seven-thirty London time. This time he used the second passport he had secreted in his cast, another Iranian one. He trusted that the Syrian officials were alert enough to notice that one Michael Adel was still in the country.

Even more important, his luck had held with the telephone call he had made from Damascus. The only person who had come to mind, the one unmarked person who might provide assistance—even though erratic and undependable—was luckily in London. And expecting him.

Now, standing in the Heathrow immigration line marked OTHERS, he longed for relief from the overpowering pain he felt. A strong painkiller, a shower, a shave and a long hot bath. He needed all of that, and sleep.

CHAPTER
31

LONDON: WEDNESDAY, OCTOBER 31: 2:05 P.M.

On Wilton Place, sandwiched between the bustle of Knightsbridge and Hyde Park Corner, stands the Berkeley Hotel. Discreetly elegant, it is one of the few remaining symbols of Britain's once-vaunted quiet good taste. To the casual observer it goes unnoticed, for it is unblemished by self-acclaim. But it does not need it: its reputation is well established among a relatively small but highly satisfied clientele.

As Adel stood in the hotel's only second-floor suite overlooking Hyde Park, he watched the tangle of traffic outside through double-glazed windows and tucked a white cotton shirt into black slacks. The painkiller and new clothing purchased by the hall porter had aroused a new sense of optimism and energy in him.

But still he yearned to stop running, to spend the week doing nothing, being cossetted by the superb hotel service. But that was a naive wish and he knew it. Once before he had ignored Allon's

171

words of caution and it had nearly cost him his life. He was determined not to make the same mistake again.

"Insure yourself. As far as possible always insure yourself. Nothing is too small."

He took his leather windbreaker from the hanger in the hallway and considered calling his brother Mark. Then he thought better of it. This time he would listen to Allon, down to the letter. There was nothing pressing about contacting Mark. Not yet. But should he place the other call? No. That too could wait. First he would visit Harrods and insure himself.

Adel walked past the crackling fireplace in the hotel lobby and picked up a newspaper from the stack that lay on the counter marked ENQUIRIES.

"Have the evening papers arrived yet?" he asked the young man behind the desk.

"I think so, sir." The young man dipped below the counter as Adel glanced at the paper in his hand. A photo of Prime Minister Menahem Begin and President Anwar Sadat laughing and shaking hands rocked him.

Adel looked no further. He remembered how it had all started and the words of Don Anderson.

"That's not possible; we can't use our own people; there's some sort of problem with it. I don't know what it is. Only thing I can think of is that the president doesn't want anything to tarnish the Camp David Agreement. He's pleased as a kitten with it; it's still too fresh and vulnerable."

"Here we are, sir," said the young man, holding out the evening paper.

"What time is it?"

"Five past two, sir."

"Thank you." Adel took the paper, adjusted his watch two hours back from Damascus time and walked away, the picture of Begin and Sadat still playing in his mind. He glanced at the evening paper absentmindedly. But it brought him no relief.

Wednesday, October 31, 1979
SHAH SELLS SURREY MANSION

The Shah of Iran's mansion in Hascombe, Surrey, was being stripped today of all its priceless antiques for shipment to America

172

where the former ruler is at present undergoing emergency medical treatment at the Sloan-Kettering Institute in New York.

Strutt and Parker, the London estate agents, believed to be handling the sale of Stilemans estate near Godalming . . .

Adel folded the papers and stuffed them in his windbreaker. He could not afford the luxury of time. At any moment now Bell and his organization would trace him. At most it would take them a day; if they were slow, that was. More likely they would be here in a few hours. That was all he had. A few hours to insure his future.

And no estate in Surrey to sell.

Outside the Berkeley he turned up his jacket collar to ward off the drizzle and hobbled across the street, toward Knightsbridge and Harrods. In front of a post office on the corner he noticed a bespectacled blonde in her late thirties step from a black de Tomaso Mini Innocenti. Her raincoat drifted upward with her skirt as she struggled to unknot herself from the cabin; beneath were revealed legs of extraordinary length and beauty. Adel noted them with pleasure, and discreetly watched them unwind. It had been a long time, he thought.

He hobbled across Sloane Street, thinking of Samira and welcoming the refreshing touch of the rain on his face. On the Brompton Road he remembered the last time he had been on this street with her; at Christmastime, ten months ago. He pressed the bell on the door marked KUTCHINSKY and waited for the buzz of the security lock. It was one of her favorite jewelers and suddenly he felt a strong urge to remind her of his love. Besides, Harrods was next door and it would only take a minute.

He chose the watch she had admired; a thick gold identification bracelet with a timepiece, studded with small diamonds.

"Are you sure this is the one she liked?"

"Yes, sir. Mrs. Adel has been in to see it several times," the formally attired salesman assured him.

"Okay, I'll take it," said Adel. "But I'd like something inscribed on . . ."

Abruptly the words caught in his throat. The blonde with the fine legs passed the window a second time. He had seen her earlier but put it down to coincidence. But a second time? Actually, it was the third time, he thought. She could have been waiting for him outside the hotel.

"Shit," he mumbled under his breath.

"What would you like put on it, Mister Adel?" the bald salesman inquired politely.

Adel stared at the window. "Ah...ah...just put 'I love you' and my initials on it and the date."

"Yes, sir."

"Oh. And...ah...can you send it to her? You have the address."

"Certainly, sir. Do we bill you, Mister Adel?"

"Yes...yes...that'll be fine," he said distractedly as he headed for the door.

On the Brompton Road he turned left toward Harrods, but immediately started across the road, weaving through the stalled traffic to the opposite side. He was careful to act like a man with a purpose, a man with a destination in mind.

He entered Richoux, the continental teahouse across from Harrods, and took the staircase down to the lower floor. Five minutes later, he placed a pound note on the table to cover the tea he had ordered but not touched and came back upstairs.

He opened the cafe door and looked both ways, up and down the pavement. Several doors down, to his right, blonde hair receded into the Rosenthal Studio House.

"Shit."

They had found him.

He crossed the street, his heart pounding, his mind racing. He needed time. Another few hours. He wasn't ready, not yet. He had to lose them, he had to shake free.

He was in front of Harrods now, directly in line with the doorway hiding the blonde. Her back was to him as she carefully studied the china in the shop window; and, no doubt, his reflection in the glass. He hailed a taxi.

"Where to, guv?"

"Hammersmith across to Barnes." He stepped into the cab, his eyes fastened on the rear window.

The fair-haired woman ran across the road, barely missing an oncoming car. She ran to the front of the taxi rank stationed outside Harrods and said a few words to the alighting passenger. Then she entered the cab and set out after him.

Adel turned to the driver. "How would you like to make fifty pounds?"

"That depends," the driver said skeptically.

"Someone's following me and I'd like to lose them."

"Like taking candy from a baby," the driver boasted as the vehicle surged forward.

"Drive over to Barnes, then."

The driver took a detour and headed up Exhibition Road toward Hyde Park. The traffic decreased as they passed Kensington and gained distance from the inner city; after Olympia they made good time. The pursuing taxi kept pace its distance, never varying between one and two hundred yards. Adel's heart pounded as he watched out the rear window. He had to lose her.

Suddenly, as they passed the former St. Paul's School compound, the pursuing vehicle turned into a side street.

Adel was surprised; it made no sense. She had been following him—he was certain about that. From the Berkeley to Richoux and then the taxi; it was more than coincidence.

Then it hit him. This was not Khomeini's rabble he was dealing with. They were professionals, real professionals. Sidewalk artists, as they called themselves.

Adel turned to look through the rear window again. "Which one of you is it?"

It was impossible to tell.

The taxi made its way past a huge church then over Hammersmith Bridge into Barnes; within a suspicious distance a motorcyclist, two taxis and a double-decker bus followed.

"Take a right," ordered Adel after they had passed a second set of traffic lights. He had to separate them; he had to isolate his predator, identify the hunter.

Only one taxi followed.

"Take a left."

Again the same black vehicle gave chase. A taxi, he thought. If that was all he had a chance. He watched for a second vehicle to appear, but none did.

"Pull up ahead."

The taxi swerved over to the curb and stopped. Adel stepped out.

"Listen carefully," he told the driver as he leaned into the window. "I want you to pick me up in two minutes at that..."

"I thought you said fifty quid, mate," the driver interrupted, full of indignation.

175

Adel gave the driver a cold, hard look. He did not want to pay the man, not even what was on the meter; he had to be sure that the cabbie would return.

"Look in your mirror," he said. "See that taxi back there?"

"Yeah."

"Well, we haven't lost him yet, have we?"

The cabbie's attention alternated between Adel and the rearview mirror.

"But we will," smiled Adel, giving him confidence. "Drive around the block and pick me up on that corner in two minutes." He pointed to the intersection ahead.

"Two minutes?" the driver asked sharply.

"Exactly two minutes," said Adel, leaning back from the window. "And not a second later."

"Two minutes it is," the cabbie said, deciding he had no choice.

Adel's eyes followed the parting cab until they rested on the predator behind. He wore a dark hat and a cream-colored raincoat; nothing else about him stood out. He was of medium height and build, and he was paying the taxi.

Adel limped down the quiet Victorian street. Except for them, there was not a person in sight; the handsome suburban street was deserted; not a sound could be heard, except the footfalls of the man behind him.

The distance to the crossroads was too short to justify two minutes at a normal pace, and his casual saunter belied the anxiety he felt. It was not designed to calm the pounding heartbeat, or relax the tension. It was meant to consume time and unnerve the man in pursuit. He stopped twice, once to admire a brass hound's-head doorknob, another to touch the petals of a late-blooming rose, but still he arrived at the corner twenty seconds early. As he stood waiting he fought the urge to turn and observe the pursuer's movements. Instead, he stood there, holding his ground, confident that the professional hunter behind him had committed what Allon called the cardinal sin—he had underestimated the opposition.

The clack-clack of the diesel engine was a welcome sound; he heard it before it came into view from a side street to his right. It pulled closer and stopped in front of him. Adel looked back at the perplexed face of his pursuer before he stepped in.

As the taxi pulled away, the hunter showed no sign of panic; he pulled a small, square object from his pocket, raised an antenna and bent his head. Then he looked up and down the street in search of a vehicle.

Adel turned to the driver. "What's the nearest underground station?" The walkie-talkie beaming its message across London left him no choice.

"Ahh...Hammersmith Station, I'd say."

"Drop me there."

Two minutes later the taxi pulled up to Hammersmith Underground Station and Adel hopped to the wet pavement. He stuffed sixty pounds in the driver's hand.

"Thanks," he said as he headed away.

He had lost them. But it would not be for long.

CHAPTER
32

HARRODS, LONDON: WEDNESDAY, OCTOBER 31: 3:20 P.M.

It was three-twenty when Michael Adel entered the radio and television department on the second floor of Harrods department store, confident that he had not been followed. En route, he had run decoy patterns to make certain he wasn't being followed. Twice he had changed trains; and twice he had lured any would-be pursuers into the open.

Now he hobbled past turntables, amplifiers, tape recorders and television sets and scanned the department's salesmen.

It was important to choose correctly, quickly and without a fuss. It took a few minutes before he spotted a young shop assistant, nattily dressed in a suit that was obviously beyond his means. Adel watched him for several minutes in search of a give away sign. But there was none; the young man behaved normally in every way. And yet something about the boy smelled of moonlighting, of subsidizing his tastes. He watched the assistant closely

177

for several more minutes but still there was no concrete reason to back up his suspicion.

He had to move quickly; he had to decide. Out there Bell had an army looking for him. Time was running out.

As he hovered beneath a sign that read AUDIO ACCESSORIES Adel decided to gamble on his instincts. He waited for the redheaded young man to finish with his customer, then moved closer.

"Can I help you, sir?"

"Perhaps," replied Adel cautiously.

"What is it you're looking for?"

Adel reached in his pocket. "Something a little unusual."

"Well, we have *almost* everything at Harrods," smiled the young man, "and if we don't carry it, we can always order it for you, sir."

"Yes. I'm sure you can. But I'm not looking for anything in particular, just someone who's willing to make himself a hundred pounds legally and quickly."

The young man's eyes flickered but he was neither insulted nor shaken. He scanned the floor for a supervisor.

"I...I...don't know, sir," he stammered. "A hundred pounds? What is it you want?"

Adel removed the tapes from his jacket. "Duplicates of these."

"Well, sir," replied the salesman, obviously mollified. It was a relatively simple task. "That's not exactly permitted, but let me see what I can do."

"That's what the hundred's for." Adel showed the five twenty-pound notes in his hand.

The redheaded salesman scanned the floor again. "Leave them with me," he said nervously, grabbing for the tapes and the money.

Adel pulled back. "That's the problem," he said, stretching the words. "I want to hear them while you do it."

CHAPTER 33

OCTOBER 31: 3:39 P.M.

The two Gale speakers erupted in a deafening, high-pitched noise in the makeshift recording cubicle. Perched on a high stool, the salesman depressed the volume lever, reducing the sound to a more tolerable level.

Adel frowned and glanced at his watch. Then he picked up the cassette jacket the salesman had placed on the deck and read the handwritten red letters: "The Trust 1975. Tape 1."

The words meant nothing.

The sounds were a drone of mumbling, intermittently shattered by laughter or a raised voice that momentarily stood out, clear and distinguishable, only to fade again.

Adel felt uneasy and confused. "Is this working at normal speed?"

"Sure." The salesman looked at him curiously. "Why?"

"It's a lousy recording," muttered Adel, his mind drifting back to Bell.

"It's all gibberish if you hear them on a normal tape recorder. To make any sense out of them you need access to a machine that can slow them down to a crawl."

Why? Why the hell had Bell lied? The tape was recorded at normal speed and it was patently decipherable at that.

"Listen," he said to the boy, "give me a pair of earphones; that way I can turn it up and the sound won't bother anyone. Bell's lie had unnerved him; he didn't want anyone listening.

"That's marvelous," said the salesman. "Because I've got to be seen on the floor, so I'll be coming and going." He handed Adel a pair of earphones and left.

179

Adel felt a surge of adrenaline as a clear voice burst through the jungle of murmurs.

"Gentlemen. I've requested this extraordinary formal session because of the grave and impending nature of the crisis we face."

Adel sat up with a start.

"I think you'll consider the inconvenience of flying in to New York at such short notice justified as the ramifications of the problem become apparent."

Adel cocked his head as he registered a hint of recognition. That voice, he thought. That inflection. He knew them. He had heard them. And what did a crisis in New York have to do with the Phoenix missile anyway? His stomach rumbled with anticipation.

"I'll be as brief as I can on the background so we can reach the crux of the matter quickly. As you are all no doubt aware, the Shah of Iran is presently on the last day of a ten-day state visit to Rumania. During the course of this period, intelligence reports started coming in indicating that top-secret negotiations were taking place between the two countries that, if successful, could shake the very foundation of our organization."

What organization? What the hell was he talking about?

"Unfortunately, these negotiations have now been successfully concluded. Mahmoudi, who went along as the Shah's finance minister, has just flown in from Bucharest. He's here on a round of previously scheduled talks with the people in Washington and he's brought with him a copy of the final accord."

"Incidentally," added the same tantalizingly recognizable voice, *"Mahmoudi is standing by next door should any of us have any questions."*

"What," asked a second voice, *"are the terms of this arrangement?"*

The first speaker responded without hesitation. *"The accord itself is inconsequential, Sol. It's a barter agreement. The Iranians are to supply one hundred and fifty million dollars' worth of oil per year and receive in return an equivalent dollar value in agricultural equipment and foodstuffs. But the ramifications, as I am sure you are well aware, are devastating."*

180

There was a momentary silence and Adel shifted on his stool. What the hell had this to do with the Phoenix missile?

The voice in the earphones continued. *"On its own the deal is peanuts. But it's the first entry into the marketplace by an OPEC nation. That is what's wrong."*

The voice was a calm, refined baritone. Deep and resonant, with a mid-Atlantic timbre. Adel frowned and leaned forward, trying to force his memory.

"Fundamentally, what the Shah signed in Bucharest last Friday—the document is dated February 28, 1975—" the voice paused, obviously for effect—*"is an assault on our monopoly."* Again it paused. *"The overt challenge, gentlemen, by an oil producer to bypass our marketing apparatus and acquire independent markets."*

God damn it! Of course he knew that voice! He knew it well. It was the voice he had heard only days ago. The voice of his friend. The man he had trusted. The man he had turned to for advice and help and guidance.

It was the voice of John Alexander Case, Chairman of the Board of Chief Executive Officers, Enerco Corporation—the largest energy company in the world.

Suddenly his worst doubts and fears were a reality. "Phoenix missile, my ass!"

There was a new voice, fragile and barely audible. Like the two which had preceded it, its inflection was American. But there the similarity ended. The voice was more elderly, more confident and assured.

"How deeply does it cut into the marketing network, Jacey?"

Jacey, thought Adel bitterly. Those were his initials—J.A.C.— John Alexander Case. Jacey to his cronies.

"The answer to that, David, is it doesn't," replied Case. *"Not significantly, anyway. But it's the precedent we've been watching for. Like everything else about OPEC, it'll lead to leapfrogging. Once the Iranians get away with this deal—and knowing the Shah he'll find some absurdly glittering manner to proclaim his achievement—every OPEC nation will seek its own market. Kuwait will*

181

want to enter Australia, Bahrain Japan, Nigeria Brazil, and so on. They'll bypass us."

"Well," said David, with a heavy sigh, *"as I understand it, this isn't altogether unexpected. Clear-cut contingency plans designed to handle just such an event have been in existence for some time. The drawback has always been our reluctance to activate them. The time has obviously come to put that reluctance aside."*

"Gentlemen, David Thorncroft has a cogent point...."

Shit! thought Adel. But there was no time to think further. The voice was a new one, unmistakably British.

"...but the reluctance is not whimsical, it's based on very valid concerns. The region is not a stable one, and the intricacies— indeed the variables—of these so-called contingency plans are both numerous and the outcome uncertain. Very high-risk stuff, all this, in what is strategically the most important area in the world. That's why this contingency thinking was always seen as a last resort. I'm not sure a miniscule barter agreement constitutes quite that."

The discussion had only one direction, thought Adel. And it sure as hell didn't include the Phoenix missile.

So far, four voices had spoken. Besides Case only one other had been clearly identified. It was the voice of one of the richest man in the world; a man who owned a controlling interest in several of the largest oil companies in the world. It was the voice of David Thorncroft.

Even worse, it was not difficult to guess the names of the others present. Not with the Christian name of one and the British accent of the other. Not when he—Michael Adel—had, at various times, and degrees of proximity, known and worked with every one of them: Solomon Horowitz, Arthur Sinclair and Baron Gerome Steendijk van Lochem. The rulers of the world's oil industry.

CHAPTER
34

At that precise moment, less than two miles from Harrods, Colonel Grover Cleveland Bell stood at the window on the fifth floor of a palatial Regency mansion on The Mall, reflecting on the history that the sprawling majesty of Buckingham Palace epitomized. After a moment he turned to the unimposing heap of Victorian buildings that stood directly in front of him, across St. James's Park. It was there, in the unimpressive heap of Whitehall, that that history had been made. And not, he noted, in the impotent splendor of the palace to his right. His reflections on the ironies of real and apparent power were cut short by the buzz of the telephone. He turned from the window and pressed a button.

"Yes, Ann."

"It's Mister Gleeson, sir."

Bell pressed another button and reclined in his swivel chair.

"Hey, Jim. How's it going?"

"We've lost him."

"What!"

"We lost him," repeated Gleeson.

Bell sat ramrod straight. "How the hell did you do that?"

"He engineered it. He slipped his tail around Barnes."

"Who," snapped Bell, "is Barnes?"

"It's a neighborhood, Grove. Just across the Hammersmith Bridge."

"Terrific. You got twenty-seven men, eleven vehicles and a fucking cripple to follow and you can't manage it. A fucking amateur!"

"He knows what he's doing, Grove. He executed the slip perfectly."

"When did it happen?"

"About an hour ago. Around two forty-five."

Bell reacted with military precision. "Call in the rest of your unit and deploy them over six areas: Soho, Mayfair, Belgravia, Chelsea, Knightsbridge and Kensington. I'll get domestic assistance to cover the rest. Circulate an exact description of what he's wearing and key on recording studios, stereo stores, tape and record shops—anywhere he could duplicate the tapes."

Bell walked to the far end of the office and back, barking orders.

"If I know the bastard he's going to double back to the areas he knows best and that, Gleeson, is the six you're covering, so for fuck's sake keep your finger out of your ass!"

"What about known associates?" Gleeson asked.

Bell stopped pacing. "If he's good enough to slip you, Gleeson, he isn't going to drop in on his aunt for tea, is he?" He paused and covered himself. "Let domestic stake the knowns. We'll interface with domestic here. I'm going down to the Sit Room now so I'll be plugged into all the communications traffic. I want to know every step you're taking, Gleeson. Have all the vehicles do a Howard Cosell. I want ball-by-ball coverage."

"Yes, sir."

"Find him, Gleeson. I don't care what it takes, find him. I don't want that mother getting close to a tape recorder."

"Yes, sir."

"Oh, and Gleeson..."

"Yes, Grove?"

"Don't forget the larger department stores: Selfridges, Fortnum and Mason, Harvey Nichols, Harrods—all of them."

CHAPTER 35

HARRODS: 3:58 P.M.

It was David Thorncroft's voice that broke the silence of the tape. *"This is a watershed problem, and I think it might help if we reflect a moment before we go any further."* He sounded assured and self-confident, without the tension of his colleagues. He seemed to be trying to appease the two different factions. It was not clear what the differences were. Only that the interests of the Americans who wanted to act and the Europeans who advocated caution were divergent.

"The essence of this Trust, indeed the characteristic that sets it apart from all others, has been its ability to retain its unity in times of stress. It might be useful to keep that in mind as we go over the intricacies of this crisis. Perhaps we should etch in our minds the preamble to our constitution: 'Only through cooperation comes power.' And remember how well those five words have served us in the past. I suspect they may be the reason behind any future prosperity we enjoy."

"Your point is well taken," replied the clipped British voice of Arthur Sinclair testily. *"No one is questioning 1928. I'm committed to it. Gerome here is committed to it, and clearly the three of you are committed to it. Yes, indeed, 1928 forms the basis of any decision we take. But in addition to cooperation, 1928 also suggests that responsibility and risk be equally . . ."* he paused and repeated the word *". . . equally distributed among the economic units. The area in question is only of peripheral interest to three of those present. To Gerome and myself it endangers all four of our sources of supply: Iran, Iraq, Kuwait and the Arab Emirates. Your prime concern—the Saudi production—would be unaffected. The pipelines you've built down to the Red Sea insure that. You're not affected by the Straits of Hormuz and its closure."*

"That's true, Arthur," Case said firmly. . . .

Adel shook his head in amazement. In 1928 the major oil companies had secretly met at Achnacarry Castle in Scotland and signed the so-called "Status Quo Agreement." An accord that eliminated all competition in the energy industry and divided the world into separate but equal sectors to be shared among the major international oil companies who were signatories to the agreement. The "As-is Agreement" was never published. In fact its existence was always vehemently denied by the oil industry. But here were the potentates of oil not only testifying to its existence, but baring its details.

Adel massaged his forehead and felt a thin moist film of fear.

". . . The contingency plans present far more of a danger to your two European units than they do to us, but that's why the reserves

185

and production facilities we intend to develop before the plans go into effect are slated to be in your spheres of influence and under your direction."

"But it's the old story of a bird in the hand, isn't it?" said Sinclair. "It's a very high-risk game we're playing. Perhaps we could still explore other less drastic options. Perhaps a more political, less violent solution."

What violence? What high-risk game were they playing? What the hell was going on?

Again David Thorncroft spoke in his authoritative voice. *"Over the years, Arthur, the power base of this Trust of ours, the essence if you will, has been its ability to recognize when the time has come to make difficult decisions. And never attempt to skirt them. We must be careful not to lose that ability."*

"Look, Art," said Solomon Horowitz, *"the circumstances in 1928 weren't too different from what we've got today. The world's economies were growing too fast; we've got that today. The oil industry was facing excessive demand; we've got that today. Supply sources had not kept up with demand; we've got that today. Competition between marketing units was getting out of hand; for all intents and purposes after the Shah's Bucharest agreement, you can say we've got that today. For Christ's sake, what we are talking about here is excessive market competition. Destructive market competition. If the OPEC people are allowed to establish a foothold in the marketing end of operations, we're finished. They have the oil; all they need is the markets."*

"These decisions," David Thorncroft said, *"do not lend themselves to emotions or questions of right and wrong."* His words were a buffer to the brisk, aggressive manner of Solomon Horowitz. *"They concern the survival of our world and way of life—the Western world of free democracies—and, incidentally, the health of this Trust. If we are going to retain our position, I submit that we must be up to the challenges of today, even if that means employing the sternest of measures and a modicum of risk."*

At length another voice broke the silence. *"Does there exist any evidence of Russian connivance in this barter agreement the Shah has concluded?"*

Adel felt vindicated. It was the voice of Baron Gerome Steendijk van Lochem, head of a Benelux energy conglomerate, a half-British, half-Continental hybrid. Adel recalled clearly the last time

186

he had seen the baron at a luncheon in The Hague. He remembered the baron's stiff, Prussian bearing and his affected, outmoded English mannerisms, his slicked-down hair, the Savile Row suit, his horsy features.

"The short answer is, yes," Case said. *"Mahmoudi claims that the Shah was flown off in the middle of the night by helicopter and that the man who negotiated on Rumania's behalf was Alexei Kosygin himself. Now you'll recall Kosygin was prominently present when we were negotiating with the Soviets. He, with Khrushchev, Suslov and Mikoyan, signed the agreement we concluded in 1962, after their ploy with Mattei ended with his fatal accident and they became willing to play ball. This Rumanian thing with the Shah is a clear breach of those understandings. It may well be a new pincer movement by the Soviets and they wouldn't do it unless they thought the timing was right. A response, gentlemen, and an unmistakable one, is imperative on more than one front.*

Mattei too, thought Adel with a shiver. Enrico Mattei, the head of ENI, Italy's oil giant, had tried to buck the system and a bomb had torn his private plane to shreds outside Milan's Linate Airport.

"Speaking on my own behalf," said the baron, *"I am not opposed, and neither have I been in any one of our previous discussions on this subject, to the concept of the dismantlement of OPEC. I see the eventual need for it. The disquieting element, as Arthur suggests, is the radical nature of the proposed operation and the somewhat uncertain outcome."* The voice sounded half-throttled, but the words and their meaning were more than clear.

"Look," said Horowitz impatiently, *"we could have accomplished every one of the things we accomplished with OPEC in other ways and without losing supply-side control."*

What did this mean?

"Now the Shah of Iran—this creature of OPEC—is going for our balls and here we are sitting debating whether his assault on the marketing end of operations is or is not acceptable."

He paused. *"Well, I'll tell you something. If he's allowed to succeed you can all rest assured of one thing: every OPEC member will seek its own market and with the discounts they can offer to acquire those markets, it'll be a bush fire. They'll nibble away until all that's left for us to play with is a couple of gas stations in Climax, Nevada."*

187

Adel closed his eyes and leaned forward as the barrage of revelations continued. A picture of Horowitz, the major shareholder in the largest independent oil company in the world, formed in Adel's mind. He was slight and sloppy in appearance. His balding head sat on hunched, narrow shoulders and its most noteworthy feature, besides the ever-present grimace, were sharp, dark eyes hidden behind photo-chromic lenses. He was variously described in the media as controversial, outspoken, brash and arrogant. The entrepreneurial skills that had taken him from a penniless Jewish immigrant from Russia to the pinnacle of American corporate power were awesome. His immense fortune, used to spread patronage and philanthropic largesse, was legendary. The Horowitz private art collection was envied and coveted by the world's major museums.

The voice of Arthur Sinclair brought Adel's attention back to the tape. *"Really, Sol, you're being rather uncharitable on the OPEC decision. Establishing OPEC has unquestionably been the single most complex undertaking we've ever attempted and its success must be close to perfect."*

Adel reeled. This was the biggest bombshell yet.

"Every one of us has benefitted enormously from it. There's no question of anyone being harmed."

"Yes," interjected Case, before Horowitz could take issue, *"your reticence regarding the OPEC option is on record, Sol, and I think I can say we've all appreciated your spirit of cooperation in going along with us. I know you've had misgivings all along. But I think I have to agree with Arthur here."*

Case was coming to Sinclair's aid. The art of diplomacy. Case was already certain of Horowitz's support; he was going after Sinclair's.

"There was no choice. We had to diversify to alternative sources of energy, and the OPEC option we triggered fifteen years ago has just about put us in reach of our goals. Without the price increases they forced through, how could we have financed the development of alternative energy sources? No, Sol, it was the right decision. And it's smack on course. By nineteen eighty-four or -five it will have served its purpose."

188

Loud and clear it was coming through: OPEC with all its swagger had all along been a ploy of the oil companies. Adel could scarcely believe what he was hearing.

"*Yes, quite so.*" It was now Sinclair hammering the points home. "*The only politically acceptable way of getting prices up to the required levels was to get the producers to do it. And the only way that could have happened was to organize them. The perfect foreign organ which seemed to be giving us a beating. Very neat, really. I can't say any of us has cause to complain.*"

"*Fine. It's served its purpose,*" conceded Horowitz grudgingly. "*But it's grown too independent now.*"

CHAPTER
36

THE MALL: 4:17 P.M.

The Otis elevator that Grover Bell entered serves only two points of the sprawling mansion on The Mall: the security clearance room on the ground floor with its visual identification procedures, and the basement which has two electronic checkpoints, one by the elevator door, another at the end of a long tunnel. These measures are additional to the two clearances necessary to enter the building itself, and the closed-circuit video camera that records all who enter and leave the room at the end of the tunnel.

No one—not the Queen of England nor the President of the United States—is allowed to circumvent the security measures that lead to that door marked 2001SX. To insure against the unlikely event of someone trying, armed marines stand by with sidearms loaded with KTW brass bullets, whose deceptively benign-looking apple-green tips coated with Teflon solutions can penetrate any bullet-proof equipment known to man.

As he went into the cave of electronic wizardry, Colonel Grover

189

Cleveland Bell felt foolish. The sophistication of the room was, he admitted, a classic case of overkill for his purposes; it was designed for far more Gordian purposes. Its capabilities were mind-boggling; all the technological marvels of the twentieth century were condensed into that one room.

It was in fact one of four such facilities in the Western world: the Strategic Air Command Headquarters outside Omaha, Nebraska; the Joint Chief of Staff Command Center in the Pentagon; U.S. Military Command, East, in Guam; and this—Strategic Command Europe—the least publicized of all.

Every military and intelligence capability that the Western world possesses is available in that one room. And all at the touch of a button. The vast electronic surveillance gadgetry (ELECTINT) of the CIA, NSA and DIA, the sensitive human grid (HUMINT) of the SIS, Mossad and SDECE, the American military satellite and land-based intelligence network, as well as the conventional security forces of law and order.

The equipment can zoom in with high-resolution satellite cameras on the havoc Afghan rebels are wreaking on Soviet troops in the Pamir Mountains; and establish with remarkable accuracy the types and quantities of captured arms and ammunition. It can listen in on Ayatollah Khomeini's domestic conversations in North Teheran, provide the exact numbers of central American rebels about to attack a government post, assess the caliber of companion any pretargeted politician might have chosen for that particular night's activity. It can monitor—and provide simultaneous translations in every language—all ground-to-ground, ground-to-air, air-to-air conversations throughout the globe, and even assess the load of a tanker at sea not by its size but by the exact level of its watermark.

It can provide the numbers, regiments and ranks of soldiers enforcing martial law in Warsaw and Gdansk, contact visually and audially the American base in Diego Garcia or a lonely soldier on patrol near Panmunjom.

All of which was of little use to Bell; he had neither the time nor the inclination to reroute satellites to search for Adel.

What he did need was the vast domestic communication capability this room contained: the ability to contact anyone at the touch of a button—the keeper in the lighthouse off Land's End, the chief constable's desk on the Shetland Islands, the prime minister, the head of M15, every government department, every public or private transportation outlet or service in Britain.

190

CHAPTER
37

The voice of David Thorncroft cut in. *"We have to be careful here to differentiate between the desirability of dismantling OPEC and the actual mode of destabilization. The mode of execution is not something we are in a position to assess. That's for Operations to decide, isn't it?"*

"Yes, it is," said Case. *"And they're fully prepared. What we need to decide is whether or not the timing is right."*

"I'm not sure the time is ever quite right for these things," said the baron after a moment's silence. *"It's more a question of whether OPEC is controllable or not. Rumania seems to suggest it isn't. Or at least it seems to suggest it soon won't be."*

"Yes," agreed Sinclair. *"If Rumania is allowed to succeed it would seem a fair bet that the Russians would at the very least seek to expand the barter concept to their other satellites—Poland, Hungary and so on. It would have a snowballing effect: unstoppable after a certain point."*

The speakers were silent momentarily. But the silence itself was worse. It drove home to Adel the claustrophobia of the small room.

"How does Operations see a project of this magnitude, Jacey?" asked Arthur Sinclair.

"Well," Case sighed, *"it's really two problems rolled up in one, isn't it? One—the issue of the Shah's future; and two—the issue of OPEC. From what I understand, Operations' plans revolve around the fact that for the most part OPEC nations need our money more than we need their oil. At least in the short term that's true. The development dreams of the producing nations are enormous and their dependence on oil revenue is absolute. That, gentlemen, is their Achilles' heel.*

"Operations suggests that if a glut scenario could be manufactured for, say, a period of one or two years, the internal fiscal pressure on every OPEC member except Saudia Arabia would be such that it would lead to pressing financial shortages and consequently a price war within OPEC. In effect, OPEC would self-destruct."

"And how do we bring about such a glut scenario?" asked Horowitz.

"Operations will be making a presentation on that shortly. It's based on the destabilization of one or both of the moderate elements of OPEC—Saudi Arabia and Iran—who between them produce half of OPEC's oil or roughly one quarter of world production. That way the moderates would lose their plurality to control; and this would lead to gradual price increases; a panic in the West as we stockpile more oil; further price increases, much larger this time; conservation and probable economic recession in the West, with OPEC left holding a high-priced baby that no one wants. In other words, a glut."

An ear-splitting siren wailed between the earphones. The chairman of the board of the most powerful energy company in the world was admitting to the largest conspiracy of all time—a conspiracy to subjugate hundreds of millions of people, entire nations, so a handful could thrive.

What was worse, Adel realized, was that his own problems had only just begun. Everything—the killings, the pain, the fatigue—were merely the prologue.

"If the choice for destabilization is between the Shah and King Khaled, it's simple, isn't it?" said Sinclair. "One's a megalomaniac, the other a reasonable man content with his hawks and his hunting."

"There are technical elements involved, too." It was Horowitz's crusty voice. "Iran has reserves of fifty billion barrels; Saudi Arabia one hundred and fifty million. Iran has a daily export capability of eight million barrels, Saudi Arabia fourteen. Iran is on the Soviet border, Saudi Arabia is a thousand miles away, separated too by a gulf."

"My main concern," continued Case patiently, "is the preliminary years. We'll have to generate a major program to increase Western reserves and supplies in order to insure adequate energy *levels throughout the transitionary period. Six million barrels of Iranian oil—that's a hell of a loss of supply."*

"It's not a problem technically, Jacey," said Horowitz. *"We can do it by carrying out some in-fill drilling in some of the existing fields. And start major exploration efforts in areas of the continental United States, Alaska and Mexico. There's so much we've located but left fallow. Once prices rise, we can open completely new areas such as the North Sea quite economically. And the Saudis will always go along with production increases. Tell 'em the incremental growth will be applied to strategic military stockpiling only. They always buy that."*

"I seem to have missed something somewhere." It was the baron. *"Why do we need to lose the Iranian production? Is the outcome that uncertain?"*

"No, Gerome, you didn't miss a thing. The thinking on that is that we can set the price program ahead a few years. If a revolution occurs and six million of the Iranian production goes off the market it would seem a natural time for a shortage to occur. That being the case the projected prices in effect at that time which are ...ah...ah..."

"Twelve dollars and change," said Horowitz over the rustle of papers.

"Yes," said Case. *"The twelve dollars or so projected to be in effect then can be engineered upward to the thirty-dollar range. That's when the alternative sources we are now so heavily committing to can be brought onstream economically. An unfriendly new regime in Iran's going to lead to a scramble for oil. The whole world's going to be terrified of the Straits of Hormuz being blocked, so everybody's going to rush to stockpile. And we, of course, can help that scare program along.*

And that, Adel thought, was exactly what had happened. On January 16, 1979—the day the Shah left Iran—the price of oil had been $12 and change a barrel. Today it had reached $30. Six months. That's all it took them. A 150 percent increase in six months. He nodded as he thought of his own fate.

Case went on confidently. *"After a decent interval, the energy glut we just talked about can be manufactured. The glut that hopefully will force OPEC nations to internal competition, discounts and, eventually, disintegration."*

193

Suddenly the door of the studio opened. The salesman entered and murmured something.

Adel did not reply. He was mesmerized.

"Gentlemen," said Case firmly, *"we must arrive at a complete and final solution...."*

But abruptly there was silence.

CHAPTER
38

THE MALL: 4:39 P.M.

"The cab dropped him off at Hammersmith Underground Station, sir."

Bell raised his head from the computer screen of the conference table overlooking the room. He looked up at the wiry young man and the clipboard he held.

He pointed. "What else have you got there?"

Christopher Capelli shook his head. "That's about it, sir. We traced the taxi through the number John had, and that's all the driver knew. Hammersmith Underground Station."

"What time was that?"

"An hour and a half ago. Two forty-five. Three o'clock. Somewhere in that time frame."

Bell glanced away, slowly scanning the eight silent film screens on the three walls in front of him; the screens that, if activated, could literally cover the world and record the smallest detail of history in the making. He bit his lower lip and swiveled on his chair.

"He's doubled back. I can feel it." His eyes narrowed, aging the lines around his eyes, crinkling the sliver of a scar on his right cheek. "To the crowds, to where he knows best." He stopped swiveling and withdrew a pack of cigarettes from his pocket.

"Patrolmen wired in this town?"

"The bobbies? Yes, sir. They carry walkie-talkie systems. Not too sophisticated, but they can be reached."

Bell stood and nodded. "It'll do. Circulate a description to every cop on the street and stress the fact that Adel's limp is barely noticeable. Then, Capelli, I want to know what happens to this town on Wednesdays. What time the stores close, if there's any late closing areas and anything else that's special about Wednesdays."

CHAPTER 39

HARRODS: 4:45 P.M.

Michael Adel watched in a daze as the salesman ejected the first cassette and replaced it. His body ached with pain; it yearned for normality. His life had been uprooted during the past week, but this latest twist was shattering.

"Any good?" the salesman asked in a friendly voice.

Adel looked at him. Have you any idea of the enormity of what you're witnessing? No, but you wouldn't have, would you? That's what it's all about; that's what makes it work for them. Our ignorance, our preoccupation with ourselves, our fecklessness. The Shah of Iran had to go, the man had said in 1975. Four years later, he was gone. Now it was OPEC's turn.

"Yes," Adel said, replacing the earphones and pointing to the salesman to start the second tape. "It's good, all right."

"Without any more ado I'm going to turn the floor over to Operations," the tape boomed. *"Gentlemen, James Farrar."*

It was the same voice as on the first tape. John Alexander Case, resonant and eloquent.

James Farrar's voice was scholarly and soft, tinged with a southern lilt. It was also highly nervous.

"The strategy for this exercise is," he said, clearly jittery, *"in a general way, always prepared. This is as true of all potential targets as it is with Iran. Each has its own particular idiosyncracies; each depends on timing and the course of events—past, present and projected—and at the point of execution, the strategy may or may not require refinement to accommodate the desired outcome."*

He cleared his throat self-consciously before continuing. *"The system we use for destabilization models is Operations Research and Analytical Logic, or ORAL, as it has come to be known. Most of you are familiar with the use of this program to problems of planning for your companies. But these same programs can be adapted to accommodate various other applications."*

Again a nervous clearing of the throat. *"The programming software is essentially the same. The computer is simply—too simply, as I present it today—programmed to simulate, to be an analogue, to the system it analyzes. In the case of this particular ORAL program, it is programmed to pretend that it is Iran—in terms of the economy, the military, the intelligence, the governmental and religious systems, the demographic parameters of all types, the communications and transportation systems, the agriculture, and so on.*

"To apply ORAL to Iran, one in effect applies a variety of potential strategies that could result in destabilization. The computer then reports the relative success or failure of such strategies and/ or a combination thereof. ORAL and similar research . . ."

As Farrar talked, Adel found a picture of Farrar forming in his mind. Fortyish, slight build with fine thinning blond hair. Wears wire-frame glasses, has eager eyes that dart swiftly beneath a large forehead. His idea of a good dinner is a barbecued steak during the halftime interval on the Monday night football games. But with wine, not beer.

". . . These strategies should hold probabilities in the neighborhood of eighty-five to ninety percent if they are to be looked at as potentially successful programs. They must, as well, be practical, both in optional and economic terms.

"ORAL, like all such operations, provides the means to evaluate practically, weigh, cross-reference and integrate enormous vol-

196

umes of data on Iran—socio-economic, cultural, demographic, geopolitical, defense, intelligence—instantaneously. We know from experience that destabilization—by definition a euphemism for an engineered revolution—is far less costly, in both human and material terms, and with a higher success rate, than traditional military methods. The cost/benefit experience with systems such as ORAL..."

The voice of John Alexander Case interrupted. *"I think most of us are reasonably aware of the marvels of the computer age,"* he said brusquely. *"Perhaps we could proceed to the actual program."*

There was a moment's silence before Farrar continued. *"Based on our studies to date, any destabilization program for Iran must take into account the following critical factors: One: The 1973 oil price increases by OPEC led to Iranian oil revenues soaring from five billion dollars in fiscal 1973 to some nineteen billion dollars last year, fiscal 1974. Even with major new investments for military equipment, the economy is unable to absorb this income."*

Adel refined his Identikit impression of Farrar. White Brooks Brothers button-down shirt. Gold Mark Cross pen stuck in breast pocket. Regulation striped tie—synthetic. Gray Dacron-and-wool pin-striped suit. Pants at half-mast. Heavy brown wingtip shoes. Long sideburns.

"Two: Lacking the necessary infrastructure, the country's economic program has been a fiasco. It has ignited wave after wave of socio-cultural shock. The bottom line is rampant inflation and a severe overloading of all support systems—transportation, communication, housing and so forth.

"Three: Dramatic public aspirations, aroused by the Shah himself when he launched his so-called 'Great Civilization Program,' have now been severely disappointed. The result is total political disaffection.

"Four: The Shah himself is demoralized by the lack of progress. The Shah's realization that his 'Great Civilization' is a fantasy has induced bouts of severe depression in the man."

Farrar was full of new-found confidence. He was at ease as he ticked off causes for the effects which were being engineered.

"Five: The historical tension between the mullahs...uh...the *clergy...and the Shah's government is always a basis for open*

197

conflict. The Shah's undermining of clerical power through land reform, the secularization of education, marriage and divorce procedures and so on have posed an increasing threat to the mullah caste. Subsidies from the Shah and the CIA to keep them in line have only added to the resentment of radical elements among the priests.

"Six: Corruption is rampant throughout the society. A general decadence, a growing sense of cynicism and a feeling of helplessness to affect the destiny of Iran permeates the professional and technocrat levels who form the core of a small but ambitious middle class.

"Seven: The offshoot of this disaffection is a level of communist infiltration that is higher than has generally been admitted. Needless to say, the communists are tactically available to participate in the destabilization of the country, albeit for their own ends.

"In short, gentlemen, Iran is fertile for destabilization."

Adel was aware of a tenseness through his body. Every muscle was hard, every vein bulged. He recognized the feeling. It was fear—a different fear from what he had felt over the past few days. That was the fear of danger, of pain, of personal loss, but there had always been a chance. The enemy was a rabble, a zealous, cruel, vindictive rabble, but nevertheless unworldly, uneducated, untrained.

These people were different. They were psychopaths with machines and psychiatrists; they had analysts and strategists; they owned organizations and companies that spanned the world; they had tentacles with trained, professional killers. And time. All the time in the world.

Hell, he thought. This tape had been made four years ago, in 1975. It was a precise analysis of every weakness in the Shah's regime, pinpointing every pressure point.

They had probably gone through the same process with him, and there was only one conclusion they could have reached.

He knew too much.

CHAPTER
40

"Domestic are getting uptight, sir. They say we're cutting into their everyday security needs."

"Capelli!" hollered Bell as he stomped across the room. "I don't give a shit what domestic think. So it'll be a good day for pickpockets, so fucking what? We have clearance."

Cappelli and the older man with him followed in Bell's wake through the frenetic activity of the buzzing room. A cacophony of electric sounds seemed synchronized to the colored wall and panel lights that lit and dimmed amid the ringing of phones and clacking teleprinters. The eight screens on the walls, too, were now alive. Maps in varying scales lit the immaculately white walls as all of London became within the reach of a button and the glance of an eye.

Orange lights followed the path of every vehicle involved in the dragnet. The cold, wet route of every policeman on a beat was being flashed in yellow, while green indicated the scattered locations of eight helicopters ready to descend upon a given point. Red flashed every potential sighting that was reported; white indicated every informer at the disposal of British security: Underground ticket offices, planted train and bus station employees, airport officials, flower, vegetable and newspaper hawkers, pushers, hookers, ice cream vans, beggars, gas station attendants and hotel staff.

What the lights and screens did not indicate was the bank of telephone and teleprinter monitoring systems being employed on the floor above. Every C.B. channel legally allowed was being eavesdropped upon, even regular radio taxi, minicab and international call to the South of France was being followed.

199

And the operation was only just beginning. Within the hour the net would expand further, to include every bus driver, conductor, taxi driver, combing the streets of London. To call girls, cinemas, theaters and pubs as they opened. The superintendents of buildings and parks and rent-a-car outlets.

Bell reached the square wooden conference table and dropped the navy blue dossier on it.

"If domestic have a gripe," he said, staring at the man accompanying Capelli, "they should call their superiors."

He held his glare for a moment before turning back to Capelli. "What do you have for me?"

"McNulty has it," replied Capelli. He motioned to the man beside him without taking his eyes off Bell.

Bell looked at the man from Scotland Yard. "Well?"

"We have three late-closing nights in London each week," McNulty said in a Scottish brogue. "Each night pertains to a different..."

"Skip the commercial, McNulty," cut in Bell icily. "Wednesday. Night. That's all I'm interested in."

McNulty seemed flustered by Bell's American bluntness.

"All areas close at five-thirty P.M. except Knightsbridge and the King's Road. They close at seven P.M." The natural pink hue of his cheeks had darkened to red.

Bell bit his lower lip. "Every other area in London closes at five?"

"Yes."

Bell glanced at his watch and then back at the Scotsman. "In thirty-seven minutes."

McNulty nodded.

Abruptly, Bell reclined on the swivel chair and locked his fingers behind his head. His eyes gradually glossed over, and he bit his lower lip again.

"He hasn't had time," he murmured, and to no one in particular, swiveling toward the bank of twinkling electronic maps on the wall. "Those tapes are over two hours long. No matter how you figure it..."

He stopped and turned back to the two men.

"How long does it take for the streets to empty after closing time, McNulty?"

"It's an attrition process, I suppose. Presumably half an hour or

200

so should see a marked decline in the pedestrian flow."

Bell nodded and stabbed the air with his right index finger. "Let's start closing the net on the two late-closing areas at five," he commanded. "Capelli. I want everyone in Gleeson's group combing those two districts from five onwards. The domestic can cover the rest. And you," he said, turning to McNulty, "after five-thirty, reassign as many men as you can from the other areas to these two parts. Just keep skeleton groups operating in the areas you think appropriate. Assign five—no, make that ten—of your people to start calling every shop with the capability of recording tapes in those two neighborhoods. If he hasn't been in, tell them to call you if he does. Circulate his description: last seen wearing black pants, black leather windbreaker, white shirt, five-ten, one hundred seventy-five, black curly hair, everything. And make it formal. Use official language . . . call him a nut, dangerous, Jack the Ripper, whatever it is that turns you people on."

CHAPTER 41

HARRODS: 5:21 P.M.

In the claustrophobic cubicle at Harrods, the voice of James Farrar droned on.

"Based on ORAL's findings, the following preliminary program sets out the optimum strategy for controlled destabilization, regrouping and establishment of a new friendly and compliant governmental authority.

"One: The annual CIA subsidy to the mullahs—*an estimated four hundred forty million dollars a year initiated at our behest in 1953 to calm the growing unrest of the country at that time— must be halted forthwith. These CIA subsidies are now obviously counterproductive to the new goals.*

There had been widespread rumors of this in Iran. But Adel had always dismissed them as foolish, and paranoid.

"*Two: The strategy depends on an extensive roster of reliable Iranian nationals to carry through key tasks at all stages. It is a list of competent individuals with a prior record of assistance.*"

"*Have these people been approached?*" asked John Alexander Case.

"*No, sir. The timing is still vague. The operation hasn't received final authorization yet. Only the preliminary phases have been activated.*"

"*Very well. Please go ahead,*" said Case.

"*Two opposing views presently make up Iranian—indeed world—public opinion. One is the sympathetic view that the Shah's errors are natural and could be expected since he had so little with which to begin. Coupled with this is the belief that external pressures on him prevented wide success.*

"*The opposing view is that in the heady intoxication of power, the Shah has blown a unique opportunity for development and modernization by attempting too much, too soon, too corruptly.*

"*The propaganda process in the West will be adjusted to encourage the latter view.*

"*To undermine the support being given to the Shah in the West, SAVAK's record of ruthlessness and torture and total disregard of human rights must be given full exposure. In due course we hope to create an atmosphere in Western public opinion that will strongly discourage continued support for the Shah's regime. This is the core of the entire program; the Shah's confidence must be shattered, turning a basically indecisive man to impotence.*"

Farrar proceeded to outline the steps that would be taken in Iran itself. Iranian "friends" with important positions in the Shah's administration would encourage the Shah toward immensely ambitious development programs, which the country's infrastructure did not have the capacity to handle. The resulting chaos, corruption and discontent would be phenomenal. It was important to involve all—he stressed the "all"—the Imperial family in the corruption and payoffs. Public discontent over a period of two to three years would be brought to fever pitch, stoked by uncontrolled economic expansion.

Eventually, in order to extricate himself and buy back the people's loyalty, the Shah would be encouraged to embark on a political liberalization program. The press would be gradually unmuzzled, politicians allowed their views, a handful of political prisoners released.

"If matters proceed as we project, that's when the dam bursts and the regime begins to disintegrate."

And how right the bastard's "projections" had been, Adel thought.

"What's the catalyst to bring things to a head, Jim?" asked Case. *"We already got the Shah to castrate just about anyone with balls. What's left?"*

"We recommend a force used often in the old days, but one that has been dormant in more modern times. We recommend the use of religion. It is singularly the most effective force to mobilize and cement a revolution in Iran. The vehicle of religion lends itself well to other parts of the Middle East if and when it becomes necessary. Iran, Egypt, Saudi Arabia, Libya or wherever else Islam is a force. It really makes no difference. Once Islamic fundamentalism is born, it's unstoppable. Armed might is ineffectual when faced with aspiring martyrs."

"How about leadership?" asked David Thorncroft.

"In that context we sought the advice of our British counterparts who, due to their historical role in the fanatical Muslim Brotherhood and other secret religious sects of the Middle East and their widespread contacts with the clergy in Iran, are more finely tuned to Islam than us. They have concurred with our conclusion. The movement must be led by a fundamentalist theologian with the appropriate personality, eloquence and charisma."

"Do we have one?" Again Thorncroft.

"Yes, sir. The man we've selected is Ayatollah Ruhollah Khomeini."

CHAPTER 42

"Gleeson's unit is forty minutes into their sweep, sir," said Capelli, pointing to the wall. "Those two screens isolate the late-closing sectors. The right is Knightsbridge, the left King's Road."

Bell closed the dossier he had been contemplating and looked up, first at Capelli, then at the wall.

The scale of the maps, he noticed immediately, had tightened. Not only were the major arteries, streets and alleys pinpointed but now buildings, shops—even street stalls—were discernible. The flashing lights were closer and more numerous—so close in some cases they seemed like ever-changing, multi-colored clusters of space invaders in an electronic arcade machine. The pace of the lights had quickened too; but that, he knew, was an optical illusion; the areas the men and vehicles were covering were smaller, their concentric sweeps shorter, their beats more concise.

The clock read 5:42 P.M. There was still a little more time, but not a lot. Enough time had passed for Adel to have listened to, even duplicated, the tapes. He studied the dark areas of the maps, those that fell out of the range of the lights or between them. He studied the mass of Harrods and Harvey Nichols and considered the heavy flow of human traffic that circulated around them on the Brompton Road, Sloane Street, Sloane Square, Hans Crescent, Hans Road and up toward Beauchamp Place and the museums.

By now Adel knew, Bell was convinced. Whether he had duplicated the tapes or not was another matter and quite beside the point. Knowing was enough.

He pointed up to the unilluminated mass within the perimeters of Harrods. "Get some more domestics in! There's too much black up there."

CHAPTER
43

"You may recall the man," said Farrar. *"In 1963 he violently opposed the Shah's land reforms and enfranchisement of women. He orchestrated widespread protest riots which were mercilessly crushed by the Iranian army."*

He paused, seeming to shuffle papers.

"Mean-looking bastard," said Case. Farrar had obviously passed round some pictures.

"This guy's got class," Solomon piped in.

"I say, very Old Testament," muttered Sinclair.

"God verdamme," the Baron said.

"Tell me, Sol, could this be the Messiah you people have been waiting for?" asked David Thorncroft.

They all chuckled and after a brief interval, Farrar continued: *"He is a religious mystic, sir, whose only motivation outside Islamic law is limited to his personal vendetta with change in any form. He is a kind of surrealist, with a bizarre conviction in his holy mission as an ascetic spiritual leader. Like the Shah, he believes he is the instrument of God and therefore above error. He is also blessed by Allah with that most impressive of talents—to arouse the masses to the rage of jihad, or holy war."*

Adel rubbed his damp forehead in despair. Mariam was right. The skeptics, the cynics, had been right: Khomeini was a company man, and his support came from outside, from the same men who had once helped the Shah.

He felt cold as he recalled the old woman's words: "If you lift his beard you'll find 'Made in England' printed underneath."

But by now nothing surprised him anymore. The last hour had numbed him.

205

"Khomeini's simplicity and lack of any twentieth-century experience makes him enormously malleable. In essence, the last person the Ayatollah talks to is the person who forms the Ayatollah's attitudes.

"It is essential, therefore, that from today onward we keep him on a very, very tight leash. We have taken the necessary steps in this direction already; several of our people, both Iranian and otherwise, with a history of opposition to the Shah, have moved to his home in Iraq. Their instructions are to provide him with organization. They are busy setting up what we have called 'The Khomeini International.' It will be a terrorist network in association with the Libyans, Syrians, P.L.O., the fanatical Muslim Brotherhood and other groups, and will operate active cells within Iran."

So that's who they were, these Ghotbzadehs, Yazdis, Bani-Sadrs, who suddenly blossomed from nowhere.

"Khomeini himself, however, is only an instrument. And then on a short-term basis. Options for the long-term government of Iran have been, purposely, kept open. It is . . ."

Suddenly Adel knew he wasn't alone in the room. Slowly the sounds of the tape faded as he hardened his body into a weapon of defense.

He jerked sharply around on the stool to face the door. In the doorway, stood a tall, well-dressed, powerful-looking man. His eyes exuded the welcome of a smiling cobra.

CHAPTER
44

Directly across the street from Harrods, less than two hundred yards as the crow flies, Jane Bennett dropped her cushy pink bathrobe to the floor and stepped down into the sunken Jacuzzi of her Rutland Gate apartment. She tested the temperature of the water on the first step before committing herself. It was, she observed as she took the remaining four steps down, a philosophy life had taught her the hard way.

She sat on the mosaic seat at one end of the bath for a moment, and lit a cigarette. Then she lowered her slim body into the turbulent water until it was submerged completely—all, that is, but her head and right arm. That, like a periscope, she held up in the air, protected from the spray of the currents below.

She took a deep drag and held her breath for ten seconds before exhaling. Then she repeated the action twice more in quick succession, only now she submerged her head, held her breath and released her breath below the water. It was another habit she had acquired. Whether at the end of a long, arduous day of shooting or the start of a lengthy evening ahead, the marijuana, combined with the sensuous, gentle massage of the Jacuzzi, relaxed, refreshed and aroused her as the occasion demanded.

She lay back and savored another drag, opening her legs to allow the bubbles to caress her more intimate parts.

It was, she admitted as she gazed at the mirrored ceiling, the essence of self-indulgence; the zenith of what her success had really brought her. She dragged once again and panned the all-white bathroom with her eyes. What a shame, she thought, that her poor mother had not lived to see these days. She had witnessed only

207

her daughter's raw climb to success, never the mellow, contented days like today.

Joan Bennett recognized the start of a morbid trip and shunned it. She took one last drag before tossing the roach into an ashtray by the tub and submerging, twisting onto her belly as she went under. Even below the water she heard the trill of the telephone.

CHAPTER
45

HARRODS: 6:01 P.M.

The icy stare of the man held interminably. He stood unmoving in the doorway, his eyes challenging, ready to pounce. Then, slowly he unbuttoned his white trench coat, his eyes never leaving Adel's.

He was trapped. Bell had found him and he wasn't ready. Not yet. He hadn't had time; he had to insure himself. He had to escape.

"Who are you?" asked the man.

Adel played for time. He smiled at the man and slipped off the earphones. He picked up the heavy microphone and started unscrewing it from its base.

"I asked you a question, young man," said the man as he moved closer. "Who are you?" He placed his hands on his hips and glared down.

Adel curled his fingers around the disengaged microphone unit and gripped it tightly. He looked up at the man and prayed he would take one step closer.

"What are you doing here?"

Adel did not hear the rest. All his attention was focused on the small rectangular green badge in the man's lapel.

CHAPTER
46

"McNulty," said Bell as the tall, bespectacled Scotsman approached his desk, followed by Capelli. "See that up there?" He shouted against the electronic noises. But NcNulty's slow movements grated.

"Yes, sir," said McNulty, studying the two bleeping electronic maps on the wall.

"It seems to me there's a hunk of black up there. Does it look covered to you?"

McNulty studied the wall at length. "Nothing is ever quite airtight, sir," he said calmly. "The Yorkshire Ripper eluded apprehension through fifty different interrogations."

Bell tried to suppress his anger. "Terrific." He glanced at Capelli, then down at the desk. "This man is not the Yorkshire Ripper, McNulty," he said in a monotone. "We are not the CID and we have one shot at it." He looked straight at McNulty. "And we have less than an hour to do it in."

The Scotsman said nothing.

"There's hunks of black up there, McNulty," Bell said, "and I want them lit up. Like a Christmas tree I want them lit up, especially the two department stores, Harrods and Harvey Nichols."

CHAPTER
47

Adel waited for the buildup of tension and violence to ease from his body. Still gripping the microphone, he turned to look up at the imposing figure. And his green Harrods badge.

"What," he asked, trying to sound like a cocky British worker, "does it look like I'm doing? Mending the equipment, that's what I'm doing."

The man scrutinized him for a moment. Then he looked around the room full of boxes and components and electronic equipment. His gaze stopped at the unscrewed microphone in Adel's hand.

"Oh," he said, less assured. "Never seen you around here before. Where's Kevin?" He was flustered but not enough to admit it to a subordinate.

"Sick," Adel said confidently, reassembling the microphone to its base. He wanted desperately to sigh, a long deep sigh of relief.

"Oh. Poor chap. Nothing serious, I trust?"

"Nah."

"Good. Well, must run," the Harrods man said. He hung up his raincoat next to Adel's black leather jacket. "Cheerio."

Adel slumped on the stool, staring at the closed door. After a long moment he turned and slipped on the earphones. Immediately the sound of Farrar emerged. But now he was on to something else.

"*...which leads to the topic of the Shah himself,*" said Farrar over the sound of pages being turned.

"*Is this the psychograph?*" asked the baron.

"*Yes, sir, it's the nonspecific summary. A full psychographic study is a lengthy, intimately detailed analysis of a specific target's*

210

*personality and behaviorial traits. It is established usually at pro-
digious cost and effort, and is constantly updated. Each sector of
a target's makeup is examined to determine its influence on his or
her life. Areas such as childhood, traumas, fixations, sexual behavior, religious upbringing, influences, response to stress, defense
mechanisms, friends and so forth.*

"What I'm reading is a very general summary. If any further
information is required . . ."

"No," said the baron. "That won't be necessary."

"That's great," said Sol.

"The summary's fine," David agreed.

Farrar started up again. He seemed to be reading. "*Mohammed
Reza Pahlavi was a shy, sensitive boy, lacking self-confidence. He
was, even in his formative years, an uncertain, vacillating child. . . .*"

Adel listened to a perceptive discourse on the Shah's history and
personality, his shrewdness and intelligence, his indecision, weakness and sense of insecurity; his domination by a ramrod father
and a ruthless, domineering twin sister; his love-hate relationship
with the West—his awe of it and the paranoid anxiety it instilled
in him.

"*Domestically, the very same traits are apparent. His regime
has a veneer of democracy but it is a very thin film. Severe personal
instability leads to fear of opposition from any quarter. This in
turn preempts adoption of any Western institutions. Checks and
balances and diversification of power are concepts alien to him.
He tends only to promote and feel comfortable with individuals
whom he can dominate. He therefore surrounds himself with sy-
cophants and opportunists of little value in matters of state. They
manipulate his weak psychological architecture, doting on him while
plundering the country.*"

There followed an analysis of the Shah's three marriages, with
special emphasis on the artistic and cultural pretensions of his
present wife, the Empress Farah.

"*The Shah's extramarital life is extensive. These activities are
primarily relationships with* filles de plaisir, *to use the French term.
They are inevitably young, blond, buxom and of the wholesome
California variety. They are invariably imported and kept at considerable (by our standards, exorbitant) cost. These events are (we*

211

*are told) not always what they are made out to be. Insecurity,
shyness and lack of confidence drive Mohammed Reza to spend
these hours in pleasant conversation and chitchat over tea. The
consensus of opinion among his female companions is that he is
pleasant, well mannered, considerate, intelligent and very, very
lonely. He is not sexually prolific.*

"That, gentlemen, is Mohammed Reza Pahlavi, the Shah of Iran,"
concluded Farrar.

*"Did you say 'tea'?"*came David's fragile voice.

"Yes," replied Farrar. *"Tea."*

*"That in itself suggests an inefficient use of resources. The job's
wasted on him,"* said David Thorncroft.

There was a roar of laughter.

CHAPTER 48

THE MALL: 6:15 P.M.

Bell closed his eyes and lifted his feet from the table. McNulty
was not being difficult, he decided. Not intentionally, anyway. He
was just ponderous and British. Every proposed action was arduous, every idea impossible, every speed slow. He had just wasted
ten precious minutes on this klutz from Scotland Yard.

"McNulty," he said with controlled patience. "We are not talking
about our field assets; no one wants to increase the number of
operatives involved. We are talking about bringing a major portion
of these assets together, in one place, at one time. We are talking
about cordoning off one section of one area. A very small and
inconsequential area at that."

"Inconsequential!" cried McNulty in a high-pitched voice. "Inconsequential!" He shook his head. "That inconsequential area you
are talking about, colonel," he said, pointing at the black mass on

the map that showed Harrods, "has a four-and-a-half-acre ground plan that affords fourteen acres of selling space, eight and a half acres of stockrooms and backup services, eighty display windows, fifty elevators, twelve escalators and over thirty-five doors of one sort or another. It also has twenty-five thousand automatic sprinkler heads, and one hundred and ninety-seven hydrants, eight hundred and forty-one fire extinguishers, nine hundred and ninety automatic fire-resistant doors, two thousand two hundred and twenty-six heat sensors and one hundred and fourteen hose reels."

He paused, withdrew a pack of Senior Service cigarettes and lit one, holding on to the burning match. "Any one of which even an amateur, as you call him, would not have to tax his brain to create pandemonium with. All it would take is just a modicum of intelligence. Can you imagine, Colonel Bell, what chaos, panic, death and injury he could cause by merely using his initiative? One wrong move in that store and there'd be a string of questions to be answered."

He took a slow drag of his cigarette, shook the match and dropped it in the ashtray on Bell's desk. "There is just one other point you might want to consider, colonel," he said grandly. "The Queen of England shops there."

CHAPTER
49

HARRODS: 6:19 P.M.

"*Domestically—in the United States, that is—*" Adel heard Farrar clarify—"*the tide of opinion is turning against the Shah. Many of the nation's top corporations, once anxious to play ball with Iran, have become disenchanted by the Shah's grandiloquence. The military and intelligence communities are concerned about an excessive reliance on one man....*"

Case's resonant voice interrupted. "*Yes, and the Shah's fortu-*

*nately managing to alienate a wide variety of other powerful in-
terest groups too. The human rights advocates, the nuclear
proliferation lobby, the oil price control lobby, the arms control
lobby, the anti-Israel lobby, the pro-Arab lobby, the Left, the
Democratic Party and the liberals, particularly the Kennedys—
they'd all be quite happy to see the Shah go."*

CHAPTER
50

6:19 P.M.

McNulty had a point, thought Bell, glancing at his watch.

"Besides, Colonel Bell," continued the man from Scotland Yard,
under the circumstances, it seems unnecesary to cordon off the
entire store; perhaps a handful of people would put your mind at
rest. After all, the manager of the radio and television department
had been contacted and he clearly insisted that Harrods does not
provide such a service. Certainly not at the speed we are talking
about."

CHAPTER
51

HARRODS: 6:22 P.M.

*"The pro-Shah element in the West—particularly the United
States—must be held in check. Many of the grandees of the Re-
publican Party, various Rockefellers, the Annenbergs, the Scran-*

214

tons, have established close personal relations with the Shah. The axis of mutual flattery between Teheran and midtown Manhattan is a powerful one. Doctor Kissinger of course lends it much respectability.

"Timing is critical. The influence of these people must be kept dormant at least until the operation has reached an irreversible stage. At a point when it is, essentially, too late for them to stop it or oppose it, or indeed, even expose it. They must be . . ."

David Thorncroft intervened. *"I don't think it's necessary to dwell on how to handle what you call the pro-Shah element."*

"I'm sorry, sir. I only meant to—"

"Yes, yes. Please proceed."

The door of the studio crashed open and the salesman appeared, gesturing nervously.

Adel withdrew the earphones and stopped the tape.

"Listen, mate, you'd better get out of here. The manager is asking about you."

Adel's mind raced. Of course. Bell would know. And out there on the streets Bell would have an army looking for him.

He glanced at the progress of the tape. It was almost finished. Five minutes, maybe ten, were left. And he needed the copies to be complete.

He rubbed his shirt to soak up the sweat and looked up at the flustered salesman.

"Five minutes," he said. "I'll be out in five minutes." He pressed the start button. As he placed the earphones back on he heard the panicky voice of the retreating salesman.

"That's . . . that's fine with me but . . . but . . . I'm leaving and I'll deny any involvement."

"The man we've chosen to coordinate this entire program—for many reasons—is Colonel Grover Cleveland Bell."

Adel felt queasy; his stomach churned as he recalled his conversation with Case; his stomach churned. He lit a cigarette and inhaled to fight the unsettled feeling in his stomach the salesman and the mention of Bell's name had created.

CHAPTER 52

The rain, the incessant rain of London, had started up again but so far it was a light shower that added a sparkle to the sidewalks, a slight blur to the lighting of the elegant shops.

Jim Gleeson scoured the pavement as the unmarked police car crawled past Sloane Street on to the Brompton Road. To his right was the baroque red brick and sandstone building that housed Scotch House. To his left, one fashionable boutique after another: Lucy's, Fiorucci, Yves Saint-Laurent, Charles Jourdan. Each packed with a cosmopolitan assortment of customers.

The rain, he observed as his eyes registered the red, blue and silver fox furs, the Blackgamma mink, the Burberry raincoats and umbrellas that flashed by, was a godsend. The faster pace of pedestrians seeking to escape the approaching downpour served to isolate the least unhurried movement—those undaunted by the rain as well as the handicapped. The movements of the arthritic, the elderly, even the slightest limp, had all become easily discernible.

"Gleeson." It was Bell's voice over the unmarked police car radio. It cut through the communications between the countless vehicles, walkie-talkies, police stations and Capelli and McNulty in the Sit Room.

Gleeson grabbed the microphone and pressed the button.

"Yes, Grove."

"Where are you?"

Gleeson looked out of the rain-speckled window of the car. "On the Brompton Road. Just outside Mappin and Webb."

"How far is that from Harrods?"

216

The CID officer driving the car pointed to the glittering department store looming up ahead.

"Fifty yards."

"Great. Go to door number five. That's in Hans Crescent. There's four of you in the car and another four men are waiting at the door. Check it out, Jim. The manager responds negative. But let's check it out ourselves."

"Sure, Grove." He turned to the driver and waved a hand. "You heard the man." He did not mention that never, not in twenty years of working for him, had he heard Grover Cleveland Bell sound so urgent. Or so worried.

CHAPTER 53

HARRODS: 6:30 P.M.

"The overriding issue that influenced our selection of Colonel Grover Cleveland Bell," said Farrar, *"is our inability to count, as in the past, on formal government support.*

"Colonel Bell's background in this area goes back twenty-five years—from the birth of the CIA and before. He's occupied pivotal positions within the intelligence community: OSS agent, planner, plotter, spymaker, military intelligence, Vietnam and, of course, finally, the coordination of the entire covert activities of the nation. Recently Bell's had more than his fair share of problems with a mistrusting president and the growing public disenchantment with the operational side of intelligence activities. Unfortunately for him, but fortunately for our purposes, he has become one of the victims of Watergate."

Adel looked at his watch.

"...intricately aware of the workings of government in London, Paris, Teheran..."

217

A minute had passed since the salesman had left the cubicle. Adel glanced at the revolving tape. There was very little left. A minute. Maybe two.

CHAPTER 54

The Rover 2600 pulled up with a screech at door number five of Harrods department store. The driver disregarded the turning heads and made no effort to park economically. He stopped at an angle, the car's tail jutting into the driving lane, its nose angling into a space barely wide enough to accommodate its width. A few yards ahead, another empty, unmarked Rover rested, half on, half off the pavement. It too stuck out and from its exhaust the vapor fumes of an idling engine confronted the damp, cold night air.

Beneath the door's wrought iron and glass awning, four burly men in varying shades of off-white trenchcoats stood waiting, blocking the movements of the heavy pedestrian traffic. As the car stopped they turned to latch on to the four alighting passengers and with barely a nod of recognition the eight men moved through the swinging doors into the massive complex. No one acknowledged the disapproving expression of the uniformed doorman. His warning about parking tickets went unheeded.

They moved quickly and silently through the crowds to the base of the escalators.

"Let's spread out," said Gleeson. He turned to his domestic counterpart, the man who had shared his car for the past five hours. "How do we cover this place, Henry?"

Henry Pearce did not hesitate. "The radio and TV department is on the second floor. And the subject has a gammy leg, so presumably his natural inclination will be to use either the escalators or the elevators. If we scatter and join upstairs we can cover eight

218

of the possibilities at his disposal. That's the best we can do, I'm afraid."

"How long do we have?" asked Gleeson.

Pearce looked at his watch. "It's twenty-seven to seven. Twenty-seven minutes."

"Fine," Gleeson said. "I'll take these escalators. You guys separate and peel off."

CHAPTER 55

HARRODS: 6:31 P.M.

The last two minutes of the tape seemed to go on for an eternity. On and on they went, grinding out compliments to Bell's organizational skills, his knowledge of the Iranian political scene, his power base in Washington, his hold on the capital's power brokers. His competence was compared to James Angleton, Richard Helms, William Colby.

"*He can, shall we say, persuade the reticent,*" was how Case put it when referring to Bell's notorious files on congressmen, senators, senior bureaucrats and lobbyists.

"*And thirdly . . .*" Case paused.

Adel again looked at his watch. But he was yanked back by the words that followed:

"*He's frankly the toughest son of a bitch any of us is ever likely to come across. He has a healthy element of the brute in him which could be useful in the more delicate moments of this operation. Please continue, Mister Farrar.*"

"*Ahh . . . yes, sir. To break down the Iranian security and armed*

219

*forces, we have elicited the assistance of the top man the army has
assigned to Iran—the deputy chief of European . . ."*

Abruptly, the steely voice vanished. The tape had ended.

Adel hit the stop buttons and leaned forward on his stool. He
closed his eyes and levered his right arm up to massage his throbbing forehead.

He was exhausted, lonely and frightened; there seemed to be
no hope, no point to it all. No point in running: sooner or later
they'd catch up with him.

He opened his eyes and despondently pressed the eject button
on the four machines. Out there they were looking for him. An
army of them. Trained men, equipped, armed and well rested
men. And what did he have going for him? he asked as he wearily
gathered the tapes.

He looked at the two dirt-stained original Sony tapes, then at
the six brand new plastic boxes with three complete copies. They
were his only hope. Somehow he had to find a way to insure himself.
He had to find someone Bell hadn't covered.

Before he could do that, though, he had to get out of here. He
had to slip through the cordon that was around the brightly lit
streets of Knightsbridge.

He walked toward the coatrack and reached for his jacket.
Abruptly, he pulled back. That's what they were looking for. A
man with a limp. A man with a black leather jacket, black slacks,
white shirt. It wasn't much in the way of deception or camouflage,
he thought, as he grabbed the white trenchcoat the Harrods man
had hung next to his jacket, but it was better than nothing. He
stuffed the tapes into its deep pocket, then put on the coat. It was
too long and baggy—perfect. He looked heavier and shorter.

There was just a chance, he thought as his heart beat picked
up. The streets were crowded. He had to get out of there before
they emptied. His watch read six thirty-six. Twenty-four minutes
before the shops closed.

He scanned the room for a pair of scissors, a razor blade, anything
sharp.

His luck was holding. He found a tape editing device and quickly
extracted the blade it held. Crudely he set to the cast, surprised
at the sharpness of the blade, pulling and tearing at the cast as he
cut. With three strokes he cut a slit through the plaster above the
knee, then ripped it an inch or two further with his hands. Now

there would be no limp; the knee could bend. It was stiff. It was painful. But it could bend.

He opened the door and looked up and down the corridor.

He felt the flow of adrenaline as he walked down the corridor and stepped into the crowded radio and television showroom. He scrutinized the room briefly, then glided across the floor, absorbing the pain but camouflaging it and hiding the stiffness in the knee that made it so hard to bend. He walked determinedly toward the far end of the room to the elevators next to the pet shop.

He hesitated at the elevator doors, then moved to the stairs directly behind. They were safer. With a cast the odds were against a man using stairs. The elevator doors he had shunned opened twenty seconds later. Henry Pearce stepped through them to greet Jim Gleeson as he walked into the lobby that separated the pet shop and the radio and television department. Neither man glanced at the stocky figure stiffly descending the stairs to their right.

CHAPTER 56

QUM, IRAN: WEDNESDAY NIGHT, OCTOBER 31, 1979

Ayatollah Sadegh Khalkhali watched as the old man shuffle-stepped down from the rooftop balcony in his white *gieveh* slippers, his arms held by a coterie of disciples.

Outside, the feverish crowd attending one of the Imam's rare *namaz* ceremonies numbered close to a hundred thousand and its impassioned roar shook the windows.

"*Allah Akbar, Marg bar Cart-er, Marg bar Shah, Marg bar Amrika* (Death to Carter, Death to the Shah, Death to America)," it chanted over and over.

It had been eight months since the victorious Imam had returned to Iran and still the crowds in Qum grew in intensity and number as they came to worship the Twelfth Saint in this holy city.

He was walking majestically down the hall now; immediately to his right was his son Ahmad and, to his left, the bespectacled foreign minister, Ibrahim Yazdi. Behind followed Sadegh Ghotbzadeh, a tall, stout man with thinning hair, a bulbous nose and what his detractors described as a constant inane grin.

Khalkhali was honored to be among such leaders. As he watched the entourage move down the hallway of the school building toward him, he was genuinely glad and spiritually uplifted to see them. It had been nearly two weeks since he had had the pleasure; and a fortnight was a long time where men of such caliber were concerned. Yes, he thought, he missed sitting and deliberating with them in this simple school building that had become the nerve center of the world.

And then, of course, there was the Imam himself. It had been such a long wait but now, Allah be praised, it was over. The Twelfth Imam, the savior sent by God to stop corruption on earth and crimes committed against Him, had arrived.

He took a deep breath and bent his head low in respect; Imam Khomeini was passing directly in front of him.

CHAPTER 57

LONDON: WEDNESDAY, OCTOBER 31: 6:43 P.M.

It was precisely seventeen minutes to seven when Michael Adel stepped out of Harrods and felt the lash of heavy rain. Instinctively he flowed to the center of the fast-moving sidewalk traffic and let it bump and carry him toward Hans Crescent.

Hyde Park, he thought, careful to conceal himself in the crowd of shoppers. He had to get to Hyde Park; the most ludicrous place in the world in this storm, but there was no other choice. His brain ticked furiously, trying to come up with a more hospitable hiding place.

He waited at the zebra crossing, his eyes scanning yet uncertain about what they sought. A crawling car, a lingering gaze, behind, in front. It could come from anywhere. A private army.

He shuddered as he saw two policemen turn and wait at the opposite side of the zebra crossing. Had Bell co-opted the police too?

The lights changed and Adel check stepped to let a wall of pedestrians precede him. Then he started across the Brompton Road, his eyes trained on the two uniformed men across the road.

He had to get to the safety of darkness. Somewhere no one existed. He had to think.

The policemen started crossing the street toward him and instinctively he added a bounce to his walk. It was excruciating but necessary. They went by without a glance.

He turned left on the other side of the road, then hard right into the darkness of Lancelot Place. It was two hundred yards to the safety of the park. Oblivious to the pouring rain, he dodged the traffic on Kensington Gore and entered Hyde Park.

What chance did he have? What chance did anyone have? And what did it matter anyway? Life and death and poverty and wealth. It was all a game. A chess game played by remote control; only the pieces were live.

In Iran thousands had died in the streets. Thousands more had been made homeless. A revolution had been promoted from afar, for profit and gain, armed with a new Catch 22: *Crimes against God and his emissaries.*

Millions had been whipped up to religious fervor by slick propaganda. Disinformation, they called it. The innocent, ignorant masses had been disinformed in the name of God.

But the reality was different. Full control over the world's energy and energy prices—that's what it came down to. Lower prices could not be tolerated. At least not for now. Not until they had cornered and consolidated a monopoly of the alternative source of energy.

In any case it was the Shah who had forced their hand; that ungrateful army sergeant's son had overstepped the boundary. Khomeini too was merely another pawn. Like the Shah, he was expendable. Another would soon follow. And another, until the wells dried. Until the wind and sea and sun had been harnessed. For the time being, however, he would do; a new Shah, only this time masquerading in religious garb. Devoid of the trappings of grandeur and anxious to please. And like a puppet, grateful for his elevation and eager to stay.

Same shit, different color, thought Adel as he snapped back to reality. He looked at his watch; he had been walking aimlessly for over two hours in the pouring rain. He had walked the park in a daze, oblivious to the dull ache in his leg.

Through the darkening twilight, the mist of rain, he recognized the Serpentine, Hyde Park's twisting artificial lake, a hundred yards off, surrounded by a forest of trees to his right.

He looked around again at the stillness, the beauty, and felt an overpowering isolation.

He needed warmth, human warmth and loving. And a little care. He had had enough of this alien world of violence and pain. He craved Sam. To talk to her and hear her innocent chatter. To feel her arms around him, protecting him from loneliness and fear. But that was a dream. It could not be.

He started walking again, limping southward toward Knightsbridge. Through the mist a children's playground loomed up ahead and Adel hobbled toward it. He sat, gently rocking on a swing as the rain subsided to a drizzle. Thinking, analyzing, weighing his options. None seemed attractive. The more he considered his position, the more restricted it looked. His only hope was an unstable one—erratic and unpredictable.

"Insure yourself. Always insure yourself," the Israeli agent had said over and over, repeating himself every hour for three days. Had the Israeli agent tried to warn him? Or was it just his mind playing tricks on him? Somehow he had to convince Bell that there was more to lose from his death than from his life. But how?

Who else, other than Jane, was there close enough to trust; close enough to risk involvement, yet too distant in the past to be linked to him, too fleeting an encounter in his life for Bell to have a record of? Someone more dependable than dear, loyal, temperamental Jane?

Sure, he would act in character; he would go to the people Bell expected him to go to; his brother Mark and his banker in Switzerland, Claude Boissy. But he would have to do more. To survive his insurance would have to be foolproof.

But who? Who else was there that he could depend on? Who else was there who was unknown even to his family and closest friends?

224

He selected, then rejected, one by one, friends and even casual acquaintances. The truth was that Bell would have gone through the same process. Except he would have done it with machines. In his computer file they would all be noted, like every detail of his life. As for his acquaintances, there was no reason why they should be loyal to him—except for money, and money generated greed which led to blackmail. Out of the question.

No, it would have to be Jane. Their relationship had been too distant, too fleeting, too anonymous to be remembered. He forced himself to concentrate. To remember the details of their relationship, to see if anything of substance had occurred to become an asterisk in his life. To be accessible to Bell.

He had met Jane Bennett a long time ago, twelve years. She had been a high-flying Paris model on the brink of fame when they had met by chance at a private party thrown by a mutual friend at Regine's. They had clicked immediately, mentally and physically. For two mad fun-filled, secret weeks they had spent sleepless nights, laughing and screwing; crazy days combing the *marché aux puces;* and weekends at a rented cottage near Deauville. They had had a ball, and the relationship had been spiced by the fact that Jane was married. It had been a whirl of two carefree spirits.

After an emotional parting marked by unkept promises, Adel had gone on to his work in Iran and she to the first of her many divorces and to a liaison with a famous English actor who fell insanely in love with her. Pouring money into film after film, he had pushed and shoved her to stardom.

But scandal after scandal erupted into headlines as the actor's jealous rages led to public tantrums; he had beaten and imprisoned her. Their careers demanded long separations for location filming and naturally the press had fanned the flames. After a year of marriage Jane's third husband suffered a heart attack that nearly killed him.

Finally, depressed and defeated, she had divorced. Like many beautiful women from humble backgrounds, Jane Bennett had chosen to fly too high, too fast. And she had paid her dues.

Adel saw her once after that, recovering from an attempted suicide at the American Hospital in Paris. Physically she had been unaffected; she was still as beautiful as ever. Maturer, with the thinnest of age lines around her eyes but still wholesomely beautiful. Inside, though, she was crushed. Appallingly broken and with little will or inclination to recover. She had had enough of her life.

"If this is what success brings," she had whispered sadly, "imagine, Michael, what failure offers."

He shuddered as he recalled that sleepless night in Teheran: What would happen to Samira? What fate awaited her if he died? Would she choose her man more carefully than Jane? Would she be more blessed? And Natalie?

He shook off his worries, forced himself to concentrate on now, on staying alive.

For the last few years Jane Bennett had dropped out of his life. At the hospital she had sensed his love for Samira and accepted it gracefully. Ever since, their once their secret affair had withered away completely.

Yes, she would do very well. She was safer than Mark or Claude Boissy. They were known quantities, marked men; traceable and controllable, and sooner or later Bell would get to them. But with Jane it was different, he thought as he stood up from the swing. During their brief time together, she had insisted on the most extreme secrecy to protect herself from her husband. There were no records of their affair. No telltale letters. No phone numbers. No pictures.

There was a chance.

As he hobbled toward the wrought-iron mass of Rutland Gate a terrifying thought struck him. What if he was wrong? What if Bell had her in his files too? And under scrutiny.

CHAPTER 58

QUM: WEDNESDAY, OCTOBER 31: 1:30 P.M.

"Have there been any new developments, ayatollah?" asked Imam Khomeini after Khalkhali had settled beside him on the floor of the spartan reception room he used for his audiences. The Imam's face was expressionless; his beard formed a halo of white around baleful eyes that stared at the floor in front of his crossed legs. In spite of the hour the Imam looked majestic. An immaculate black cape covered his daunting figure and his black turban was carefully angled to hide a receding forehead.

Khalkhali bent his head respectfully. "Yes, Hazrat Imam. Lamentably it is worse than we imagined. Far worse. An old woman was buried in a shallow grave in the grounds of the Adel house, her mutilated body barely cold. Two other corpses were found thrown in a well. They too were viciously murdered."

"Who were they?" asked Khomeini, his voice passionless, barely audible.

"They were American Embassy officials, Holy One. Their identification showed they were Americans and this was confirmed by their embassy. But it is a matter of some mystery. Everything points to an alliance between this animal, Adel, and the Americans and yet there are two dead Americans in his house. There is no doubt a simple explanation, but time has been short and we wish to be very careful in our investigation."

Khomeini sat motionless, his face without expression. Khalkhali was not concerned by the Imam's cold bearing; he had come to expect it. The Imam was always calm. Even when his infant daughter had died, thirty years ago, the Imam had shown no weakness. Khalkhali had looked into the Imam's eyes that day, knowing how he adored the child, but neither sorrow nor hurt nor longing had marred the saint's bearing. His strength on that occasion had been almost unnatural.

"He who gave the child has now recalled her," Khomeini had said as he knelt to pray. Those were the only words he uttered on the death of his beloved youngest daughter.

He wore the same expression now—calm, passionless, serene.

"But we found no tapes, Holy One," Khalkhali went on. "We searched the house from top to bottom and there is no sign of them."

Khomeini's frail hands shook as he reached for the plate of goat cheese and mint leaves. "Was anything else revealed in your labors?" His voice was low and gravelly.

This was the moment Khalkhali had been waiting for, the moment to capture the Imam's attention and arouse his interest, the moment he would recapture his own power.

"Yes, sir," he responded, looking into the Imam's eyes sincerely.

"The car we found in a nearby alley has been positively identified as an American Embassy vehicle. No one came to claim it so we approached their embassy. The officials there professed ignorance as to why the car was in Farmanieh."

Khomeini nodded and Khalkhali continued. "The equipment Adel used was scattered in various hiding places on the grounds. We also have definite proof now that he was the man who entered the *komiteh* building through the underground *qanat* between the two buildings."

Still there was no reaction from the Imam.

"Everything we've found suggests that he has been generously assisted by the Americans. Many, many things suggest that, Holy One," Khalkhali lied.

To obtain full authority to handle this affair his way, without interference from that fool, Prime Minister Bazargan, it was imperative to arouse the Imam; and the only way to do that was to link Adel directly to the Americans. Khalkhali was confident, as he wove fact and fiction, that no one could dispute him. He alone had interviewed Salim on his deathbed.

"The Palestinian, Salim, was a dying man, weak and mumbling, but he was very clear on this point. He said Adel told him that the tapes were to be delivered to the American Embassy. Surely it is safe to assume Adel made that delivery after his escape. And if so, the tapes are still there—in the embassy's compound. We moved very quickly, Holy One. The Americans did not have time to dispatch them out of the country. No diplomatic pouches have left Teheran since this incident."

Khomeini raised his bushy black eyebrows. It was the first sign of emotion he had shown. He leaned forward, and Khalkhali bent closer.

"Why would Adel want to kill the two Americans, then?" the Imam whispered.

Khalkhali answered cautiously. The old man was shrewd. He instinctively spotted weak links in the arguments of his associates. And he was a highly suspicious man, too.

"That is a more difficult question to answer without first interrogating Adel, your eminence. The scientists believe that the evidence points a finger directly at Adel. They say the bullets that killed the two Americans are of the same variety as those used in the assault on the *komiteh* building."

"Is that unusual?"

"The experts claim it is, Holy One. They say the bullets are special ones, designed expressly for assassins. They travel faster than the normal variety and, what is more worrying, such bullets do not exist in Iran."

Khomeini lifted his eyes from the silk Kashan carpet and nodded. "But that does not explain why Adel would want to kill his American employers."

"Perhaps there was some sort of falling out among them, your eminence."

"Perhaps," said Khomeini doubtfully.

"We will not know the answer for sure until we interrogate Adel, Holy One. And that, *insh'Allah*, is only a question of time. We've clamped down on every exit from the city: the roads, the trains, the airports. Every vehicle, pedestrian, even mule, is being searched with a microscope. I've also instructed the opening of diplomatic pouches of every embassy in case the Americans should try to use one of their surrogates to export the tapes. The only country not to comply with my instructions are the Russians, and they withdrew their pouch; they did not..."

Khomeini's whisper interrupted him. "Adel is unimportant."

Khalkhali was surprised; he shifted his rump to the other cheek on the hard floor.

"But the tapes. That is another matter. They are very helpful."

Khalkhali made no attempt to mask his puzzled expression.

CHAPTER 59

LONDON: WEDNESDAY, OCTOBER 31: 9:00 P.M.

The front door of the flat opened in answer to his ring and her eyes glistened with delight at the sight of him. Adel slumped against the wall.

"Michael!" Jane Bennett shrieked, her face lighting up further as she grabbed and hugged him.

"Hello, Jane." He placed an arm tentatively around her and peered into the flat beyond, instinctively continuing the cautious approach that had included an efficient surveillance of her building before entering.

She pressed him close. "It's so lovely to see you," she said in his ear.

Adel stepped away from her embrace. "I did call to give you warning."

"And what a terrible line. Where were you ringing from?"

"A long way away."

"Come in. Come in," she said, pulling his arm.

Adel was eager to respond. He needed warmth. He needed friendship. And she looked stunning.

"My God, Michael!" she exclaimed as he limped in. "You look terrible. What's wrong with you?"

Adel negotiated the three steps up to the sitting room.

"That's exactly how I feel." He pointed to the damp patch on her dress and said lightly, "You should watch who you hug these days."

"What happened to you? What's wrong with your leg?" She glanced down at the stains on her red silk dress.

"If you don't give me a towel, the whole place will look like that."

She looked at the water dripping onto the thick white carpet and pushed him into a corner of the room.

"God, you're a mess. Just stand still."

She began removing his clothes, pushing away his shaking hands.

"You need a bath. That's the first thing. Then some food. A good hot bowl of soup is the best thing for you."

She gave him a luxurious soft towel robe. "Regular mother," he muttered, as she left the room again. He felt relieved; the tension was subsiding.

Within minutes she was back. "The soup's on the stove," she smiled.

"Great."

She bent down and kissed him lightly on the lips.

This was the difficult part, thought Adel. Her crush had never completely died; it was he who had always discouraged and resisted

230

it. But tonight that was going to be difficult to do; tonight it would be impossible.

"I need a joint," he said, knowing, unless things had changed radically, she kept a stock of therapeutic goodies.

She smiled, walked to the cabinet and withdrew a cherrywood humidor. "What's wrong, Michael? Why are you in such a state?" She offered him the box.

He took two joints and looked up at her. "First the bath."

He inhaled on a potent stick of high-quality Acapulco Gold as he soaked in the bathtub. A warm, relaxing sensation suffused his body. His mind was both sharp and befuddled as he gazed at the water in the tub. Was the water hot or cold? He splashed his face and the scent of the jasmine bath salts from Floris filled his nostrils. Flashes of reality flickered across his mind. He saw Mariam's wrinkled face as he buried her, interposed with Khomeini's diabolic eyes. "Made in England" printed under his beard, Mariam had said. How she had chuckled. The water was too hot and he turned it to cold. It felt better and he rested his torn cast on the stool more easily. He could feel his body unwind, his mind turn away— from the horrors of reality—if only for a moment. Slowly he sank into oblivion.

He awoke suddenly. The touch of Jane's caressing hands had startled him. A tray sat across the tub.

"Thanks," he slurred, dazed but hungry.

She pulled up an egg-shaped plastic stool and sat close to him. "I won't insist you tell me what happened—that beaten look, the broken leg, walking about like a madman in the rain. Of course, if you want to tell me, I'll listen."

He spoke between spoonfuls of ham and pea soup. "You're an absolute wonder. You're worth a hundred shrinks."

"Well?"

"Well what?"

"Well, are you going to tell me what happened or not?"

He closed his eyes and dropped the spoon into the bowl. He was tired and it was far more than an explanation he would have to give her. It was a trap he had to lay. A noose tied tightly around her neck.

"Not tonight, Jane. I'm tired and...Maybe tomorrow," he said as he clumsily grabbed for the edge of the tub.

231

She smiled and gently clasped his penis.

"We'll see," she said, tugging it gently.

They laughed as she helped dry him and then led him into the bedroom. She stripped the gold-patterned chintz bedcover to reveal black satin sheets.

Adel fondled the shiny material. "What the hell is this?"

She looked at him with surprise. "What's wrong with it?"

"Nothing. I've just never been seduced in a coffin before."

Tomorrow he might regret this brief interlude of warmth and loving. But what the hell, how many tomorrows were there?

They made love without inhibitions. At first he was passive, memories flashing, intruding, keeping him tense. But time had neither doused nor reduced the burning sexual attraction they had once enjoyed.

She went down on him, slowly at first—licking, nibbling, teasing—and gradually he loosened up, transforming his pent-up remorse and anger to energy. Her tongue darted everywhere, building his desire, increasing his need and at the same time arousing her own body. He lay back, savoring the flickering massage on his nerve endings and letting her build to a frenzy.

But his needs were more than animal. He needed loving and warmth and nearness. He brought her head up and kissed her. It was a long passionate embrace, and they held it as they rolled over in the king-sized bed, the soft, slinky satin sheets caressing their skin, lubricating the sensuality of the moment.

Abruptly he entered her. At first she relished the moment, clinging to it and making it last. Then slowly she let it slip. She slid down on him gently, her face an open book of delight. Just as suddenly her mood and needs changed. Like a savage mare, she started bucking wildly as she closed her eyes and bit her lower lip, digging her nails into his shoulders. As she gradually increased her ferocity, Adel forced himself to hold back—to wait—until finally she gasped and cried out again and again. Only then did he arch upwards and let the juices flow from his body.

CHAPTER
60

"Ah, but the Occidental mind is simple," sighed Ayatollah Khomeini, a contemplative smile on his face. He reached for the *tasbih*, worry beads, that lay on a side table beside the old-fashioned telephone, and his fingers toyed with the one hundred green *jovain* beads, moving them one at a time, first in one direction, then back again. The movement was as slow and deliberate as the words he uttered.

"They have a marvelous ability to judge everything by their own false standards. They have never had the flexibility of thought to adapt to the subtle nuances of Islam. Some have done better than others... the English, the French. But the Americans, they do not comprehend the beauty and joy of Islam; they see it as a religion not unlike their own."

The old man seemed suddenly tired. Tired and saddened by the unwillingness of some to heed his warnings.

"Islam is not a religion; it is an all-emcompassing way of life. It is not an empty slogan like Christianity. It is a rigid, serious way of life and since it is the government of God, it must adhere to the principles He has clearly outlined in the Good Book. We do not need man-made laws and punishments, we have no use for Western playthings.

"But," Khomeini sighed deeply, "they cannot comprehend us. And I am the representative of that which they cannot understand. It suits them better to think of me as some sort of prime minister, or president, or pope—anything that fits their own simple understanding. They refuse to believe the divine destiny with which I

233

have been charged. They cannot comprehend that my government is Allah's government and that it is the first lawful government on earth in twelve hundred years."

Khomeini's right hand brushed and stroked his bushy white beard. He sighed deeply. "They compare me to the Shah," he said, with a scornful chuckle. "But they are wrong, Aghayeh Khalkhali, and do you know why?"

Khalkhali knew the Imam was not seeking an answer; he remained silent.

"The human soul, my son, is complex. It cannot be satisfied simply. It needs profound nurture. The Western culture creates an atmosphere of dark despair in which avarice is its color and greed its shape. Their people are mentally and emotionally deprived. They spend their lives subsidizing this esthetic void by amassing great fortunes: large houses, expensive cars, colored stones, airplanes and boats and silk apparel. They do this to give their empty soulless lives meaning because that is what they have been brainwashed to believe—*programmed* is the term, I think. Success, they are taught, is material wealth and hedonistic pleasures.

"The germ of greed once planted, my son, is difficult to remove." The old man raised his eyebrows, his gaze fixed on Khalkhali. "But they never achieve happiness, because the path they embark upon, encouraged and indoctrinated century after century by their corrupt governments, in partnership with their misguided churches, is wayward and devoid of meaning.

"They are not blessed with the way of Allah. Instead of meditating and looking inward, like stubborn rams they butt their heads against the wall of material wealth in search of a security and happiness that cannot be found on this earth."

Khalkhali was puzzled at the Imam's speech. What had this to do with Adel and the tapes? He listened intently to catch every word.

"And so, of course, they are awed by death. They are in terror of it. The state where aches and pains disappear, where troubles evaporate, where the comfort of total luxury and the warmth of constant security and relief from labor mesh together with unlimited meditation and rest to form true happiness. The state of communion with God."

He shook his head and smiled. "*Halah man-ra tahdid mikonan.* Now they threaten me with death, my friend; they seek to frighten

234

an eighty-year-old priest with martyrdom." The smile turned to laughter and his chest bounced with joy. "I who value death above all else.

"They are children, are they not?" he asked rhetorically, as the laughter subsided and he reclined on a large silk pillow.

Khalkhali sat waiting; the Imam had not finished.

"My son, we worked together recently, the Western world and I. It was a marriage of convenience; we needed each other to remove the cancerous regime of the Shah."

Khalkhali listened intently as the old man outlined how he had allowed the Americans, as they thought, to manipulate him. How he had permitted Ayatollah Beheshti to play along with them in the negotiations—conceding point after point on the post-revolution power structure of Iran, its government, intelligence organizations and armed forces.

"Now they want to blackmail me with exposure of this past relationship, believing my people will be disappointed to learn of my association with the West in defeating the Shah. Of course, Allah forewarned me; I knew such a day would come. It is something I, with the help of Allah, have prepared for."

"*Allah Akbar,*" said Khalkhali.

"Six months ago in France that creature of corruption, Ali Mahmoudi, passed word to me that he had information on tapes secreted somewhere in Iran which recorded the relationship between the Americans and us. He seemed to have stolen it from the Americans in some fashion. That despicable wart on God's earth desired to sell us these tapes. Naturally we ignored him. Undoubtedly he has now sold them back to the Americans or they have found out about them somehow. Clearly they now wish to retrieve them for their own purposes."

Khalkhali nodded but said nothing. He did not know what to say in the face of the Imam's revelations.

Khomeini frowned and the monotone continued. "Actually it is unimportant where these tapes are, for I am sure the Americans have copies. And I doubt you will find them no matter how efficient and dedicated your efforts."

"Then how must we stop them?" Khalkhali asked cautiously.

Khomeini turned toward his disciple. "My son, never fear the mighty," he said with exquisite calm. "For the mighty are not motivated by victory. They are preoccupied by defeat."

A smile spread slowly across Khalkhali's face. "As with the Shah, Holy One."

"Precisely, my son. The Americans, this nation of infants, have provided us with the very stick with which to beat them and all they have stood for in this country."

"Holy One, by what means?"

"I will inform you. I will inform you at the appropriate time."

CHAPTER
61

"American Embassy, good morning," said the female operator.

"My name is Michael Adel and you have fifteen seconds to connect me to Colonel Grover Cleveland Bell."

Immediately the line clicked and Adel knew that his guess had been right.

"Congratulations, Michael, you did very well. I must admit your speed and efficiency surprised even me. I suppose you called to finalize this whole thing?"

Adel watched the moving second hand on the Imhof clock beside the telephone. "Sure."

"There's a small house in Shepherd's Market, near Curzon Street. It's off the beaten track and quite safe. Are you familiar with the area?"

"Birds of a feather flock together," mumbled Adel.

There was a moment's hush before Bell responded. "What was that?"

Adel thought the length of the silence exaggerated. "I know the area. It's where two-bit hustlers walk the streets."

There was another, longer pause.

"Things turned out well, Michael. It's all over now. We don't

236

need to fight about it. The location of the house is safe, nothing else."

Adel's eyes were riveted to the clock. "Safe for whom, Bell? If you're worried about me, I'd prefer to meet somewhere more public, some place swarming with people. Besides, there's a couple of things that might interest you, things that might persuade you that my well-being is in your best interest."

"Back to that again," sighed Bell.

When they were one minute ten seconds into the conversation, Adel said: "Let's say the lobby of the Berkeley Hotel."

"Half an hour suit you?"

"Only if you're willing to wait several hours. No. Let's say six o'clock this evening, colonel. And alone. No bodyguards, advisors, *consigliori* in drag as waiters or doormen."

"That suits me fine," Bell agreed. "Tell me, Michael, was it easy getting out?"

The elapsed time of their conversation stood at a few seconds over two minutes and Bell was patently trying to stretch it out. Adel pictured computers buzzing and clicking and humming in a desperate search to make the right connection.

"Six o'clock, Bell," Adel replied and hung up. He checked the clock and then looked at the telephone. "Bastard," he spat.

"Is that your way of saying good morning?" came the sleepy voice of Jane Bennett.

He turned in the bed and kissed her. In the dim light, two flawless dimples receded attractively on the small of her back. Warmth spread slowly through his body as desire took hold. He swung the cast over the smooth heart-shaped curves of her hips and she arched her back in assistance.

By three o'clock, Adel had finished his letters. One was addressed to his brother Mark, the second to his banker-friend Claude Boissy in Switzerland. Both were attached to heavily taped envelopes that, as the covering letters instructed, were to be kept sealed until his death. Each manila envelope contained two tapes, clones of Mahmoudi's originals. There was also a note identifying the voices and companies on the tapes.

The covering letters requested that, in the event of his death, the tapes be transcribed and duplicated, then sent to selected journalists, newspapers, writers and scholars of the whole political

237

spectrum—leftists, rightists, radicals, conservatives. Adel stressed that the tapes and transcripts were to be released only on his death; and they were to withhold any information or knowledge of the tapes from even their closest confidants.

At any rate, he told himself, he was only going through the motions, acting in character. He had no choice; both men were known to Bell; they were the obvious choices; Bell would intercept them.

He sat for a long time wondering if he was actually exposing the two men to danger. He decided he wasn't. Besides, it was a risk he had to take. And what did it matter if Boissy faced a little danger? Boissy had made enough money off him over the years. Now he could earn it.

His brother Mark was another matter. There he could take no chances. Mark was more than a brother to him. Since childhood they had been true friends. He couldn't bear the thought of endangering him. He would have to make certain that any insurance policy he took out with Bell covered Mark too.

From Jane's living room he dialed Mark's number at his house less than a mile away in Chelsea. It rang for a long time before there was a response.

"Hello." It was Mark's longtime housekeeper.

"Hello, Theresa. Let me talk to Mark." He would be expected to call Mark. So even if Mark's phone was tapped, he would have to go through the motions. But quickly, before they could trace the call. "I'm afraid he's not here, Mr. Michael. He's not in London at the moment."

"Where is he?"

She hesitated a moment too long. "I . . . I don't know, sir. Probably the States."

Adel frowned; Mark was never out of touch with his home. As an independent consultant, specializing in commercial risk analysis, he usually worked from his house and since he had never married, Theresa acted as his conduit. She always knew where to contact him.

It didn't make sense, thought Adel. It was highly unusual—especially in view of their close relationship."

"I need to talk to him urgently, Theresa. When do you expect him back?"

"He didn't say. Not for a few days, sir."

Adel thought for a moment. "Listen, Theresa. There's a letter

238

I've got to get to him. I'll send it round in a little while. The important thing is for him to contact me as soon as he sees it. I have to go over a few of the details with him. I'll send it over by taxi shortly."

If the phone's tapped, that should do it.

"Very well, sir. I'll be in all day."

Adel was puzzled. Why was Theresa reluctant to tell him where Mark was? It made no sense. Or was he being unduly suspicious, paranoid? Maybe Theresa really didn't know where Mark was. Perhaps she was making something out of nothing—God knows she did that often enough. To her, secrecy was a door to romance. Mark was probably off to some conference or other, and she was being, as usual, self-important.

"Now, what do you want to talk to me about?" said Jane, interrupting his thoughts. She walked into the sitting room dressed in a skin-tight black leather pantsuit that set off her blond hair. Her red T-shirt added color to her pale English skin, making it glowing and translucent.

"You look great," he said.

"It's all for you, sir," she said, pirouetting on the ball of her foot.

He patted the couch beside him. "Come here."

He talked to her as though she were a bright pupil. "I need your help," he said. "But you have to listen carefully and memorize everything. You can't write anything down. You think you can do that?"

"I'm an actress, remember? Memorizing is the nuts and bolts of the business."

"Good. Now listen, Jane, this isn't a joke. It's probably the most important thing that's ever going to happen to either of us. So be serious. I'm going to give you two cassette tapes and two different addresses. I want you to hide them. Do you have a safe deposit box at a bank?"

"Sure. Yes," she stammered, surprised by his gravity.

"Good, bury them there. Put them in the vault and forget about them until the right moment. Or should I say the wrong moment."

"But why? What are they?"

He pointed to the envelopes on the coffee table. "I'll get to that in a minute. The first thing you have to do is to forget about me. I mean completely. You mustn't mention my name again. Pretend, act, do anything you want, but make damn sure no one finds out we ever knew each other. Just like before. Repeat: no one must

239

ever know we've seen each other or know each other."

Her face took on a serious, questioning look. Her eyes searched for reassurance and guidance, but they found none.

"Are you serious? What's wrong? What kind of trouble are you in?"

"Yes, I'm serious, but you don't want to know. Not about this, Jane. Just trust me and do as I say. Don't mention my name, for your own sake as much as mine."

Adel stood and limped toward the fireplace to gain distance from the hurt he was about to cause.

"Why? Are you and Samira having problems?"

"Hell no, it's nothing like that. It's a long story and, as I said, you don't want to know. It'll only make things more dangerous for you."

"Dangerous! Are you being serious, Michael?"

"Very."

Jane frowned and moved forward to the edge of the couch, her body tensing. "What danger? What's all this about?"

Adel ran his fingers through his hair. "There's a lot to it, Jane. And I need your help."

He glanced at her but she said nothing.

"If anything happens to me I want you to take the tapes from your safe, duplicate them and send a copy to two people."

He pointed again to the papers on the table. "You'll find two names and addresses in the letter I've written for you. One is to an old friend of mine here in London. He's a writer and a good one, but I don't want him touching this material unless something happens to me. The other is to an address in the States. He's a friend, too, but he's a little more devious and dishonest. If anything happens to me, maybe he can make life hell for them."

Again he pointed to the table. "I didn't have time to duplicate enough tapes. So you'll have to make a copy for the American address, if and when the time comes. Don't make any extra copies for yourself. Under no circumstances must you do that. Just do exactly as the note says. No more, no less. And don't do it before the right time, don't touch it before... before..."

"What's all this about, Michael? Who are 'they'?"

He looked at her for a long moment before answering. "Jane, I'm trying to make this easy. I'm trying to keep you as far out of it as I can. Don't ask questions. You don't want to know."

"First you tell me I'm in danger, then you tell me I'm better off not knowing why. Does that make sense to you?"

It was getting difficult. "No, it doesn't. But that's the way it has to be."

She stared at him suspiciously and squinted as the sun broke through London's cloud cover and washed through the window, catching her in its golden path.

"Does that leg have anything to do with this, Michael?"

"In a fashion."

"How?" she asked, the color draining from her face.

"Drop it, Jane. The less you know the better off you are."

"I don't believe this," she said, looking away. "You make all these dark statements about secrecy and tapes and danger and you don't want me asking any questions?"

"Exactly."

"Why, damn it, why?"

"Because that's the only way I know for both of us to survive."

She was silent, confused. She reached for a cigarette and fumbled with the gold Dupont table lighter as she lit it. "He is serious," she whispered to herself.

Adel said nothing. He felt only guilt and sorrow as he watched the slow disintegration process unwind. He had to remind himself that there was no other way, that it was a scene that had to be played.

"What's going to happen, Michael?" she asked in a whisper.

"Nothing, I hope. It's just a precaution, Jane. Sort of an insurance policy. Just trust me and do exactly as I say and it'll be all right."

She walked away from his approach and then swiveled around to face him from a distance. "I don't like it, Michael. You're frightened yourself and you're getting me involved. Why? Why do you need me?"

There was nothing to say, there was nothing he could do.

"What's wrong, Michael?" her voice pleaded. "Please tell me. Please explain."

"You're right. I am scared," he said softly. "But I can't tell you any more than I already have. Not without making it worse. How can I convince you?"

"You can't," she said, her face taut and angry. "I'd just like you to leave."

"It's too late for that, Jane. I can't go and I can't tell you about it either," he said. "Not if you want to live."

She gasped—a choke of terror that made the veins bulge in her

241

neck. Her eyes filled with tears and her hands formed a cup around her quivering lips.

It was against everything in his nature, everything he believed in. He wanted to cross the room and hold her, console her, but an alien urge stopped him. It told him that it would do no good. That it would only make things worse. It would expose her to more than she could handle. And it told him he had no choice.

Even worse, it told him that this was the moment in which he would succeed or fail. It was now that he had to drive the point home; now that he had to make certain she fully understood the importance of silence.

"The only way you'll stay alive is if you do exactly as I tell you. Otherwise they'll kill you. And not a person in this world will ever know why," he said without compassion. His words were past threats. "So just stick to exactly what the letter says."

She crossed her legs and squeezed the armrests until her knuckles were white. "Why, Michael?" she whispered as tears flowed down her cheeks. "Why did you have to get me involved? Don't you think I have enough problems of my own?"

It was a fair question.

CHAPTER 62

LONDON: THURSDAY, NOVEMBER 1: 5:35 P.M.

Michael Adel stepped cautiously into the lobby of the Berkeley Hotel. He scanned it quickly, searching for a Bell surrogate.

The foyer was elegantly decorated, with light orange walls and gray and white marble floors. A blazing fireplace extended into the foyer, forcing visitors to pass the Enquiries Desk to the left, the Hall Porter's counter to the right. Three steps up was a cocktail lounge, furnished with high-back leather armchairs and polished wooden tables, positioned to insure maximum comfort and privacy.

He glanced at his watch; it read 5:37 P.M. It was pointless searching the place, he thought. He was powerless to change anything,
even if it was out of line. Besides, it would be impossible to detect
any of Bell's men; they were professionals. In spite of the warning
Bell was sure to have covered himself. At the very least, the en-
trances of the building would be watched and guarded. And word
would have already gone out that Adel had arrived.

Convincing Bell would be the hard part. He chose a comfortable
leather chair at the entrance of the room, overlooking the foyer.

"Mister Adel?"

Adel froze. His body stiffened as he turned.

"I'm afraid ties are required," the waiter said politely.

Adel sighed with relief. "Yes... yes, of course they are."

"I can serve you in the breakfast room across the hall, if you
wish, sir."

"Thank you." Adel followed the waiter's glance across the foyer
to the room reserved for the hotel's more "informal" American
guests.

"Glenlivet and water, please. No ice," he said, limping away.

The breakfast room was just as good a vantage point with an
equally good view of the lobby; he couldn't miss Bell from there
either.

At precisely six o'clock Colonel Grover Cleveland Bell came
through the revolving door. He stood unobtrusively to one side of
the lobby, stiff and upright, his pale blue eyes slowly sweeping the
area as his hands adjusted the black knitted tie at his throat. He
straightened the jacket of his gray tweed suit before spotting Adel.

"It's difficult to get a taxi at this time of day," he said as he
extended a firm, dry hand. "Especially when it's raining."

"Drink?"

"That sounds rather good. Let's see... ah... something to drive
the chill out of the bones. Vodka, I think, vodka martini."

Adel signaled the waiter and ordered the martini and another
whisky for himself. Bell smoothed his already flawless hair, then
rubbed his hands together vigorously.

"Damned weather. Don't know what it is about London. Tem-
peratures seldom drop below freezing but the chill goes straight
through you. Probably age," he added, chuckling affably. "What's
wrong with your leg?" he asked with what appeared as genuine
concern.

243

Adel felt a tinge of anger. Bell knew exactly what had happened to his leg. He knew an hour or two after it had happened. Or however long it took George Clark to contact him from Teheran.

"Let's get this over with," he said.

"Very well, very well," Bell said, ignoring the hostility.

"I don't know much about your profession, colonel, but I know more than I did two weeks ago," Adel said. "And you were right. I seem to have some natural built-in ability. I've learned quickly. Had some good on-the-job training too. I've killed seven people, give or take a few, and I've betrayed and endangered the lives of at least three more. And I don't think I'd stop there." Adel's stare was hard and angry. "You were right about that, too. To survive you seem to stoop to any level."

"Most people do, Michael. It's instinctive. If you look at it, though, every profession has its unpleasant side. Doctors only save lives if they're paid. Lawyers defend the most terrifying homicidal maniacs, if the rewards are rights. Accountants are used to rip off the government. There's always a nasty side. One has to do a certain amount to protect the things one believes in. Unfortunately, the end does justify the means."

Adel looked at the distinguished public servant sitting in front of him, coolly enjoying his martini. Elegantly dressed. Establishment. But that was the veneer. Inside was a madman, a psychopath who compared assassins to doctors and accountants.

Adel forced himself to relax.

"Perhaps," he said. "But you're conditioned to this type of life. I'm not. It's alien to me, a way of life I can't take." He meant to say hate, despise, abhor, but checked himself. All that was beside the point. He had to convince the man to let him live. He put his hand in his jacket, brought out the two original tapes and placed them on the table in front of Bell. The colonel's face showed no reaction.

"In my world, it's rather different, colonel," he went on. "I don't lie. I don't believe in deception as a way of life. Not for me, anyway. It's important you understand that and believe me because if you don't—we're probably both dead."

The threat did not register on the colonel's face.

"Those are the tapes from Mahmoudi's safe. They're yours. And that's my side of the bargain. Your side is to leave me and my family alone. And I expect you to keep to it."

He let his words hang. He wanted Bell to digest them. "There's a redheaded young man, who works in the radio and television department in Harrods. I don't know his name, but he'll vouch for the existence of three copies of the tapes you have in front of you."

Bell's steely blue eyes opened a fraction. He picked up the long-stemmed glass and sipped his vodka martini.

"I've distributed them in such a way as to insure the widest possible exposure should you choose to renege on our bargain."

Bell's lips held a glint of a smile as he shook his head. "That wasn't very wise of you."

"I'll tell you why first, colonel. You've only been told half the story about Teheran, I'll tell you the rest. I doubt that you've heard it all." Adel felt his anger returning; he wanted to forget about survival, to tell the son of a bitch why he couldn't trust him, why he was a two-bit thug.

"Your man Khan and a doctor friend of his overdosed a seventy-year-old woman to get those damn tapes out of me. Not just any old lady, colonel. A lady I loved. And I killed them for it."

Bell looked at him placidly. "Yes, I thought as much; I thought it was probably the result of some sort of falling out among you," he said calmly. Then his face took on a more serious, concerned air. "But why would they kill this lady? Aren't you letting your imagination run away with you again?"

Adel ignored the barb. "You were certain of getting the tapes. Who gave them the authority to go around me, colonel? To go for a shortcut?" He didn't wait for an answer. "Well, whoever gave them the authority killed them."

"Why would I have an old lady killed to get information from you? Why wouldn't I just have them get to you?"

"Ah, colonel. What was it you said in Cannes? 'Options.' You had to keep your options open, didn't you? The risk element was too high. If you'd tried it on me with the same result you'd be in a lot of shit now, wouldn't you? You'd have lost the tapes again, perhaps for good. But with the old woman, there was just a chance that she knew. And if she had—" the image of Mariam's corpse flashed before his eyes. "—well, poor soul, she'd be dead anyway." He stared coldly at Bell. "But so would I. They'd have taken me right then and there—in my sleep—wouldn't they, colonel?"

"That's hogwash, Adel, and you know it. Why would we kill you when we control the strings? That's poppycock. The product of a warped mind."

"I don't know. Maybe the exit part of my trip bothered you.

Maybe you wanted to get your hands on the tapes through the diplomatic pouch. Maybe you knew I wouldn't just take your word for it, that I would listen to the tapes. I don't know. You tell me."

"Look, Adel, no one gave any such order and I don't know a damn thing about any of this. I gave my word and I'll keep it."

"Yeah... well... just in case you change your mind, I've insured myself."

Bell looked hard at Adel. "Have you listened to them?"

Adel smiled and shook his head. "Yes, colonel, and it's all gibberish. You can't make a word out of it," he said, his voice dripping with sarcasm.

"Michael, these things are dynamite. They contain the most sensitive, dangerous material imaginable. If there's an error in your judgment and they're made public, they'll set off a chain reaction that could shake the entire structure of the Western world. There would be a scandal of unprecedented proportions; it could lead to the destruction of the whole system: governments toppling, economies crumbling, intelligence networks dissolving, our entire system of alliances undermined. The chaos could lead to the power vacuum the Soviets have long been projecting and waiting for."

"I doubt it, colonel. The Western world is strong enough to excrete its crap without damaging itself to that extent. Perhaps it'll even grow stronger."

"Listen, Michael..."

"No, you listen for once, colonel. I want to live and you're not exactly a man who elicits trust. Leave me... us... all of us, including my brother Mark... alone and there'll be nothing to worry about. No one will ever see the tapes, much less hear them. They'll stay buried in vaults and your scenario will be avoided.

"It's an unnecessary risk, Adel," said Bell. "You're not protecting yourself this way. You're making it worse."

"Don't threaten, colonel. Listen. Let me explain so there's no misunderstanding. If anything happens to me or my family, it'll set off a chain reaction in which your oil company friends will become the sole targets. Even if you track down one or two of the tapes, you won't find them all. Not in time. That's the way it's set up. And if they do come out... if the shit does hit the fan... not even your government cronies will be able to help or protect you or your oil company friends. If the exposure is right, they'll be forced to turn on you. And I assure you, colonel, it's right. The exposure I've set up is total. Once the dam breaks, the flow of dirt—fifty years of dirt—will be impossible to stop. It'll create a scandal so staggering, so immense, that your usual tactics of lying, stonewalling, getting rid of evidence or even killing won't do you any good. It will be too late for all of that.

"In a nutshell, your government friends will turn against you. They'll come in and split your Trust apart seam from seam because they'll have no choice. They'll make you and your Trust the scape-goats so they themselves can survive."

Bell gulped his drink and wondered: How did this clown slip the net? It had all been arranged: they had picked him up at Heathrow Airport and then lost him. For twenty-four hours they blew it, giving him the opportunity to wreak all this havoc. It had all been projected, of course, but no one had any idea that a man with no previous experience could slip a full coverage net of profes-sionals. Professionals, he mocked silently. They were clowns.

He said: "Presumably you think you're protecting yourself this way."

"Can you think of something better?"

"Use your head, boy," Bell said, slapping the table hard.

Hastily he covered his outburst by raising two fingers, indicating two more drinks to the surprised waiter.

Then he turned back to Adel. "All you're doing is lengthening the chain, increasing the possibility of a weak link and the chances of a leak. A simple clean operation is getting totally out of control because of your paranoid suspicion and mistrust." He shifted in his chair and brushed the sleeves of his jacket. "Look, if you did make copies, you'd better go round them up and get them back to me before it's too late. Before it blows up in your handsome face." He leaned forward, resting his elbows on his knees. His complexion, Adel noticed, had gained a shade of color.

"I wouldn't trust you as far as I could spit, colonel."

"You refuse to take my word; everything is conspiracy with you, isn't it, Adel? Well, if you believe the world can survive without order, you're a dreamer. A child. The 'great conspiracy'—as you would think of it—is merely an attempt to give the world and its affairs rationality and order." Bell felt in his pockets for a cigarette. "It controls chaos and avoids waste. It means that you can forget about World War Three. It means that none of this can happen because it would be destructive and counterproductive to mankind

247

and the coterie of wealth that runs the world. It means, Adel, that without order the world would destroy itself. It means I would have no reason to lie to you."

"You wouldn't stop at genocide, would you."

"I'm surprised at you, Michael, at your naïveté. Those are words. Mere words in the overall scheme of things." Bell stuck a cigarette in his mouth and lit it. "There's no such thing as genocide because there are no genotypes left. At least, no such thing as an American, or an Englishman, or a Frenchman, or even an Iranian—they're all mosaics, genetic mosaics. What you in your self-righteous smugness fail to see is the overall scenario. It's the march of time and the imperatives, the priorities, the weights of every second of that march. Order is the only imperative, and it doesn't come from God. He left in despair a long time ago, Adel. It's up to us now. And if control is not exerted every second, every hour, every day, the world would slide toward anarchy and chaos..."

"And for the moment the imperatives are that the industrialized world is running out of resources and America doesn't have a resource pot to piss in. Is that it?"

Bell inhaled and let the smoke leak out of his nose. "Look, Adel, we can't engage in an undergraduate discussion on ethics now. There isn't time. Be reasonable. You can't fight this. No one can. Tell me where the tapes are. Tell me where you copied them and if anyone else heard them."

Adel smiled nervously and lit a cigarette. Bell was mad. But within his crazy scheme it was all logical, everything had a place. Order, as he called it. And now he, Michael Adel, was disturbing the great order. His only hope was the tapes. Without them he was dead.

"I told you. They were duplicated at Harrods. Three copies, and there was a redheaded salesman in the room off and on but he wasn't listening. I mailed the copies to various corners of the world yesterday, with letters outlining clearly what should be done if anything happened to me."

"Mailed yesterday?" Bell's voice seemed to come from a distance. "Well, it's still possible to retrieve them. I need to know where you mailed them from. And where you sent them. The redhead's no problem."

"What?"

Bell smiled his lopsided smile. "It means you killed him, Adel.

That makes a total of eight notches on your gun. Unless you wish to take the credit for the death of His Excellency Ali Mahmoudi and his daughter, Gina, too. And there'll be more...."

Oh, my God. He's killed Gina. Images of Natalie's mother flashed before his eyes. The young Gina. The girl he had loved so desperately once, shared his youth with and his daughter. The woman who had caused so much happiness in his life. And pain. He remembered their first kiss at the house in Teheran. And their last at the Hotel George V in Paris. Her bounce, her lust for life.

This madman had killed her. And Mahmoudi, too. He'll go on killing. He'll kill Mark...and he'll kill...Jesus Christ Almighty, stop him...he's a lunatic...I'll give him the bloody tapes...just tell him to leave...to get out of my life...to leave me alone....

But no. He'll never do that. Even with the tapes he won't stop. If he gets his hand on them, he won't let anyone live.

"Those tapes are all I have to protect me and my family from you. Or from worse...if there is any worse. There are three duplicates out there, you can't stop it," he pleaded. "Leave it alone, colonel."

Bell finished his drink and looked directly into Adel's eyes.

"Tell me, Adel, what makes you bigger or better than the Shah? Let me answer that for you. Nothing. We had him by the balls, so you're no problem at all. If I can topple a man of his stature, just imagine what I'm going to do to you." He picked up the tapes from the table and slid one in each breast pocket.

Adel looked at the tall, distinguished man looming over him and felt the cold ice of hate.

"You're a reptile, Bell. A slimy snake that slithers and grovels in filth."

Bell looked down at him and smiled.

"The only difference is I have feet, Adel. And no matter where you go, I'll be there."

CHAPTER
63

At the Berkeley Hotel, Adel had tossed and turned all night, images of pain and fear were joined by a new despair—guilt and sorrow. Guilt about Jane, the hurt and damage he had caused her. Genuine sorrow at the death of Gina, who was after all Natalie's mother and a woman he had once loved. The nightmare seemed never ending. It had no beginning; it had no end. It was a constant journey along a recurring path on which scattered and mutilated bodies of the dead and dying lay, haunting and accusing.

At five-fifteen, frustrated and tormented, he threw off the bed covers. There was nothing he could do about it, he thought as he hobbled from the bed toward the bathroom. He could not change the past and there was no guarantee for the future. In a few hours he would be home, to Samira, to Natalie, to warmth and security. Perhaps there, in time, the images of the past would fade. Perhaps, too, there would even be a future.

CHAPTER
64

The five men had arrived at the detached, two-story, neo-Georgian red brick house on the north side of Hyde Park by different routes. They had reached their destination at predetermined times, between seven-thirty and eight-thirty, to coincide with the arrival of other carefully selected dinner guests.

The middle-class residence in the Paddington district of London was, like several of its neighbors, celebrating the weekend. The ground-level double reception room glowed with bright lights that filtered through the lace curtains. The rise and fall of voices and laughter came through the partially opened windows.

Unlike the other neighborhood parties, however, the celebration at 18 Sussex Gardens was camouflage. The windows that fronted the street were half an inch thick and bulletproof, and the building itself was a deception—a safe house, as it is called in the trade.

Inside the five men, who had mixed with the guests for a suitable period, were now gathered in a basement that did not show on the house plans available at the city and borough planning departments. Nor did it show on the designs at the real estate agents in Kensington who had originally sold the building in 1966, when it was constructed. In fact, none of the high-security additions to the building were visible or on file anywhere. They had been added by a branch of the U.S. Naval Intelligence in 1972, when the house had been purchased by the Central Intelligence Agency. The lead-lined basement walls to offset electronic eavesdropping, the bulletproof glass, the heavy steel-sheeted doors, the narrow tunnel that burrowed under the road to the private park across the street, were all well-kept secrets. The outdoor high-resolution camera and microphones were camouflaged, but the dozen television cameras inside provided a 360-degree view, with zoom ability to pinpoint anything within view. An electronic net added audio surveillance with extensive mix and isolate capability for the immediate surroundings.

"What do we have on Adel?" asked Bell, looking at the wiry blond young man opposite him at the round table.

"On him personally, sir? Or the whole background report?" The man was nervously thumbing through the pages of a folder in front of him.

Bell glanced at the swarthy, sun-tanned figure sitting next to him, then back at the young man.

"All of it," he said curtly.

The younger man shuffled the papers again.

"Well, Adel left for the South of France this morning. British Airways flight 342 to Nice/Côte d'Azur airport at eleven o'clock, to be precise."

251

Bell nodded and waited, his head angled to the right, his eyes scrutinizing the dark, scholarly-looking man to his left.

"We've recovered both tapes, sir," said the younger man. "The first set of documents was recovered, as you suggested, from the Cheyne Walk address in Chelsea, the residence of a Mark Adel."

The young man paused, then continued. "The package contained two Narela cassette tapes. Numbers seven-four-five-three-seven dash E stroke R dash forty-six dash seventy-eight and seven-four-five-three-eight dash E stroke R dash forty-six dash seventy-eight. It also contained a five-page handwritten letter, a summary of which I'll get to in just a minute, if that's all right with you." He looked around the table for approval.

"The second package was located with the assistance of our British counterparts. We could have waited for its receipt by Claude Boissy in Switzerland before retrieval, but at your suggestion, colonel," the young man nodded deferentially at Bell, "it was decided to put an early stop on it here in London, even before it got to Boissy. This was done for two reasons. First, while Boissy was classified as 'cooperative' and 'safe,' it was determined that an appreciable reduction in the risk factor could be obtained through the prevention of his exposure to the contents of the package—if, that is, it could be achieved. The second was a sizeable reduction in the time factor. It was determined that early access to both packages would increase our cross-check capabilities and thereby accommodate and increase the accuracy factor of our comparative analysis. This we believed would substantially improve our chances of understanding fully the planned offensive in the shortest time frame."

The younger man looked up at his audience; they were attentive. "Through our British counterparts we placed an immediate stop search on all parcels to Switzerland above the size of a letter. X-ray scanning on four thousand one hundred and eighty-three packages, destination Switzerland, point of origin British Isles, in the last twenty-nine hours isolated and recovered the target package at the Foreign Sorting Facilities at Mount Pleasant.

"The second parcel was almost identical to the first. It contained two Narela cassette tapes numbered seven-four-five-four-zero dash E stroke R dash forty-six dash seventy-eight and seven-four-five-four-one dash E stroke R dash forty-six dash seventy-eight . . ."

"Capelli," Bell interrupted. "Just give us the gist of your report.

We can go through the details with you individually if we need to later."

He had been through all this before and the meeting was bound to be a long one.

Christopher Capelli cleared his throat and continued. "The package also contained a letter. The two letters were remarkably similar; if there was a difference, it was in the wording. Boissy's version was more formal and more detailed. Under the circumstances, this has been adjudged normal," said Capelli, looking up to check Bell's expression. "The letters instruct the recipients that, in the case of unusual circumstances regarding the subject's well-being and safety, the tapes are to be made available both in audio and transcript form to an assortment of outlets: governments, institutions, a broad spectrum of the media, lawyers, writers, radicals and a variety of companies, both friendly and otherwise. The word *unusual* is defined by the subject in the broadest terms.

"Some of those listed are not in our sphere of influence. On the contrary, if one or two of these outlets found access to this information it would be impossible to contain." He looked up again at Bell, who nodded slightly.

"As for the Narela tapes, their point of origin is the C.K.Y. manufacturing plant just outside Tokyo. The first series of numbers of their identification tags which I partially read indicate the number of the production run. The E stroke R indicates they were manufactured specifically for the European market. The forty-six indicates they were made in the forty-sixth week of 1978, which is identified by the last digits.

"C.K.Y. manufactures high-quality tapes under a variety of brand names; it has no distribution arm of its own. These tapes and other C.K.Y. products are shipped to London by container, warehoused and distributed throughout Europe by various distribution companies under a variety of brand names. Narela Corporation is a British distributor and is considered top of the line."

Capelli placed the papers on the table and looked around. "In a nutshell, that's the gist of the task force findings. The originals—tapes, letters and our assessments—have been forwarded by courier to Washington for review and in-depth analysis. We should get their result and recommendations back in thirty-six hours."

Bell nodded and leaned forward until his elbows rested on the polished table. There was a moment's silence as the group digested the information. Two of those present had a more abiding interest. They were careful, meticulous men, experts on the human psyche, its weaknesses and strengths; and for them a person's past determined his future.

Bell turned to Capelli. "See if you can get Washington to speed things up. What's a realistic minimum?"

Capelli thought for a moment. "Another twelve hours. Say sometime tomorrow morning. Afternoon at the latest."

Bell looked around. "Are there any questions for Capelli?"

The emaciated man to Bell's right shifted in his seat. He was the more senior of the two scientists present—men trained in the area of covert operations but specializing in one exacting aspect.

"Yes, John," said Bell, anticipating a comment.

Dr. Johan Brandt withdrew his glasses from his bony face and placed them on the red folder in front of him. Below a bushy, disheveled mop of white hair his eyes were half closed, watery.

"I wonder, Mister Capelli..." he said in a heavy Germanic accent, "...where was the letter to ah...ah..." his hand shook as he replaced his glasses and referred to his notes, "...Mister Boissy mailed from?"

"Sloane Street," Capelli said promptly.

"Yes. Good...good...good. I wonder, did you put a stop on the other mail from that box, Mister Capelli? Presumably if the subject mailed anything else, which is doubtful, it would not be unreasonable to assume that he mailed them at the same time as Mister Boissy's package, would it?" He blinked frequently behind thick curved glasses that distorted the shape and size of his eyes.

Capelli smiled back but it was an uncomfortable smile. The doctor's gentle questioning was unsettling, especially since Capelli had only recently read his personal file. Like the others around the table, the doctor was an intelligence expert, but the similarity ended there. He and his colleagues sitting opposite him were a different breed of specialist. Their expertise lay in a rapidly emerging new science—human behavioral engineering. Part doctor, part psychologist, part interrogator, the two men were manipulation strategists who correlated the likelihoods, odds and percentages of an individual's future behavior based on past patterns. They analyzed his loves, hates, desires, fears, but most of all his weaknesses and vulnerabilities...and which stimulus would produce which result.

Capelli answered cautiously. He knew the two men were analyzing every word and the thought unnerved him.

"Sure it occurred to us," he nodded at the doctor. "But let me
explain the logistical problems involved with that. We had a clean
handle on Boissy's letter. His name was one of two hundred thirteen we had isolated and targeted. We knew the approximate time
it had to have been mailed. And we knew its destination. If those
two parameters are available it is always, relatively speaking, a
simple task to isolate a specific piece of mail. It was a chicken and
egg problem. We intercepted the package because we had a potential destination and enough time to locate it. When we did so,
then, and only then, did we identify Sloane Street as the mail drop,
but of course by then something like six to eight hours had elapsed,
during which the mail from that box had been sorted and mixed
with the ah...ah," he flicked the package of his folder, "...one
million, two hundred thousand other pieces of mail that on average
leave this country daily.

"As soon as we were aware of the Sloane Street drop we put an
immediate stop search on all mail originating there. But practically
speaking, it was too late, the pouches had already been sorted and
mixed by destination. We're trying to isolate the Sloane Street mail
back again but it's a horrendous task. The British are more opti-
mistic about the outcome than we are, but then again they're very
efficient at this sort of thing. They have dozens of people working
on it and we should have an answer by the morning."

Johan Brandt nodded his head as he doodled. "If we had another
parametric characteristic...a destination...a name...something,
I'd feel far more confident myself. But you thought about it, did
you?" he asked, nodding and smiling.

"Yes, doctor."

"Have you considered stopping all the outgoing mail?"

Capelli smiled nervously. "In essence that's what the British are
doing. Although perhaps 'delaying' is a more operative description
than stopping."

"I have no other questions, colonel."

Bell looked around the room from right to left. "Any questions?"

The dark, scholarly-looking man puffed at his pipe and shook
his head.

"Thank you, Capelli. Wait with the others."

There was silence as Capelli closed his folder and left the smoke-
filled room.

Bell waited for the door to close. "Well, Johan," he said to Brandt, "what do you think?"

Brandt peaked his white eyebrows; his pouted lips were a criss-cross of wrinkles.

"It's an interesting one. This man is behaving awkwardly. In fact, he's acting downright unpredictably," he said, his accent thicker now. "Perhaps there has been a change. Maybe we missed something. It is unsettling; the fact is, up to a given point, in every single instance he acted as projected. We have to presume that that was because the created stresses resulted in a controlled environment that was predictable. He had no choice; he had no alternative but to cooperate with us. First and foremost he had no means with which to fight back, and second he had quite a considerable amount to lose. So naturally he reacted in the expected manner. The question is, why did he veer from that pattern of behavior? Why does he feel so confident now under the very same conditions that have theoretically existed all along? I don't know.

"The possibility does exist that he has found this so-called third outlet and no longer feels the pressure so overwhelming. Perhaps this third source has reduced the insecurity factor. Either that or he has succumbed to the rather lengthy period of high-stress to which he has been subjected. If that is the case, then it would mean, I'm afraid, that projecting such a person's behavior with any degree of accuracy under a continuing high-stress state would be a most difficult task. It would mean that he is now unbalanced and totally unpredictable.

"It's worth thinking about, isn't it?" he asked, his voice worried but his eyes alive with professional interest. "He's certainly a challenge."

Edward Rogers, Brandt's colleague sitting opposite him, looked at the doctor and said, "I don't know, John, I see it a little differently. The key part for me is that in retrospect it's pretty clear that, from the start, the program has been just a little off and all the misjudgment has been in the obeisance factor. Adel simply hasn't been as compliant as projected. No, that's not exactly true. He did act predictably at the very outset, when his daughter was threatened. Since then he hasn't, though; he's been fighting every step of the way. He didn't accept our field operatives," he said, ticking the points off on the fingers of his left hand. "He didn't keep to the schedule. He killed two of our operatives. And while we clearly projected the likelihood of his duplicating and then retaining copies of the tapes if he had the opportunity, we had no idea he would go so far as to mass-distribute them to this extent. Now, as Grove tells it," Rogers pointed to Bell, "even his daughter has taken on a secondary importance."

Brandt turned to Bell, aware of the practical problem at hand. "Basically, colonel, we need something we don't seem to have— time. We need to go back and take another detailed look at all of this in the lab. See if a possible third source exists in London or if it's simply a product of his imagination. It's possible that he is a more complex person than we perceived him to be."

"Let's call a spade a spade," said Rogers. "Someone in Operations blew it. No matter what the behavioral deviations have been, we projected very clearly that he would duplicate if he could. From the start we insisted that a high-coverage grid be placed around him from the moment of his departure from Iran; in fact, we even suggested that his surveillances should start from the moment he laid his hands on the tapes. That's where the fatal error was committed. This problem should never have come up."

He looked at Bell for a reaction. While the colonel looked more haggard than usual, he betrayed no emotion.

"True, he's not acting specifically as we projected, Grove," Rogers continued. "But all the deviation relates to one specific factor; we've been accurate in every other dimension. The fact remains that a rank amateur was selected to execute a highly technical and dangerous task based only on capabilities and personality traits as displayed in quite different areas of endeavor. And it's been a highly successful operation. Let's not forget that side of it. The question is, as you point out, John, is there a third outlet?"

Bell's index finger played with his lower lip as he studied Rogers. The analyst had, for two decades, weighed and evaluated statistical data on human behavior.

"What do you think, Ed?" he asked through splayed fingers. "Deep down do you think that the projections are wrong? Do you think there's someone..."

"That's the sixty-four-thousand-dollar question." Edward Rogers smiled but the smile faded quickly. He tugged at his blond curls. "No, Grove, I don't believe that we're that far off. There is nothing to suggest a third outlet. In London, anyway, there isn't. Remember, you're not talking about a simple favor from an acquaintance.

You're not playing with the kids in the alley. You're talking about deep personal involvement in a highly dangerous game of life and death. Hell, there's nothing to suggest the existence of such a person here. If I had to bet on it, I'd say he's bluffing. But it's a dangerous poker game we're playing."

"In a sense, he's right," said Brandt, nibbling at the arm of his glasses. "The chances are he's lying but I would suggest we wait for Washington to respond. That is a more cautious approach. Let them study the knowns at length in the laboratory where they have access to the computer files. Meanwhile we can all sleep on it. Give it time to..."

Bell interrupted impatiently. "We have severe time restraints. He's already left for France. Every hour of indecision extends the circle of exposure and correspondingly the risk factor. We can't afford that. Either we do something quickly or we might as well forget it. It'll be too late. We can sit back and wait for it to blow up in our faces."

"Yes, Grove," Rogers broke in. "But on the other hand, of you eliminate the man and find he's got the royal flush..."

Bell gently dropped the yellow Ticonderoga pencil he was twirling over and over in his right hand onto the table. It bounced on the eraser at one end and fell to the floor.

The swarthy man now spoke for the first time. "The risk is too great. There are too many ifs involved. For a start there is a good chance he didn't mail anything; he could have hand-delivered the third set via a courier. After all, that's what he did with one of the recovered packages." He gave no indication that he, Mark Adel, was the recipient, even though he was aware that the others knew.

"Then there's also the possibility of him asking someone— whoever—to mail the package in a week or two, or ten. That would hardly be too much to ask anyone, would it? It wouldn't require a good friend or even a close acquaintance. Under those circumstances he could approach just about anyone. A hall porter, a secretary, virtually anyone."

"Yes, that's true," said Brandt, rubbing his forehead. "The fact is something is wrong. It was never thought the subject would behave so erratically The question of multiple sources was never approached. That was an error on our part. In fact..."

The swarthy man broke in. "We're all sitting here talking as if the manipulation of a human being is an exact science with proven laws upon which one can depend. It is not. It is a crude art in an embryonic stage. Let's stop getting carried away with its accuracy and dependability. The fact is that the success of Operation Peacock in Iran—the changing of a regime—had nothing to do with this so-called science of human manipulation. That, gentlemen, was a planned military and intelligence operation. Only in part—a very small part at that—did it rely on the manipulation of one weak and terminally ill human being—the Shah. It would be fatal to continue to ascribe proven propaganda and destabilization tactics and their successful execution to this... science of human manipulation, or whatever it is you call it. You can't sit here and project exactly what anyone is going to do—ever. Let alone a complicated, sensitive, tough human being who is fighting for his life."

Johan Brandt looked at Mark Adel. "Yes. Well, if we are restricted by time I suggest we use what little we have constructively. I don't see this man's behavior as being radically divergent from the original projections. Divergent, yes, but not so radically as to suggest a total departure from the program. It is impossible to project an individual's behavior exactly," he said, glancing superciliously at the swarthy man. "With the existing state of this science it is, anyway. Perhaps someday we will reach that level of accuracy. And we all knew that from the start. It has been ninety percent accurate up to now and I can live with that sort of success level.

"Given the complexities you have, colonel, I would recommend that we wait for Washington to respond. Let them run the data again to see if there is a correlation between the recipient list the target has provided in his two letters and the known acquaintances we have on file. In addition, the lab could scour the names again and see if there is a distant girl friend, a former business acquaintance, tennis partner or karate teacher, someone we might have missed."

Bell held his gaze on the doctor for several moments but his mind was elsewhere. He thought: Mark Adel is no longer a valid input. His personal involvement is blinding him to the realities and dangers of the situation. As one of the foremost military strategists and an outside consultant to the Agency on the Middle East and Iran, he was one of the key planners in Operation Peacock. But he was a leftover from that project. It was wrong to have brought him into this operation, however unfeeling and professional he actually was. Even now he's showing no emotion or personal interest. That's what's incongruous about his behavior. He's trying to argue professionally, strategically, and it doesn't make sense.

He stored the information and turned to Rogers. "What about you, Ed?"

Rogers followed the doctor's lead and tilted his chair back onto its hind legs.

"I think we should all try to remember," he said, "without getting emotionally involved, that this man is no longer a stable human being. The strains of the last few days must at the very minimum have caused considerable shock. After all, it was an alien and frightening experience for him. The result is, we may well have a lunatic out there armed with enough information to destroy our entire system of democratic government. I submit that, even if we do not call his bluff, even if we leave the matter totally alone, let him go his own way, never see or touch or talk or contact him again, that there is a sector—a proven sector—of this man's character that we must not forget. I'm speaking, of course, about this man's sense of revenge and determination. Look at the elaborate lengths he went to for the recovery of his daughter Natalie.

"This is not a man who will sit back and take defeat graciously. I submit to you that in the days ahead, the resentment he feels will turn uncontrollable. It will devour him and force him against us. At some point he will be unable to stem that drive; it is an integral part of his makeup, his *hubris*, as the Greeks put it. At that point—and it is impossible to predetermine it—he will come after us."

"Terrific," said Bell, as he watched Mark Adel shift in his seat.

"I further submit that this vengeance might take a different form. He could simply publicize the information contained on those tapes, even if he is lying and there is no third set of tapes. With time, he will recall or piece together much of the information contained on those tapes even if he doesn't have an actual copy. Perhaps the proof will be missing but the facts will be there, available and ready.

"He must not be given that opportunity; we must not give him time to plan a strategy that would be difficult to neutralize; let's face it, he is a competent man."

There was a hush around the table; no one could argue with the wisdom or logic of the words, not even Mark Adel.

The meeting lasted until midnight, but nothing new emerged.

Bell, Brandt and Rogers talked around the various options but Mark Adel stayed silent. He had nothing more to offer.

At one in the morning Colonel Bell saw the three men to the door. Mark Adel departed first; he nodded, mumbled brusque farewells and left quickly. He was followed by Dr. Brandt, who was in better spirits. Ed Rogers shook the colonel's hand.

"There's one more thing, Grove," he said. "I didn't want to bring it up in front of ah...everyone. If you go through with this, be careful. There's no room for error. He's the same in enmity as he is in friendship; he gives it everything he's got."

Bell looked deep into his colleague's eyes and nodded before the two men turned in opposite directions.

The colonel walked back into the wood-paneled room toward his desk. He needed facts, figures, odds, percentages, ratios. Judgment calls were dangerous, anathema, in this business. He reached for the telephone.

He knew that Adel was lying; he could feel it in his bones. Brandt and Rogers agreed with him; they had to but, like him, they were concerned about the risk. And they had no actual proof, no hard evidence. If anything went wrong all hell would break loose.

And this time, he thought wryly, there were few candidates for scapegoats. He picked up the phone and pressed a button.

"Tell Gleeson to come in." He leaned back on the swivel chair, closed his eyes and stretched his feet on the table, locking his hands behind his head. "Judgment calls," he spat in disgust.

There was a knock and Jim Gleeson entered.

"What happened with the sales clerk?" Maybe, with repetition, something new, a scrap of information forgotten, would emerge.

"He was in the room, Grove, taping the duplicate copies while Adel listened to the tapes."

Bell said nothing, waiting for more detail.

"Claimed he hadn't heard them himself. He said Adel had listened to the whole thing on earphones. But he gave a hell of a description of Adel. Right down to the dimples-when-he-smiles."

"Terrific." Bell's eyes were still closed.

"He knew enough to be dangerous. After our visit and the attention it must have aroused, it would have been dangerous to leave him lying around."

Bell opened his eyes.

261

"He won't be a problem, Grove."

Bell looked away. "If the kid had been that smart he would have remembered how many copies of the tapes he'd made. Now the only one who knows is Adel."

"We tried everything, Grove. He just didn't remember whether it was two or three copies. The problem was, since he was working a fiddle, there was no receipt from the store to show the sale of four or six tapes. He claimed he was out of the studio most of the time and Adel could have popped extra tapes into the apparatus without him knowing."

Bell swung his feet to the floor, sat up straight and gave Gleeson a penetrating look.

"This is a rough one, Jim," he confided. "A mother! We have to wait awhile to see what Washington comes up with. The problem is, we can't afford the time."

He sighed and bit his lower lip. "Have you set up the surveillance grid in the South of France?"

"Yes, it's all in place."

"Okay, you better get down there and activate it. Keep your eye on the bastard."

"Sure, Grove."

"Get down there as soon as possible and keep a tight leash on him; we don't need another fuckup like London. Remember, Jim, this thing is critical; it's as big as anything we've ever handled, probably bigger. Keep everybody on their toes. The man's no fool and we don't need him spotting it. I want him to relax, to unwind and feel like it's all over. I want him to drop his guard and perhaps that way we can learn something. If he spots it like the last time..." Bell hesitated and looked away from Gleeson.

"We know what to expect this time, Grove."

"Well, it's encouraging to know that after twenty years in this business, you're still learning. I suppose all we can hope for is that Adel isn't a faster learner."

Gleeson turned away from Bell's piercing stare.

"Okay, you better get going."

"Oh...ahh...Jim," Bell called.

Gleeson turned to face him.

"Wait for Davis. He'll be coming with you."

Gleeson nodded and left the room.

Bell rested his elbow on the table and rubbed his eyes, which were tired and bloodshot with fatigue.

Was there a third set of tapes? Was there a third outlet? The nagging question went around and around in his brain.

The Harrods salesman had no reason to lie. He had insisted that there were three sets of tapes. Three, four or forty, it made no difference to him. Davis and Gleeson had gone too far, especially Davis, he thought, making a mental note to reprimand him. Between them they had mixed the fool up, repeatedly asking him if he had included the original tapes in his figures or not. Had he made three copies or was it three in all? Four with the originals or three? On and on until the poor fool's brain jammed. The young man had no reason to lie. His original answer had come out forcefully, without hesitation.

And Michael Adel? He thought as he walked to the conference table. Who on earth could he have found in London who was not on the records? No one. Absolutely no one. There were only three sets of tapes and all three were already safe. The bastard was bluffing. Adel was lying.

He picked up a pack of cigarettes from the mahogany table and lit one. Besides the cigarettes the spread-eagle emblem on the blue leather folder caught his eye. He fanned the pages absentmindedly. He didn't need to read what was on them. He had read them so often that he had memorized them. Abruptly he turned his back and started pacing the floor.

There was nothing to be gained from the papers. Not even a hint of a third person, especially in London, and even outside there was no one. Only his wife, Samira. But that he would never do. He would never involve her.

"He's lying," he said aloud as he picked up the phone and dialed. "Theresa, let me talk to Mark."

There was no third person, he thought again as he waited. Michael Adel had very few friends; that was another reason he had been chosen in the first place. No, the facts were indisputable. He crushed his cigarette and lit another.

"Hello," came the deep English accent.

"Mark, I'm relieved you went straight home," Bell said.

"Good." The tone was sharp.

"Mark. The more we delve, the more it looks like your brother is lying. There's simply nothing to substantiate the existence of a third person in London." He added quickly, "Without our knowing."

"We went through this at length before the meeting, colonel.

Whether he's lying or not, the risk you're taking isn't justified. You've become too involved in all of this. It's become a personal vendetta. My advice, and that's what I'm here to give, remember, is to let it cool down. Wait for Washington to get back to us. There's nothing to be gained by acting rashly. And a great deal to lose," he added coldly. "You're exaggerating the time restraints."

"The timing is critical," Bell snapped. "Every hour his exposure increases. Besides, as for personal involvement..."

"Don't be rash, colonel. It's the logic that's wrong. It has nothing to do with personal involvement." The perception of these people was off, he thought angrily. It was offensive. An insult to his professionalism. They saw a weakness in him that wasn't there. And he was powerless to convince them. No matter how persuasive his logic, they saw it as an attempt to save his brother. An emotional issue. And they were wrong.

"I want your professional judgment, Mark."

"Okay. You want a formal response," said Mark Adel, his voice cold and angry. "Here's my professional opinion. Carve it in your brain because it'll come back to haunt you. I don't know who the third person is, but I don't think he's lying. Nothing you have proves otherwise. Until you do, the risk is not worth taking. That, Colonel Bell, is my formal response. I'll have it to you in writing in the morning."

Bell felt a shudder. What if Mark was right and he was wrong? What if there was a third outlet?

"Look, Mark, this has been a horrendous task. It's gotten to all of us. I really do understand your position. They should never have involved you in this. It was too much to expect," he said, trying to sound conciliatory.

Mark Adel bristled. "When I was assigned to this project, I made up my mind to be impartial. To help you, colonel. And that is exactly what I'm trying to do. I have tried endlessly to explain to you that there are things above and beyond facts and figures and computer analyses. There's a thing called feel and it comes with years of close proximity. You can't acquire it by feeding a machine and playing with variables. Especially with this human being, you can't."

He fell silent, then went on in a calmer manner. "You are all right, colonel, when you talk about my brother's fascination for the concept of revenge. We've discussed that at length but you refuse to listen to the man who knows him best. Even so, you're only partly right; there's a major portion you've missed. It's not revenge that drives him. It's something totally different. It's winning. And to win you have to be cautious, calculating."

He waited to let Bell absorb this, then continued. "None of that shows up on your computers, does it, colonel? That's the part you missed—the critical part—and you refuse to listen to me. He's not bluffing; there is a third outlet. He's too careful to gamble without it. Michael won't lie down and die. Not without being reasonably certain that one way or another he'll eventually win."

He's a cold fish, this one, thought Bell. In all his years in this business, he had never known anyone quite like Mark Adel. The man really wasn't pleading for his brother. He was merely pressing a professional viewpoint. What was bothering him was not the danger his brother was in. He was pissed off because the voting was going against him.

Let's test him, thought Bell. "Mark, all that's well and good but it has nothing to do with a third outlet. You're worried about your brother and that's understandable. But we have time restraints and we know he's lying."

Mark Adel let out a lungful of air. "You're wrong, colonel, on both counts. I keep trying to tell you, there's no emotion involved. In this profession, emotion is a bad habit. And there is a third outlet."

There was something eerie about Mark. Something Bell couldn't quite put his finger on. He was cold and humorless, constantly scowling behind his scholarly, controlled features. From the very beginning he had felt uncomfortable with Mark. Nothing he could isolate or classify, just a sixth sense of discomfort, of distaste.

"He's lying, Mark. I'd bet my life on it."

There was no hesitation as Mark Adel said, "You probably are, colonel," and hung up.

Bell looked at the dead receiver, surprised. He replaced it and leaned back in his chair. The guy has a point there, he thought.

He picked up the phone again.

"Ask Gleeson to come in. And Davis, too."

Holding the receiver, he clicked the phone dead. The antique Victorian clock read two-thirty. It was a good hour for what he had in mind, even better when the extra hour was added to get French time. He dialed the thirteen numbers for the South of France and

265

listened as a staccato of clicks made the connection. His palm was sweaty and he switched the receiver from one hand to the other in nervous excitement.

He would tell Michael Adel that his offer was acceptable. Better yet, he would tell Adel that his superiors had overruled him, that they had ordered him to accept Adel's offer. That it was all over. The choice was unattractive, the risk of exposure too great.

"Adel residence," a sleepy voice finally answered.

"I'd like to speak to Mr. Michael Adel," said Bell.

"Who may I say is calling?" a polite male voice inquired.

"Bell. Grover Cleveland Bell."

The response came immediately. "Mr. and Mrs. Adel are out for the evening, sir."

Bell looked at his watch. "It's three-thirty in the morning down there," he said incredulously. "What do you mean, he's out?"

"There is no curfew in the South of France, sir," replied Usher, his voice calm.

"Yes . . . well . . . tell him I called to let him know we've accepted his offer. Tell him that we've agreed to his proposal. And ask him to call me."

Bell hung up and reached for another cigarette. It didn't make sense. It wasn't normal for a man under this kind of pressure to be out with his wife at three-thirty in the morning.

"Come in," he shouted angrily, in answer to a knock. Adel's behavior made no sense, he thought as Gleeson and Davis approached his desk. He lit his cigarette and waited for them to settle in chairs.

"We've got to move, Jim," Bell said, looking at Gleeson. "It's too risky to let it just hang."

He bit his lower lip and looked at his watch again. "Set it up for tomorrow, Jim. We'll have the report in from Washington by then so if need be we can always abort. If not, we'll go ahead.

"Oh, another thing, Jim. I want to be there myself. I want to be certain there's not a trace left of him."

CHAPTER 65

Et la vie sépare
Ceux qui s'aiment,
Tout doucement,
Sans faire de bruit.

Et la mer efface
Sur le sable
Le pas des amants
Désunis.

Adel hugged Samira close on the crowded dance floor of Le Pirate. They were not dancing; they swayed in tight embrace to the strains of a Spanish guitarist vocalizing in French. To Adel it was bliss. The suffering and violence had eased, replaced by love and desire. He squeezed Samira tighter, feeling her firm breasts through the thin black chiffon of her Renato Balestra dress, feeling his excitement as their hips pressed together.

"Where did you hear that before?" he whispered into her ear.

She caressed the black curly hair at his neck. "Boulevard Saint Germain, the day we met."

He smiled and kissed her forehead. "Who said you were just a pretty face?"

"God, I love you." She pulled his head down and kissed his lips. "I've missed you."

"Let's see how you feel next week."

The trio broke into a fast samba and Adel motioned to their table. He guarded his damaged leg as they made their way through the chic Monaco crowd that packed the small dance floor.

"*Salute.*" Samira raised the glass of Dom Perignon before she sat.

"*Cento anne,*" he answered without thinking. A hundred years? A shiver moved up his spine as he thought of Bell. He would settle for much less if he was pushed.

"There," said Samira. "That's the look I was talking about. It crosses your face every now and then. You seem so troubled."

"Nonsense," he said, a little sharply. He tried to cover himself. "I need a joint. I'm a little uptight, that's all."

"So have one," she shrugged. "Why are you so tense?"

Her large brown eyes stared into his. They were worried eyes but still sparkled in the candlelight. Her thick, full lips glistened, setting off the long black hair that fell to her shoulders. It was an open, trusting face, yet exotic and sensuous, the result of perfect cross-cultural mating.

He picked out a joint from a box of Marlboros and lit it.

"I don't know. I guess I'm tired."

"It scares me, Michael. It really does. I've never seen it on you before."

"It shouldn't. I'll be all right in a couple of days." He looked at her provocatively. "Besides, it could be something else."

She smiled, a flush appearing. "Me too."

Suddenly an orange flare illuminated the restaurant's private beachfront. Instinctively Michael Adel snapped his head toward it as his body shied away. He ducked, waiting for the explosion to follow the flash of burning phosphorous.

It did not come.

Quickly he tried to camouflage the violent movement, but Samira was staring at him, her eyes filled with suspicion and worry.

Mercifully the strains of a waltz sounded, cutting off conversation.

> *Oh, how we danced*
> *On the night we were wed.*
> *We vowed our true love,*
> *Though a word was not said.*

The vocalist and his accompaniment serenaded an elderly couple sitting next to the windows overlooking the brightly lit beachfront. Outside, the restaurant's traditional anniversary ceremonies were unfolding. As the waves crashed against jagged white rocks, two swimmers emerged from the freezing Mediterranean with bright flares held aloft. They ran across the narrow beach and up the inclined steps into the restaurant. Inside the amplifier was turned up and the waiters moved from table to table, pouring champagne. "Compliments of the gentleman," they said, pointing to the couple.

The song ended noisily. Clapping and shouting and laughter were accompanied by the kind of music played at Italian weddings, and suddenly the room was filled with chatter and laughter. The *patron,* the musicians and the customers fused together to celebrate the couple's twenty-fifth wedding anniversary as waiters bustled in with fresh bottles wrapped in fluffy white napkins. Le Pirate was at its best. The lush, loud, decadent spirit was difficult to resist. Even more as the marijuana took hold.

Samira stretched across the table and took his hand. "It worries me, that look," she said, refusing to be sidetracked. "And your lying makes it worse."

Adel looked out the window and lit a cigarette. Nothing would be gained by telling her. She would only worry herself sick, be dragged into the quagmire like the rest of them. He pressed her hand.

"You're making a mountain out of a molehill. I'm tired and jumpy and the leg hurts a little, that's all," he said, patting her hand. "But don't go on about it."

"Is that all?"

He closed his eyes impatiently. "That's all I know."

She held her look for a few seconds, then relaxed. "Okay. Enough said." Her lips stretched into a delicious smile.

It was nearly sunrise when they arrived home; and quite some time later before they slept.

CHAPTER 66

QUM: SATURDAY, NOVEMBER 3, 1979: 7:00 A.M.

In the austere reception room that was soon to mesmerize the entire world, Ayatollah Khomeini frowned and his sullen features took on a sinister expression as he reached for the traditional Iranian *ghand palou* tea. He selected a sugar cube and dunked it in the hot tea before placing the lump in his mouth, using the rich brew as a chaser to wash down the sweetness. His frown lingered, his forehead was a twist of furrowed lines.

"So the *pasdaran* militiamen have been infiltrated too?"

Ayatollah Khalkhali said deferentially, "It would seem so, Holy One."

"The fact that this Adel has been escorted out of the country confirms that the Americans are still everywhere in this land. From the prime minister on down."

Khalkhali nodded. "You will be satisfied to learn that at midnight last night we tried and executed Hossein Mikhchi and Samad Nafti, the two American spies who worked at the airport."

Khomeini brushed aside the reassurance. "If Adel took these tapes out of the country, it can only mean one thing: that the Americans are in a hurry. There would be no reason to risk rushing them through the airport if they were not concerned with time. They could have simply and safely slipped them through our unguardable borders like we used to do."

Khalkhali remained silent, trying to anticipate the Imam's mind.

"No, my brother, they wish to use these tapes against us," continued Khomeini, his eyes downcast, one hand toying with his beard.

"They wish to blackmail us with our own flock, trying to show that we collaborated with them. No doubt they will attempt to entrench their puppets again — lackeys like Bazargan, Yazdi, Ghotbzadeh — in our midst."

Khalkhali was amazed how calmly the Imam was unfolding his thoughts.

"But did I not say they are like children? They have done for us what we have sought to do since the success of this revolution. They have given us the opportunity to eradicate their stooges forever. And more. Much, much more."

The Imam lifted his gaze from the floor and looked at the whitewashed wall at the far end of the room. "This peanut grower has handed us the perfect tool with which to carve anti-Americanism into the very souls of our people."

Khalkhali looked at the Imam with awe. "How, Your Holiness?"

Khomeini turned slowly. The piercing eyes that were soon to hypnotize the world locked in rage on the man beside him. "We

270

shall take their embassy. We shall take their spies hostage. And we shall hold them. And hold them. We shall hold them until those tapes are useless to Mr. Carter and his cronies. Never again will either East or West dominate our land."

CHAPTER 67

CANNES: SATURDAY, NOVEMBER 3, 1979

It was ten-thirty in the morning when the sleek *White Leopard* yacht drifted out of the gateway to Port Cano. Serenely the twenty-one-meter Italian vessel turned outward toward the Estorel, Les Iles Lerins to her port, Le Vieux Port de Cannes to starboard. In spite of the bright sun, a light haze clouded the shimmering glass surface.

Once clear of the harbor, Michael Adel pushed forward the two levers beside the wheel and instantly the twin diesel Caterpillar D/334 engines picked up momentum, raising the vessel's majestic bow and belching a stream of turbulent froth from its stern. Adel handed the wheel to the captain and headed aft, down three steps, past the kitchen and into the lounge. The new cast on his leg felt looser, more comfortable, and he adjusted easily to the boat's movement.

He slid open the cabin door and stepped in.

"Damn!" He felt a surge of pain move up his leg. He grimaced and he hopped into the cabin and slumped on the suede sofa. He glared at the door sill as he hoisted the cast atop the lacquer coffee table and stretched to massage the bruised toes below the cast. A video tape deck flickered French cartoons competing with music from Radio Monte Carlo. Adel used the remote control switches beside the sofa to silence them.

"Are you all right?" asked Samira.

"I guess so."

271

"You really have to be more careful. Stop moving around so much."

The whiff of freshly brewed coffee filled the cabin. "John," he called to Usher in the kitchen, "can I have some coffee, please."

Samira was relieved by the quick recovery. She picked up a cushion and made light of the incident. "I wonder how much damage you're going to cause the furniture before you're better," she said, as she placed the pillow between the cast and the table.

Natalie giggled at him; it was a game father and daughter played when either was scolded.

"Think that's funny?" he asked, looking at her in mock seriousness.

"Uh-huh," she nodded excitedly, smiling, her eyes playful and naughty.

"Thank you, John." Adel took a cup of steaming coffee from the wicker tray Usher held and placed it on a side table. Then he turned back to Natalie and looked at her for a moment. Someday he would have to tell her about her mother. Somehow he would have to explain it all to her. And the only thing he could do to soften the blow was to insure that his little daughter had warm, loving memories of her mother. In his mind he promised her that. It was the least he could do.

But not now, he thought. Not today. He wasn't up to it. And he was far too young to understand or absorb the nuances of the tragedy.

Instead he wagged his finger at her. "Come here."

Natalie dived onto the sofa next to him and he caressed the side of her face.

"How would you like me to start Sam on all the homework you should be doing right now?" he whispered in her ear, loud enough for Samira to hear.

"Oh, that's not fair," she pouted. For an instant her face reflected deep thought. Then she whispered even louder than he had, "I'll be on your side if we can eat at Tahiti Beach."

Samira and Adel smiled involuntarily. It was Natalie's favorite restaurant, serving charcoal broiled corn on the cob dipped in butter sauce.

"Come on, that's enough whispering," said Sam. "Natalie, fetch the backgammon set and I'll play you."

Natalie ran from the room, even before Sam had finished her sentence.

Sam turned to Adel. "Michael..."

Adel put the cup down and looked at her. She sat cross-legged on the floor in a white jump suit studded with golden buttons. Her large doe eyes, youthful and innocent without makeup, held a worried air.

"You really have to snap out of it. It's starting to affect Natalie. She's asking a lot of questions."

"Like what?"

"Like, why didn't you call when you were away? Like, why are you so quiet now? Why are you sad? It's all fairly obvious, you know. I have to live with your explanation. I'm not very happy about it but I figure you'll tell me when you're ready. Children are different, they don't think that way. They respond on simple, emotional levels and she senses something. I told her it's some trouble with your work."

Samira dropped her eyes, her fingers picking at strands of the dark green carpet. "But it wasn't good enough for her. She thought about it—you know the way she does—and said, 'Well, dad should get different work then.' I didn't want to bring it up again, Michael; it's obvious you don't want to talk about it. But if you don't change, it'll affect her."

Adel felt irritated; he was tired of acting. He was sick of performing and camouflaging his despair and depression. Over and over he had had to do it. Mariam, Jane and now Samira and Natalie. There was no end to it. And besides he wasn't exactly doing a masterful job. He closed his eyes and disciplined himself once more.

"Sometimes it has to be that way," he said. "Sometimes you're better off not knowing. I hope you believe me because that's all there is to it."

She offered no reply for a moment, but when she did, her voice was severe. "I don't think you have the right to make that kind of judgment. What's better or worse for me, or for us, is something you have no right to decide alone and privately. We share things, good and bad. Besides, we aren't talking about me."

"Presume you're right," he said harshly. "Presume there is some goddamn thing wrong. You're not doing anyone a favor by going on about it. Leave it alone."

She stood and moved to him, nestling her head in the curve of his shoulder and embracing him.

"Please, Michael," she whispered. "I hate this feeling. I can't

273

stand it. I don't know what it is, but it scares me. You're frightened, I see it in your eyes constantly. And then, sometimes, it's even worse. It makes you untouchable, unreachable. And you won't even tell me what it is." She kissed him on the neck. Is it all over at least?"

He wanted to tell her. To scream that he did not know, that he would never know, not until it was too late. A split second before a bullet smashed his forehead. A flash before his car blew up, tearing his body to shreds. Or poison tore his guts apart. He would never have the luxury of living without the fear of death hovering over him.

Instead he caressed her face and kissed her. "I think so. . . ."

Natalie cut him short in midsentence. She rushed into the cabin, clutching a backgammon set and talking.

"Let's play in turns. You know, whoever wins plays the next guy."

"Okay," he said, eager to be alone. "You play Sam first. I have to go on deck for a second. I'll play the winner."

A frown crossed Samira's face. "Come on, Natalie. We'll play," she said good-humoredly.

Adel kissed Samira's forehead and offered her a reassuring wink. She gave him a cool look.

The sea air was fresh and clean. Using the wooden railing, he made his way up to the bow, ignoring the strong headwinds that tore through his windbreaker and an occasional spray of sea water. He sat on the teak surface at the tip of the bow, his back to the sea. A mile or so off to starboard he could make out Porte la Galere with its shining white stucco buildings and red tiled roofs, tranquil and stately.

He thought about Sam and knew that he could never tell her. It was enough that his own life was haunted by death. To make Sam a party to his fear and guilt would be more than he could bear. She would become another partner in his misery, another accessory targeted for death. But she was right about one thing: it couldn't go on like this. He was nervous and uptight, a coiled spring ready to unwind, snapping and snarling at random. Nothing was enjoyable. Nothing and no one.

He had been through it a thousand times, but the conclusion never changed. The fact was, there were no guarantees of anything. There was nothing to depend on. No security; no peace of mind.

274

His whole case was built on the shifting sands of credibility. That and the fear of exposure of the tapes. Credibility and fear, two qualities Colonel Grover Cleveland Bell knew little about. And there was little else to cling to.

He shrugged and lifted the wall phone.

The captain answered.

"Gerrard, est-ce que Usher est là?"

"Oui, monsieur."

There was a moment's silence before Usher answered. "Yes, sir?"

"John, have you been able to contact my brother yet?"

"No, sir. And not for lack of trying."

"Thanks." Adel hung up.

And that was another thing. Where the hell was Mark?

CHAPTER 68

NICE/CÔTE D'AZUR AIRPORT: NOVEMBER 3, 1979:
11:00 A.M.

"What time is it set for?" asked Bell as the three men stepped out of the airport door marked DOMESTIC.

"High noon," replied Bill Davis, glancing at his watch. "We picked up Adel's conversation with the captain on the wiretap. He called for a ten o'clock departure. Even if there's a delay, it's built into the safety factor."

"An hour," said Bell, more a statement than a question.

"Yes, sir," replied Davis.

The three men crossed the access road and made their way to the apron in front of Nice/Côte d'Azur Airport. To the spectators on the observation deck, it was apparent that two of the men were American. One could not mistake the loud check trousers cut shorter than the continental fashion. It was more difficult to identify the

275

third man from his clothing; he wore a gray, conservative Savile Row suit.

"Not even transportation to and from the planes in this damned place," Bell grunted.

"Only when it's raining, colonel. Conservation of energy; something we're learning back home rather quickly," said Jim Gleeson, who wore the conservative suit. He pointed to the clear, turquoise sea. "Besides, with the Mediterranean surrounding you on three sides, it sure is pretty enough for a short walk."

Bell flashed a quick look at the sea and then at Jim Gleeson before lengthening his stride to the ramp.

"Have we got the vessel sighted?" Bell shouted above the whine of the AB-206B helicopter jet engine.

"We've got a radar track on it, sir. It left just over thirty minutes ago." Davis stepped aside to let the others precede him up the narrow ramp.

The pilot, wearing Ray-Ban reflector glasses, gave the men a casual salute, asked them to fasten their seat belts, then engaged the motor and watched the tachometer crawl upward. After a brief exchange with the control tower, he lifted the sky-blue helicopter forward and upward toward the Estorel.

CHAPTER 69

"Who's winning?" asked Adel as he stepped over the sill and closed the cabin door.

"I am," Natalie said. "And I'm playing really well."

Adel slid onto the couch next to Samira and smiled at her atrociously placed pieces.

"I'd throw in the towel if I were you."

She looked at him coldly. "There's a lot of things you'd do if you were me."

276

Adel was silent for a moment.

"You're right, Sam," he said softly to hide the tension. "But you'll have to bear with me. Just give me a little time."

Samira threw the dice. "It's not me you have to worry about." She glanced at Natalie, then turned away.

"Now you, dad. Now you!" cried Natalie.

Adel forced a smile and busied himself positioning the pieces in their appropriate spots. "I'm going to have to do something about it."

"I hope so," said Samira gently. "For all our sakes."

He placed his hand on hers and pressed it. "It'll be all right. Don't worry."

She smiled wanly. "I hope so. I honest to God hope so."

CHAPTER 70

The sun shone into the helicopter as it gained altitude to 2,500 feet and flew on a gyrocompass reading of 227 degrees due southwest with the airspseed indicator hovering at 170 knots.

Colonel Grover Cleveland Bell felt nervous and uneasy as he looked through the window at the hazy sea below beating against the tip of Cap d'Antibes. Visibility was slightly impaired, but still good enough for visual sighting. And that was why he was here, he reminded himself as he tried to discipline the emotions which had no part in his professional life. He did not want to rely on the airplane instruments no matter how reliable or how efficient. He was here to see the last act for himself.

But his uncertainty refused to budge. It had stuck to him for several days and now it fought back with vigor. It seemed to feed on itself, growing and spreading dark pessimism until it produced an even more distasteful emotion: the need for reassurance.

He turned uncertainly toward Jim Gleeson. He studied his col-

277

league for several minutes before pushing the intercom transmitter button. What the hell, he thought. What's the harm?

"What do you think, Jim?"

Gleeson turned slowly to face Bell. He was more surprised by Bell's worried tone than the question; he had no idea how to react to it; he had never heard it before.

"I don't know, Grove," he said carefully. "I just don't know. It might be premature."

"Even after Washington?" Bell's habitual superior smile was twisted.

"Washington was vague, Grove. They didn't really take a position, did they? It seems to me they just threw the ball back in your court. It's the 'establish veracity' part that gets me," he said, unable to hide his anxiety; and unwilling to take a position.

"'Without risk of exposure'—they said that too," Bell said testily. "And this asshole's touring the world."

"Yeah, Grove," Gleeson agreed with a sigh. "That's true too. It's a bitch."

Bell turned toward the window. What if he was wrong? He didn't want to think about it. He couldn't be wrong. There was no third set; there was no third outlet. There couldn't be. They'd been back to ORAL again and even Operations Research couldn't find a new lead. Friends, former classmates, ex-girlfriends, business associates, a couple of whores, even another relative—but nothing. Zero. Every one of them had an alibi. Besides, none of them was close enough to him for Adel's kind of dependence and trust. And risk. No, if there was a third set it was down there, close to him, within easy reach. Either that, or it was at the house in Cannes. That was human nature and the odds lay in human nature.

"There's your boat. Up ahead there," shouted the pilot over the clatter of the engine. He pointed ahead a few degrees to port.

Below, the sleek white yacht glimmered in the hazy sun, cutting a path through the calm sea.

"Keep well away," ordered Bell.

Instantly the pilot veered starboard toward the land mass on the horizon.

But what if he was wrong? What if there was another outlet? The doubt returned and ice-cold needles punctured his body. Again he called on his iron discipline to suppress the weakness, the doubts. He wasn't wrong; he couldn't be. The facts were there.

The intercom came alive; it was Gleeson.

"What gets me, Grove, is that Mark. But I guess it's natural for him to see things differently."

The mention of Mark Adel's name made Bell wince. Even now his Oxford intonation came through as clearly as Gleeson's voice over the intercom.

"It's not revenge that drives him. It's winning . . . and to win you have to be cautious, calculating . . . He's not bluffing . . . There is a third outlet . . . He's too careful to gamble without it."

Bell shuddered as he recalled Mark Adel's words. He was ice, thought Bell, dry ice. Cold and heartless. And he only moved in the background; anonymously, silently, efficiently, and without a shred of feeling.

He bit his lower lip and turned to the window.

CHAPTER 71

"I'll come with you," Natalie said to her father.

"Get your coat on then."

"Meanwhile I'll get presentable for Saint Tropez," said Samira.

Adel followed Natalie up the ladder to the upper deck. The Perspex windshield in front of the upper controls was the only protection against the cold headwind. As they sat on the pilot's bench the steady drone of a helicopter filtered through. Adel was curious; he looked around but the glaring haze obstructed the view.

"Can I drive, dad? Please, please," Natalie clapped her hands in excitement.

"Sure," he smiled, caressing her windswept hair.

He picked up the intercom. "We'll take it up here for a little while, Gerrard," he said into the mouthpiece.

CHAPTER
72

The earphones in the helicopter suddenly erupted above the roar of the engine.

"Gibraltar Ground Control to Dragon One. Gibraltar Ground Control to Dragon One. This is urgent. Repeat urgent. Do you read me? Over."

"The pilot pushed a button. "Dragon One to Ground Control. Dragon One to Ground Control. I read you. Over."

"Gibralter Ground Control to Dragon One. I have an urgent call for Barracuda. I have an urgent call for Barracuda. I'll proceed to patch it through. I have instructions to inform you to switch to scrambler. Do you read me? Over."

"I read you. Barracuda standing by. Repeat Barracuda standing by. Scrambler activated. Over." The pilot motioned to Bell to take over.

"Colonel Bell?" A voice demanded.

"Yes," said Bell. He did not recognize the voice.

"Hold on please, sir."

The next voice that came through the scrambler was easily distinguishable. It was refined and confident, but no longer calm.

"Colonel Bell, can you hear me?" It was John Alexander Case, chairman of the Trust.

Bell pressed a button. "I read you. Over."

"Good, I hope I caught you in time. There's a tape missing. At this point we have in hand two original tapes and four copies. I am talking to you about the copies. We have Narela seven-four-five-three-seven and eight. We also have Narela seven-four-five-four-zero and one. Please note that Narela seven-four-five-three-nine is missing from the sequence. We believe that there is a third set and that this missing tape has a mate most likely sequential in

280

nature. We have reason to believe that seven-four-five-four-two is its mate.

"This information has only just been observed. No sales slip exists. But unfortunately the store confirmed less than an hour ago that these six tapes are missing from both the stock and the sales records and that they were indeed part of a batch received by them. Since only one number is missing from the sequence the possible existence of a third set is high. Too high. Consequently all plans must, repeat must, be postponed until this point is clarified. I repeat, abort all plans immediately and indefinitely. Do you understand me? The man must be left alone until clarification is made. Until we are certain. Do you understand?"

Bell's face registered shock. He sat uncomprehendingly at the control panel, unable to move.

"Do you understand? Do you hear me?"

Bell was paralyzed.

"Goddamn it, Bell! Can you hear me?"

Bell slowly grasped the microphone. He adjusted its already perfect position. "It... it may be too late," he whispered, searching his mouth for moisture.

There was a moment's silence before the voice spoke coldly. "I don't think you can afford that, colonel. There has already been one serious and unnecessary blunder."

Bell looked at his watch. It was 11:55.

"Over," he said curtly and hung up the microphone. He grabbed at the pilot's leather jacket. "How long would it take to get onto that boat's frequency?" he said, pointing at the yacht below.

"A couple of minutes," said the pilot.

"We don't have that kind of time. Drop down and I'll use the bullhorn." The pilot went into a steep dive even before the words were out of Bell's mouth.

CHAPTER
73

"That's called a depth finder, darling. It tells you how deep the water is."

Adel found himself talking steadily louder, competing with the ever-increasing roar of a jet helicopter. Suddenly he realized that the noise was far too close. Quickly he turned, his slitted eyes scanning the bright, hazy sky.

Then he saw it and his heart missed a beat. Instinctively his mind formed a picture of Colonel Grover Cleveland Bell.

A blue chopper swayed from side to side two hundred yards behind the boat and only a few feet above the sea. But it was closing in quickly. Adel grabbed Natalie and pushed her beneath the bench wedged between two wooden lockers. It was not too much cover but it was all that was available. His heart was speeding now, pumping violently as he felt fear. He picked up the phone.

"Take over the boat and tell Samira to stay down there," he shouted at Usher. There was no way down. Not with Natalie anyway. He crouched beside her, gaping at the recess dead center beneath the closing helicopter. It was a machine gun and it was trained directly on the bench.

"*Adel. Michael Adel. Listen to me.*" Even through the uproar the voice was recognizable.

"*Get off the boat! There's a bomb aboard!*" the voice boomed as the chopper swayed only a few feet from the stern.

"*It's set for twelve o'clock.*"

Adel looked at his watch. Two minutes to twelve.

"*Get off. We'll pick you up.*" Bell's voice sounded louder, closer.

What bomb? Who put it there for Bell to drop from the sky to become his savior?

Adel thought of Sam and Natalie. What if it was a ploy? A setup?

A lie? What if he didn't pick them up? What the hell would he do with his two girls, in the middle of the sea, two miles from shore.

He couldn't think. The questions were coming too fast. It didn't make sense.

"Dad, dad, what's going on?" asked a petrified Natalie.

He looked at her sprawled beneath the bench. Her eyes bulged close to tears.

"Nothing, darling. Just stay there," he shouted over the clatter.

He looked up again at the helicopter; it was following only fifty yards away. Suddenly Sam's face appeared through the hatch. She was dripping wet, with only a pink bath towel shielding her from the chilly winds. He stood up and pulled her down beside them. When he looked back up the helicopter had dropped back and gained altitude.

"*Listen, Adel, you have less than a minute. Jump. For God's sake, jump!*"

Adel could hear the alarm in Bell's voice. But was it feigned? Dear God, was it feigned?

"What is it, Michael?" screamed Samira. "What's going on? What is that man saying?"

"I don't know. I . . ."

"*Michael!*" boomed Bell's voice. "*It's a mistake. There's a bomb in the engine room put there to kill you. But it's a mistake. It was put there by mistake. . . .*"

The helicopter was dropping back and gaining altitude.

"*I know what you're thinking,*" said Bell. "*And you're right. We were wrong. Just get off with your wife and daughter. I'll explain everything. Please. Just trust me.*"

There was urgency in that pleading voice. And panic. And the helicopter was dropping back too. It was close to two hundred yards behind. There had to be a reason for the lengthening distance.

"Dear God Almighty," Adel dragged Natalie to her feet.

"Jump, darling. Jump!" he shouted at Samira, pushing her toward the railing with his free arm. He picked up his petrified daughter and handed her to Samira. "Hold her, Sam, and don't let go. No matter what happens, don't let go. I'll throw you a raft."

"What about . . ."

He pushed them hard, to clear the vessel's wake. From the nearest wooden locker he grabbed an orange life raft and pulled

283

the black knob at the top. Instantly it began to inflate. He threw it overboard toward them. Twenty yards behind he could see their heads bobbing above the water.

There was one more thing to do. Then he would join them. He turned back swiftly to the control panel and picked up the intercom.

"Gerrard," he barked. "There's a bomb on board. Tell Usher and get off the boat. Jump. And do it quickly."

He dropped the receiver and ran toward the railing.

CHAPTER 74

Bell, Davis and Gleeson strained their necks as they watched the three frantic figures dashing toward the yacht's upper railing. From above the movement seemed in slow motion as Adel hurled his wife and daughter into the sea and turned back toward the boat. Their necks craned even farther when he dropped the raft overboard and ran to the control panel.

"Fuck them, man, jump," said Davis as Adel picked up the intercom.

"Come on. Come on. Get out of there," pleaded Gleeson. "Jump!" he shouted.

"Way to go. Yeah. Way to go," Davis encouraged the scrambling figure as he dashed toward the railing.

It worked, thought Bell, feeling a cool breeze on his soaking body as Michael Adel climbed the railing. He slumped back on his chair and closed his eyes. That was too close for comfort, he thought, thanking the god of luck. He touched the corner of his right eye to still the twitch and took a deep lungful of air.

His relief was premature. Only by seconds, but it was premature. The force of the explosion smashed into the helicopter, driving it backwards, the engine unable to rise above the torrent of air that blasted it.

The roar followed later, deafening the four men as the helicopter was battered by flying debris. Only their seat belts saved them as the pilot rode the turbulence and climbed with it, up and to the rear.

When he straightened out at 900 feet the debris was still rising like dark confetti drifting in a whirlwind. All that could be seen of the proud vessel was a small fire where the engine room had once stood. The remainder of the structure was obliterated.

The three men were speechless. They felt a sense of catastrophe, of utter defeat, and knew they would be held culpable. In their line of work bad judgment was never pardoned.

After a lengthy shocked silence, Bill Davis could control himself no longer. He turned his eyes from the two figures in the choppy waters struggling to board the lifeboat to the shambled heap that was Colonel Grover Cleveland Bell.

"Shall we have them picked up?"

Bell was silent a moment, his head drooping, forcing the tired, defeated skin of his neck into a double chin. Then he gazed through the Perspex of the cabin into the distance as a tape of Mark Adel's voice played over and over in his mind. *You can't rely solely on machines...you can't rely solely on machines...it's not revenge that drives him. It's winning...it's winning...it's winning...it's..."*

"No," he whispered, his eyes locked on the confetti shimmering in the distance. "Leave them alone."

"What'll happen to Egypt and Saudi Arabia?" mumbled Jim Gleeson. "What will happen to those projects?"

But his question fell on dead ears.

CHAPTER 75

CANNES: SUNDAY, NOVEMBER 4, 1979: 6:00 A.M.

One of the three men accompanying the sleepy, bathrobed figures of Gleeson and Davis slipped his brass master key into the Fichet lock, eased the wooden door open and reached for the light switch. The two Americans entered the sumptuous hotel suite and froze.

It was the dull gaze on the dead man's face that shook them the most. The fixed, dilated eyes locked on the ceiling. A stream of blood trickled from the pebble-sized contusion at the man's temple, past the scar on the right side of his face, forming a pool on the light green carpet. A Smith & Wesson .38 service revolver lay on the floor beside the corpse.

"Call the police," said the short, slim manager of the Carlton Hotel to one of his security men.

Davis and Gleeson rushed forward, but the two hefty French security men blocked them.

"You will touch nothing," said the manager. "You will leave the room."

The two Americans looked up from the prostrate body of Colonel Grover Cleveland Bell. Then a pale, angry Gleeson swung around to face the manager. "Listen, asshole, this is over your head. You better contact the DST security people in Paris before you go any further."

The manager reached into his breast pocket. He withdrew a small, worn leather wallet and snapped it open. Beneath the bright red stripe and his picture were the words *Direction de la Surveillance du Territoire*.

"My instructions are to escort you to Nice airport. You will board a flight to New York which has been arranged for you. Any further explanation will come from the other end."

Gleeson and Davis looked at each other in astonishment. Before they could say a word, the manager of the hotel held out a folded copy of *Nice Matin*. "Perhaps this will explain something," he said.

Gleeson stared at the Frenchman. Then slowly he dropped his eyes to the glaring headline being circulated at that very moment on the dark streets of the Côte d'Azur.

EXPLOSION MYSTERIEUSE D'UN YACHT
CINQ PERSONNES SAUVÉES
PAS DE MORTS.

There were no fatalities. All were alive.

EPILOGUE

At 3:03 A.M. Washington time on Sunday, November 4, 1979, the United States Embassy in Teheran was occupied by Iranian students, "Followers of the Imam's Line," they called themselves. Sixty-five United States Embassy officials were taken hostage. Two weeks later, thirteen of the hostages—five women and eight black men—were released. The other fifty-two remained in captivity for four hundred and forty-four days.

International Herald Tribune—January 19, 1980 (LAT)

SHAH SAYS OIL FIRMS HELPED TO OUST HIM

WASHINGTON, Jan. 18—Mohammed Reza Pahlavi, the deposed Shah, charged in an interview broadcast yesterday that international oil companies had sacrificed his regime to reduce Iran's oil production and thus drive up prices.

. . . The Shah said that two years before he was overthrown he had "Heard from two different sources connected with oil companies that the regime in Iran would change. We believe that there was a plan to ensure less oil was offered to the world markets in order to bring about a price rise." He added: "One country was to be chosen for the sacrifice . . . It seems that the country chosen to drop its oil production was mine."

International Herald Tribune—March 4, 1980

CARTER IGNORED CIA CUTTING
IRAN ISLAM PAYOFF, JOURNAL SAYS

WASHINGTON, March 3 (UPI)—President Carter abruptly halted CIA payments supporting Iran's Islamic religious affairs in 1977

287

despite warnings that the cut-off would undermine the Shah, according to Politics Today magazine.

Daniel Drooz said in an article that details of the events were provided by six agents, former agents and intelligence analysts with connections in Teheran, the U.S. State Department and the White House.

Mr. Drooz said that the CIA payments began in 1953 following the overthrow of the Shah by Premier Mohammed Mossadegh. The CIA assisted in restoring the Shah to the throne and began payments to the country's ayatollahs and mullahs—in essence buying support for the Shah.

"For the next decade the Shah and Iran's religious leaders coexisted more or less peacefully, while the CIA quietly sent regular payments to help support the mullahs," claimed Mr. Drooz.

He also alleged that one source contended that the amount paid had reached $400 million a year, though other sources said that figure was too high.

The payments came to an abrupt halt shortly after Mr. Carter became president in 1977, when the Washington *Post* revealed payments of $10 million a year to King Hussein of Jordan.